Incident on the
Road to Canterbury

VINCE PANTALONE

NEWMAN SPRINGS PUBLISHING
320 Broad Street
Red Bank, NJ 07701

First originally published by Newman Springs Publishing 2018

ISBN 978-1-64096-099-2 (Paperback)
ISBN 978-1-64096-101-2 (Digital)

Cover Design by Tyler Okomba, Lebanon Valley College
Map by Emily Graf

Printed in the United States of America

To my wife, Carla,
who has defined *love* for our entire family

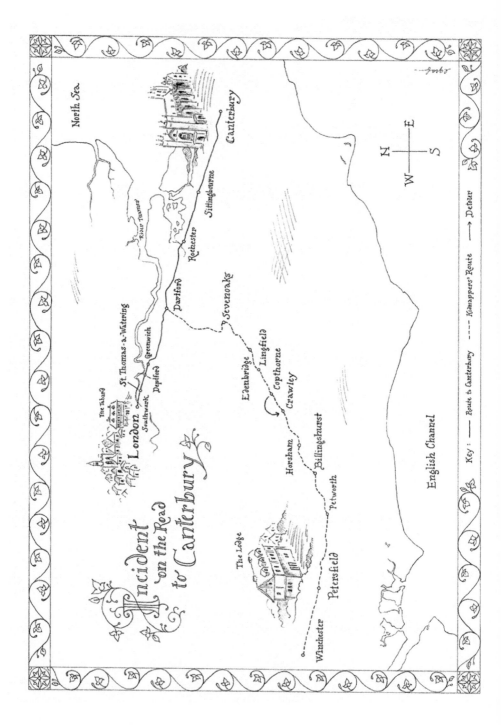

Incident on the Road to Canterbury

North Sea

River Thames

Canterbury
Sittingbourne
Rochester
Dartford
Greenwich
Deptford
Southwark
St. Thomas-a-Watering
The Tabard
London

Sevenoaks
Edenbridge
Lingfield
Copthorne
Crawley
Horsham
Billingshurst
Petworth
The Lodge
Petersfield
Winchester

English Channel

N
W — E
S

Key :   ——— Route to Canterbury   - - - - Kidnappers' Route   ——→ Detour

CONTENTS

CHAPTER 1

TWO REQUESTS

The bells on the church tower in Winchester had just chimed, signifying nones, prayers between midday and sunset. Outside, the sun was shining, making the usually cold February day in Southern England almost comforting. Local merchants and farmers kept their wooden stalls open later than usual, hoping the balmy weather would keep the customers a little longer in the marketplace, near City Centre, one of the oldest sections of Winchester. With its narrow streets and overhanging buildings, City Centre had a narrow entrance that opened into a wide area that held the weekly marketplace.

Hovering above the northern and the eastern side of the marketplace loomed Winchester Cathedral. Less than a quarter of a mile from the busy City Centre, the grand cathedral stood in the midst of the city. From one of the towers, a barrage of pigeons flew to another perch near the center of the cathedral above the nave. As the seat of the Bishop of Winchester, the cathedral boasted the largest nave in all of Europe.

At the chapter house, right beside the great cathedral, Prior Gilbert Berners awaited a guest. Even though the sun was brilliant outside, one could not tell from the Prior's office. The windows had been covered with rich tapestries decorated with the images of Christ's apostles. The tapestries were a gift to Father Berners from a rich merchant in town. As they were costly and beautiful, imported tapestries kept the cold air from creeping through the mosaic windows of the office, but today made the office hot and stuffy.

The office was unusually large, a gift from the bishop as a token of thanks for Prior Berners's thorough work in the day-to-day workings of Winchester's monastery, the largest in England. Beside the decorative tapestries, the room boasted a hearth that covered an entire wall. Prior Berners, prone to illness in the cold weather, made sure the hearth blazed with heat while he worked in his office, even on a warm day. Stacked next to the great hearth stood a massive pile of wood, and by the hour, one of the young monks of the monastery would tend to the hearth and its continuous fire.

Prior Berners owned a desk made of a varnished walnut. It, too, had been a gift to the prior from one of the builders in Winchester. The desk had a smooth top inlaid with bright beads in the form of a cross. Three secret drawers glided on tracks made by a local blacksmith—another gift to Prior Berners. The chair, imported from Portugal with richly adorned Latin carvings from more than half a century ago, had also been a gift to the prior from a local noble-man, grateful to Prior Berners in the handling of a delicate situation between the nobleman's son and a peasant girl from a seedy side of Winchester.

Since the windows had been covered with the fine imported tapestries, Prior Berners needed an unusual amount of candles to keep the room properly lit. The blazing fire from the hearth aided in the lighting of the room, but not enough to help the prior with his daily letters. Near the desk, a dozen sets of candles were kept lit whenever the prior was working in his office. It was up to the young monk who tended the fire in the hearth to also keep the candles fresh and lit for the fussy Prior Berners.

Prior Gilbert Berners had great skill in handling the day-to-day matters in running the largest monastery in England. He had intelligence, shrewdness, and proficiency in his work. But what the bishop valued greatly was Berners's ability to handle all of the bish-op's unpleasant duties. Prior Berners dealt daily with monks' misbe-haviors, a rich builder's unwed pregnant daughter, or a merchant's misplaced merchandise on church grounds. These duties were of a wide variety and were usually problems no one wanted to handle. Prior Berners skillfully dealt with them in such a discreet way that the bishop himself had no or little knowledge of the problems or situations at times. Hence, Prior Berners operated in a lavishly adorned office and accepted other accommodations by the bishop, merchants, tradesmen, and local noblemen.

William Edington, the Bishop of Winchester and one of the most famous men in England, had served the king in many capacities to include the Royal Treasurer, the Keeper of the Wardrobe and Lord Chancellor of England. His reforms in the royal finances had greatly contributed to the English military efficiency in the early stages of the long war with France. At one time, he was also the Chief Royal Chaplain, a personal advisor to the king himself. And now as Bishop of Winchester, a post he had held for twenty years, William Edington controlled the largest Catholic *see* in England.

Bishop Edington was a highly literate man who had served king and country. Now as Bishop of Winchester, he was able to use his power and influence to run one of the great cathedrals of England. He took pride in the rebuilding of the cathedral since his appointment, and he was especially proud of the Augustinian priory he was building in the small village in which he was raised. It was even named after the bishop, the Edington Priory.

The bishop was a man with great vision, so he took it upon himself to surround his table with able clergymen to run the day-to-day affairs of the cathedral, the monastery, and the town of Winchester. For the most part, the men he appointed were masters at their crafts. They performed their services as directed, paid all due respect to the church and the bishop, and ran their assignments proficiently. By coincidence, they all were handsomely compensated for their work. Gifts, bribes, and allowances were given to the men on a day-to day-basis. Bishop Edington knew about the graft occurring, but as long as his officers kept a low profile and did their jobs, he let them continue in their ways. Prior Gilbert Berners was one of Bishop Eddington's most trusted officers.

The prior sat at his desk, finishing a letter he transcribed for the good Bishop of Winchester. Berners blew on the fresh ink as he reread the letter. Satisfied, he placed it on the desk. Reaching for his kerchief, he wiped the colorless drop running from his nose. The drip was a constant nuisance ever since his accident three years ago. Berners looked at the sleeve of his cassock and wiped a smudge. His appearance had always been important to him. He had his cassock made by a tailor. His hair and beard were kept neatly trimmed. Still, the bend in his nose was a constant embarrassment to the priest, who had considered himself a handsome man before the unfortunate accident that had also led to a broken jaw.

"Come in," Berners quietly answered the knock at his door.

Father Richard Pauls, his secretary, stepped into the room. "Prior, Lord Berkley is here."

"Send him in," Berners said, rubbing his upper jaw that had never healed after the accident. And it still caused pain if Berners raised his voice or spoke for too long.

"He has others with him," Father Pauls questioned, not sure if Father Berners would see Sir Berkley alone or with his party.

"They can wait outside, Father Richard. Send in Lord Berkley."

"As you wish, Prior." Father Pauls exited, closing the door behind him.

The prior got up from his desk, wiping his nose automatically as he drew near the door.

Father Pauls returned, motioning for the guest behind him to enter. Sir Edward Berkley was a big man with an infectious smile. He wore a scar above his left eye. It was almost hidden by the long unruly greyish hair he kept. As Berkley entered, he extended his left hand, for his right hand was disfigured. The damaged hand always stayed clenched, the nerves damaged from a blow of a battle-ax years ago.

"Gilbert, my friend," he exclaimed, grabbing Berners's hand and shaking enthusiastically.

"Welcome, Sir Berkley, welcome," Berners said uncomfortably. Berkley's size and physical presence made Prior Berners a little nervous. Berkley's intimate use of Berners's name also made him uncomfortable, especially in front of Father Pauls.

"May I offer you some wine, Lord Berkley?" Prior Berners nodded to Father Pauls who closed the door and moved quickly to the side table that had a bottle of wine already opened. It was not the usual sacramental wine made by the priests in the monastery, but was imported secretly, since England was at war with France. Father Pauls poured two glasses, while Berners guided his guest to a chair in front of Berners's desk.

"Thank you, Father." Berkley nodded to Father Pauls, accepting the goblet of wine. "May I propose a toast?"

"Perhaps a prayer, Sir Berkley?" Prior Berners interrupted with a feigned sincerity.

"Of course, Prior Berners. Of course."

Berners raised his glass. "To the Holy Catholic Church and the forgiveness of sins, and to your spiritual health, Lord Berkley."

They both drank from their goblets.

"Father Richard, that will be all," Berners ordered as he put down his wine.

Pauls bowed and exited quietly, closing the door softly.

Lord Berkley tasted more wine. "I was under the impression that the Lord bishop was going to meet with me."

Prior Berners took the kerchief to his nose and paused until he took care of his dreadful drip. "The Lord bishop asked me to handle your request, Sir Berkley. Your problem seems to be best handled by secular courts. Asking the Church for help in this regard is a delicate matter. The Church must stay out of governmental courts. So to keep the bishop out of our conversation protects the Church and his position of Bishop of Winchester."

"Even though the bishop will be made rich by my proposal?" Berkley asked with stern voice.

"It is a delicate situation, Lord Berkley. The bishop has instructed me to help you but with discretion. No one is to know that the bishop is involved."

"So you are doing the bishop's dirty work?"

"Not dirty work, Lord. Just his delicate work. I have been instructed to hear your plan. If I think it will work for the betterment of the bishop and the Church, I will give you permission to proceed. If I do not think it will benefit the bishop or the Church, I will say so, and you will not be able to get any help from the Church."

Suddenly, Lord Berkley smiled and gave a hearty laugh. He drank more from his goblet, got out of his seat, and refilled his glass.

He laughed and shook his head. "The Church has all the angles, does it not, Prior Berners? And I said *angles*. It occurred to me just now that it also has all the *angels* too!" Berkley laughed at his own pun.

Berners smiled politely and dabbed at his nose. "So what do you want from the Church, Sir Berkley?"

Berkley did not sit. Goblet in hand, he made his point. "As you may or may not know, Lord Appleton owns a parcel of land adjacent to my own. Years ago, my great-grandfather, for whatever reason, sold his great-grandfather one hundred acres of land. I want the land back."

"Is there a record of the transaction?" Berners asked as he sipped his wine.

"Oh, they have the document. I do not doubt that it was legal at the time. But my great-grandfather was deep in debt when he sold Lord Appleton the land."

"Have you tried to buy it back?" Berners inquired.

"Indeed, Prior Berners. Indeed. In fact, I have offered a substantial amount of money for the land."

"And?"

"Lord Appleton would not accept my offer. He refuses to sell the land at any cost," Berkley answered with apparent frustration.

"May I ask why the land is so important to you, Lord Berkley?"

"At one time, the Berkley and Appleton lands were separated by the Alban River. Our families shared the rights to the water. However, my great-grandfather sold the lands that bordered the river. By selling the lands adjacent to the river, he gave away our water rights. We have no water for our farming, for our livestock, for our homes."

"And he will not sell the lands back to you?"

"We must pay rent if we use his water, an expensive rent, I might add."

"I do not see how this pertains to the Church or the bishop. Perhaps you should have an audience with the local judge. I am sure that a franklin could help with your case."

"Tried going that way, Prior. Did not work. In fact, I have tried negotiating, going to secular courts and even petitioned the highest court in London. But nothing has helped."

"What can the Church do?"

"Grant me absolution."

"Absolution?"

"Yes, absolution. For a sin I am going to commit." Lord Berkley stared at Father Berners with a glare. "I am going to order the kidnapping of a church official."

Berners's eyes squinted hard. As he looked into the suddenly cold eyes of Lord Berkley, Prior Berners felt a chill. Drawing his breath, he asked quietly, "I am lost, Lord Berkley. Please explain."

"I want to confess my sins, Father Berners."

"Confess? Now?"

"Will you hear my confession?"

"Yes, of course. What about your plan?"

Berkley put his goblet on the table, got down on his knees, and crossed himself. "Bless me, Father, for I have sinned. You see, Sir Appleton has six children, two boys and four girls. His sons are knighted and fight for the king in France. His three older daughters are married to noblemen from areas north of London. But the youngest daughter lives close by. She is a nun, a prioress. I have hired men to kidnap her. With her as a captive, I will negotiate a deal with Sir Appleton to regain the water rights my great-grandfather squandered away." Berkley paused and let the idea form in Berners's mind. "For this sin and all the other sins of my life, I am heartedly sorry."

Father Berners stood silently for a moment then made the sign of the cross in front of the kneeling sinner. "For these sins and others, you are forgiven. Now, rise, Lord Berkley."

Berkley looked up and slowly got off his knees.

"By confessing your plan to me, you are assured I will not tell anyone, not even the bishop."

"Not even the pope himself?" Berkley smiled.

"So what do you want from the Church?"

"I want you to sell me an indulgence, Father. I want to be pardoned for this sin. I do not want to be excommunicated for the action I am about to take. Can you do that for me?"

Father Berners did not answer. His mind was racing. "Do you have a plan?"

"Since I am still in the confessional, I will tell you. The prioress is to go on a pilgrimage to Canterbury in the spring. I have hired men to go along as pilgrims. When the time is right, they will kidnap her and bring her to me. And we will negotiate with Sir Appleton on my terms!"

Prior Berners took another sip of his wine. He dabbed at his nose. "If I grant your request, Sir Berkley, the Church will be accused of attending to secular matters."

"Believe me, Prior Berners, when the deal is made, I will make a public showing of my sorrow in the form of penance and your pardon of my sins. I will also make a considerable contribution to your priory and your private coffers."

"That being said, I believe we have a deal, Sir Berkley."

"Excellent, Prior Berners—"

"Now I have a request for you."

"Anything, Prior."

"There will be a priest going to Canterbury with the prioress. He will be travelling with her small group. I am requesting you do me a favor."

"Name it."

"As your men kidnap the prioress, perhaps one of your men could accidentally greet this priest for me."

"Greet? I am not sure what you mean, Father Berners."

"I want him 'greeted' in a most hostile way. I want him hurt, hurt badly. And if he should die from his wounds . . . well, so much the better, Lord Berkley," Berners said as he wiped his nose.

Berkley blessed himself.

"Of course, I will issue you a pardon for 'greeting' the priest," Father Berners added. "And that pardon will be free."

CHAPTER 2

LAST RITES

Old man Richardson was dying. For weeks, he had been battling a crippling cough, thinking it was a common ailment that was making its way through the village. But the cough would not leave him. It only worsened, upsetting his stomach daily so that he could barely eat. The cough seemed to worsen at night, preventing Tommy Richardson from getting the proper rest he needed to allow his body to heal. And then the fever came, forcing him to his straw bed in one of the back rooms of his tavern, The Harp.

A widower, Tommy Richardson had to rely on his daughters, Thea and Emellye, to run the tavern in his absence. At first, Tommy was able to run the tavern from his bed, dictating special recipes for the kitchen fare, giving advice in keeping the ale in the kegs fresh and dealing with the buying of victuals and supplies for the day-to-day business of The Harp. But the fever worsened, demanding Tommy to sleep more. In a week, the rising fever put him in an incoherent state. His daughters feared for his life.

There was no doctor in the village of Harper's Turn. Thea, the older of the daughters, called for Rose Freeman, the village midwife, who was called upon to help with ailments, sicknesses, and broken bones. Thea hoped Rose's use of local herbs and roots could somehow bring her father's fever to a halt and make him well again. Rose visited the ill innkeeper and gave him a mixture of her finest herbs, dry roots, and natural medicines. Together, Rose and Thea had a difficult time trying to make the feverous patient swallow the antidote.

Rose visited for five days in a row. Tommy grew worse. It was time to call the village priest.

Father Merek Willson had been assigned to the village of Harper's Turn three years ago to run St. Mary Magdalene Church, a small run-down building the size of a chapel. A priest in his late twenties, Father Willson was unusually tall, almost a head taller than the villagers he served. The priest had a broad, thick chest and was uncommonly strong. His hands were large and strong, able to crush a walnut between his thumb and forefinger. Merek wore his black hair long. It fell to his shoulders, but he kept it tied in the back to keep his ears uncovered. His brown eyes were dark, made darker by his black eyebrows. His high cheekbones and unusually straight nose made him a handsome man in the eyes of the women of the village. But his faith and deep love of the priesthood had not led him to disobeying his priestly vows.

The villagers of Harper's Turn knew of Father Willson's strength, for they were always asking Father Willson to help when it came to digging out large rocks in fields, or when beams on new huts had to be held in place for carpenters to finish their jobs. Old man Richardson used Father Merek to help him carry his kegs of ale into his tavern, The Harp. No one knew why or how Father Merek had such strong arms, a broad chest and hands that could crack a walnut in a flash. No one questioned him, nor did they ever think to ask him. But he was unlike any priest they had ever met. Little did they know, Merek had another life before the priesthood, a life he kept a secret.

Merek entered The Harp and was led into the back by Thea. Tommy Richardson lay in his bed fast asleep in a deep fever. Upon entering the dark and stuffy room, Merek could see the fever rising from the dying man. Merek liked Tommy Richardson. The tavern keeper had an infectious smile and devil-in-his-eyes demeanor that allowed him to live a joyous life. Short, thin and full of energy, Tommy resembled a legendary leprechaun with his sparse red hair and freckles. He laughed loudly and often. Despite the daily routine of village life with all the hard work and heartache, Tommy enjoyed life. His tavern was very popular, not because it served the finest ale or delicious homespun food, for Tommy treated all his customers like royalty. If you came into The Harp, you were served with a smile, a laugh, or a joke.

Tommy was the first villager to greet Merek upon his arrival three years earlier. Father Willson had just entered the run-down chapel that would serve as St. Mary Magdalene Church. It was in ruins, for a priest had not said Mass there in twenty years. The few benches that served as pews were broken; the altar was indescribably dirty from the vagrants and animals that had used it over the years on cold winter nights. The roof leaned in a dangerous way. The littered altar had collapsed, and the walls of the church had openings where animals had burrowed their way in to escape the winter temperatures.

"Could use a little work, Father." Tommy smiled as he walked into the chapel.

"Did you bring a broom?" Merek countered.

Tommy laughed at that. His laugh made Merek smile, and a friendship was underway.

"They say the Muslims have invented a powder that can blow things up. Could use a bit, do you think, Father? Start from scratch, eh." The tavern keeper jested with a wide smile.

"Great idea, sir. If you have not heard, the English have such powder. We would not have much trouble obtaining some," Merek added. "I am Father Merek Willson." Merek moved to Tommy, and they shook arms.

"Tommy Richardson, Father. I own The Harp, the tavern over yonder. Say you amble over to my tavern for a meal, and we will talk about the demolition of the church."

Father Merek remembered that first conversation as he began the sacrament of extreme unction, last rites. He placed his scapula over his shoulders, brought out the holy chrism and his rosary beads. He began to pray over his friend, whose fever could be felt by the priest standing beside the bed.

Thea entered the room quietly and felt her father's head. She laid a wet cloth on Tommy's head. She tried not to cry, but her whimpers began to escape her. She knelt and put her head on her father's chest.

Merek let her cry and continued with his duties, praying quietly. As he prayed, he thought of the banter between Tommy and him.

"You know, Father Merek, they do not make priests like you anymore." Merek was lugging a keg of ale into The Harp, setting it behind the bar. Tommy continued, "You might be the strongest priest I know." Tommy, with that big grin and generous laugh, watched Merek struggle with the keg by himself.

"Tommy," Merek answered as he placed the keg in the assigned place, "I am the only priest you know. Besides, I have to be strong physically, for my spiritual soul is weak from hanging around inn-keepers like you."

And Tommy howled with laughter.

Thea stopped crying and stood next to Merek.

"Henry Barber was in here and wanted to bleed poor Father to rid him of his fever," Thea said with a quiet anger. "I threw his arse out, Father." She faced Merek. Her anger melted as she said, "By God, Merek, he is dying." She crossed herself and added a plea, "Please help him."

"Thea, I can only administer to the soul," Merek replied, trying not to stare into Thea's hazel eyes.

"Then do so, Father." She made the sign of the cross on his forehead and left the room.

Alone with Tommy Richardson, Merek began his litany of prayers Merek Willson was in his sixth year of the priesthood. He had entered into the vocation late, receiving his vows at the age of twenty-two. Had there not been such a shortage of priests because of the bubonic outbreak in 1348 and the war with France, Merek might have been turned away for his age. But England was in dire need of priests, and so he was ordained at the age of twenty-two.

Merek continued with the sacrament, anointing Tommy's fore-head with the holy oil and saying his prescribed prayers. Merek knew well the sacrament of the dying. How many villagers had he per-formed it on in his three years, he could not remember.

"Oh, Merek, must you be so loud," Tommy suddenly snorted. His eyes opened, and for an instant, Merek saw the mischievous look and grin that were Tommy's trademarks. The look made Merek pause in his prayers. He could not hide his smile.

"Tommy, you must not interrupt me when I am trying to save your soul," Merek replied with a grin. "I was just bargaining with the Lord for your angel's wings."

"Father Merek, may God bless you for the intercession of my soul, but everyone knows that a tavern keeper is Satan's best friend."

"Not true, Tommy. Not true. Someone who can make such a fine barley soup as you could not know the devil as a brother." Merek reached out and touched Tommy's hand.

Tommy smiled and closed his eyes. He seemed to drift off. Merek continued with his prayers and the sacrament at hand. By the standards of the day, Tommy was an old man, having celebrated his fiftieth birthday two years ago. Some considered it a blessing to live past forty, for death was all around. Merek, at twenty-eight, was "middle-aged." It was not an easy life, even for a prosperous tavern keeper.

As Merek prayed, he begged the Lord God to return to him the feeling of sadness surrounding death. He stood beside the bed of a man whom he considered his best friend in the village, yet he could not find sadness in his heart. He wanted to feel the sadness, but it would not come. Merek begged God to give him heartache and pain again regarding death. In Merek's life, he had witnessed so much pain and death that he had become inured by it. It was not healthy for any man, especially a priest, to be callous toward death. Father Merek could show the humble villagers his sad and serene face at the death of a loved one, but it was a hollow look, a look without feeling. How he hoped someday to feel that pain again!

Merek knelt beside Tommy and continued his rosary. He remembered the awful plague of 1348 that swept through Europe. He was only a boy and had contracted the deadly disease, as did his parents and brothers. For three days, he suffered incredible pain and high fever, as did the rest of his family. On the fourth day, his fever resided, and he slowly began to recover. Members of his family were not as fortunate. He ended up burying them all.

Tommy was sleeping when Merek completed the sacrament. As he made the sign of the cross on Tommy's forehead, Merek could feel the heat of the fever pouring out of the tavern keeper. Sitting on the side of the bed, Merek listened to Tommy's shallow breathing. It was quiet in the back room of the tavern, and Merek with his rosaries in his hands watched the dying man. He almost found himself smiling at the man lying on the straw bed. Merek's mind was playing tricks on him. The withered figure on the bed could not be Tommy Richardson, the mischievous and fun-loving owner of The Harp.

Before long, Thea entered the room and sat beside Merek. At first, Merek did not notice Thea's entrance. When she sat beside him, Merek turned to her. "Father Merek," she said softly, "can I get you something from the kitchen?"

"Not yet, Thea. Maybe on the way out."

Thea put her hand to her mouth, trying to stop a whimper. "How much longer?"

"I am not a physician, dear Thea." Merek took her hand and held it. He knew he had just lied. He had witnessed too many deaths. He knew the signs. Tommy would pass to the next world soon. "I can tell you that your father is ready to meet his Maker. He will be with God."

Thea did not say a word. They sat silently. Merek continued to hold her hand. It began slowly, but Thea began to cry. Her shoulders shook, and then her head sank. Merek stood up and took her hand. She also rose from the bed and wrapped her arms around the priest. Her cry turned into a deep sob. And Merek let her cry, holding her and trying to comfort her. The couple stood beside the bed of the dying man. Thea continued to cry as Merek sought God's mercy to help him to feel her pain.

When she was done crying, she continued to hold onto Merek. Her grip was tight and strong. It was a hold that did not want to let go. Thea raised her head and let her cheek rest against the priest's. Her crying had stopped, but her grip continued. Suddenly but slowly, she stepped back and looked into his eyes. "Thank you, Father Merek. You are a great friend to my father."

"As he is to me, Thea," Merek answered.

Thea came closer again and grabbed Merek fiercely. She placed both arms around his neck and held him tightly. Merek could feel the tears on her cheek against his face. Thea was strong and would not let go. Merek did not try to pull away. The grip lasted less than thirty seconds, but it defined her feelings for him. Both knew there was an attraction, but this was the first time it had ever been allowed to rise. She slowly pulled away from him and kissed him softly on the cheek. "Forgive me, Father," she said. "The impulse to kiss you was too great for me to let go. I am sorry."

It was an uncomfortable moment, as both were unhinged by their mutual awareness of themselves. Merek was quick to intervene, but it took him a second to gather himself.

"Dear Thea, let us go to the kitchen. I am suddenly hungry for some of that famous barley soup."

Thea wiped her eyes and smiled, knowing for the first time that Merek had feelings for her. He had not said anything, but Thea knew by the way he held her and looked into her eyes when they pulled from the embrace. Taking a breath, she led Merek to the kitchen.

The kitchen of The Harp was a room just behind the serving area. It was not large but had an unusually open stone hearth against the outer wall of the tavern. With a fire blazing constantly, it was always the warmest room in the tavern. A stack of wood for the hearth stood neatly on the other side of the room from the fire, making sure its proximity could not induce an unwanted fire in the remaining part of the kitchen. At this time of night, no meat cooked on the spit in the fireplace. A small pot hanger with a cauldron attached hung on a hook above the embers of a dying fire. The cauldron was filled with rich barley soup. A three-legged cauldron with the day's meat gravy stood by itself in front of the great hearth. All the tools needed, from the poker tending the fire to the ladle for scooping the soup into wooden bowls for serving hung on hooks to the side of the great fireplace.

Merek and Thea entered the kitchen. As Thea went to the stone hearth, Merek sat on a stool close to the warmth of the fire. Thea took the soup ladle and spooned some barley soup into a wooden bowl for the priest. As she handed Merek the bowl, she allowed her hands to touch his as they exchanged the bowl. The touch was only a second, but she was sure he felt her fingers.

Merek tried to ignore her touch, but his red face could not. Fortunately, the red in his face was hidden by the fire's glow. He took his spoon quickly and filled it with soup yet brought it to his lips slowly, for he could feel the soup's heat immediately. As expected, the soup was excellent.

"Your father's batch?" Merek asked between mouthfuls.

"No, Father Merek. Mine. I made the soup. For the past few months, it has been up to me to ready the tavern for business."

Merek took another generous portion to his mouth. "Ah, it is excellent, Thea."

Tommy Richardson had three daughters. His wife had died a decade ago. Thea, the oldest, was the real caretaker of The Harp. The middle daughter had run away with a huntsman a year or two ago, but her whereabouts were unknown. The other sister, Emellye, was a great help to Thea but was too young to have the savvy to run a tavern. When Tommy passed on, it would be up to Thea to make The Harp run.

Even before Merek found that he was physically attracted to Thea, he had a great regard for her. Thea was blessed with Tommy's ability to handle people and was strong enough to run a business in a "man's world." She was not book smart, having no formal education, but Thea Richardson had talents and the wherewithal to know her world around her. She could be gentle and caring if the situation warranted it, or she could be tough as nails and throw an unruly patron from the premises.

"That one," Tommy sometimes called her, "is the one you do not cross, Father Merek. Thea is hell 'n the wind if she gets her temper up. I swear it is her red hair, just like her mother's."

Thea did have red hair, although an artist would have called it auburn in color. And when she let it, the hair cascaded down from her shoulders in a most beautiful way. She had a handsome face set off by her dazzling hazel eyes. Her nose was straight, offsetting her mildly crooked teeth. Her smile could inspire the angels, but when she became angry, her crooked teeth could scare off the most drunken of patrons.

Thea was taller than the average village woman. Built with a solid frame, Thea had the strength any woman of the village would need to perform the daily chores of village life. With large hips and strong legs, Thea could help her father with the heavy kegs of ale. Tommy Richardson had taught her to stand up against any patron who would seek to rob or damage The Harp. And Thea did, sometimes wielding a small mallet to knock sense into some drunken patron. She had a reputation in Harper's Turn as a lass in which one did not trifle.

When Merek first met Thea through Tommy at The Harp, he could not believe that such a beautiful woman was not married. He soon found out that she had no steady beaus or boys in Harper's Turn who were interested in her. As he began to know Tommy Richardson and his daughter, Merek soon realized why Thea was not engaged or in a relationship. In the poor village of Harper's Turn, she intimidated all the unmarried young men of the village. Her beauty and presence were no match for her resolve and her strong personality. And now that she was twenty-two, she was "an old maid."

The tavern was quiet on this night when Merek sat in its kitchen eating barley soup and worrying about his friend Tommy Richardson and what would become of his daughters. There were only two customers sharing a pint of ale in the main room. Thea's sister Emellye tended to their needs as Merek and Thea sat in the kitchen. Merek treasured each mouthful of the barley soup. He ate it slowly, for the kitchen was nice and warm. Soon, he would have to cross the village to the cold, damp church in which he stayed.

"Father Merek, I have a rather unusual question to ask you," Thea said quietly, breaking the quiet thoughts of Tommy's death.

"Thea, what is it?" he answered. Merek put the soup down and gave her his full attention.

"Father Merek, you have been a good friend and a blessing to the Richardson's. It never seemed to matter to you that we ran a tavern, something Mother Church would frown upon."

"The Richardson's are good, hardworking, and honest people. That means more to me than how you make your livelihood." Merek meant every word he said. Brother priests would never have been caught in a tavern, let alone making friends with the tavern keep and his daughters. Merek was not the usual priest, though. Late to the priesthood, Merek had been exposed to the real world and its "vale of tears" more so than the usual village priest. The son of a serf, Merek was raised in the real world. He hunted and farmed for a feudal lord. No, Merek was not the common priest. He tried not to judge, did not condemn, and took people for what they were. He had a secret side the normal priest had not experienced. Merek had been a soldier before entering the priesthood.

And he had killed. Before his life as a priest, Merek had fought in the king's war with France. He had been in battle. Merek had seen the grizzly face of death and war's aftereffects. With his skill with the longbow, he had taken men's lives, had caused pain and injuries to hundreds of others, and was accustomed to the horrors of war. He had not told his parishioners of his previous life of being a soldier in the deadly art of the bow, not wanting them to know his sinful past. Had the villagers known, they would have understood Merek's broad chest, his thick arms and strong hands were from his years of training in the proficient use of the longbow.

"If you please, Merek, let me finish," Thea interrupted. Merek smiled, for he and Thea had conversed before. They had had long conversations from every topic under the sun. There were times when Thea forgot to address Merek with his religious title, something Merek did not mind, especially when he felt their vibrant attraction. Thea continued, "To keep this tavern will require a lot of hard work, a good business mind, and perseverance."

"Three business virtues you have an abundance of—"

"Kind of you to say, Merek, but what this business needs is a male proprietor."

"Are you going to sell it?" Merek asked, not understanding her point.

Thea did not answer. She only looked at him in a way that focused on Merek's entire being.

And he knew that look. Merek's instincts on many levels were good, from hunting with a bow to reading people. He knew Thea was attracted to him. He knew that she scorned many suitors because she wanted Merek. And he dreaded what she was going to ask him.

"Merek, have you ever thought about giving up the lonely life of a priest to become the proprietor of a busy tavern?"

Merek blinked and said nothing. He knew it was more than a business proposal. It was a real temptation, for her look was genuine and her beauty was real. Against the fire blazing from the hearth, her auburn hair and hazel eyes had a stunning look that mesmerized the smitten priest. No, the temptation was real. Merek knew he had feelings for her, too, and only recently acknowledged them to himself.

He fought the feelings. But they were there. For three years, he had worked in the village, done his priestly duties, and obeyed the rules of Saint Benedict. Merek lived for poverty, chastity, and obedience. Getting to know Tommy Richardson had allowed him to be a friend to Thea and Emellye. And in those years, he had secretly fallen in love with Thea. He had never told her, never acted on it, and prayed constantly to the Holy Spirit to help him with the temptation.

He never told her, but she knew. "Thea, I have given my life to God," he said, trying to convince himself more than her.

"Does not Our Lord work in mysterious ways? Could He not pardon a selfless priest who gives up his 'flock' to serve a different kind of 'flock'?"

Merek could only manage a smile. In his heart, he wanted to hug her, kiss her, and make love to her. With the strength of the Holy Spirit, he did not. Each night, Merek prayed to the Holy Spirit for strength through temptation. And with Thea around, he prayed constantly for that strength. It actually made him a better priest, for he found that if he stayed busy with his priestly duties, he was less likely to think about Thea and his feelings for her.

"Thea, you are asking me to be your partner?"

"Indeed, Merek. As proprietor, you would be housed and fed and have a handsome salary, not to mention other 'benefits' that come with the job." She smiled at the last comment.

Merek blushed, and she could tell, even though the candlelight in the room was not strong. He took another long sip of the barley soup. "Thea, you honor me. But I must not, cannot go back on my vows to the Church. They are sacred."

"Merek," she countered, "you must be the last clergyman to cling to your churchly promises. Tell me of another clergyman who has clung to his vows of celibacy! It is unnatural."

Merek had an argument, but it did not come out. It was stuck as a lump in his throat. Thea had made a point about Merek's vow to the Catholic Church and God. But right now, Merek was thinking about how he could keep that vow, for the temptation was stronger than ever.

"Thea, I made a vow to God."

"You mean, a vow to the Church, a corrupted Church, none-theless. Merek, do away with the cassock, the white collar and move in with me."

There it was, plain as day. There was a moment of silence. And Merek smiled. So did Thea.

"Thea, if I ever consider thumbing my nose at the Church and my sacred vows, you will be the first I seek."

"Fair enough, Father Merek. It shall be a standing offer then. Until then, I shall attend my father's business, while you attend your Father's business."

"Agreed, dear Thea. Agreed." Merek finished his barley soup, looked in on Tommy one last time, and blessed him. Merek left without another word to Thea. But they looked at each other.

Tommy died before the morning cock crowed.

CHAPTER 3

THE MEETING

Lord Berkley and his most trusted men-at-arms rode to the hunting lodge in the far northeastern corner of Lord Berkley's land. There were a dozen men in all. Each man was heavily armed, for there was always a risk of running into bands of robbers and criminals hiding in the forests. In addition to a personal servant and a cook, a livery man accompanied the party to service horses that carried a selection of bows and hundreds of arrows. It was Lord Berkley's idea. Although they were going to the hunting lodge for business, they would do some hunting when the business was concluded.

It was a cold February morning, and the frost was all about, hanging from the limbs of the many trees leading to the lodge and upon the road. Lord Berkley and his men rode at a leisurely pace, not wanting to chance a spill on the icy ground. Having left before dawn, Lord Berkley wanted to get the early morning meeting out of the way so that he and his men could spend the rest of the day hunting boar. The men would hunt till dark, spend the night at the lodge, and return to the manor in the morning. Despite the cold morning and the chilling frost, the men were in good spirits, especially Lord Berkley, who loved a good hunt.

The hunting lodge stood in a large clearing amongst a small forest of trees. Although Lord Berkley used the hunting lodge for his favorite pastime, he had designed the building as a formidable defensive structure if it were ever needed as such. The hunting lodge stood in the exact middle of the clearing, with one hundred yards of open ground on all four sides of the building. If an enemy would attack the lodge, he would have dangerously open ground to cover without protection.

The hunting lodge had an enormous fireplace in the center that heated the main room and the two separate bedrooms on either side. The fireplace had two openings, for the backside opened to the kitchen. There meat could be roasted on a spit while there were cauldrons, pots, and kitchen utensils ready to prepare a proper meal for the lord of the manor. The hunting lodge had a window in every room that could be reinforced with strong wooden boards to fend off attackers. There was a ladder in the main room that led to the roof, where defenders could fire arrows under the cover of a wooden railing that ran the perimeter of the building. Lord Berkely had even paid for a well to be dug at one end of the lodge and had designed the kitchen to be close to the well and its precious water. Lord Berkely found it ironic that he could find water at this remote hunting lodge but could get water where he needed it most, near the manor and his lands of farming.

Arriving at the lodge, the men secured their horses and inspected the building. In the past, they had found trespassers hiding in the building, either for its protection from the elements or its protection from the law. Either way, blood was usually spilled. If the trespassers were vagabonds looking for shelter, they were beaten by the men-at-arms as a warning not to come back. If they were found to be criminals, Lord Berkley would send for the constables in Petersfield, the nearest town. With Lord Berkley's permission, the constables sometimes hung the captured bandits right on Lord Berkley's property. As the men-at-arms inspected every inch of the property, the servant began to unload the bows and arrows. The cook went to work immediately. His first task was to start a fire in the great hearth. Starting a fire was not an easy task, and once started, it would be up to the cook and the servant to keep it going.

Lord Berkley was a little nervous about the impending meeting. His visitor had a reputation for being thorough, yet his reputation also had a ruthlessness attached to it. Lord Berkley did not feel threatened by the man in a physical way, for he had his men with him. But the plan, the kidnapping and the negotiation following made him a bit anxious. Once Lord Berkley put his illegal plan in motion, there would be no turning back. It was a risky plan, one with great benefits. However, if it did not work, dire sacrifices would have to be made.

"Lord, a rider approaches," one of his men-at-arms announced, breaking his revelry.

Lord Berkley went to the large door of the hunting lodge and opened it. He stepped out onto the large porch protected from the overhanging roof and watched the solitary rider approach. The rider rode a handsome stallion, dapple-gray in color. It was a young horse and must have cost the rider a fortune. The stallion ambled easily toward the hunting lodge, seemingly unworried about the slippery frost on the ground. As impressive as the stallion was, Lord Berkley was not impressed by the appearance of the rider.

The rider seemed to be plain. His clothes were not of a nobleman, but that of a common worker. A rider of a gray stallion should be dressed as a prince or lord, not a commoner. The rider was very slender, and as he drew closer, Lord Berkley could see the man was muscular and carried himself with confidence. The rider wore no hat. His hair was cut high around the ears and clipped short in front like a priest.

"Good day, my lord," the rider said as his horse reluctantly stopped in front of the lodge. The horse seemed to want to keep going; its youthful energy not ready to be still. The rider calmed the horse with a stern pull of the reigns. He looked around at the dwelling and the men-at-arms in front of him. It was a quick glance, but Lord Berkley could tell the man was taking it all in and assessing the situation. Lord Berkley was pleased. It was the sign of a professional. "May I dismount?" he asked without a smile.

"Please do. My men will take care of your fine horse. Please join me in the main room where the fire will warm us."

The rider dismounted and ignored the man-at-arms who offered to care for the horse. The rider tethered his horse himself and walked into the lodge. Lord Berkley was surprised by the man's height. He was taller than expected, but not as tall as Lord Berkley. His legs were long and lean. He wore a long upper coat with a certain blue dye that the lord was unfamiliar, for the color was not seen in this part of England. The rider also had a knife. It was large but had a rusty blade. It was tied to his waist with a rope.

Inside, the rider neared the fire for the moment and turned to the lord of the manor. The two men were alone, as Lord Berkley wanted. Lord Berkley offered the stranger some wine, for Lord Berkely had brought plenty, hoping to celebrate the killing of a wild boar or two. The stranger put his hand out and shook his head. It did not stop Lord Berkley from pouring and drawing from his own goblet.

"You come highly recommended, sir," Lord Berkley began, putting his goblet on the table.

"Thank you, my lord," the rider said without emotion.

"No doubt, Lord Pennington in Norfolk told you of my situation," Lord Berkley added.

"Somewhat, Lord Berkley. I was hoping you could bring more detail to the plan."

"I will speak plainly with you, sir, about the plan and the situation. But I need to know your name and more about you."

"I am called Oswald. I serve as Lord Pennington's reeve in Norfolk. I have been in his service for many years. On occasion, he loans me to other lords for the services I render. These services, as you know, are quite unique. And because they are unique, can be expensive."

"Yes, I know Oswald. Lord Pennington and I have already agreed upon a price. When your mission is completed, you will receive your cut from Lord Pennington."

"As is the custom, Lord Berkley."

"Yet, I tell you that if all goes well, there will be a bonus for you that I shall give to you personally. And it will be between us." Lord Berkley smiled.

"Very good, my lord," Oswald answered softly. "What specifically do you want me to do?"

Lord Berkley looked around. He wanted to be sure his men were not hovering at the door. He wanted no eavesdropping. In the kitchen, the cook was working on the noonday meal. Lord Berkley poked his head into the kitchen and nodded for the cook to go outside. The cook left immediately. Satisfied that no one was in hearing range, he began, "Each spring, Christians make pilgrimages to Canterbury to pray at the tomb of St. Thomas a' Beckett. Are you familiar with these pilgrimages?"

"Indeed, my lord, I have heard of them, never having made the trip myself."

"Sometime in March, just as Lent begins, the prioress of Norwood is to make a pilgrimage to Canterbury. The trip should take three days to get to the city of Canterbury, and three days for her to return to Norwood. During that time, I want her kidnapped and brought to this hunting lodge."

Oswald did not say anything for a moment. It was as if he were processing the plan. The hesitation caused Lord Berkley a moment of nervousness.

"You hesitate, sir?" Lord Berkley inquired.

"Lord, please do not confuse my hesitation with regret in undertaking this mission. On the contrary, ideas like this need thought and consideration."

"Good," Lord Berkley smiled, relieved and impressed with Oswald's intelligence.

"I have undertaken notions like this before, Lord Berkley, and have been successful in each endeavor. But each time a kidnapping occurred, it took proper planning and execution."

"I understand, Oswald. May I ask, will you do this alone?"

"No, Sir Berkley. I have a crew of men that I use for just the occasion. I assure you they are all competent and will perform to my satisfaction."

"Outstanding, sir. Outstanding. However, Oswald, it is imperative during the mission that the woman does not get harmed in anyway."

"Rest assured, Lord Berkley, that my men and I will do our best in that regard. However, if there are members of her group or pilgrims alongside who try to interfere, we cannot guarantee their safety. She is our target, and no one will be allowed to get in our way."

"Yes, Oswald. Understood."

"And we will bring her to this lodge, lord. When we have the woman and are close to the lodge, I will send a messenger to you. We will wait at the lodge with the woman until you arrive."

"Excellent, Oswald. Excellent. And when my men and I arrive at the lodge, I will have your bonus ready for you."

"Very good, Lord Berkley. Is there anything else?"

Lord Berkley hesitated. "Yes, there will be a priest travelling with the prioress. In the course of the kidnapping, he is to be hurt, and hurt badly."

"Sir, that is an unusual request." Oswald's eyes squinted with seriousness. "Besides, there will be other priests on the pilgrimage. How will we know which is to be the target?"

"I am told he will be in the direct company of the prioress. I am also told he is a large man, one whose size will stand out."

"Do you have his name? I want to be sure of the target."

Lord Berkley smiled. He liked Oswald's earnest way of wanting to perform the task correctly. "I assure you, it is not for me, Oswald. It is for a very interested party, one with great power. The target is to be beaten to an inch of his life. In fact, if he were to die from the injuries he sustains, our interested party would be very satisfied." Lord Berkley scribbled on a small piece of parchment and handed the piece to Oswald. "That is his name. Can you read, Oswald?" Lord Berkley asked as an afterthought.

Oswald took the piece of parchment and looked at it. "I can read this, my lord. Nevertheless, attacking or killing a bystander was not a part of the original deal, especially a Catholic priest."

"Oswald, hurt the priest badly, and I will double the bonus intended for you only. If possible, I do not want Lord Pennington to know of this 'extra' duty."

Oswald said nothing. He was thinking again, taking it all in. "It shall be done, Lord Berkley. We will bring the prioress here as you wish and leave the mangled priest on the road to Canterbury."

CHAPTER 4

THE PARSON

Harper's Turn was a small village nestled between vast fields of farming and a small forest. Before the plague of '48, it was nothing more than a gathering place for the local feudal lord's market. The reeves, who sold crops and livestock for the lords of the manor, set up a marketplace in an open field near a creek that wound its way around the field. Glenside Creek was a narrow creek but was deep enough for small boats to navigate all the way to the Thames River, and so the marketplace was a fine spot for local lords to bring their crops to be shipped to London and the surrounding areas.

Tommy Richardson saw the marketplace at the "turn" as an ideal area to construct a tavern for the traders, farmers, and lords to stop by as they did their business. And when he called his tavern The Harp, the area became known as Harper's Turn. Soon, other small businesses began to set up shop, and so by the time of the plague, the village was established around the field that contained the marketplace.

The plague of '48 changed the feudal system of all of Western Europe, and Harper's Turn was no different. With so many lives lost to the plague, changes were made. Feudal lords and their entire families, in some instances, perished in the plague. The lands surrounding Harper's Turn, once owned by various feudal lords, suddenly had no owners and no one to manage them. So the peasants who were once the serfs of the land became the owners and the caretakers of the lands. Essentially, the feudal system died out. Yes, death hit the village, but it also set many peasants free.

And so by 1366, Harper's Turn was a thriving village, continuing to use the small port to ship crops and goods to London and its surrounding areas. From an old path used by reeves to bring cows to market, a road was widened and named Harp's Road. Cottages were constructed near the marketplace and were quickly established as local businesses. Abe Blacksmith set up his shop there, as did Jacob Tanner. Other businesses took hold, and at the insistence of visiting friars, a church was built. Once the small church was built, the town took on its own identity and seemed to thrive with trade and a steady flow of visitors to the marketplace.

The church in the village was named St. Mary Magdalene, after the woman who attended Jesus at the Last Supper. It was Mary Magdalene who discovered the empty tomb three days after Jesus was crucified by the Romans. The church was more of a chapel, as it only held fifty followers at a time. It did not have pews but did have benches. Kneeling was difficult, for the stone floor was rough. There was only one window in the church, and it was placed right behind the altar. Twice a year, the window presented a dazzling light at sunrise that seemed to bring the Holy Spirit to the humble church.

Father Merek Willson lived in a small room attached to the church. The room had a tiny fireplace that housed a fire that could not adequately heat the room. Even though the villagers kept the priest with a good supply of wood, the fireplace never could furnish the heat to make the room comfortable. Father Willson slept on a straw mattress on the floor. Since he did not own a change of clothes, he had no use of a closet or dresser of drawers. It was a barren room. He did have a solitary chair and small table with a candle for reading. Merek never complained, for he felt it was part of his priestly vocation. His humble discomforts kept him grounded on his role as a priest to serve his villagers.

Father Willson said Mass every morning at six. It was after the early Mass that he was told of Tommy Richardson's death. With a few village women, he went to The Harp to say some prayers over the body of his friend. He spoke to Thea and her sister, Emellye, and tried to comfort them as best he could. There was no further discussion between Merek and Thea about the dialogue they had the night before. The village women took care of the sheathing of the body and readying it for burial. It was a task the women were well-adept. They moved the body to the forefront of the inn so that Tommy could have the customary "wake."

Thea had insisted on placing her father's body in a wooden coffin, an expensive cost that not many villagers could afford. Ned Woodman was contacted to begin the construction of the wooden box. Most villagers who passed on to the next world were placed in a shroud, a thin fabric designed to hold a body for a short period of time. Only the rich could afford more costly arrangements, especially a wooden coffin.

As by custom, the wake would last all day and into the next. Family and friends would gather at the deceased house and literally wait to see if the deceased did indeed awaken! While they waited, the host family was expected to provide food and drink. Rumors and old stories of people buried alive terrified the common villager. Persons who were thought dead and were actually in a deep sleep or a trance could be prematurely buried. Thus, the wake, just to be sure.

Father Willson did not believe in the need for a wake. He did recognize that a wake did indeed bring the villagers together. And that, he liked. A wake brought an end to the common ordinary day. Willson knew that most of the villagers worked from sunup to sundown six days a week. A wake provided a needed distraction from the common week. And usually, the family who hosted was glad for the company.

The death of a tavern owner brought the wake to another level. The food and beverage would not only have been uncommonly good; there would also be a great abundance of it. For that reason, Father Willson decided to watch over the wake and to make sure the villagers did not take advantage of the situation. At least, that is the rationale Merek used to stick around longer than usual. He tried to justify his long stay at the wake as protection, but truth be told, he enjoyed being around Thea.

Tommy's daughters afforded a fine menu for the villagers attending the wake. Spread about the main table for the villagers to eat were roasted capons, a few rabbits, and pheasants. A pig had been slaughtered earlier in the day, and the pork was available in large quantities. Bread and cheese were also offered along with Tommy Richardson's own ale. It was a feast of which Tommy would be truly impressed.

At midday, Merek momentarily left The Harp and walked back to the church. He saw some village boys with bow and arrows running into the woods. Merek Willson paused and remembered a moment in his childhood. Ever since he could remember, he had a bow in his hands. His father had run a farm for a feudal lord, and so he would send his four sons out to hunt game for the dinner table. Merek was only six the first time he was given a bow to join his brothers for a hunt. By the time he was ten, he could outshoot his brothers and all the other boys in the nearby village. He had a gift, and it was with the bow.

Although he was the youngest of the four brothers, his gift was recognized by his older brothers. On a hunt, they always made sure Merek got "the shot." Their father did not care who made the kill shot; he only wanted the meat for the dinner table. The older brothers knew that, so they put their pride aside and let Merek work his craft.

The brothers would set Merek up by driving a herd of deer past where Merek was stationed. His aim, his strength, and his intuition would always deliver a kill. And the family ate even in the winter. As most families had meat once or twice a week, the Willsons would have meat almost every night. And at the dinner table, especially after the kill of an extraordinarily large deer, their father would ask who had the kill shot. None of the brothers would say a word, but they would all look to Merek. And the father knew.

Merek reached the church and walked in. It was time for his midday prayers. Genuflecting, he crossed himself with some holy water and approached the rail in front of the altar. He kneeled and began to pray. His prayers were quickly interrupted by thoughts of Thea and her offer. Compared to his lonely barren room at the church, living at The Harp would significantly change his lifestyle. However, bedding her would undoubtedly alter his soul's future! And so he prayed harder to ward off the temptation of accepting Thea's offer.

Finishing his prayers, Merek slowly arose, genuflected, and turned to exit the church. To his surprise, kneeling in the last pew was a fellow priest. Merek had not heard the priest enter. The priest was deep in prayer, head bowed, hands clasped at his chest. Merek walked to the bench in which the priest knelt in front. The priest did not look up but only continued in his silent prayer. Merek waited patiently for the priest to finish.

After a minute or two, Merek felt awkward waiting in silence. After three minutes, he felt the circumstance to be strange. Five minutes later, Merek quietly exited the church. The priest continued in his silent prayer, never looking up or acknowledging Merek's presence. Exiting the church, Merek could only wonder what the man was doing at Harper's Turn. In his three years at Harper's Turn, Merek had only seen friars come through the village, no other church officials. In fact, the friars had stopped coming to Harper's Turn shortly after Merek's arrival. Word had gotten out to them. Do not go near St. Mary Magdalene and Father Willson.

Friars were priests who had a territory to cover with no home parish. Friars took the usual vows of obedience, poverty, and chastity but were supposed to really stress the "poverty" element of their vow. They were to go from village to village spreading the word of God, administering the sacraments, helping the poor, and assisting the small village priests, like Merek Willson. Friars were supposed to only carry the clothes on their back and the sandals on their feet. If the villagers did not feed them, they went hungry. If the villagers did not offer them shelter, they often slept outside under the moon.

But they stopped coming to Harper's Turn. Three months into Father Willson's assignment, a friar came to the village. He was greeted warmly by Merek Willson and was allowed to stay in the St. Mary Magdalene's that night. Merek caught the friar stealing from the alms box and promptly dragged him to the edge of the village. Merek's size and strength were no match for the friar, who protested madly that he had a right to the alms as an official of the church. Merek disagreed and, as he dragged him through the village, announced that no church official was going to take from the good parishioners of St. Mary Magdalene's.

A few men and a host of village wives saw the incident and gained an immediate affection for Father Willson. And when they followed and saw Merek grab the friar by the scruff of the neck and top of his pants, they were in awe of Merek's strength, for he literally threw the friar down the road! Landing on his face, the friar turned over coughing and gagging from the dust he had swallowed. As Merek headed back into the village, the friar slowly stood and began to shout scripture about one's treatment of his fellow man. The friar stopped when Merek suddenly turned. The friar ran and stumbled as Merek began to walk toward him. The begging priest was never seen again.

A few months later, another friar entered the village. He made his way through some of the huts and shops before Merek was given word of his arrival. Merek went to meet the friar, a seemingly good man of God. Merek took the friar to dinner at The Harp that night, and both men were guests of Tommy Richardson's hospitality. The friar and Merek spoke of a variety of subjects, from the commandments to the pope's latest edicts. It was, all in all, a good dinner and welcomed conversation.

At one point in the dinner, Merek had to excuse himself to visit the privy. On his way back, Tommy Richardson stopped him.

"Father Merek, the priest with you," Tommy said, gently pulling on Merek's cassock to stop him. "I don't trust him."

"Tommy, why would you say that? He is a good man, a holy friar," Merek answered, a bit surprised by his friend's warning.

"I'm tellin' you. He's all wrong," Tommy said quietly. "I run a tavern a long time. I know 'evil' when I see it," he added.

"Nonsense, Tommy. You have any proof?" Merek smiled.

"I only know what's in me gut feelin' is all," Tommy muttered and let Merek go.

Merek Willson shook his head and smiled. He walked back to the table and sat with his guest. He and the friar continued with their conversation. An hour later, they left. Merek made a pallet for the friar to sleep on, and so the rest of the night went without incident.

The next morning, after Mass, the friar shared some of Merek's breakfast. Afterward, he said his goodbyes, gave Merek and the church a proper blessing, and made his way out of the village, saying he had one more stop to make before leaving. He said he was going to stop at Widow Thomson's hut to give her his blessing, for her husband had died only a month before.

Father Willson bade him farewell as the friar left. Merek thought nothing of it. A half hour later, Merek found the friar's belt satchel, a small leather purse that fit on the belt of the cassock. It could hold small items or even food for the traveling friar. There was nothing in the purse, but it was obvious the friar would need it. So Merek hurried to the hut of Widow Thomson.

As he approached the hut, he heard a loud woman's voice. When he drew closer, he heard the woman's voice pleading. He heard a man's voice trying to shush her. And then Merek heard the scream. Merek barged in to the hut. There, on the bed, with her woolen skirt hiked up to her shoulders lay Widow Thomson, a poor thin lady in her early thirties, crying. The friar, with his cassock hiked up to his waist, was on top of her, rutting himself on top of her.

"What is the meaning of this, Father?" Merek roared, and he made his way to the bed. He took the friar and threw him to the floor. Widow Thomson, still crying, pulled her woolen gown to cover herself.

The friar tried to gather himself and pick himself off the floor. But Merek gave him no chance. Hoisting the friar to his feet, Merek punched him squarely in the face. The friar would have fallen, but Merek had kept a clenched hand on the friar's cassock. He punched him again and then a third time. Blood from the friar's nose went everywhere, including Merek's cassock. With the third punch, he let the friar hit the floor of the crude hut.

"In the name of God!" Merek shouted.

"He said he would forgive my sins if I let him have me," the widow said as she found her composure and her voice. "He said he would cleanse me of my sins by injecting me with his holy seed," she cried.

"Holy seed? Holy seed?" Merek bellowed. He picked the bleeding friar up and threw him out in the dust of the path that went through the village. The friar landed hard, damaging his shoulder. He lay on the ground, groaning and bleeding.

By now, some of the villagers had heard the commotion and began to make their way to the Widow Thomson's hut. When they saw the friar tossed through the widow's doorway, they came running. They did not get a chance to get too close, for Merek stormed after the fallen friar.

He was not done. His temper was up. Someone had accosted one of his parishioners. And it was a fellow priest! Grabbing the injured priest, Merek hoisted the injured friar to his feet. The friar was defenseless, bleeding and trying to grab his injured shoulder. Merek saw that his left shoulder was aching and was a little misshapen. With all his might, as if he had a hammer in his hand, Merek closed on the injured shoulder with his fist as a hammer. The friar screamed in pain and fell to his knees.

"May God damn you, brother!" Merek shouted as he stood the traveling priest on his feet again. Grabbing the friar by the back of his neck with one hand and his other hand grabbing the lose rope around his cassock, Merek escorted the bleeding man toward the river. The crowd followed.

Merek held the battered priest upright on a small embankment ten feet above the creek. The crowd that followed drew near, not knowing what their mad priest was going to do.

"Please, I cannot swim!" the battered priest whimpered. "Please do not throw me in."

"Nonsense, brother. The waters of the Glenside will cleanse your sins," Merek announced.

Without another word, Merek sent the priest flying into the waters of the Glenside. The friar emerged from the water crying and gasping for help. The swiftly moving water was pulling him to the middle of the river. The injured priest's head bobbed up and down as he flung his arms wildly, trying to stay afloat.

Merek stood on the edge of the bank and watched with the crowd. He turned as he faced his parishioners, his temper now at rest. "Brothers and sisters, I ask for your forgiveness for my brutish behavior. It was un-Christian of me to attack that man. I am afraid I am not a good example of Christian love or charity."

Someone in the crowd pointed to the water, and all looked. The drowning priest had secured a floating log and was hanging on, gasping for air and moving swiftly away from the village.

Merek turned from the river and walked through the crowd. It parted quickly as he passed. A few of the villagers said, "God bless you, Father," or "We are with you, Father," as Merek passed. That Sunday, the congregational turnout to Mass was extraordinary. There was no room even to stand. And St. Mary Magdalene had its largest collection of offerings ever!

Lost in thought, Merek had walked across the village and was standing in front of the Harp. The hair on the back of his neck was standing, just thinking of the corrupt friar and his rape of the Widow Thomson. Merek was aware of his temper and, for the most part, had kept it in check since he had taken his vows. But every once in a while, it erupted.

"Pardon me, Father," a voice behind Merek said quietly.

Merek turned and saw it was the mysterious priest who had been praying so deeply in the church.

"My name is Father Colman, Leo Colman," the priest said, his head bowed and his hands clasped together in front of him.

Merek put his arm out. "I am Father Merek Willson."

The priest took Merek's arm and shook it in a most gentle way. Father Colman bowed as he shook Merek's arm, never allowing his eyes to meet Merek's. Even though Merek was indeed taller than the priest, Father Colman's perpetually bowed stance made Merek even taller. And it made Merek uncomfortable.

"Come, Father, I am not a bishop," Merek quipped. "Must you be so formal?"

"I bring news from the bishop. It is in a sealed envelope. If you follow me, Father, I shall get it for you," the priest said quietly.

Father Colman began to walk back toward St. Mary Magdalene. As Merek followed, he took note of the priest. Father Colman's cassock was old, worn, and had a multitude of stitchery that seemed to hold the garment together. His sandals were worn from long use. Even though Father Colman gave the appearance of being frail and bent, Merek took notice that his gait was strong. And Merek had to hurry to keep up.

Father Colman had ridden into the village on a cart horse. The horse was aged and did not need to be tethered to a post to keep it in one place. The horse was brown with a shabby mane. A crude saddle was tied to its back, and from a lone saddle bag, Father Colman pulled a sealed envelope. He gave it to Merek.

Merek was surprised by the letter. It had been over three years since he had seen the official seal of the bishop. The crimson seal was beautiful, with a bishop's figure holding a sword and standing defiantly over a serpent. Merek looked at it in awe.

"I felt the same way when I received mine, Father," the priest broke the silence.

Instinctively, Merek made the sign of the cross. Father Colman, taking Merek's example, blessed himself too. He slowly began to open the letter, first by breaking the seal. He took his time and opened it with the utmost care.

"Father, forgive me," Father Colman said in the most humble way, "are you able to read?"

Merek nodded. "Some." Of course, he could read. However, it was not always that way, for the son of a poor serf was never offered an education. But Merek's time in the monastery had offered him the time to learn to read and write. In time, he was a valued clerk and actually served the bishop in that capacity. Serving the bishop seemed a lifetime ago.

And now he held the document in wonder. The words did not amaze him. The fact that it came from the Bishop of Winchester, arguably the richest and strongest bishop in all of England, amazed him. To think that the bishop took time to send Merek a message was unfathomable. Merek was just amazed that the bishop knew where Merek was serving the Church. How could the bishop possibly know where Harper's Turn was?

The message was in Latin:

Father Willson, please report at once to the priory of Norwood. You are to accompany the prioress, Madam Eglantyne, and her entourage on her pilgrimage to Canterbury. Pray at the tomb of St. Thomas a' Beckett and begin the Lenten season with our Lord in your heart. Yours in the faith of Christ, Bishop William Edington, March, MCCCLVI (gb)

Father Colman allowed Merek to read the message a few more times before he made a comment.

"We are to leave immediately, Father," the older priest said quietly.

Merek did not reply. He was amazed. He had been praying for help from temptation in regard to Thea, and his prayers had been answered! A trip to Canterbury would take weeks, maybe even a month. It would be a month away from Harper's Turn and Thea.

"How fast does God work?" Merek mumbled to himself.

Father Colman smiled and replied, "Our Lord's ways are not always mysterious." He smiled again.

"But why me? Why has the bishop chosen me?" Merek asked.

"Chosen us," Father Colman answered softly. "We do not question our Lord, bishop. We are servants to our Lord, and the bishop is our superior."

"I understand. But who will take care of the village?" Merek looked about.

"I too had to leave my 'flock' behind. It is not what I wanted, but I—we—must obey. They are sending a friar to attend the village in which I serve," Father Colman tried to reassure Merek.

"I doubt that will happen here," Merek added confidently. Obviously, Father Colman did not know the history of friars entering Harper's Turn. Merek was sure his 'flock' would be unattended.

"Will you be able to secure a horse?" Father Colman asked. "It is a long way to Canterbury."

"I will have to rent one," Merek answered, thinking of the villager who could spare a horse. He could only think of one.

Father Colman and Merek had been walking as they talked. They had returned to the front of St. Mary Magdalene.

"Father Colman, I cannot leave today. I must tend to the funeral of one of our villagers. I was hoping you would help."

"Gladly, Father Willson. Gladly."

"I must warn you, Father Colman, that the villager is the owner of the tavern over there," Merek said as he pointed to The Harp. Merek knew that there were certain clergy who would balk at participating in a service for an innkeeper. After all, "innkeepers were the devil's brothers"!

"Every soul needs God's tending, no matter how he makes a living," Father Colman answered with his head slightly bowed. "I will assist in any way, Father Willson."

Merek liked this priest. There was a spirit of humility and servitude in his speech, his mannerisms, and in his apparel. This priest was no hypocrite. He was a man who loved God and served his people. Merek did not worry about this priest misrepresenting the Church.

"Thank you, Father," was all Merek said. He smiled and led him to the tavern. They would break bread together.

CHAPTER 5

THE CONFEDERATES MEET

The Stag's Inn had been serving ale for almost one hundred years. One of the largest taverns in the southern part of England, The Stag's Inn seemed to grow every few years as more and more rooms were added for meetings, celebrations, or to accommodate travelers wishing to spend the night or only an hour. The owners of The Stag tried to accommodate all, for a customer at The Stag could eat, drink, and pay to be merry by the homemade ale, the delicious food, or the host of women who made themselves available for pleasure.

In the large tavern that housed benches and a bar, a group of five men sat around a small table against the far wall of the entrance. Each had a mug of ale in front of him, but unlike the other customers of The Stag, the men took their time to drink their ale. They sat quietly, observing all the activity that was occurring in the busy tavern. At one end of the bar, a group of men sang an old ballad of a man married to a shrew. At a bench nearby, men gambled with dice and seemed to scream as the dice spun on the bench. In a corner near the bar, a couple kissed passionately, the woman's leg wrapped around the man's waist. The bartender had a man, clearly drunk, by the scruff of his neck and was slapping the man for not paying for his drink. Suddenly a woman approached the table of the five men, trying to ply her trade. One of the men told her to take her business elsewhere. The group of men was not interested, at least not this night.

A keen observer of the group would have observed a few things about the men: They were all about the same age, mid-to-late twenties. The men owned clothing that was old and worn but kept neatly and with stitching smartly used. The five men wore pants with a similar brown color. Each had a vest with a tan color. The men carried weapons, all concealed. A few had daggers hidden in their boots while the others had small swords tucked neatly in the coats that covered their vests. Their boots had a similar look, for they were made by the military. The men all had beards that were well-kept. They did not wear hats inside the tavern. At one time, they had all served in the king's army.

On the other side of the room, on a bench by the bar, a curly-headed man with a large belly sat with a young woman on his lap. They were sharing a cup of ale, clearly enjoying its taste and each other's company. The man was young, had a curly brown beard and brown hair, and gave a hearty laugh when the girl on his lap spilled a mouthful of ale down her front. Not missing a beat, the man pretended to try to lap up the spilled ale, placing his face between her breasts. And then she too laughed.

The man with the girl on his lap tried to stand up, had his feet entwined with the woman on his lap, and they both fell over backward to the floor. More laughter ensued, not just from the fallen but from those around them. Slowly the man arose and helped the lady to her feet, giving her a kiss and hug. There was more applause from the patrons around them. The drunken man helped the lady to her seat and then stumbled to the bar to refill his mug of ale.

Oswald entered the inn and stood near the bar, watching the raucous crowd. Soon he caught the attention of the owner. The two conversed briefly, nodding as they parted. Oswald was sure to give the owner a few coins. The owner disappeared into a backroom. Oswald sipped his ale and studied the crowd. He glanced at the five men sitting quietly near the back of the tavern amongst the crowd's chaotic behavior.

Soon the innkeeper reappeared and nodded to Oswald. Oswald thanked the owner and made his move. Gliding through the inn, he approached the table of the quiet men, close enough to catch the eye of one of the men. Oswald nodded to the man, and with his hand, he gestured to a room behind the bar. The man at the table nodded back and said something quietly to his mates. They all got up at once, brought their packs, and followed the first. As they approached the bar, they were careful not to bump into the curly-headed man carrying a pint of ale back to his tipsy woman. The drunken man, stumbling with the pint of ale, bumped into the last of the men who were joining Oswald in the back room. The drunken man with the curly brown hair apologized, bowing and, adding insult, poured some of his ale on the man. Angry, the man shoved the drunken man, who fell to the floor, spilling the rest of his ale all over himself. The patrons observing the action roared with laughter. The man did not stop, nor did he offer to help the drunken man to his feet. He merely followed the others into the back room.

Oswald was seated at a table in the back room when the men entered. He did not get up when they walked in and set their packs against the wall. Nothing was said as the four men sat down at the table. The fifth entered a few seconds after the others, wiping his coat from the spilled ale. A servant girl poured each man a cup of wine. No one spoke as she poured. It was not until she left did the discussion begin.

Oswald spoke first, "Glad you could meet me here, Thaddeus. I know it was out of your way."

Thaddeus, the group's leader, answered, "No trouble at all, Oswald. You need our services. We are here. What is the mission?"

Oswald did not hesitate. "I have been hired to perform a service in which a noblewoman is to be held ransom. It is a tricky endeavor, one which will try your planning and skill."

Thaddeus nodded. "Go on. Tell us more."

Oswald continued, his voice continuing in a businesslike monotone, "There will be a group of pilgrims heading to Canterbury in the next few weeks in which a prioress, the daughter of a high-ranking nobleman, is to be plucked from the group, brought to a lodge a distance away, and kept for ransom."

Thaddeus answered without emotion, "Seems simple enough. What is the catch?"

Oswald answered directly, "No one on the trip is to be harmed, especially the woman."

"But if someone on the trip interferes or tries to be a hero?" one of the men of the group asked.

"Well, then perhaps he must be incapacitated for the good of our cause," Oswald said with a sly smile on his lips.

"If the group in which she travels is large, there will surely be a soldier or two," another was quick to point out. "Those soldiers might offer resistance."

"If they do, you will use any means to secure the woman," Oswald replied. "I just want to be sure there is no unnecessary violence toward the other members of the party."

"Understood," Thaddeus replied, looking sharply at his men. "We understand."

"Good," Oswald said quietly. "I have it on authority that the lady will be traveling with another nun and a few priests. They are to meet other pilgrims in Southwark at the inn of Harry Bailly. You will join them there, pretending to be pilgrims. You will meet them, travel with them, and get a feel for the others traveling with you. The trip to Canterbury should take two or three days. I want you to wait until the return trip from Canterbury to make your move. By then, you will have an idea who will interfere and who will not."

"Under what guise are we to travel?" Thaddeus asked.

Oswald threw a small purse on the table. "Use these coins to purchase new clothes. I want you to give the appearance of guildsmen." From his sheath, Oswald pulled out patches of cloth. "Have these patches sewn onto your new clothes. I want it to seem that each of you represents a different guild. There is a patch here for a weaver, a dyer, a carpenter, a tapestry maker, and a haberdasher. I want to make it seem as though you are successful guildsman."

"May we assume the usual wages, bonuses, and payments for our services?" Thaddeus asked.

"As we have worked out before," Oswald assured him. "In fact, there will be an extra payment if the kidnapping produces the desired result. Our employer is a most considerate and anxious man to have this deed accomplished. I feel we will all profit handsomely."

"How will we communicate with you?" Thaddeus asked.

"It will be easy. I am coming along as one of the pilgrims. But I assure you, I am there only to observe and help in any way you may need me. Thaddeus, this will be your operation. Her abduction from the group will be your way, your plan. Once the prioress is brought to the appointed lodge, I will take over. Thaddeus, once we are underway to Canterbury, I will give you a map of the lodge in which I want the woman brought."

There was a faint knock on the door.

"Come," Oswald said loudly.

The door opened, and the drunken curly-headed man entered.

"I am here at your disposal Oswald," the curly-headed man said in a quiet tone, far from the loud, boisterous carouser he was seen in the tavern.

"Gentlemen, this is Albert. He will also be going on the trip to Canterbury," Oswald said flatly.

The men looked at one another with concern.

"In what capacity?" one of the men asked.

"How will he aid us?" another asked.

Thaddeus interrupted, "Oswald, my men have concerns about this man. We have seen him in the tavern behaving in a most uproarious way. He seems to be a drunken whoremonger. In our line of work, how shall we trust a man like that?"

Oswald nodded to Albert, who spoke in a most sober way, "I assure you, gentlemen, that my behavior out in the tavern was an act, a subterfuge to portray me in a way that no one will take heed of me in any important way. And that is my role on the trip. I will be a drunk, a clown, and gain the mistrust of all on the trip, so much that some will not care what they say in my presence, for I am the silent mouse that no one notices, the eyes and ears that report only to you."

Albert took a dagger from his pocket and gave it to the man he stole it from moments ago. "I believe this is yours, sir." He smiled, giving it to the last soldier in the group.

Oswald continued, "Albert can be of use to us. He is an actor and a splendid pickpocket. And, believe it or not, he is a cook. Once we get to the lodge with our prioress, Albert will provide us with the nourishment we need to wait out the paid ransom. You will like his cooking. His blancmange is the best I have ever tasted. On the trip, Albert will travel with you. He will be the cook that your guild has sent along. That is how we will play it."

The men looked at Albert in a new light. He appeared to be stone sober while earlier he was completely drunk out of his mind. His clothes gave the appearance of a drunkard, with stains and rips all over. Although no one said anything, they each noticed that he had an open sore on his knee. Puss was seen where the sore was located, indicating that the wound was not only opened but was not cared for. The men did not think much of the wound. All had been in the war and had seen far worse.

"Me, I will meet you at The Tabard once I verify the prioress's schedule. Thaddeus, I will communicate with you in the usual way. We will meet there and proceed with the group to Canterbury. Is there anything else?"

No one said a word. Each of the five soldiers exited, no one saying anything more. When they had gone, only Albert remained.

"They seem up to the task," Albert said calmly.

"Those men were dependable soldiers. I feel confident that they will accomplish the mission. It will be our task to stay out of their way," Oswald replied. "Albert, there will be a man waiting outside the door. On your way out, send him in."

"I will," Albert replied. "By the way, how will I know when to proceed to Southwark?"

"Just keep in touch, Albert. Keep in touch."

Albert nodded and left the room. In his place, a man entered the room. He was a tall, lean man with eyes that smiled. Oswald felt a small chill looking at the man's eyes, for they seemed to smile, yet there was something sinister behind them. The man had a beard, a beard that came to a point on his chin. He had an unusual color to his face, like one who had spent too much time in the sun.

"Ah, you are Anglicus?" Oswald asked.

"I am," the man said with a broad smile. "At your service."

Oswald noticed that the man wore a woolen gown that stretched all the way to his knees. The gown had small holes near the man's waist and looked as though he had worn it for a long time. Around his neck, the man had a long strap that fit around his arm and torso. A dagger, large and somewhat rusty, was attached to the strap. Even though the dagger was rusty on the surface, Oswald could see the blade was sharp, for there was a small shine to it.

"I am Oswald. You come highly recommended by some of my colleagues. I am surprised that you are available for this appointment."

"Appointment?" Anglicus laughed. "Now, that's a different way to express what I do."

"As a man of the sea, I was surprised you were available. That is all I meant."

"Not to worry, sir. Our 'friends' tell me that you are a man who delivers, and that the pay for such a job is quite high. So I make myself available to you."

"So be it," Oswald replied. Oswald was suddenly uncomfortable around this man. Anglicus's eyes had malice in them, even though his mouth was smiling and his manners were polite. Oswald knew people, and he instantly knew that Anglicus was dangerous. "Will you be in port for the next month or two?"

Anglicus smiled. "If the price is right, I shall make myself 'in port.' What is the job?"

"A group of 'pilgrims' will be travelling to Canterbury to worship at the tomb of St. Thomas a' Beckett in the next few weeks. One of them is a priest. This priest has an enemy, and this enemy wants to hire you to hurt this priest very badly. I mean badly. In fact, if the priest dies from the wounds he receives, that is an accommodation our employer is fine with."

"A priest?" Anglicus smiled. "I am to hurt a priest, perhaps hurt him so badly that he dies from his wounds? How hard can that be?" He genuinely laughed.

"But you must comply with my plan," Oswald added. "For we are all being paid by my employer. You must fulfill your part according to what I want."

"Continue," was all Anglicus said.

"Your part of the plan must wait until I give the go sign. You must wait until the first part of my plan is exercised before you do your part."

"And what is your plan?"

"That, I cannot tell you. However, this I can tell you. You will meet us at The Tabard in Southwark and travel to Canterbury with the pilgrims and me. And on the return trip, you and I will coordinate our missions at the same time. If you are successful, you will be richly compensated. But it must be timed with my operation. Are we clear?"

"Assuredly so. And where am I to meet with you and the others?"

"Meet us in Southwark at The Tabard. It is an inn there, owned by a man named Harry Bailly."

"So be it. I will comply with your wishes. By the way, does your employer care in what manner the pain is given?"

"I doubt he cares. He just wants it delivered in a harsh way."

CHAPTER 6

TOMMY'S WAKE AND FUNERAL

Tommy's "wake" went without incident. As expected, the entire village turned out to pay respects to the popular tavern keeper, eat his delicious food, and drink his homemade ale. Even though the wake occurred on a weekday, the villagers made it a special "holiday" and declared no tedious work would be done until Tommy Richardson "awoke" or was buried. The body lay on a bench near the back of the tavern with the lid of the casket open. In the front of the tavern, the villagers ate, drank, told Tommy Richardson stories, and paid their respects to the two daughters. At the end of the day, Tommy did not "awaken." Father Willson performed some last rites again in the back of the tavern and declared the burial would be early the next day. He dismissed the villagers, not wanting them to drain the kegs and eat all the food, for the girls would have to be able to run the tavern without their father and would need every penny to make a go of it. The villagers left The Harp after the announcement. Father Colman stayed and prayed silently with Father Willson. Merek was glad for the company. He did not want to be alone with Thea.

In the morning, both priests helped some of the men of the village dig the grave for Tommy Richardson. The ground was hard, for the winter had been unusually cold, and the beginning of March had not been much different. The men used picks to break the ground and shovels to turn the dirt away. But as they began digging, it began to rain. The more they dug, the harder the rain fell. It turned into a cold drenching rain. Merek tried to encourage the men and thank them for doing their Christian duty. Each time he looked around,

53

Father Colman was right with the other men, digging and picking in what was becoming a thick cold mud of clay and soil. The humble priest did not stop, nor did he complain about the chore of digging. Neither did the other men. And so they dug.

Despite the constant downpour of rain, the villagers turned out for funeral. It began with the service in the church, with both priests cocelebrating the Mass. Afterward, the funeral processed to the graveyard, a piece of property near the church grounds that was already heavily populated by the former villagers. Fortunately, the rain had let up after the church service, but the briskness and the cold wind made Father Willson hurry through the graveside prayers and blessings.

After the graveside ceremony, Thea and her sister invited the villagers back to The Harp for a midday meal. As Father Willson led the villagers to the tavern, Thea held on to his arm, pretending to need his arm to keep her balance in the muddy road. Merek knew better but did not fight her closeness. After the somberness of the funeral, her touch was most welcome. As they entered The Harp, Merek and Thea paused to let the procession of villagers enter before they did. Thea continued to hold on to Merek's arm and snuggled close as they stood greeting the guests to The Harp. Once the last villager passed the couple and entered the tavern, Thea looked at Merek with tears in her eyes.

"Seems natural standing next to you and huddling so close," she said. Despite her tears, Thea smiled and entered the tavern, leaving Merek alone for a brief moment.

Merek did not reply. His tongue was tied. Deep down, he knew she was right. It did seem natural. At one point, he wanted the line of villagers to be longer. Merek took a deep breath and forced himself back to reality. What was he doing? What was he thinking? "Enjoying the moment" was wrong. It was the devil's temptation. Suddenly he was thankful for his upcoming trip to Canterbury. Distance would only help his mind get right and rid himself of this carnal temptation. Yet as he climbed the small tavern stairs to the entrance, fully aware of the temptation Thea posed, the thought of her on his arm crept back in his mind.

The mourners were glad to get out of the cold and huddled close to the enormous hearth of the tavern. The ladies of the village helped the sisters serve the meal while some of the men manned the kegs and poured the fresh ale. Father Merek said grace, and all began to eat and drink in honor of Tommy Richardson. It was a quiet meal, with a sincere somberness to the occasion. Tommy Richardson would truly be missed.

Merek sat with Father Colman near one end of a long-crowded bench. It seemed the men had crowded to one of the long benches, and the women another. There were some more Tommy stories told with laughter and smiles, but not in a raucous way. The stories were almost told out of respect for fun-loving tavern keep. The villagers would have agreed, in a time where sorrow and suffering were the norm, Tommy Richardson's love of life was a true anomaly.

Father Colman waited for the stories to end and addressed Merek, "Father Willson, I think we should leave in the morning."

Merek was lost in thought thinking of Thea's beautiful eyes.

"Father Willson."

Merek came back to his senses. "Sorry, Father Colman. Go on."

"We should really leave tomorrow, perhaps before the first light. It is a long trip."

"I understand. I have concerns."

"Concerns?"

"Who will look after the villagers when I am gone? This pilgrimage might take weeks, maybe even a month. Who will say Mass and deliver the sacraments?"

"I am sure a friar will happen along. Perhaps the bishop will send one."

"Perhaps," Merek answered with a wry smile. He knew better. Travelling friars avoided Harper's Turn ever since Merek threw the last one in the river. He made no mention of this to Father Colman but drank from his mug of ale.

"The bishop has given us an order, Father Willson. We are bound to obey."

"You are right, Father Colman. Yes, we must obey."

"Do you have a horse? I am afraid that mine will not carry us both. But I will share if you cannot get one, Father."

"I am thinking that one of the good villagers will lend me a horse."

"Excellent." Father Colman looked around. He began to stand. "I am going over to the church, Father. It is near nones, and prayers need to be said. Will you join me?"

"I will be with you shortly, Father. I must procure a horse before leaving on our journey."

Father Colman nodded, sought out Thea and Emellye, blessed them, and left the tavern. Thea looked over at Merek and nodded, her eyes intent on showing Merek her affections for him. The look made Merek's stomach flip with nervousness, for he knew the ale he had drunk made him susceptible to temptation. It was not Thea's temptation that worried Merek. It was his own.

Merek had to gather himself before he approached Thea. He knew her father's death had an emotional toll on Thea on this day, and he did not want to do anything that he would regret, like giving into his desires for her. For although she was vulnerable, he was even more vulnerable. At that moment in time, Thea looked beautiful.

"Did you get enough to eat, Merek?" she asked as Merek approached.

"Plenty, Thea. Thank you. I am sure no one will leave the tavern hungry . . . or thirsty," Merek said. "I need to ask a favor."

"You have thought about my proposal?" she asked with a smile.

Merek had to gather himself at her directness. He only smiled. "Truly, Thea, I cannot even think of your proposal. But I do ask a favor."

"Name it, Merek."

"I need to borrow Sir William." Sir William was Tommy's horse, a beautiful black palfrey that Tommy had purchased from a trader a few years back. Tommy had named it Sir William after the great warrior king, William the Conqueror. Tommy did not know much about King William, but he liked the name and wanted to give his horse a noble name.

"You are leaving?" Thea asked with a sudden seriousness.

"Church business. I have been ordered to Canterbury on a pilgrimage of sorts. As it is a long way, I seek the comfort of a horse."

"How long do you propose to be gone?"

"Weeks, perhaps a month."

"And who will tend to the villagers and their spiritual needs?"

"I am sure a friar will be along to help."

Thea laughed a full-throated laugh. "God's arms! After what you did to the last friar, I highly doubt that another will come around."

Merek agreed with her but did not let on. "The bishop has ordered me to go. I must obey."

Thea stopped laughing and simply smiled at Merek. "You take orders from a man you have never met. He asks you to take a long trip without means of transportation, and he unwittingly leaves a village without its spiritual rock! Is that correct? Is it not irresponsible of your superior to send you away and leave us poor uneducated villagers alone to fight off the evils of Satan?" Thea said the last sentence with a sardonic grin, using every bit of a sarcastic tone she could muster.

"Indeed. Indeed, it is," Merek answered, understanding her sarcasm. "God help the devil if he enters The Harp and runs into the likes of you. He will not have a chance. It is the devil who will seek out the good bishop for help," he said with a straight face.

Thea laughed, got up from her seat, and gave Merek a kiss on the cheek and a hug. "Take Sir William. Just make sure you bring him back," she said in his ear. "Just come back," she repeated and hugged him again for what seemed like a long time.

Merek did not answer. As they broke from their embrace, Thea simply gazed at Merek. Her stare was unnerving, for Merek suddenly felt pangs he had not truly felt since his ordination years ago. He had to go.

"Thank you for the use of the horse" was all Merek could think to say.

"Yes, take Sir William. But I shall require a rent for his use," she said with laughter in her eyes.

Merek regained his composure and countered, "Thea, I am sure that you understand that I am handicapped when it comes to money. Surely I will not be able to pay a month's rent on a horse."

"Who said anything about money, Merek?"

Merek's face turned bright red. And Thea laughed. "Take Sir William. But upon your return, I shall require a service from you."

Merek did not reply immediately. Thea laughed again. "Do not worry, Merek. I will ask nothing of you that will endanger your priestly vows."

Merek looked at Thea, and now it was he who laughed. She joined him.

"I shall pick up Sir William at first light."

"Fine. Now go pray for all us sinners." Without another word, Thea walked up and hugged Merek tightly again. He could feel her cheek next to his. "Just make sure to come back," she whispered.

Thea let go and went about helping her sister in the tavern. Merek nodded to some of the villagers, shook some hands, and turned to go. He looked back one time and saw Thea looking at him. There was love in her eyes. He did not really know that look, for no woman had looked at him that way before. But he knew. And then he exited the tavern and made his way back to the church.

CHAPTER 7

THE TRIP TO NORWOOD

Merek knew it was not a good idea to travel the roads south of London alone. Robbers, thieves, and road pirates made short work of a lone traveler. And there were many. And even though Father Colman accompanied Merek on the trip, it did not sit well with Merek. He felt vulnerable. Father Colman was a true priest, older in age, and with a sense that God would protect them from criminals of all sorts.

Unfortunately, Merek knew better. His experience in France had taught him that it was great faith to have in God, our Lord Savior, Jesus, and the Holy Spirit. But faith was held stronger when you were able to defend yourself with proper instruments. And so, as they readied their horses for the journey, Merek packed his longbow. The shaft of the bow was made of a fine ash. The ash gave the bow sturdiness yet allowed it the deadly flexibility to launch arrows. Merek did not keep the bow tethered. The cord was made of hemp, finely wound to give it the tense pull it needed to bend the shaft. Merek knew the more he kept the bow strung, the weaker the hemp cord became. The cord was kept in a small bag attached to the sheath of arrows on his saddle.

Merek kept a dozen arrows in the sheath attached to his saddle. The sheath was canvas and totally covered the arrows. It kept the arrows dry and did not let any fall out. In battle, an archer would have had the canvas sheath tied around his waist, but Merek was satisfied to have it tied to his saddle. The arrows were made of yew, a sturdy wood that could be made straight with little work. To help the arrow fly straight, Merek used goose feathers called fletching. When choosing his fletching, Merek was certain to choose the feathers for an arrow from the same bird, even the same wing. By choosing the arrows from the same wing, he could be sure they were curved the same way. Half of Merek's arrows were tipped with the conventional arrowheads made of iron. The other half were tipped with bodkins, an unusual tip that was developed during the war with France. The bodkin tip was uniquely square at the end for the purpose of penetrating armor. Merek had saved the half dozen bodkin tipped arrows from his time in France. Fortunately, he had not used one since he had returned to England.

The two priests mounted their horses and left Harper's Turn just as first light of dawn was seen in the east. The morning was cold, but fortunately, the air was still. As they left the village, the horses' hooves crunched on the frost-covered road. Both priests wore the hood of their cassocks in an attempt to keep their heads warm. They began at a brisk pace leaving the village but after an hour slowed their horses.

Father Colman saw the longbow and the sheath of arrows Merek tied to the saddle of his horse and waited until they slowed their pace to a walk.

"I must ask you, Brother Merek. Why the weapon? Do you not believe that the Holy Spirit will guide and protect us?"

"Yes, Father Colman, of course. I worry that some of the vagabonds of the forest we may encounter have not heard of the Holy Spirit, and that He does protect us. The bow will be a sign to the thieves that we are protected by Our Lord." It was Merek's attempt at lightening the situation, for having spent time with Father Colman, he knew there was a chance that Father Colman would launch into one of his sermons.

"I see. And do you really know how to use the instrument?" Father Colman asked.

"Somewhat," Merek answered in an understated way. He had not told Father Colman of his life before the priesthood. He truly had not told anyone, not even Thea. He had not told them that he had been an archer in the king's army, had fought in the war with

France, and had taken many lives. Merek, in fact, had been a killer with the bow. His skill was unmatched in the company in which he served.

The villagers of Harper's Turn might have guessed as much. In the three years in which Father Merek had served the village as its priest, they had had the opportunity to witness his prowess with the bow. In fact, he had been a regular on their hunting trips. His presence guaranteed that if there were a shot at a deer or boar, Merek's proficiency with a bow was almost always a sure thing. The villagers had seen him draw the mighty string on the six-foot bow and unleash the blinding arrow with accuracy and death.

Ironically, it had been the king's orders that had first shown Merek's skill. He had only been serving the village six months when the local constable showed up at Harper's Turn with the latest edict from the king. The edict stated that each village in England would have weekly practice with the longbow. The king had seen the destruction the longbow had in France and wanted to ensure England's superiority of its use in the years to come. Therefore, he ordered that each village, town, and city would have weekly time set aside to practice the art of shooting the longbow. No other country in Europe could match England's proficiency with the longbow, and the king wanted it to remain that way.

The constable read the law and waited for the villagers to give him a plan of action as to how they would obey the king's law. To disobey would be horrible, for fines would be levied. The poor villagers would be unable to pay the fines and would end up in jail. It was not a good situation.

"I say," the constable announced, "this village will need an instructor to lead the village in its weekly drill of shooting the longbow."

"But we are farmers," one of the villagers said. "We have no knowledge of the longbow."

"Nevertheless, it is the king's order that each village and shire shall practice with the longbow in case the war with France comes to our fair shores. Now, if no one in the village can be a proper teacher, I shall send a proper master who shall lead in the teaching of the use of the longbow." The constable paused. "Of course, the master shall need compensation for his travel to the village. He shall need room and board."

The villagers were not happy. There was great murmuring amongst them.

"Wait," Merek stepped in front of the crowd. He was still in his vestments, just having finished Mass. "I will teach the use of the longbow."

The constable did not laugh, scoff, or smile. He was a wise man who had learned over the years that sometimes the unexpected was the expected!

"Father, my name is William Kint. I am the constable for the king in this area. I have not seen you here before."

"I am Father Merek Willson. I have been serving Harper's Turn for only six months."

"You have skill with the longbow?"

"Some," Merek understated. Merek's answer was simple, but the look in his eyes told Kint everything he needed to know. Kint had looked at Merek's size, the broad shoulders and big chest, and guessed what Merek had been in another life. Yet, he played Merek's game.

"Perhaps, Father, you could give us a simple lesson in the use of the longbow?" Kint smiled, playing along.

"Surely, sir. If you will let me get my bow."

Kint nodded and smiled.

The villagers were confused. Their murmuring amongst themselves amused Kint. They do not know, he thought. He continued to grin as Father Merek returned with a longbow. The priest had taken off his vestments and was in his daily cassock. The villagers were mystified by the length of the bow. It was six feet in length! Yes, they had bows and hunted frequently but had never seen a longbow. Some had heard about it, but none had ever seen one, let alone used one.

Merek quickly strung the bow and prepared to launch an arrow.

"Choose, Master Kint," Merek said quietly.

Kint pointed to a tree twenty-fives yards away. The arrow was loosed quickly and hit the tree dead center. The crowd did not know what to say. As they turned to Merek, he had already tethered another arrow and let it fly at a tree fifty yards away. Another solid hit. The third arrow hit a tree squarely at one hundred yards.

Suddenly the villagers cheered. Merek unstrung the bow and held his hand up for the villagers to stop their applause. "Have you seen enough, Master Kint?"

"Oh, I have seen enough, Father. I have seen enough. You will do."

And the villagers cheered again.

Later, Master Kint and Father Merek had dinner together at The Harp. They became good friends. Merek knew Kint to be an honest constable who looked after his territory and treated the people fairly. And Kint knew that Merek was no ordinary priest. They would remain friends.

And Merek kept his part of the bargain by having longbow sessions each Sunday afternoon. The villagers, particularly the boys, were eager to learn. Merek found that by teaching the art of the bow, he not only served his country, but his God. The boys' skills with the bow improved over time, and Merek, as their instructor, had their attention and respect. He noticed they attended Mass more regularly and helped him with the minor duties of running the church.

Merek and Father Colman were miles from the village. As they were about to enter a thick forest, Merek noticed that the path narrowed so that the horses could not walk side by side. The forest was thick with mighty elms. Underneath the elms, smaller ferns and grasses grew sporadically. The hair on the back of Merek's neck stood up, for he knew the multitude of thick elms would give proper cover to highwaymen or thieves. Merek chose to be in front, so when the horses entered the path that narrowed, Merek hurried his horse forward. By being in front, Merek would be able to see any awaiting ambushes or trouble. At the same time, he made his longbow ready. He pulled it from the saddle and strung one end. He loosened the drawstring that held the cover of the canvas bag holding his arrows. If attacked, he wanted to be ready.

It was then that Father Colman wanted to have a conversation. He was oblivious to the potential danger of the thick forest and the threat of attack on the two travelers. "Father Willson, I feel a need to ask you a question, priest to priest," Father Colman began.

"I am right here, Father, no need to be so loud," Merek said patiently. He did not want their voices to carry and draw any unwanted attention to any potential trouble.

"I want to ask you about tithes and tithing," Father Colman continued.

"By church law, a parishioner is to give one-tenth of his earnings to the Church," Merek recited by memory. "What is your question, Father?"

"Not a question, Father Willson, but a concern. You see, the villages I serve are poor and destitute. They have very little to begin with—"

"And you have a hard time collecting their tithes," Merek interrupted. He turned and looked at Father Colman behind him. Father Colman was astonished, as if Merek could read his mind. "So do I, Father Colman. So do I."

Father Colman felt immediate relief. "Oh, Father Willson, I thought I was the only one breaking the church's law by not demanding tithes. I have truly wrestled with the problem. I have prayed to our Lord time and again yet have anguished over the issue all the time. For a while, I demanded the tithes but then would turn around and give it right back to my parishioners in the form of food and clothing."

"Did you feel guilty for giving it back and not sending it the holy bishop?"

Father Colman did not answer right away. He was thinking. "No, Merek, I did not," Father Colman finally replied. Merek noticed it was the first time Father Colman addressed him by Merek's first name.

Merek turned and smiled at Father Colman. He really liked this priest. Although they were not the same kind of priest, they both served the poor, and Merek felt a great respect for Father Colman.

"And there lies the problem, Father Willson. I should feel guilt for not upholding the church's law. I do not collect tithes. If I do, I give them back to the poor people of my villages. Yet, I feel strangely good about it. And that troubles me."

Once again, Merek turned in his saddle. "Father Colman. It is my humble opinion that you are a good man, and the decisions you make for your villagers are the way Our Lord and Savior, Jesus Christ, would have acted."

"Thank you, Merek. I feel the Lord's presence with us today."

Merek did not answer but turned his attention to the path and the forest in which they travelled. Merek realized that his conversation with Father Colman had taken away his attention to watching for trouble along the road. As they passed through the forest, Father Colman's feeling that the Lord was with them must have been true. For the two priests did not encounter anyone in the five miles through the forest. And they travelled without incident.

Perhaps the Holy Spirit was indeed with them.

CHAPTER 8
THE KNIGHT, THE SQUIRE, AND THE YEOMAN

Near midday, the priests came to a crossroads. There was a sign at the crossroads, but years of weather had disintegrated the words on the sign. Both priests were aware that they were to head east, so they knew which road was theirs. At the crossroads was an old inn, The Moritz. It was named after the man who had built it one hundred years ago. Samuel Moritz had been a carpenter by trade, but as he aged, his hands could not do the necessary carpentry skills to complete the jobs needed to support his vocation. So he and his sons built the tavern, their very last job involving carpentry. They had done a magnificent job, for it had stood the test of time.

The Moritz was not a large inn, small compared to the inns of London, but the wood work on it was awesome to behold, exhibiting the skill of Samuel Moritz and his sons. The entrance to the inn sported a wooden statue of a great warrior holding a sword and shield. The statue stood on top of the door leading into the tavern. Behind the bar, Moritz and his sons had carved a battle scene from Hastings. All around the perimeter of the inside of the tavern, wooden swords had been carved and placed for patrons to hang hats, coats, or other articles. Even the benches had intricate carvings on their surfaces. No two were alike. The inn could house many more visitors than could meet the eye, for the master carpenter had used every square inch of the structure for a purpose. Even though it was south of London, it was well-known.

The priests guided their horses to the inn, having agreed to have their midday meal there. Actually, it was Merek who wanted to eat. He was famished. Father Colman, although hungry, had told Merek that he was trying to fast in preparation for the holy trip to Canterbury. Merek suggested a small bowl of soup would not anger the Lord in a time of fasting. Father Colman actually smiled when Merek made the suggestion.

Since it was midday, there were not many horses tethered outside of The Moritz. The priests saw only one man outside. He seemed to be tending to the hooves of one of the horses. Merek and Father Colman brought their horses near to where the man was bent, checking a single hoof.

"Good day," Merek said, getting down from his horse.

"Good day to you sirs," the man replied, standing upright and looking at the priests.

By his dark skin, the man appeared to be a Moor. Merek was surprised by his English accent. He was dressed in green from head to toe. Although his clothes were not new, they were well-kept and clean. He wore a hood, but it was not covering his head. As Merek tethered his horse to the rail, he tried not to stare at the man. Yes, he had seen dark-skinned people before, but they were rare in this part of England.

"A fine day, young man." Father Colman smiled at the attendant.

"Indeed it is, Father." The man smiled back, continuing to inspect the horse.

Merek took a good look at the attendant in green. The man was not tall but had a thick chest and arms. Looking at his horse, Merek noticed he had fine weapons. As Merek waited for Father Colman to tether his horse and gather himself, he took a closer look at the man who appeared to be a Moor. Merek was impressed with the bow that was hung on the man's saddle. Although it was not a longbow, it looked strong and seemed to be well-kept. The feathers on his arrows were expertly made and, like Merek's, were of the same color, indicating they came from the same bird. The attendant also carried a knife, a large one in his belt. When the man bent down to check another hoof, Merek noticed he had another knife hidden in his boot. Merek knew the man had military training.

Merek also saw the scabbard of a fine sword. He knew the look of a sword like that. It belonged to a warrior, a knight, a nobleman. How would a man dressed as a forester own the sword of a nobleman? Did he steal it? Did he win it in battle? Or was the nobleman inside the inn, and this man was a servant, a bodyguard? Having been a soldier fighting in foreign soil, Merek knew how to look for details when encountering strangers.

"Good food inside?" Merek asked, trying to gather some information.

"Aye, Father. That is why my lord is inside, with his son. I am sure they will like the company of two priests," the attendant said quietly and with sincerity.

"Thank you, sir," Merek said, a little relieved in the man's answer.

The attendant added, "I will keep watch over your horses, Father."

"Bless you," Father Colman said as they walked toward the entrance.

"Will you be coming in?" Merek asked.

"No, Father," the brown-skinned man said, continuing to inspect the hooves as the priests entered the inn.

Upon entering the inn, Merek looked around and began to compare the inside to that of The Harp. There was no comparison. The interior of the inn was far superior to the outside. The craftsmanship to every detail of wood was remarkable. It truly did look like the work of a master who was doing his last job.

Near the door, two men were seated at a table, eating a mutton stew and sharing a cup of ale. A few other patrons shared a bench on the farside of the room. The tavern keeper was nowhere to be seen.

"Good morrow, sirs," Merek said politely to the two men seated at the bench near the door.

"And to you, sirs," the older gentleman answered. And then he corrected himself. "Pardon me, Fathers. I did not realize you were men of the cloth until I looked closer. My apologies."

"No apologies necessary," Father Colman was quick to answer.

The younger of the two quickly got up and gestured with his hands to join them at the table.

"Please join us, Father . . . and Father." He bowed quickly.

"Gladly," Merek said. "But we do not wish to disturb your meal."

Now the older gentleman rose. "Please, join us."

"Is the tavern keep about?" Merek asked.

"In the back. I am sure he will be out presently," the younger gentleman answered.

"Thomas, go summon the keep," the older man asked gently.

"Yes, Father. I will." The young man walked into the back of the inn.

Merek knew from an instant the older gentleman was a noble. And thinking of the fine horses out front, Merek could guess he was wealthy. But there was more. Without really trying, the man exuded a nobility, a dignity that many noblemen he had met lacked. No, this man was impressive.

Just as they sat, Thomas brought out the tavern keeper. Merek ordered a stew with vegetables and mutton. Father Colman was hesitant to order, so Merek asked the tavern keeper to bring out two portions of the stew. Father Colman began to protest but was interrupted by the nobleman. "I am Sir Robert of Ganse," he said, holding out his arm. Merek hesitated, then took his arm, and shook. It might have been the first nobleman he had seen who would actually shake a common priest's arm. He did the same with Father Colman. "And this is my son, Thomas."

Both priests shook Thomas's arm. Merek introduced Father Colman and himself, while Thomas poured the priests a cup of ale to share.

Merek studied Robert of Ganse more closely. Speckled gray hair populated his long mane. There was a scar above one eye, but it was not easily seen. Sir Robert's eyes displayed a spark of youth and energy but at the same time displayed the stress of age and experience. His arm shake and smile were genuine and displayed an inner confidence that told Merek that this man was accomplished. Sir Robert was tall, not quite as tall as Merek, but taller than the average man. His fustian tunic had stains, and Merek could see the marks where his armor had been worn to protect him. After seeing the sword, the horses, and now the man, Merek knew that Sir Robert had been to war.

"You are travelling priests, may I ask?" Thomas asked quietly. Unlike his father, Thomas was not dressed modestly. He wore a linen shirt with very wide sleeves. His hair was long and parted in the middle with curls dangling freely. The gown he wore was short, displaying the powerful legs of youth. Merek guessed he was eighteen or nineteen years old. Merek also guessed that he was a squire, in training to be a knight. Despite the fancy clothes, Merek saw a powerful young man.

"No, Thomas, Father Colman and I are simple village priests."

"Father, would one of you give us and our meal a blessing?" Sir Robert asked.

Merek looked at Father Colman, who gladly gave the blessing. Near the end of the blessing, Father Colman added a blessing for the journey that he and Merek were on.

"I hope that the two of you are not travelling alone. Even for the clergy, this area can be dangerous. It is notorious for brigands and thieves," Sir Robert warned.

"Yes," Father Colman said. "Father Willson has warned me. However, our lord bishop has called on us to perform a pilgrimage, and so we must. I trust the Lord will protect us on our journey."

"Might I ask where you are going?" young Thomas asked.

"Canterbury," Merek said.

"Canterbury! That is our purpose too," Thomas added. "You see, Fathers, we have just returned from overseas and want to thank our Mighty Lord for our safe delivery back to England," Sir Robert added. "We head to Canterbury at the present. Will you join us?"

"We would be grateful, Sir Robert. Father Colman is going directly. I, however, by order of the bishop, must stop at a priory near London and accompany a prioress and her nuns to the cathedral in Canterbury."

"Well, if my directions are correct, we still head in the same direction, Father Willson," Thomas said. "Perhaps you can travel with us for part of the way?"

"I would like that, Thomas."

So it was settled. The priests would travel with Sir Robert, son and servant, eastward. In the town of Bentzway, there would be a crossroads where their paths would separate. Father Willson would head north to Norwood, while Father Colman would continue to travel with Sir Robert and Thomas toward Southwark. Traditionally, pilgrimages to Canterbury began in Southwark, just south of London.

The priests' meal was served. There was pleasant conversation. Sir Robert did not talk much about the places he had been, but Thomas was eager to tell of his father's deeds. He was a proud son. Apparently, Sir Robert had been a soldier for the King of England all along the Mediterranean coast. From the eastern part of Europe all the way to Alexandria, Sir Robert had been a leader in a number of battles. Thomas was with his father in northern Africa, particularly in Granada, Algeciras, and Anatolia. They had fought the heathen Turks in Tramissene and the Bey of Balat. It was easy for Merek to see that Thomas admired his father, for he spoke with pride of his father's service to God and king.

Merek found Sir Robert's humility quite unusual and refreshing. As Thomas spoke of his father's exploits, Sir Robert rarely looked up from his bowl on the table. He sat solemnly and let the young squire talk. Finally, he touched the squire's arm and said, "That's enough, Thomas. Let the priests eat in peace."

Thomas obeyed his father; the meal was finished. Sir Robert insisted on paying for the meal, which was a great relief to Father Colman, who had no money and was "fasting" because of it. The party left, with Thomas bringing out food for the bodyguard, whom Sir Robert referred to as his yeoman. Mounted, the group led the horses from the Moritz Inn toward another thick forest.

As they began the journey together, Merek purposely rode beside the yeoman. Merek felt a certain unwritten kinship toward a man who carried such fine weaponry, especially the bow and arrows. Merek had learned from conversation with Thomas that the yeoman, a true forester, was accompanying Sir Robert and son, not as a fellow pilgrim to Canterbury, but as a bodyguard. A noble knight like Sir Robert would go on his pilgrimage without his weapons. It was a holy retreat, after all. But travelling in this part of England could be dangerous, so it was necessary to take precautions. The yeoman was the "precaution." Merek looked at the giant sword that hung in the scabbard hanging from the yeoman's saddle. It had to be Sir Robert's.

The yeoman ate quietly as they rode. Sir Robert and his son took the lead. Father Colman rode by himself behind the father and son. Merek and the yeoman brought up the rear. When they came to the next forest, the road narrowed again. Thomas took the lead. Merek noticed that Thomas had all the weaponry that a squire would have: a sword and an assortment of knives. Although Thomas was on the same pilgrimage, he did not have the same beliefs his father had concerning travelling on a pilgrimage. Thomas looked like he was ready for battle.

The men rode at a leisurely pace single file along the path that led through the forest. Thomas and his father conversed freely, so Merek felt at ease and did not seem to have a worry about silence. Except for the yeoman, the men spoke freely on a wide range of subjects, from pilgrimages, church laws, and battles.

"The yeoman does not speak much," Merek said as he smiled at the bodyguard in green.

"If you look closely, Father Merek, he does speak loudly with the weapons he holds and the manner in which he carries himself," Sir Robert spoke, not turning in his saddle.

Merek smiled, for he knew what the nobleman meant. Nevertheless, he turned in his saddle and spoke to the yeoman, who took up the rear of the party, "Sir, may I ask your name?"

The yeoman looked at Father Merek a moment before he spoke, "I am Hugh. Hugh Bowman." He said it as a matter of fact and then returned to the business at hand, keeping a sharp eye out for trouble.

"Hugh and his family have served my family for two generations now," Sir Robert interjected. "Hugh's father has been with me for years. Hugh's mother and father were originally from Spain but resettled in England. I was fortunate enough to hire Hugh's father as my livery master. I have watched Hugh grow from an infant into the man he is today. Hugh has accompanied us on our travels overseas and has fought in the same battles we have fought. He is a forester in whom I absolutely trust."

"A servant you can trust is worth his weight in gold," Father Colman spoke.

"Oh, Father Colman, Hugh is a freeman, just like his father."

"Oh, I am so sorry, Hugh," Father Colman apologized.

Hugh just smiled.

"But he is your bodyguard?" Merek asked.

"Yes. As is Thomas," Sir Robert said. "I felt this pilgrimage to Canterbury was necessary, for the last encounter with an enemy had made my living a rare miracle. So we travel to St. Thomas's shrine to give thanks to our Lord. I go without weapons on my person, but the young men carry the weapons, just in case. Speaking of weapons, Father Merek, I see you carry a bow with you."

"For game, Sir Robert, just in case I need nourishment."

"Perhaps, Father, but I know a military longbow when I see one. You must forgive me for saying, but it looks truly out of place on the saddle of a priest."

"Actually, Sir Robert, I keep it for game and for those who will not convert to the Holy Catholic Church."

The men laughed at that. Even Hugh smiled. Father Colman did not smile but was wholly confused.

"Please, Sir Robert. Tell us more about the places you have been," Merek asked, trying to avoid the issue of the longbow on his saddle.

As the small parade wound its way through the forest, Sir Robert indulged the priests. He told them of his travels, the sights he had seen and the battles in which he fought. And yet, he did so in a most humble and gentle way, never bragging or making himself take center stage. His descriptions of the lands he had seen reminded Merek of his travels to France. Sir Robert's descriptions of battles were glorious and full of honor and glory. At this, Merek knew better. He had been in battle and knew the hell that went with it. There might have been honor and glory with the noblemen, but there was nothing more than blood, guts, and death from what Merek remembered.

But Sir Robert's descriptions were almost poetic, so Merek let him talk. And so they rode.

As they rode, Thomas would interject on what his father was saying, sometimes adding details or telling about something his heroic father did. Each time Thomas would begin to tell of his father's heroism, the knight would humbly ask his son not go any further in his story. The knight would remind his son that priests were men of God, and a story about taking another man's life would not befitting for a priest to hear.

Merek wanted to hear more but did not say it aloud.

It seemed the group of travelers found themselves in the middle of the forest where the road narrowed even more. Large elms stood on either side of the path, bringing perpetual shade to the area and providing cover for robbers or highwaymen. The narrow path led to a small hill that had a copse of younger elms. A single man stood on the hill amongst the trees. He stood in plain sight. "If it pleases you, sirs, there is a toll for riding through this section of the forest," the man said nonchalantly. The man had no visible weapons, wore a ragged cloak, and seemed to be in his early forties.

As he spoke, the yeoman and Thomas instinctively moved their horses off the path and came abreast of Sir Robert. Hugh Bowman idled up next to Sir Robert on the left. Thomas backed his horse and rested on Sir Robert's right side. Without hesitation, Merek moved his horse through the thick brush alongside Thomas. Merek understood the tactic. He had seen it before, in France, in war.

Father Colman, unaware of the danger, sat behind the party. Merek contained a smile. There was no doubt that the highwayman did not know who he was dealing with.

"Like I said, sirs, there will be a toll," he repeated in a smug way.

"And what will the toll be?" Thomas asked loudly and distinctly. His blood was up.

"Each of you will pay a few shillings to use the road," the man answered cockily.

"By whose authority?" Thomas asked. Merek found it interesting that Sir Robert was allowing Thomas to do the talking.

"Ours," he smirked. Two more men came out of the brush and stood beside their leader. Each carried a sword and gave a third sword to the leader. From the bushes to the left, another man with a bow emerged, arrow drawn. To Merek's right, yet another man appeared with his drawn bow. Finally, two more men stood behind the party with clubs.

"Come to think of it," the leader continued, "I doubt a few shillings or even a pound would loosen your purses too much." He was grinning, as were the men standing beside him.

Merek knew it was serious. He could feel it. He heard the men laughing, even the ones behind them. He glanced to the bowman on his right. While the others were laughing, the bowman on the right was not. He seemed worried. And the bow did not look right in his hands. Merek knew the look. The others might be brazen, but the thief to his right was nervous. And nervous was good.

Thomas spoke, "Sirs, we want no trouble. In fact, we travel with two priests."

"Surely we can compromise, brothers," Merek said amicably. "You would not want to rob a servant of the Lord."

"Brothers," Father Colman announced, getting down from his horse, "I am sure we can rectify this misunderstanding. In fact, Father Willson and I will hear confessions and say Mass for you—"

The leader lost his smile and interrupted the pious parson. "Mass, confessions? Servant of the Lord? God almighty! How can you even say there is a God? No, God has forsaken England, Father. Did you not witness the plague years ago? Where was God when my wife and children were dying a painful death from the cursed plague? No, there is no God. And even if there is a God, I curse him and the church. God damn all of you."

"We all lost family in the Great Plague," Merek assured him. "But it is through God's mercy that we live and continue our mission here on earth."

Father Colman, letting go of his horse's reigns, began to walk around Merek. It seemed he wanted to confront the highwaymen.

Merek knew exactly what Father Colman wanted to do—make peace. Try to save souls. But Merek also knew the look in the eye of the leader of the bandits. The leader of the bandits did not want God; he wanted blood.

"Leo, get back on your horse," Merek demanded in a quiet but stern way. Father Colman stopped and looked at Merek with confusion. "Get on your horse," Merek said sternly, but in a low tone.

Father Colman hesitated and then, still confused, got back on his horse.

"I am certain we can come to an agreement," Merek said to the leader, trying to mask his orders to Father Colman to get back on his horse.

"Say what you want, priest, but it will do no good." The leader paused and looked at his followers. "In fact, it has just occurred to me that the toll for this party might just be a little higher." To the others, "I believe we have encountered a bit of a jackpot here, lads. Do you see their fine horses? And the clothes that they wear will keep us warm in the winter, especially the priests' garments."

The man was smiling again, a cocky smile that angered even Merek. Merek glanced at Father Colman, who was back on his horse looking worried and silently muttering a prayer.

"And so, sirs, get off your horses and begin to strip," the leader said with authority.

Merek was thinking. He knew there were times when he was not a good priest. He admitted it. He had given his life to God in thanks for saving him from the perils of war in France and the deadly plague that had entered England in his lifetime. But he had seen death, had killed and had seen his anger get the best of him. And his anger was beginning to show. And he did not pray to God to have his anger lessened.

Thomas spoke with a caution for the highwaymen, "Be wary of us sirs. We do not want trouble. Let us pass. But I will tell you, we are not giving up our horses, nor are we stripping for the likes of you. And let me make our intentions clear to you- we are not paying a toll."

Thomas spoke with a confidence that added to Merek's rising anger. There was going to be a fight. God help the highwaymen.

"Aren't you the bold one," the leader spoke, "with all your fancy clothes and hair? But we not only outnumber you but have you surrounded. Do not underestimate our skills with weaponry and our surrounding position."

Sir Robert spoke quietly in Latin, "I will take the leader and the men in front. Thomas, take the men behind us. Hugh, when I signal, toss me my sword. And take out the bowman on your left."

Merek added in Latin, "I have the bowman on the right."

Sir Robert, Thomas, and Hugh looked at Merek with surprise. Thomas, with fire in his eyes, managed a smile. Hugh and Merek quickly dismounted and strung their bows. Father Colman, seeing Merek dismount, did the same. He stood by his horse.

Sir Robert finally spoke to the leader of the highwaymen, "Will you reconsider and let us pass peacefully? I will gladly contribute a toll for the welfare of your families."

The leader shook his head. "No, that will not do." He and his companions began to walk toward Sir Robert and Thomas.

"Now!" Sir Robert shouted.

Hugh tossed Sir Robert his sword. Sir Robert caught the sword and charged the leader and his companions. Thomas wheeled his horse around and made for the men behind. Hugh loosed an arrow at the robber to the left, hitting the robber squarely in the belly. The robber dropped in pain. In seconds, Hugh had loosed a second arrow, hitting the robber a second time high in the chest between his heart and his shoulder. The man fell behind one of the elms.

Merek raised his bow at the nervous robber to his right. The robber, a young man with horribly ragged clothes, was surprised by the sudden action. He had trouble notching his arrow in his string. Merek, in the meantime, was poised with his arrow ready to fly. The robber, shaking, released his arrow prematurely, and it dropped harmlessly on the ground. With tears in his eyes, he looked at Merek.

"Go!" Merek shouted. "Run away!"

The robber hesitated then stooped to pick up another arrow. Merek let his arrow fly, striking the robber's hand that reached for the arrow that lay before him. The arrow went through the hand near the ground and stayed, making a gruesome sight. The robber, with arrow sticking through his hand, screamed. The arrow had pinned his hand to the ground. He screamed trying to loosen it from the ground. He pulled the arrow free from the ground after a few tugs. With the arrow through his hand, he turned and ran into the thick of the forest screaming.

Merek saw him run and turned to the direction of Sir Robert. The experienced knight had charged into the middle of the three men and was warding them off with his mighty sword. Merek wasted no time and sent an arrow at the man on Sir Robert's right. The arrow struck the bandit in the side of the chest, and he fell immediately.

From his horse, Sir Robert made short work of the leader, using his sword to make a mortal slice across the chest of the fighting man. The leader fell with a cry of pain and did not move. It was the third man who was the problem. The third man had been cut off by Sir Robert's initial charge. He had fallen off the small hill, rolled away, and now was in position to attack Sir Robert from behind. So when Sir Robert felled the leader, the third robber stood and tried to stab Sir Robert from behind. But before he could do so, two arrows found him. Merek's arrow hit him in the front of his chest, while Hugh, from another direction, had sent his arrow to the robber's back. The arrows hit the man simultaneously, and he dropped.

It was over. Sir Robert, seeing the arrows in the third robber, turned to Merek and nodded. He also did the same for Hugh. Still on his horse, Sir Robert approached Merek and Hugh. Father Colman was on his knees crying and praying simultaneously. It dawned on all the men that Thomas was nowhere to be seen.

At the beginning of the fight, Thomas had done what his father had ordered. Thomas charged full speed at the men with clubs behind them. But in the ensuing fight, no one had seen what had happened. As the men looked to where he had ridden, they saw a dead body on the path. It was easy to see that it was one of the brigands. The other bandit and Thomas had disappeared into the thick brush beside a giant elm.

"I will find him," Hugh said quietly. Mounting quickly, he spurred his horse to where Thomas had been. Merek began to mount his horse in hopes to join Hugh in search of Thomas. Suddenly, Thomas emerged from the dense brush, sword bloody and still held in the ready position.

"The fools never had a chance," Thomas remarked as he drew closer to the group. "Did they think we were going to give into them?"

Sir Robert looked at Merek. "Father Willson, you are a man of surprises and skill. I believe you saved my life."

"Sir Robert, Hugh was also equal to the task," Merek answered, nodding at Hugh. Hugh smiled at him, an acknowledgement between warriors.

"Seems to me you have military training," Sir Robert spoke again.

"I have served our lord, the king, in France. I was an archer."

"You have not lost your touch, Father." Thomas smiled.

"Aye, but I am afraid I have sinned and will count on Father Colman to hear my confession," Merek answered.

"These men meant to do us harm," Thomas said. "What should you have done?"

"Make peace. Try to give them the Word of God," Father Colman suddenly interrupted. He looked at Merek as he spoke. "We are priests, representatives of God the Father and the holy Catholic Church. And you, Father Merek, have killed. You have killed while wearing your priestly robe!" Father Colman went to his knees and bowed his head. Tears were coming from his eyes.

Merek did not feel guilt about the killings until Father Colman spoke. As Merek's anger subsided, he began to understand what Father Leo was saying. Merek was no longer an archer; he was a priest. Yet, his instincts as a former warrior had been right. The brigands wanted blood. Now he was really confused. Should he have let the brigands rob him, possibly kill him and die a martyr for the church, or should he have fought for himself and remained alive?

Sir Robert interjected. "With all due respect, Father Colman, do you have a village in which you serve?"

Father Colman was puzzled by the question. "Sir?"

79

"Do you serve a congregation?"

"Yes, Sir Robert. In fact, I have several villages in which I serve."

"Does Father Merek do the same?" Sir Robert asked in a gentle voice.

"He does," Father Colman answered.

"And do the members of both your congregations depend on you and the services you provide?"

"Why, yes, they do," Father Colman answered, still a little confused by the questions.

Sir Robert said, "Then let me say to both priests. The men here today meant to rob and kill you. If they had succeeded, think of the countless villagers who would have missed your very service to their souls. Think of all the people you will serve in these villagers in the future. Think of the souls you shall save. To become a martyr in some unknown edge of a forest seems pointless. By sending these men to meet our Maker, you have prolonged your vocation to God and His holy Church here in England."

Merek looked at Sir Robert with earnest. Sir Robert's voice was gentle, but the look in his eyes was hard. Merek could not think of a retort or some scripture to counter what Sir Robert was saying. The old warrior in Merek understood that the brigands had to be dealt with, but his priestly vocation told him that killing was wrong. It was another test of his priestly vows. Merek felt the "tests" came more often from Thea's looks to using his bow as a weapon.

Father Colman was still on his knees. His head was bowed. "Can we at least give them a proper burial?" he asked, getting to his feet.

Sir Robert was quick to answer, "Father, we can gather the bodies so that you and Father Willson can pray over them. But that is the best we can do."

Before Father Colman could protest, Thomas interjected, "Father, these men are not alone in these woods. And we know that one is still running." He looked at Merek and nodded. "Though I am not sure how far he will get."

"And we have no tools for burial," Hugh added. "And there are many."

Father Colman did not try to argue but only nodded. The men gathered the bodies by the side of the road. The priests said prayers and anointed the dead with holy oil that both priests carried. At the end of the shortened prayers, they all crossed themselves, even the yeoman.

The group mounted their horses and left the area without another incident. They rode steadily for about three miles to distance themselves from that part of the forest. Had they remained, more trouble would have arrived. Brigands in the woods travelled in large bands for protection and profit.

As they rode, Merek made a silent confession to God for his part in the attack. In his mind, he knew what he did was justified. In his heart, God told him to love his neighbor. Later, he would ask Father Colman to hear his confession.

When the pace slowed, and the group felt it was out of danger, Thomas rode up beside Father Merek. "Father Willson, your skill as an archer is impressive. If I may ask, how do you keep your skill at such a proficient level? Since you are a priest, I mean."

"Thomas, our lord, King Edward, has issued a law that states that every man shall practice his bow once a week. So that my villagers do not get fined by the local magistrate, I lead them in practice."

"Lucky for them." Thomas smiled. "And lucky for us."

"Perhaps it was divine providence, son," Sir Robert remarked.

"Indeed, Father," Thomas replied, and the men kept on riding. Thomas kept talking, entertaining the group as they rode. He spoke of the places they had been and the many battles they were a part of. He even sang songs he had written. His songs were about young maidens, love and lust. He was a young man and in love with life itself.

Merek was entertained by the young man. Even though his songs were about love and lust, Merek laughed. He remembered what it was like to be in love. In fact, as the songs were sung, they reminded him of his affections for Thea. And suddenly, the guilt showed up, and he was embarrassed by the complexity of being a priest and being a man at the same time.

Finally, the group came to a crossroads. Merek would have to depart the group. He was travelling north to Norwood. The others would travel east to Southwark where pilgrims met for the trip to Canterbury. Since Father Colman had no orders to follow the prioress, he stayed with Sir Robert's group and agreed to meet Merek on the road to Canterbury.

Pleasantries were not enough as Merek parted the group. Sir Robert and Thomas gave their eternal thanks for Merek's part in the confrontation with the bandits. They sincerely hoped they would all meet again. Even Hugh smiled when Merek parted and began riding north by himself. All agreed they would either meet on the road to Canterbury or meet at the cathedral itself. Merek gave all a blessing as they parted.

And he slowly rode to Norwood alone.

CHAPTER 9

NORWOOD

It was customary for Catholics in England to make a pilgrimage in the spring, during Lent, to begin a new Church year in the good graces of the Lord, Jesus Christ. Some went to Rome, the home of the Holy Catholic Church. Some went to Jerusalem, where Jesus Christ walked, preached, and died on the cross. But for those of simple means or little time, the cathedral in Canterbury counted as a solemn pilgrimage.

To pray at the altar in the cathedral in Canterbury where St. Thomas a' Beckett was murdered was a powerful way to start the Lenten season. To ask God forgiveness at the cathedral was a solid belief in the stillness of the troubled soul. Persons of all kind and station made their way to the shrine every spring since 1170.

Stories of miracles also enhanced the legend of the sacred altar in Canterbury, where four knights of King Henry II brutally murdered the Archbishop of Canterbury. The knights split open the bishop on the very altar in which the Holy Mass was being said. It was not long after Beckett's murder that devout worshippers began their pilgrimage to pray to God for special intentions, blessings, forgiveness of sins, and even miracles.

And so it was in the spring of 1366, almost two hundred years since the holy martyr's death, Father Merek Willson travelled alone to Norwood to fulfill his assignment to the bishop and accompany the prioress of Norwood and her companions to Canterbury. Although Merek was not keen on the idea of going in the first place and leaving his villagers without a spiritual leader, he felt a real need to go to

Canterbury after the killings in the forest. The archer in him knew that the killings were justified, but the priest in him made him doubt his actions. What better way to cleanse one's conscience by making a pilgrimage and praying at the sacred altar?

Merek's path was along farm fields that were not being attended to. It made Merek realize how England had changed since the great plague of 1348. Merek was but a boy in the 1340s leading up to the plague. His father, Will, had worked on a great estate of a powerful feudal lord. His father was given land to till, to sow, to weed, and to reap. His harvest belonged to the feudal lord, who doled out a small recompense for all the backbreaking work. Merek's father was a serf, and so he and his family were bound to the land.

Merek remembered that his father did not even have a last name in those days. He was known simply as Will. Truly, he did not even really need a last name, for Will and his wife never travelled more than five miles in their lifetimes from the land they served. Merek and his brothers helped their father with the farming—work that Merek did not like. When his father would give them time to hunt, Merek and his brothers would be in their glory. Will's family ate better than most families bound to the land because of the hunting. There were even times they would sell the extra game to willing buyers.

But the Plague came and altered life forever, not just for Merek's family, but all of Europe. Serfs and landowners alike perished by the thousands. It attacked the cities, as well as the towns and hamlets. In some cases, a great feudal lord and his family would die; yet, the serfs remained alive. With no one to oversee the serfs, they either fled the land or stayed and claimed it as their own. Harvests would be their own; crops to do with what they wanted were theirs entirely. Their profits were their own.

After Merek's family succumbed to the plague, a local farmer, who knew Will's family, took Merek in, mostly because they knew of his ability to fire a bow. Merek was allowed to stay with the farmer and his family, provided that he kept them with fresh meat. This pleased Merek, for it was his love to hunt, and it made his skill with the bow even more proficient. For three years, he stayed with the farmer.

At the age of fifteen, he joined the king's army. He did not have to lie about his age, for when the officer-in-charge saw him shoot an arrow, he was in. For the first time, Merek had to have a full name. Merek Willson was how he enlisted.

Four hours after leaving Sir Robert's group, Merek arrived at Norwood. He was hungry and tired. The sun was going down, and Merek could feel the temperature was plummeting. As was customary in England, the spring evenings could bring a chill in a very fast way.

Merek's first impression of Norwood was that of a small feudal manor. The abbey itself looked like a small manor house, neatly nestled near a copse of trees. It was not large and ornate like a feudal manor, but it was well-kept and in good repair. There was a barn directly behind the abbey and a few smaller buildings surrounding the barn. Norwood, even in the fading light, looked beautiful, nestled among a series of open fields.

Beside the abbey was a small church made of stone. The church looked much older than the abbey and was in dire need of repair. Compared to the living quarters of the nuns, the church was needy. It seemed odd to Merek that the living quarters of the nuns was in such fine shape, yet the house of worship was not. As Merek came closer to the church, he noted that as the Norwood church was in need of repair, it did not come close to the condition he had found St. Mary Magdalene a few years ago.

A figure was exiting the church as Merek approached on the mare. It was a fellow priest. Merek did not want to frighten him, so he hailed him quietly.

"Evening, Father," he said, for the priest did not see his approach.

As it happened, Merek did surprise the priest. Yet, the priest caught himself and replied, "Evening to you, sir. May I help you?"

"I am Father Merek Willson of the small village of Harper's Turn."

"You are a priest? Forgive me, Father. I did not see your priestly garb."

"Understandable, Father. Please, no apologies needed." Merek dismounted from the horse.

"I am Father Richard Smithton," he said, holding out his arm. Merek shook it. "Village priests are rare visitors to Norwood." He was friendly, but Merek could tell he was confused by a priest at this time of the evening. He seemed a little tense, noting Merek's formidable size.

"I have been sent by the Bishop of Winchester to accompany the prioress of Norwood on her journey to Canterbury," Merek said, trying to ease the priest's uneasiness.

Father Smithton was puzzled. "Funny, the prioress was also given a directive from the good bishop to take the trip to Canterbury. I do not think the directive mentioned an escort by a village priest."

"Will she travel alone?" Merek asked.

"Oh no, Father. One of her nuns will accompany her, as well as I. But I forget my manners. It's a bit late. Let's take care of your horse. You can stay in the priest's quarters behind the chapel. Are you hungry?"

"As a matter of fact, I am. Should I tell the prioress I am here?"

"In the morning, Father. In the morning. I think it a bit late to have an appointment with the Lady Prioress. Come, let's look after that horse. Then we shall find some food for you in the kitchen of the priory."

Merek knew Father Smithton was correct, for it was too late to announce a visitor to the head of the priory. It was about time for evening vespers, anyway, and by the time the prayers were over, it would be time for bed. Merek took notice of Father Smithton's choice of words. They were unusual to Merek. Smithton said Merek would need an "appointment" with the prioress. And he called her "Lady Prioress." Very unusual. Merek began to think he had been in an obscure village too long and was not in touch with the times and the way to address church officials.

Father Smithton helped to care for the horse, giving the horse an abundant amount of oats. Once the horse was secure, Merek followed the priest around the back of the building to a door behind the priory. They entered the kitchen. Merek could feel the heat in the kitchen as he entered. The heat was welcomed. Near the fire in the hearth stood a nun scooping some soup from a kettle that hung near the flames.

"Evening, Sister Anne," Father Smithton said.

The nun turned with the cup of soup in her hands. The cup almost fell when she saw Merek. Her eyes widened with surprise.

"Good evening, Father Smithton," she said meekly. She managed to recover and tried to smile at Merek.

"This is Father . . ." he was having trouble remembering Merek's name.

"Father Merek Willson, Sister," Merek interjected. "The soup smells delicious."

Sister Anne was young, not more than eighteen. She was small of stature and very thin. It was hard to see her face, for she kept the bowl of soup near her face.

"Please, Father. Have some. It is a freshly made soup of vegetables and rabbit meat," Sister Anne said, stepping aside. As Merek passed her for the hearth, she looked at his enormous stature. "Forgive me for being bold, Father Willson, but I must say I have never seen a priest as big as you."

Merek was ladling some soup in a bowl. "The village in which I serve feeds me quite well," he joked.

Sister Anne smiled. She put the cup down as she smiled. Merek noticed the horrific scar that stretched from her forehead to the cheek on the right side of her face. It was if someone had raked her face with a knife. Her eye on that side had a fog-like look to it, indicating the eye was blind. Merek did not mean to stare, but it caught him off guard.

He was quick to recover. "Forgive me, Sister Anne. I did not mean to stare."

Sister Anne kept her smile. "Think nothing of it, Father. I am used to it."

Merek smiled, and they enjoyed the soup in front of the hearth. Father Smithton partook also. They made small talk, not wanting to eat more soup, but enjoying the heat of the fire. It was Sister Anne who took Merek's empty bowl of soup and refilled it for him.

"Surely, you are still hungry," she said pleasantly.

Merek thanked her.

"Father Willson will be going to Canterbury with the Lady Prioress," Father Smithton said.

"Going with us?" Sister Anne asked.

"You go also?" Merek asked.

Father Smithton was quick to reply, "There are four of us travelling to the tomb of St. Thomas a' Beckett. Father, you will be the fifth in our company."

"It will be a parade then." Merek smiled, finishing his second bowl of soup.

The priests said goodbye to Sister Anne and left the confines of the comfortable kitchen. They made their way to the dorter, a small building used for priests serving the priory and guest priests who needed a place to sleep. It was one large room with beds against each wall and three in the middle of the room. It was quite a change from the small closet Merek slept in behind the church back in Harper's Turn. Merek was used to sleeping on a bed of straw on the floor heated by a small hearth. This dorter had beds constructed of wood that allowed the priest to sleep off the floor. Sleeping here would be a real pleasure.

Merek made note of the bed's simple construction. He was thinking of getting one of the village carpenters to help him build a small platform for his own bed when he returned to Harper's Turn. One of the villagers would help, he was sure.

Merek found the bed comfortable yet did not sleep well. He was tired but kept thinking back to the fight in the forest. Was there something he could have done to prevent the killings? That thought troubled him. But the thought that troubled him all the more was that the "killer" within him had reemerged. That was troubling. And he prayed that God would forgive him for allowing that dark side to come out.

He turned and tossed in his bed, wondering if he should awaken Father Smithton to hear his confession. Just before dawn, Merek fell into a deep sleep. He was awakened by Father Smithton. It was time for matins.

CHAPTER 10

THE PRIORESS

Getting dressed for matins and then for Mass, Merek felt a chill in the air. The fire in the hearth had lost its flame, and there were only the dying embers littered about the enclosed floor. Merek gathered a few small logs to keep the fire going. He knew Father Smithton would approve. It was easier to keep a fire going rather than starting anew.

Merek did not have a change of clothes. In fact, he had slept in the cassock in which he travelled. He had tried to get rid of some of the grime, stains, and sweat the day before at a creek. The washing helped, for the long garment was rank, especially after the conflict in the forest. Once a solid black, the cassock had been worn so often and washed so many times that the color had begun to turn a dark gray. It was not the kind of garment a priest would want to wear on a pilgrimage to Canterbury. Yet, Merek had no choice. A humble village priest, Merek would wear the cassock, for it was all he owned.

Mass was held in the priory chapel. The chapel was small but decorated with tapestries of various saints. Near the front of the chapel, a large wooden crucifix stood as a reminder of Christ's ultimate sacrifice. Since Merek was a guest priest, Father Smithton invited him to say Mass. Merek agreed gladly and was touched when Father Smithton allowed Merek to use the chapel's vestments. Fully dressed and ready to begin, Merek had an unusual thought. Could it be that Father Smithton was allowing Merek to say Mass to prove Merek was a priest? The thought made Merek smile.

The bell rang, and Mass began. It was still dark in the chapel as Merek approached the altar. There were nuns in the pews, but Merek could not discern a number. If the prioress were there, he could not tell. It was a short Mass with no sermon and little singing.

Afterward, as Merek was disrobing, Father Smithton entered. "Father Willson, we are invited to breakfast with the Lady Prioress," he said quietly with a smile.

"Very well, Father. May I ask a question?"

"By all means, Father. Ask."

"Perhaps I have been in my village too long and have been out of touch with the Church and its customs. Since when do we address a prioress as *Lady* prioress? I ask you will all due respect to the prioress."

Father Smithton smiled. It was a genuine smile. "It is Madam Eglantyne's wish that here in the priory of Norwood that she be addressed as lady." Merek noted the slightest hint of sarcasm in the priest's voice. "We usually follow her wishes."

Merek noted the smile on Father Smithton's face and understood. With the vestments properly hung and the tabernacle fittingly closed, the priests made their way to the refectory to have breakfast with the "Lady of the Manor."

The priests made their way to the refectory, a room the clergy used for eating. When the priests arrived for breakfast, there were eight nuns waiting at a long table with benches for seating. The men sat on the benches beside the nuns. There was a chair at the head of the table. It was vacant. Madam Eglatyne had not yet arrived. The priests took their seats, and all waited for the entrance of the prioress, who had yet to enter the room.

Some of the nuns were making small talk, unashamedly pointing at Merek. The younger nuns smiled, but the older ones used their eyebrows to show their distrust of the stranger. Merek was strangely amused at the ladies. He wanted to introduce himself but waited for Father Smithton to do the honors. Father Smithton did not bother to introduce Merek, so they took their seats. All seemed to be waiting for the prioress. Merek saw Sister Anne and nodded. She smiled and nodded back. And then the prioress entered.

Madam Eglantyne entered the room slowly, with grace. Everyone stood. Merek was slow to recognize that all had stood, and so he was last to stand. The others also bowed, but Merek did not. He did not bow, for he was ignorant of the standard set at Norwood. He was not bowing to a lady of the court. "Madam" Eglantyne was a nun. Last he heard, nuns were not given the courtesy of a bow.

As the table bowed and curtsied, Merek found himself smiling. It was if he were at court, and the wife of an earl or lord were entering the room. He smiled at the whole absurdity of the moment! It took discipline not to laugh out loud.

"Please be seated," the prioress said in a most kind and gentle way. "I see we have a guest with us." Merek instinctively knew she had said it as an admonishment for his failure to bow to her.

"I am Father Merek Willson, Madam Eglantyne," he said slowly, walking to her. She held her hand out, and Merek kissed her ring dutifully. If he were going to get a hearty breakfast, he would play along. He knew to kiss the ring of the bishop, but of a prioress? He was uncertain but did it anyway. It seemed to please her.

"Thank you for saying Mass this morning, Father Willson." She smiled. Merek found her smile genuine. Up close, he looked at her face for the first time. Her eyes were captivating, glass-gray in color. Merek stared at them for a moment. He had never seen eyes of that color before. They were alive and gave Merek the impression she was glad to have him at her breakfast table. The prioress wore a specially tailored veil, for it highlighted her wide forehead.

"Father Smithton informs me that you will be accompanying us to Canterbury. We are pleased to have you in our company, Father Willson," she said with an aristocratic air. Her voice had a nasal quality to it, yet it was not unpleasant to hear. Her mouth was small but soft and red. She added, "I must say that I have never seen a priest of your size, Father. I feel safe from bandits with you travelling with us."

The others laughed politely at her last comment, including Merek. He was charmed by her grace and beauty.

"Thank you, Dame Eglantyne," Merek responded. *Dame* was the more appropriate way to address a prioress.

"Please be seated, Father. Will you say grace?" she softly asked.

Merek said grace, and the breakfast was served. A few novices served fresh eggs and bread, a real treat for Merek. Fresh cider was also served. When the ham was brought out, Merek was loath to take a large portion, for he was famished and did not want to take too much. He was careful to eat slowly and make sure all had their fill until he went for seconds.

The conversation through the meal centered on the prioress asking Merek questions. Merek answered each of her questions honestly. As Merek answered each question, the prioress responded with her own comments. Merek noted how the others at the table politely listened to him but hung on every word the prioress said. It was if she were "teaching" the others about the comments made in the conversation. Yet, she did not lecture and was not overbearing. Rather, Merek found her comments to be quite witty and entertaining. The prioress had a worldly sense about her, and Merek found himself quite fascinated by her commentary and anecdotes.

Of course, the more the prioress talked, the more Merek helped himself to the food available, especially the ham. As Merek ate, he took notice of the prioress. Her table manners were that of a high-born lady. Once in a while, she interspersed some French in her discourses. Merek was amused at this, for her tone and enunciation of words sounded French, but Merek could not understand their meanings. From being in France, Merek thought he knew a little of the language. But the prioress's use of the language baffled Merek. He had never heard some of her words or phrases before, especially when he served in France.

Merek guessed the prioress to be in her late twenties. She made it known to him that she had "taken the veil at fifteen" and had worked her way up the Church's hierarchy to be the prioress of Norwood. The prioress impressed Merek. She was quite a conversationalist and made Merek feel like the most important person in the room.

The small dogs she kept about her were most annoying. As she spoke, the prioress would frequently feed them scraps from the table. As Merek continued to eat seconds, and sometimes thirds, he noticed how the prioress fed her dogs a little more, thinking that the big priest would leave no scraps for her pets.

"Well, Father Willson, it has been quite a pleasure to have you with us this morning," the prioress stated, giving an indication that the breakfast was over. She stood. All at the table, including Merek, stood also.

"Mother Prioress, I am honored and thankful for such a hearty meal," Merek said.

"It will be good to have you join us, Father," she said to Merek. To Father Smithton, "If we leave by noon, will we be able to get to Southwark before dark?"

"Aye, Lady Prioress, by all means," he answered quickly.

"Very well. There will be five of us?" She smiled.

"Indeed, my lady," Father Smithton answered.

"Until then, I have some preparations to make. Sister Anne, will you help me?"

"Of course, Lady Prioress" was Sister Anne's quick reply.

As they exited the room, all kissed the prioress's hand. Merek was last. Although he found the clergy's treatment of the prioress as a high-born lady quite amusing, he played along and tried to keep from showing his amusement.

"Noon, Mother Prioress," he said with a smile, adding his own quiet protest of the situation. As he left the room, he noticed the prioress was wearing a large brooch. The lettering on the brooch said *"Amor Vincit Omnia."* It was Latin for "Love Conquers All."

CHAPTER 11

MAKING AN ENEMY

After the breakfast, Merek returned to the dorter and began to assemble his personal items. There was not much to assemble, but he did take some time to inspect his precious bow and the arrows with him. Father Smithton had not inquired about the weapon when he brought them in, so Merek nonchalantly tended to their care.

He was alone, checking each arrow and began to think about his beginnings as a priest. Upon returning from France and seeing the horrors of war, Merek became a priest to thank God for his survival. He wanted to understand the gospels of Jesus and serve for the love of God. He also wanted to find a belief in mankind after seeing the horrors of war. Merek had witnessed not only the deadliness of battle but had seen the ruthlessness of an army that wished to rage war on the countryside of France. Merek had also seen the raping and pillaging of innocent villagers by the English army, and it soured Merek's stomach on humanity. He had hoped that giving his life to God would help rekindle his belief in the humanity of man.

He studied earnestly in the seminary, learned to read and write in Latin and English, and gave his vows of poverty, chastity, and obedience. He attended to his studies and services quickly and at the age of twenty-two was ordained a priest. In his studies to become a priest, he learned to discipline himself in containing the nightmarish thoughts he had toward his fellow man. He had also learned to tame his fiery temper and his indifferent attitude about killing his fellow man, qualities that had made him a good soldier and deadly archer.

By the time he was ordained, he felt in control of his inner demons of war and suffering.

Merek did so well in the seminary that he was assigned to be a clerk to the bishop of Witton upon his ordination. Witton had a large cathedral with a monastery and hospital within its walls. The town of Witton grew up around the cathedral and had become large with five thousand villagers. Although Merek had seen London and Paris from a distance, Witton was large.

Merek was not a monk but lived in the monastery. He was one of many clerks in the service of the lord bishop. Since Merek could read and write in Latin, he wrote and copied letters for the bishop. New to the clergy, he thought it was a true honor to work for the good bishop of Witton. Inwardly, he yearned to serve a small village but was content in his role in Witton. Merek worked hard, prayed diligently, and was given more and more duties by the bishop, who recognized his skills.

Before long, Merek was transcribing letters directly from the bishop. He often took the words of the bishop personally and put them on parchment. The bishop trusted Merek's integrity and diligence. The bishop also liked Merek's lack of politics. He was confident that Merek would do his job without looking for favoritism from outside influences. Soon, Merek was the only clerk who transcribed for the bishop. He had become the chief clerk, an honor for a newly ordained priest. Soon, Merek was reading and reporting what other bishops were sending to the bishop of Witton. On more than one occasion, Merek transcribed a letter from the King of England.

And in so doing, Merek began to learn the art of politics.

The bishop was an elderly man and had many priests for his advisors. Each priest had an area in which he oversaw for the bishop. One priest was in charge of the cathedral as a building, while another priest controlled the services within the cathedral. The prior managed the monastery, while the chief doctor ran the hospital. Each man had his own agenda. And so often, each man's "agenda" was about power and money.

As the bishop gave Merek more and more duties to perform, he found that the priests in charge of their areas would try to use Merek for their own gain. It did not take long for Merek to understand their ways. He learned quickly how to play the game. But he was always sure to be loyal to the bishop. That was always a priority.

These priests felt that Merek had the bishop's ear and would quietly ask for favors. They would tempt him with bribe money or favors. Although he was new to the priesthood, Merek had had enough experience with similar officers in the king's army. He was somewhat prepared for the viciousness of the priests' agendas and greed. Merek's belief in God and Church early on was strong. His faith and his loyalty to the bishop made it easy for him to withstand the temptations of the greedy clergy. This strength was both a blessing and a curse, for although his conscience was clear in his duty, he made enemies.

He should have known better. He had seen how petty jealousies had undermined the army in France that served the king. Officers were more concerned about gaining land and titles than winning battles. These officers would often make rash or poor decisions without regard to the common soldier in their ranks. Knowing these officers would sacrifice the common soldier for land or title made an indelible mark in Merek's mind. With that in mind, saying no to priests who wanted to advance themselves or line their pockets with gold was rather easy for Merek.

On one occasion, the chief administrator of the town of Witton came to the church offices near the cathedral. This man was the priest who ran the town. It was he who dealt with the guilds, including the merchants, the builders, and the alderman. This administrator was ambitious and dangerous. He wanted wealth and power. And by manipulating the building and trading contracts of the town, he had accumulated both. Builders needed his approval, so they showered him with gifts. Merchants would give him fine wine and food for favors. Even the town council would treat him like royalty.

When the chief administrator first walked into office where the clerks all worked, Merek was seated at his desk transcribing a letter for the bishop. The administrator had a priestly garb that boasted of his wealth. His cassock was made of fine material. His cloak was lined in fur. The rings on his fingers were rich and gaudy. The cross around his neck was golden. His beard was neatly trimmed. He had a handsome face and walked with confidence. His whole appearance was a blatant show of money. Just walking into the room, Merek could feel an air of superiority given by this man.

"Who is in charge of the daily treasurer report?" he demanded.

The clerks were clearly intimidated by this priest. They stood immediately when he appeared. One sheepishly pointed at Merek. The administrator walked to Merek's desk. Merek did not rise, as was the custom when speaking with a church official of rank. Merek continued to write as the administrator stood at Merek's desk and looked down at him.

"Are you the priest in charge of the daily treasury report?" the administrator asked, trying to hold his temper.

Merek purposely did not look up. "I am, Father." Merek still did not look up.

"Do you know who I am?" the administrator shouted. "Why do you not rise when I speak to you? I say, rise!"

Merek calmly looked up at the angry administrator. With a feigned look of regret, Merek rose.

Immediately the administrator took notice of Merek's size. Merek was a foot taller than the administrator.

The administrator gathered himself quickly and began his bullying tactic. "When you are addressed by a church official, you shall rise and answer his questions. Do you understand, Father?"

Merek answered softly, "Yes, Father." Inwardly, Merek rolled his eyes. This short, hot-tempered priest was going to try and intimidate him. Little did the administrator know Merek had stood in the face of a charging French cavalry? If one survives a battle like that, there is little else in life that intimidates.

"I want a draft for a deposit of twenty pounds to be written for the Ash brothers for their work on the bridge in town," the small administrator demanded.

Merek paused before he answered. Something inside him wanted to battle this haughty administrator. In fact, Merek wanted to infuriate this corrupt priest. "I am sorry, Father, but twenty pounds is a lot of money. I will need to ask the bishop for a sum of that amount."

"Nonsense, young man. Do you know who I am?" he shouted.

Of course, Merek knew who he was. But he did not want to let on. "No, Father. I do not know you. Forgive me, for I am new."

"I am Father Berners, chief administrator of the town of Witton. You must be some blithering idiot not to know who I am. Not only do I have the authority to demand money from the church coffers, I do not seek the bishop's approval!"

"Perhaps you do not need the bishop's approval for such a sum of money, Father, but I do," Merek spoke softly but with confidence. "I cannot write the draft without the bishop's approval." Merek stared into Berners's eyes with a look that caused the administrator to pause. It was a look that indicated that Merek might hurt him. Berners was taken aback momentarily.

There was a pause of silence. Merek could feel the old demons rising from his inner hell, and he quickly prayed to God to sway his intentions from hurting this peacock of a priest.

Berners stepped back. His intuition could feel an intense presence from this young priest. Berners was not a man easily intimidated. Quickly, he regained his composure and said softly, but with authority, "Do you understand the consequences if you do not give me what I command?"

The pause allowed Merek to catch himself. His temper passed quickly as Berners spoke in a normal tone. In his mind, he quickly thanked God for allowing him to come to his senses.

"I only know, Father, that I answer to God and our lord, the bishop. And the bishop has given me orders about such large drafts," Merek answered calmly but with steadfastness.

"What is your name?" Berners asked.

"Willson. Merek Willson."

"When I speak to our lord, the bishop, I will tell him of your insolence toward me." Berners kicked the basket near Merek's desk and stormed from the room.

Merek took a breath of relief. The clerks around him mistook the breath of relief as a sign that Merek had been frightened. They did not know that his breath of relief was that he had not lost his temper and hurt the proud administrator.

"Why did you not give him what he wanted?" young Walter asked.

"I am afraid you have made an enemy," another clerk said quietly.

"So be it, brothers," was all Merek said. These young priests had never been in a mortal battle. Men like Father Berners do not put the fear of God in you. He was just a little man with big shoes.

The following day, Merek was called to the bishop's quarters. He kissed the bishop's ring and stood before him. "At your service, Your Excellency," Merek began.

"Father Merek," the bishop said with a smile. Bishop Robinson was nearly seventy, and although his eyesight was failing, his ears were sharp. "I understand there was an irate visitor in the scriptorium yesterday."

"Yes, Bishop Robinson, there was," Merek began apologetically.

Bishop Robinson interrupted. "No need to apologize, young Merek. You were only following orders, my orders. Father Berners has his agenda, and for the most part, it keeps the town running. But sometimes, he gets ahead of himself. You were right to refuse his order."

"It is my hope that it does not put you at odds with the good Father," Merek answered with sincerity.

"Nonsense, Merek. Father Berners and I go way back. He is a very good administrator, but sometimes he has an agenda that goes faster than the Church desires. It is good we slow him down at times."

"I was only obeying your orders."

"None of the other clerks would have stood up to him, Merek. That is why you are my chief clerk. You are a man I trust."

"I am humbled, Your Excellency."

"From now on, you will also be my personal clerk. See to the treasury full-time and work in a private office next to mine. Do you have an objection?"

"I will serve God and you, lord Bishop, in any way you wish."

One month later, Bishop Robinson was dead. He died peacefully in his sleep.

John Baget, the prior of the monastery, became the new Bishop of Witton. He was a competent administrator but was much different than Bishop Robinson. Merek knew him and did not respect Baget's integrity to God.

Father Baget was always seen with an expensive robe, had numerous rings on his fingers, and like Father Berners, had a high opinion of himself. Yes, he ran the priory with efficiency, but more like a business instead of a holy community it was supposed to be. Somehow, Father Baget was making a profit from the day-to-day routine of running a priory.

And Merek knew how. If there were a problem with a leaky roof, or a wall needed mending, several town builders were called. They would bid the job, and Prior Baget had the authority to award the job to the builder with the lowest bid. The town builders craved the jobs from the Church because they were guaranteed to be paid. To gain Prior Baget's favor, the builders would add a few coins to Prior Baget's purse or give him gifts of worth.

Merek saw evidence of the bribes in his work as chief clerk. All records and transactions with the cathedral of Witton ran out of his office. It was easy to see what Prior Baget was up to. The richest builder in town was getting all the work in the priory. The same merchants and suppliers were used for the kitchens and refectories. Yes, Prior Baget and Father Berners both had their own agendas and were making money from the Church.

Once Prior Baget became Bishop of Witton, Merek was demoted. Bishop Baget had his own personal clerks he trusted. Merek had a reputation that did not suit Bishop Baget's agenda, so Merek was removed. He was transferred to the scriptorium where manuscripts were copied. For hours at a time, Merek copied text, a tedious and bothersome duty.

Merek had been in the scriptorium for two months when he was summoned by the priest in charge of the scriptorium. Merek was ordered to take a manuscript into town to Father Berners. Apparently, Berners had been given permission to present a valued manuscript to one of the merchants in town as a "thank you" from the Church for the merchant's many years of service to the Church. The priest in charge of the scriptorium was unaware of Merek's run-in with Berners a few months back. Merek gladly accepted the duty, simply for the excuse to get out of the scriptorium and his duties for a time.

As Merek began to walk into town with the manuscript, he wondered about the irony of being asked to deliver to Father Berners's "home." Priests were not to own a home, yet everyone seemed to know that Father Berners owned one. Merek wondered if Bishop Baget owned one too. The hypocrisy of the clergy was beginning to make a mark on Merek and his commitment to the Church. He saw it first-hand all around the cathedral and the monastery surrounding Witton. Perhaps the clergy out in the villages were still pure in serving the Lord? It made Merek think.

It was a beautiful spring day. Flocks of pigeons flew from rooftop to rooftop looking for a spot to land and eat the crumbs left by the people of Witton. The streets were crowded, merchants taking advantage of the beautiful day to sell their wares. The hustle and bustle of the town was refreshing to Merek, who was cooped up in a room all day copying endless manuscripts. He ambled through the streets, taking in all the sights. Merek made sure to take in the fresh air of the day, and as he did, smiled at the commoners and merchants he passed in the streets. Even if Father Berners gave him a hard time, the break from the scriptorium, the warmth of the sun, and the escape from the routine would make it all worthwhile.

Merek walked to the far end of Witton. He was given an address, but the streets were not well-marked, and he became lost. Thankfully, several citizens guided him to a lonely street just inside the town limits. Simple cottages lined a street near the city woolers. On that street, Merek found the house in which he was to deliver the document. Merek approached the house and noted how deserted the street was, particularly after he had gone through the busy streets of the marketplace. Except for two cats fighting over the scraps of a dead rodent, the street was surprisingly vacant for the time of day. Merek knocked gently on the door.

Father Berners's aid, a young priest named Father Richard, opened the door. Father Richard was tall and slim, kept his black hair cut short and rarely was seen away from Father Berners.

"I have been instructed to deliver this manuscript to Father Berners," Merek said quickly.

Father Richard had opened the door a crack and looked at Merek suspiciously. Merek did not understand Father Richard's hesitancy or suspicion. It was the middle of the day, so Father Richard could plainly see Merek's cassock and know it was not a brigand knocking at the door. Secondly, it would only be hospitable to greet Merek with an open door.

Instead, Father Richard just opened the door a little more and put out his hand, snapping his fingers. He did not say a word.

Merek did not give him the manuscript. It would have been too easy. The priest's rudeness suddenly brought out Merek's stubborn side.

"Father, I was told to give the manuscript to Father Berners," Merek said, stepping back a little.

"I will see he gets it," Father Richard said nervously. He opened the door a little wider now and stuck his head out. He glanced up and down the street as if looking for someone.

Just then, a cry came from inside the house. It was a female cry, and it startled Merek. "What was that?" Merek demanded.

"Nothing. Nothing of your concern. Just give me the manuscript and be on your way."

Another cry, and then a scream. Merek stepped forward. Father Richard tried to close the door, but Merek burst through the door, knocking the slim priest to the floor. Inside, the cottage was unusually dark, but Merek could see a closed door leading to the back of the cottage. He was sure the scream came from within that door.

Father Richard was scrambling to get up, trying to stop Merek from going inside the second room. He grabbed Merek from behind. Merek turned and pushed him with a force that bounced the priest off one of the walls. Father Richard sank, his breath leaving him.

Merek did not knock on the inside door. He burst in. A young girl, nor more than ten, was lying on the bed, her arms and legs tied to the four posts. With the commotion, a figure in a robe was taking himself off her as Merek entered the room. The robed figure was quickly pulling the robe down to cover the lower half of his naked body. It was Father Berners. *"You!"* he screamed. "What are you doing here? Get out, this instant!" As he screamed at Merek, he tried to assemble himself.

The girl cried hysterically.

Merek said nothing. Dropping the manuscript on the floor, he moved toward Father Berners, who was on the other side of the bed. Berners tried to say something more as Merek came closer, but it would not have mattered. Merek grabbed the priest and threw him against the wall. Father Berners hit the wall hard, but before he fell to the floor, Merek had him again. This time, he threw Berners against the other wall. Father Berners smashed into the wall and fell to the floor.

"You will be imprisoned and excommunicated for attacking a superior!" Father Richard said as he stood in the doorway.

Merek leaped across the bed and was at the door grabbing Father Richard before he could move.

"You knew this was happening and did nothing to stop it!" Merek yelled. Merek punched the priest in the stomach. As Father Richard began to fall forward, Merek grabbed him by the neck and seat of his pants and threw him headfirst into one of the corner posts of the bed. Father Richard dropped to the floor.

Merek was not done. Father Berners was slowly getting to his feet. He was dazed yet was trying to grasp his authority over Merek.

"I demand you leave this house," the priest said weakly, getting to his feet.

Merek looked at the young whimpering girl on the bed. He saw the ropes and how they had rubbed her wrists and ankles raw. He also saw the blood from her pubic region. And then he looked at Father Berners.

It had been a long time since Father Gilbert Berners had known fright. Merek's look brought it back.

"Look, I was trying to help this girl," Berners pleaded as Merek slowly walked toward him. "She has an evil spirit inside her, and I was trying to rid her of it."

Merek grabbed Berners by the robe and punched him squarely in the face. Blood splattered everywhere. Berners would have fallen, but Merek still had a hand on the robe. He punched him again, breaking Berners's nose and cheekbone. Berners was whimpering but still had not fallen to the ground. Merek still held him by the robe. The third punch broke the man's jaw. Merek let him tumble to the floor. Despite the beating, Berners was not unconscious. He cried quietly in pain.

Merek turned and undid the ropes that held the girl. He put a blanket over her and instructed her to get up. She did wearily, still crying softly. He found the girl's kirtle and linen shift in the corner of the room and gave them to her. Merek tried to comfort her by talking to her gently, but she was near madness because of the incident. He told her to put on her clothes, and then he went out to the other room to find a hot soup or drink to give her. As he was looking in the outer room, the young girl, clothed, went running out of the cottage. Merek hustled to the door to see which way she ran but did not see her.

He went back in to check on the two priests. For a second, he was fearful that he had killed Father Richard. Merek checked on the young priest. He was not dead, just out cold. Father Berners had sat up in the meantime and was trying to stand.

"You shall pay for this attack," he muttered despite his broken nose and jaw.

"And you shall go to hell," Merek answered, throwing the manuscript at the bleeding priest.

Merek spent the remainder of the afternoon looking for the girl. He made inquiries, stopped at the priory hospital, and wandered the streets until dark. She was nowhere to be found. He did not return to the scriptorium that day. He was clearly tempted to just walk away from Witton, walk away from the Church and his duties. But he had made a vow, and at that point in his life, the vow meant something.

***

The next morning, in the scriptorium, Merek was greeted by two men-at-arms and a priest. They were to escort him to the bishop. Merek was expecting the summons and said nothing on the way. He was worried about his audience with Bishop Baget. Merek knew he had to look and sound remorseful to have any chance of leniency from the bishop. What scared him was he had no remorse. Merek doubted he could act sorrowful to what he did to the two men.

Bishop Baget was in his great "chair" in the middle of the spacious room. Two solemn priests stood beside the bishop. On either side of the bishop, two clerks sat at tables ready to record the meeting. If charges were to be brought on Merek, the scribes would write all the testimony of the meeting. It was quite an audience.

The two men-at-arms walked with Merek to the middle of the room where he stood face-to-face with Bishop Baget. The men-at-arms had their duty to protect the bishop, but they looked comical standing next to the towering Merek. One soldier was old and thin, while the other was overweight and balding. Both had been given a duty that normally had little business to do with danger. Both men had worried looks on their faces standing next to Merek, but they did not leave Merek's side.

Merek stepped forward to bow and kiss the bishop's ring, but he did not get far. Bowing, he approached the bishop's hand but was pulled back by the soldiers, who did so almost apologetically.

"You shall not kiss this ring, Father Willson," Bishop Baget scolded. "Striking a priest is a formidable offense, but striking a superior is unfathomable! This charge will not only get you thrown out of the priesthood, it will send you to the stocks and prison. Father Berners is in the hospital. They tell me you cannot recognize his face. Father Richard is also in the hospital, suffering a grievous head wound. He has been in and out of consciousness since the incident. Father Berners is chief administrator of the church!"

"Does that give him the right to rape little girls?" Merek responded. "In the privacy of a home he is not allowed to own?"

Bishop Baget was momentarily speechless. "What is it you say?" he finally said softly.

"You heard me, Your Excellency," Merek answered with sarcasm. And to the scribes, "Suddenly, you are not taking notes. Do you need help with the spelling?"

"Stop!" the bishop commanded. "Father Berners told me that he was only trying to counsel the girl by the request of her parents. That she may have had a demon inside her."

"Oh, there was a demon inside her, Your Excellency!" Merek responded.

The bishop did not understand the pun at first, but his eyes became large when he realized what Merek was saying.

"How dare you?" he thundered. "Father Berners is a man of God. Exorcism is a way the Church rids demons from the corporal body. Who are you to pass judgment on Father Berners's choice of instrument?"

Merek could not help himself, for his anger was rising. "Father Berners's use of his 'instrument' is not mentioned in the books of St. Augustine or of St. Benedict."

"Why do you show such a lack of respect for a man of the cloth?" the bishop asked, bewildered by the conversation.

"Why do you cover for a monster who hides behind the cloth of the Church? Is it because you too have a private house for proclivities of your own?"

"I have had enough of your blasphemy," the bishop announced.

"I will have my day in court," Merek was quick to reply. "And I will seek a trial in a secular court, not an ecclesiastical one."

"You will—" Bishop Baget began.

"And my voice will be heard, Your Excellency. By the town and community. And here is my guess: more victims will come out. This was not the first little girl that that evil man raped. There are others. And when my voice is heard, there will be justice," Merek answered with conviction.

"I have heard enough!" the bishop screamed. "I want the room cleared."

There was a pause, and then the room emptied, men-at-arms, clerks, priests, scribes, and any servants. As the door closed, Merek just stared at the bishop.

"Let us talk plainly, Father Merek."

Merek simply nodded.

"What you say you 'witnessed' must have been a mistake, a misrepresentation of the counseling of the young girl. Perhaps it was an ancient form of exorcism that you witnessed."

Merek was beginning to smile at the absurdity.

But the bishop continued, "Surely, with a clearer head, you could recant your story."

"Why would I do that?"

"You almost killed those men."

"They were raping a little girl!"

"You word against them, Father Merek. There are two of them. Two who will testify that you attacked them without any cause."

"I saw what I saw."

"But there is no other witness. Where is the girl? Who will collaborate your story? The evidence is plain. Father Berners is in the hospital with a broken jaw, a broken nose and is missing a few teeth. Father Richard is in and out of consciousness because of what you did to him."

Merek's mind was racing. He knew the bishop was holding all the cards. Merek only had the truth. And the truth was not enough. In this case, the truth would not set him free.

"You did not clear the room to tell me all this," Merek finally said, trying to understand what the bishop was after.

"Father Berners is a priest with authority. His role as chief administrator of the town brings order to the town and prosperity to the cathedral. Businessmen seek Father Berners's audience. They need his blessing. The town grows because he is who he is. By his keen service, Father Berners makes Witton one of the fastest-growing sees in this part of England."

Merek knew where this was going. And it turned his stomach.

"Father Merek, you may not know this, but Father Berners has many of the surrounding nobles as his personal friends. If you take this to court, these nobles will hire the best lawyers to defend Father Berners. You will have no chance."

"I will take that chance," Merek said with confidence.

"And when you lose, you will be jailed for life or hung on the gallows."

"I will not lose."

"Stop being naïve. Are you thinking you are going to get a fair trial with the rich noblemen on his side? They will hire the jury and pay them for your guilty verdict."

"But my voice will be heard."

"Yes, it will be heard, but nothing will be done about it. You will be a noisy gong that will excite the village and town for a day or two. And when you are executed, you will be forgotten a week later."

Merek did not know how to answer. He knew the bishop was right. "You have a solution?" Merek asked.

"Recant your story. I will convince Fathers Berners and Richard to drop the charges. Do you want to die a martyr?"

"Perhaps I do."

"Nonsense. You will be forgotten once the lawyers prove your story to be false."

"If I recant?"

"I shall assign you elsewhere. I shall assign you to some small village far from Witton where you can truly be a servant of God. You will serve a multitude of villagers for years doing God's work instead of dying on the gallows for violence against a church official."

Merek said nothing.

The bishop countered. "By your silence, I assume you agree. I will have one of my scribes draw up the papers for the transfer. I will have chosen a village by then. I want you away from Witton tomorrow at dawn."

Merek only looked at the bishop.

"And Father Merek, do not enter Witton again. I never want to see your face again. Now, get out of here." The bishop watched Merek leave the room. He sighed in relief that Merek had not called his bluff. The bishop had heard rumors of Father Berners's proclivities but had done nothing about it. Deep in his heart, he knew Merek was right. Yet, he had to protect the Church. That evening, the bishop planned to draft a letter to the bishop of Winchester asking to transfer Father Berners from Witton.

Merek left the office and walked away. He knew the bishop was right. He knew that he had no chance in court. Yet, he secretly hated himself for taking the cowardly way out. How many young girls had the priest molested? How many more were there to be?

The next morning, Merek left Witton as a priest not steeped in faith. In his journey to Harper's Turn, he thought about giving up the priesthood. Yet, he continued to the village. Once there, he immersed himself in his priestly duties and gradually began to exorcise his own demons by serving God and the people of Harper's Turn.

CHAPTER 12

CHAUCER'S CHOICE

It was late in the evening, and the man was tired. For the past few hours, he had thought of nothing more than lying on his own bed in his own small room. He had been away for almost two months on this last mission. And after hours of riding, his party had finally made its way back to the palace just as the sun went down. Walking his brown palfrey to the stables, the man made sure the animal was watered and fed. The traveller took his belongings and walked slowly to one of the side entrances of the palace meant for servants. In the back halls of the palace, he was greeted by the busy servants who were cleaning the floors and walls from the daily dirt and grime. Some greeted the man by name; others just nodded as he passed them. He was one of them, a servant. Yet he was much more.

The man walked by the kitchen and was instantly drawn to the smells of a roasting pig on a spit, rotating slowly for the following day's dining. The man could not help himself but stopped at the kitchen and took in the aromatic flavors of the soups, bread, and pastries already prepared for the next day. One of the cooks, seeing him at the entrance, tossed him a small hunk of bread and pointed to the roasting pig. The man did not hesitate but took the bread and walked toward the great hearth. There he took the bread and slowly wiped the side of the pig, hoping to let the sizzling drippings find their way into the bread. The man stepped back and took a bite of the saturated bread, letting the delicious taste equal the intoxicating smell of the roasting pig. The man let the piece of bread lay in his mouth. He shook his head at the sensation, nodding to the cook

110

and smiling. The cook nodded back and continued with his chore of plucking the feathers from a dead goose. The man took another swipe of the bread against the roasting flesh of the pig and finished the piece of bread he was given. Walking by the working cook, the man patted him on the shoulder as a way of thanks. The man left the kitchen and walked to his room.

He did not have to walk far. His room was next to the kitchen. Its proximity to the kitchen had many benefits, especially if one had a voracious appetite. Secondly, the constant fire burning in the great hearth of the kitchen made the man's room warm in the cold winters. In the summer, the man was sometimes unable to sleep in the sweltering room, but it was rare in England to have too many days of great heat and high humidity. Thirdly, the room was for one occupant. It had a single bed with an old oaken dresser. There was a small table by the bed that held a solitary candle. The servant who occupied this room was indeed lucky, for he must have had a special duty for the lord of the manor.

He lit a candle by his bed and began to unpack his small valise. He had just opened his travelling case when there was a small knock on his door. The man opened the door. It was one of the special servants to the lord of the manor. The servant brought a message. The man was to see the lord of the manor. And he wished to see him immediately. The man left the valise where it was. He tidied himself as best he could, blew out the candle, and followed the servant.

The man felt it was good to be back in England. For the past several years, he had been on diplomatic missions for England's hierarchy, including the king and his sons. The missions were not numerous but usually took months to complete. And he travelled. The man had been to Italy enough times to begin to speak the language. Earlier that evening he had just returned from Spain.

In his midtwenties, the man wore a tight-fitting tunic with a dagger attached to his belt. He wore long stockings and black boots, dirty from the long trip. The man had a pleasant face, and if he found humor, a merry laugh. It was a laugh that made others do the same. The man was a bit overweight but still was youthful enough to use his brief military training if he had to be physical in art of swordplay. As a boy, he had been extremely shy, but years of service to royal households allowed him to grow out of his timid state. Since he was entrusted with various missions abroad, he learned to have confidence in his voice and his ability to represent the royal family. He had come a long way from the time he had begun his years as a page in the royal household at the age of twelve.

As he followed the servant to meet the lord of the manor, the tired traveler prepared himself to give a report to the lord of the manor with enthusiasm, adding a story or two from his travels. The servant was not walking toward the great hall but led the man to the lord's private apartment. The meeting would be private. He had met the lord there many times. As they approached the door, the man wondered if the lady of the manor would be there too.

The servant knocked, and a second servant opened the door from the inside. Both servants smiled at the traveller as he was escorted into the room.

"Geoffrey, so good to have you back." The older servant smiled.

"Oh, Ralf, it will be a treasure to sleep in my own bed tonight," Geoffrey answered.

Ralf nodded and welcomed him into the lord's private apartment. Geoffrey walked in and waited for the lord. The servants had a welcoming fire ablaze in the hearth. Geoffrey looked around and noticed new tapestries on three of the four walls. Each tapestry depicted hunters chasing different game. Geoffrey made a mental note of the tapestries. From travelling in Europe, he could tell they were imported and expensive.

There was a fine oak table near the fireplace. It was a massive table with the ornate feet that exhibited a carpenter's adept skill in carving wood. There had been times when the massive table had a multitude of nobles surrounding it as the lord held meetings and proposed strategies. The nobleman was seated at the table with a glass of wine. He stood as the traveller approached.

Geoffrey bowed. "Your highness."

The nobleman laughed and walked toward the traveler. "*Dilectus vallettus noster!*" The nobleman smiled loudly. "'Our beloved yeoman.' Is that not the name Father gave you?"

Geoffrey blushed. "Aye, my lord. Most nicknames can be brushed aside, but when the King of England proclaims the nickname, it must become a law of sorts."

The remark made the nobleman laugh genuinely. "Oh, Geoffrey, how I miss your wit when you go abroad! It is so good to see you."

The men shook arms, and the nobleman offered Geoffrey Chaucer a seat.

"Come, have some wine," the nobleman commanded, pouring a glass of claret, a fine red Bordeaux. As he poured, the nobleman motioned for the servants to leave.

"It is good to be back in England, sir." Geoffrey smiled, sipping the wine. In his lifetime, he had never tasted such a rich and delicious wine.

"And how was Spain?" the nobleman asked.

"Very pleasant, sir, for this time of year."

"No, Geoffrey, you misunderstand me. I asked 'how was Spain'?" the nobleman smiled.

Geoffrey put the glass down and looked about the room.

"Do not worry, Geoff. Blanche is not around."

"I am afraid you misunderstand me, Sir John. I said 'it was very pleasant.' Spanish ladies are most comforting."

It took a heartbeat, but Sir John got the message. He barked a laugh and pointed a finger at Geoffrey. "You see. I miss that wit whenever you leave. How good to see you! Come, drink some more." Sir John filled Geoffrey's glass. "You must tell me about the women, Geoff."

"Sir John, I pray you. Do not make me. I am not free with words to properly tell of their beauty, their ways, and their gifts."

Sir John took a large gulp of wine.

"My dear Chaucer, it is the 'gifts' in which I am most interested."

Chaucer smiled. "Sir John, do you not agree that the best gifts are those that are kept secret?"

Sir John nodded.

"Then it would be best if the 'gifts' I have seen be kept a secret. Then when you do travel to Spain, you will discover them yourself."

"I swear by the saint's bones, Geoff, that you are a scoundrel!"

Sir John suddenly stood. The lady of the manor had entered the room. Even though his back was to the lady, Geoffrey Chaucer stood and faced the lady.

"Welcome home, Geoffrey," she said sincerely.

"Lady Blanche." Chaucer bowed, taking her hand and kissing it.

"We missed you, Geoffrey. I see it did not take long for you to get my husband laughing and cursing again," she said with feigned anger.

"Apologies, Madam." Chaucer smiled.

"Did you bring back a joke or story from Spain that made my husband raise his voice so?"

"Indeed, madam," he calmly said, looking at Sir John, whose eyes showed concern as to what Chaucer would say.

Lady Blanche sat at the table near her husband, who poured her a glass of wine. "Proceed, Geoffrey," she ordered, motioning for him to sit also.

Chaucer sat, took a sip of his wine, and looked at Sir John, who was giving a worried look. "The king—" Chaucer started.

"You mean, Sir John's father, my father-in-law," Blanche interrupted, feigning her own importance. "Yes, go on."

Chaucer did not miss a beat. "Indeed, my lady. King Edward sent me on a diplomatic mission to the province of Navarre, Spain. It was not a top-secret mission by any means, so I may tell you that I was sent to offer the king of the province a trade agreement concerning wine. Apparently, King Edward had gotten word that the people of Navarre made a special brand of wine unique in all of Spain, especially in the Ebro River Valley.

"And so I was sent to Navarre. I will spare you the details of the trip. But once we landed off the coast of Spain, we had to travel inland for two days to reach the capital, Pamplona. May I tell you that the Cathedral of Saint Mary in Pamplona was one of the greatest feats of architecture I have ever seen? It even rivals their Roman brothers in Italy.

"There was a festival going on in Pamplona while we were visiting with the king. One afternoon, we were meeting with the king's emissaries and working on the trade agreement when the Spaniards suddenly called a stoppage to the negotiations. At first, we thought there was something wrong, but the emissaries rushed us from the room to a balcony at the palace that overlooked the main street of Pamplona. They pointed to the street below.

"We were not sure of what we were to look for, but one of our translators directed our attention to the far end of the street where a crowd had formed. As we watched, the crowd suddenly began to run in our direction! There was yelling and screaming, but there was also lots of laughter. As the runners got closer, we could see that there were five or six bulls chasing the men who were running!"

Sir John, relieved that Chaucer had changed the subject, laughed and said, "Bulls? Bulls, Geoff?"

"Bulls, lord. Turns out, it is a custom made popular years ago in Pamplona. Apparently, the farmers would transport the bulls through the town to take them to market after the breeding in the fields had been done. As they herded the bulls through the streets, young boys would try to show their mettle by running with the bulls. It was a sign of their bravado, I suppose."

Both listeners were smiling at the story.

"Was anyone hurt?" Lady Blanche asked.

"I am afraid one poor lad tripped and was run over by one of the bulls," Chaucer said quietly.

"Was he killed?"

"We thought so, my lady. He lay still until all the bulls had passed. A lady waited for the bulls to pass and ran out with a goblet of wine. She held his head and poured some of Navarre's favorite wine down his throat. We waited anxiously for any movement from the man. Suddenly, he grabbed the wine, finished it, and gave the woman a most ravenous kiss, much to the delight of the crowd."

Both Sir John and Blanche laughed aloud.

"We knew right then and there that the wine was very special, and we sped up negotiations!" Chaucer smiled at his own joke.

The couple laughed with him. More small talk was made.

Sir John of Gaunt, was the fourth son of King Edward III. As the Duke of Lancaster, he cut an impressive figure. Not a very tall man, the duke had an air of confidence that was mirrored in the way he dressed and handled himself. Of all the brothers, he was the most learned and was known for being an intellectual. His enemies would call his confidence a type of arrogance, but John of Gaunt would not care.

He had married Blanche of Lancaster in 1359. Blanche's father, the Duke of Lancaster, died in 1361, and John of Gaunt became heir to half of the father-in-law's lands. Eventually, King Edward III would name John the Duke of Lancaster, giving him the rights to all the lands of Lancaster. By 1366, John of Gaunt was one of the richest men in England.

And Geoffrey Chaucer was his friend. From the time Sir John had met Chaucer, he was drawn to Chaucer's charming personality, his wit and natural ability to serve. At the time of their first meeting, Chaucer had been working for John's older brother, Sir Lionel, Duke of Clarence. Chaucer had been with Clarence for more than two years and gained the respect of Lionel and his wife with his dependability, personality, and thoroughness. Chaucer could be counted on.

Later, Chaucer was given more duties, not just by Lionel, but also the king himself. As one of the king's diplomats, he had travelled to France, Spain, and Italy. Most of his duties included carrying personal letters from nobleman to nobleman, minor trade agreements, and even matchmaking. In time, Chaucer served most of Edward's family in one way or another, including John of Gaunt.

After a half hour of catching up with small talk and more wine, Blanche excused herself for the evening. As she rose to leave, both men stood. She gave her husband a customary peck on the cheek and allowed Chaucer to bow and kiss her hand before she left.

"You know, Geoffrey, my wife is fond of you," Sir John joked as his wife left the room.

"Perhaps she is amused by my stories," was Chaucer's reply.

Sir John motioned for Chaucer to sit. "I know it is late, and you have travelled far. Would you sit, Geoffrey, for I need to talk?"

"Lord," Chaucer answered immediately, sitting. He smiled as Sir John filled Chaucer's glass. "You are trying to aid my sleep with the wine, sir?"

"Indeed."

They tasted the wine in short silence.

"May I speak to you about a personal matter, Geoffrey?"

"By all means, lord."

"And it shall remain between us?"

"Aye. Of course, lord. It is understood."

"You have been around my father's court from time to time. Are you familiar with Philippa Roet, one of my mother's ladies in waiting?"

"I know who she is, lord. But I do not really know her personally."

"She is in a bit of a predicament, Geoff."

Chaucer took a sip of wine and said nothing.

"Philippa is with child. As you know, an unmarried lady in waiting who becomes pregnant loses her place and income."

Chaucer could not help himself. The wine had loosened his tongue. "And you, lord, are the father?"

Sir John looked surprised by Chaucer's question. "There are rumors? How do you know?"

"No rumors, lord. Not to my knowledge, but then I have been abroad the last few months."

"So why is your guess so accurate?"

"Lord, a lady in waiting has a very private personal life. If she were to become pregnant, it would be kept out of the ears of everyone, including noblemen. I deduced that if you were privileged to this knowledge, you would have a stake in it. I say this with all due respect, lord."

Sir John chuckled softly. "Geoffrey, your insight and wisdom baffle me."

"Lord, since we are alone, and you ask me, may I add that I am not that clever, knowing your attraction toward the opposite sex. Once again, in all due respect, Sir John."

Sir John took a sip of wine, shaking his head at Chaucer's observation. "And so, hear what I propose." Sir John sat up in his seat with his hands on the table. "Do you know Philippa by sight, then?"

"Yes, sir. She is a most attractive woman."

"Will you marry her?"

Chaucer was caught by surprise. He tried to hide it but was unable to.

"Lord?"

"Marry her, Geoffrey, so she will keep her place at court."

"We do not know each other, lord."

Sir John laughed. "Ha, next you will tell me that you are not in love with her!"

"No, lord. I know enough about courtly marriages to know that very few involve love. Most are arranged politically."

"Indeed, Geoffrey. Why should this be any different? Lady Philippa will keep her honor at court, will be happy to have 'your' baby, and she will retain a sizable pension from me for the rest of her life. Of course, you will too. I will make sure that for the rest of your lives, I will provide means of income for you two and my offspring."

Chaucer took another sip of his wine. His mind was flooding with thoughts and questions. "Sir John, you have caught me off guard. I do not know what to say."

Sir John laughed aloud. "It is not too often that I have been in your company without a witty comeback from you, Geoff."

Chaucer smiled. Behind the smile was a serious thought. Say yes and become a partner in life to a woman he did not know. Say no and risk making an enemy of one of the richest and most powerful men in England.

"Lord, with your permission, may I have time to think about it?"

"Of course, Geoff. Of course."

"On my way to the palace tonight, I was thinking of making a trip. A personal one."

"Oh?"

"Yes, lord. A pilgrimage. To Canterbury. I have never been to Canterbury and was planning on worshipping at the shrine of St. Thomas."

"Ah, yes, of course. A pilgrimage in the spring is most customary."

"My plans were to leave within the week. Would you allow me to give you an answer upon my return? What you ask will change my life, and seeking guidance through prayer would help me in my decision."

"Geoffrey, by all means. Make the trip. Think on this as you travel. Consider marrying Philippa. It will improve your standing in court, guarantee both of you a prosperous life, and you will be doing me a personal favor."

"Indeed, sir. All of those factors will be considered."

CHAPTER 13

THE MONK AND THE FRIAR

True to her plan, the prioress was ready to leave Norwood at noon. With the help of Merek, Father Smithton readied the horses of the prioress and Sister Anne. They walked the horses in front of the refectory and waited for the nuns. There, Merek was introduced to another priest, Father Gilbert Towns, who would accompany the group on the trip. Merek was to learn that the prioress had asked Father Towns to join them, for she was nervous about such trips without the proper escort.

Merek observed a large ax bolstered to the saddle of the horse on which Father Towns rode. Father Towns was not a tall man, but he was round. His large belly supported a thick chest. However, Merek noticed the large priest had small thin arms that did not seem to match the rest of his upper torso. Regardless of the size of the man's arms, Merek had a sense that the priest knew how to use the ax. As they gathered and waited for the nuns, Merek found it odd that the priest did not come up and introduce himself. So Merek walked over to him.

"I am Father Merek Willson," he said plainly, putting his arm out.

The man gave him a curt shake and went about the business of readying his horse. He seemed to ignore Merek.

"He is Father Gilbert Towns," Sister Anne interceded, exiting the refectory and grabbing the reins of her horse. "Please do not be insulted by Father Towns's apparent rudeness, Father Merek. He is somewhat deaf."

Merek looked at Towns and then at Sister Anne. The scar on her face seemed more pronounced in the sunlight. Merek was quick to check himself from staring at her.

"Thank you, Sister Anne. Glad you told me."

"Father Towns is a great help to us here at Norwood. He does the bulk of the heavy chores and is somewhat our protector. He is especially protective of Madam Prioress."

"Very good, Sister. It is always good to have an extra hand when travelling," Merek answered, still looking at Towns adjusting the saddle on his horse.

"I see by the position of the sun that it must be near noon," the prioress said with enthusiasm as she approached her horse. "Come, everyone. We must make for Southwark before dark."

Father Towns helped the prioress on her horse. He turned to help Sister Anne, but Merek had already helped her. The group made their way to the road that would lead to Southwark. Father Smithton and Merek led the way. The prioress and Sister Anne followed behind, and Father Towns rode behind the group.

It had been a cold morning, but by midday, the temperature had risen. Yet, there was a chill in the air as the group left Norwood. The road was wide just out of Norwood and well-suited for travelers. Two riders could easily travel side-by-side without the danger of low tree limbs or wayward jagged bushes tearing at their clothes. In the beginning of the journey, the road led them through some open fields, where farmers could be seen readying their fields for the spring planting. The openness of fields gave comfort to travelers, for attack by robbers would be minimized for there was nowhere to hide or surprise victims.

It did not take long for the prioress to begin chatting to the group. She made it a point to engage everyone in the group except for Father Towns. Every so often, she would turn and smile at the deaf priest to let him know she knew he was there. Once, when the prioress turned, Merek happened to be looking. He saw Father Towns smile back at the prioress. It was the only time Merek had seen the man show any emotion.

The travelers made their way down the road for two hours, entertained solely by the prioress's stories, theories and philosophy about life, love, and God. Merek was quite entertained by her unique views and opinions. He kept thinking to himself, "This is a nun?" Once in a while, he would counter an opinion she had, and it would spark more animation and energy from her. The others let her talk. They only spoke if she asked their opinion. The prioress seemed to enjoy Merek's opposition to her and furthered her digressions on a variety of subjects.

Langley Inn stood on the main road that led to Southwark, and the prioress halted her group to take a break from the road. Father Towns attended the horses as the others entered the inn. Even though it was not quite three o'clock, the inn was busy. The bench-like tables were crowded but not full. Ladies attended the benches, serving ale, wine and an assortment of meat platters and cheeses. The room was noisy with talk and laughter, but was not a raucous crowd. The drunken patrons would come later in the day.

Father Smithton made room for the party at a crowded bench, explaining to a few Christian patrons that the nuns were tired and in need of rest and nourishment. The men were willing to make room, not just for the nuns, but also Fathers Smithon and Willson. The patrons stood and greeted the nuns as gentlemen and then slid down the benches to make room. As they sat, Merek noted that except for the waitresses, the prioress and Sister Anne were the only lady patrons in the tavern.

A few of the patrons sitting close to the group began to stare at Sister Anne. She noticed them staring and put her head down, blushing. Merek, observing this, got the men's attention and shook his head in disapproval. The men got the message and turned their attention elsewhere. Merek made a point to engage Sister Anne in conversation so that she would forget their stares.

Father Smithton had small flasks of wine and ale brought to the table, and the group shared a cup of each. When the cup of ale was passed to Merek, he offered it to Sister Anne first. She politely refused and waited for the cup of wine to come her way. Merek took a deep drink of the ale. It was unusually good, and he had to be careful not to overindulge, for they had still some travelling ahead of them.

A monk approached the group with what looked like another priest. Actually, he did not look like the typical monk. He wore an expensive robe that was colored in a deep green. It was fur-lined! He was bald, and the hair he still had was cut in such a way befitting a monk.

"May we join you, Sister?" the monk asked the prioress.

"By all means, Father," the prioress smiled.

More room was made, and the monk and another priest joined the group. As he sat, Merek noticed the monk wore an expensive robe. Merek had never seen material so expertly woven and surmised the robe had been imported, probably from Flanders. He also noticed that the monk's hood was connected to the robe with an expensive golden pin that was tied into a lover's knot! Merek almost laughed aloud. Hoods were a common article of clothing and had to be fastened to the garment one wore in public by a very specific knot. How one tied a knot to the hood would indicate if one were married or not. This monk had tied his knot into a "lover's knot" indicating he was not married and was free to love! Merek shook his head and grinned to himself.

Questions flooded through Merek's mind as the monk made conversation with the prioress. How did a monk get such an expensive robe? Why is he advertising that he is free to fall in love? What about his vow of chastity?

Merek had missed the first part of the conversation between the monk and prioress. He came into the conversation as the monk was introducing the man beside him.

"And this is Father Hubert, Madam Prioress. Like me, he is a priest of our Holy Catholic Church. Father Hubert is a friar and serves some of the local villages to the southeast of here," the Monk said cordially.

"A pleasure." The prioress smiled, holding out her hand as the friar kissed it.

Friar! Merek thought. He did not trust either man but kept his opinion to himself.

"And so," the monk went on speaking to the prioress, "will you consider letting us join your party for the rest of the way to Southwark?"

"Yes, of course," the prioress answered. "Do you have any objections, Father Smithton?"

"No, Madam Prioress," Smithton answered. "None at all."

Ask me, Merek thought. But he said nothing.

Father Towns never did enter the inn. He had stayed with the horses, and Father Smithton was sure he brought out some ale when the party vacated the inn. Towns did not look happy that the two other priests were joining the group, for Merek saw the look in his eyes. Merek tried to give Towns a look that said he agreed, but Towns never glanced Merek's way.

Before they left the inn, the monk introduced himself to the group as Father Richard Quinn. Quinn's palfrey was as brown as a berry and was well-taken care of. The palfrey was young and spry and was fit for a nobleman. How could a monk own such a horse? Merek could not help noticing the beautifully supple boots Quinn wore along with his fine black robe lined grey squirrel fur. *So much for the vow of poverty,* Merek thought.

Merek also noticed that Father Quinn had a beautifully shaped bow and a quiver of arrows. The bow was not the warlike longbow, but was a hunting bow, and it was a fine weapon.

"It is quite a bow you have, Father Quinn," Merek could not help but say.

"Aye, Father, it is my pride and joy. I am very fond of hunting, you know." Father Quinn smiled as the group began a slow trot down the road.

"May I see one of your arrows?" Merek asked.

"By all means, Father," the monk answered, giving Merek one arrow from his quiver.

Merek took the arrow with great care and examined it. The arrowhead was wedge-shaped with a fine metal for killing game. Merek had a few of the same kind. However, most of his arrows Merek had were formed with the heavy bodkin tip, used specifically for penetrating a knight's armor. The head of the bodkin tip was formed into a small square that could kill a knight in full armor.

"A fine arrow," Merek said, handing the arrow back to the monk.

"I noticed your longbow," the monk said, taking the arrow. "Can you use it?"

"A little," Merek answered. "I hope that the sight of the longbow will scare any would-be evildoers from bothering us. I pray that I will never have to use it."

The monk smiled. "If they had any sense, they would be wary of it. Forgive me, Father. We all introduced ourselves in the tavern, but it was a bit noisy, and I did not hear your name clearly."

"Merek Willson."

"Indeed, Father. And I am Richard Quinn. Let us hope our ride is uneventful and our skills with the bow are not tested."

"Agreed, Father Quinn. Agreed."

Quinn nodded and advanced in the procession, which had now slowed to a walk. Merek found himself in the middle of the pack. He looked behind and saw Father Towns in the rear. Father Towns rode with a type of grimace on his face, as if he were in pain. Merek noticed he kept a hand on the large ax attached to his saddle.

Up ahead, the friar, Father Hubert, was riding alongside Sister Anne. He was talking in an animated way while she said little and kept her head down. After a few moments, Merek could see that the man was bothering the young nun. Merek began to move his horse toward the couple. His attention was to ride right between them. As he got closer, Father Hubert was pulling something from the sleeve of his robe. It was a trinket of sorts, no doubt meant as a gift to the embarrassed Sister Anne.

Merek had no use for friars on the whole, and this friar was no different. One did not offer a gift to a nun unless one wanted something. Even though Merek was a priest, he was also a man and knew the friar was "hunting." Therefore, Merek had no qualms in breaking the moment for the friar. Intentionally rude, he rode right between the two of them, grabbing the trinket from the friar. Merek pulled his horse close to the friar's not wanting Sister Anne to hear their conversation.

"What is the meaning of this?" the startled friar began.

"A special pin for a woman's hair, no doubt," Merek said casually, examining the "gift."

"Father, I do not like your intrusion," the friar countered.

"And I do not like the temptation you offer Sister Anne," Merek answered. "Surely, Father Hubert, you must be aware of the vow of poverty Sister Anne has taken? She cannot accept your gift. It goes against her vows."

"It is but a small trinket," the friar answered.

"Aye, it is but a small gift. Yet"—he lowered his voice even more so that only the friar could hear him—"by accepting this gift, you will expect her to disobey her vow of chastity too."

The friar's eyes became large with sudden anger. "How dare you suggest that I would—?"

"Save it, Father. I know your kind and how you use your holy orders for your own gain. Save your trinkets and your charm for the young village girls you no doubt seduce at your whim."

By now, the procession had stopped. Merek's voice had gotten louder than he wanted. Father Smithton, who was leading the party, rode back to where Merek and the friar were still on their horses but were face-to-face.

"Father Willson, is there a problem?" Father Smithton asked.

"No problem, Father Smithton. Father Hubert and I are discussing our differences in opinion concerning the vows of poverty, chastity, and obedience," Merek stated loudly so all could hear.

"Sounds like a marvelous discussion, men," the prioress intervened. "Perhaps we can continue to move as we all add to the philosophical discussion?"

There was a little hesitation. As a prioress, Madam Eglantyne was the ranking church official of the group. She held rank, and all were to heed to her wishes.

"By all means, Madam Prioress." Merek broke the tension. "We are ready to continue the journey," he added, still looking at Father Hubert.

Father Smithton moved his horse to the front of the procession, and all began to follow. Merek kept his horse as a block to Father Hubert's horse.

In almost a whisper, Merek leaned toward Hubert. "You bother Sister Anne again on this trip, even to Canterbury, and I will thrash you."

Father Hubert was startled by the threat. "What kind of priest are you?"

Merek turned his horse so that Hubert could move forward. "Not a very good one," was all he said.

As so, the group of seven made their way to Southwark. Southwark, just south of London, was traditionally the beginning of the pilgrimage to Canterbury. Pilgrims would congregate in various inns in Southwark, form large groups, and make the two- or three-day trip to Canterbury together. There was safety in large numbers from robbers, thieves, and highwaymen. Southwark was the place to find and join a group to travel on down to Canterbury.

CHAPTER 14

THE TABARD

Harry Bailly was a busy man. As the owner and innkeeper of The Tabard, he had a multitude of duties. Presently, he was preparing his main hall for a large meal. As one of the foremost inns in Southwark, The Tabard was a customary inn for pilgrims travelling to Canterbury to gather and organize for the trip. Harry Bailly was expecting a swarm of pilgrims in the next few days. It was April, and April meant the Lenten season, the time for pilgrimages. Although The Tabard was a thriving business for Harry Bailly, March and April were always his busiest months. They were the months he made his greatest profits.

"Adam, I want you and Simon to get this room ready. The benches and tables all need a thorough cleaning," Harry instructed his young hired hands.

"As you say, Master Bailly," Adam returned. "We will get right to it."

Adam nodded to Simon, and both began their duties. Both young men had been newly employed. They liked Master Bailly, for he treated them well and, more importantly, fairly. They did what he asked and did it well. They knew they would be compensated well.

Harry knew the boys would begin work immediately. He did not stay in the great room but moved to another part of The Tabard. There were always other details to attend. Harry climbed the stairs of the inn that led to the back bedrooms. One of the rooms had a large hole in the ceiling, and Harry had called in a man whom he trusted with such problems.

"Edgar, how goes it?" Harry asked.

Edgar was invisible in the hole in the ceiling but poked his head through the hole. "On its way, Harry. Will get this corrected in the time it takes for the good king to take a shit," Edgar said with a smile.

"Carry on, Edgar. Do a fine job. I want no leaks on my incoming clients, you see?"

"Understand, Harry," he said plainly and got back to work.

Harry moved on. He descended the stairs to another area of The Tabard, a wide-open area that served as the marketplace. It was an open area, and local farmers would begin bringing their wares into the area for sale. It was nearly the weekend, the time for farmers to sell their goods in Harry's open area.

"Joselyn, please make sure the farmers pay their fee before they set up," Harry instructed.

"As you wish, Master Harry."

"Marcus," Harry called to a young man crossing the marketplace.

The man, not more than twenty, immediately made his way to Harry Bailly. "Aye, Master Harry." He smiled as he approached Harry and Joselyn.

"Marcus, stay with Joselyn as she collects the fee from these farmers. Since she is a young lass, they might try to cheat her."

"Aye. Will do, Master Harry." Marcus smiled.

"Very good, then" was all Harry said as he moved toward his next stop.

Climbing down the stairs under the tavern area, he needed to check on the kegs of ale he had in store. Making a count, he saw the kegs that were ready for the customers, and those that were not. As a brew master of his own ale, he knew exactly which kegs were ready for consumption and which were not. Satisfied that there were enough kegs ready for the steady stream of visitors he was about to receive, he climbed the stairs to the tavern.

Perkins was behind the bar with a towel, cleaning and keeping order. Harry noticed a few of the patrons; some were seated at the benches and a few standing near the bar. Perkins was a mainstay in Harry's tavern. A big man, Perkins had the perfect temperament to be the barkeep. He was a large man with hands as large as Harry had ever seen. Perkins had an easy laugh, could talk down potential problems with drunken customers, and was extremely handy in defending himself from quarrelsome drunkards. Of course, regular customers to the Tabard knew Perkins had a large club under the bar for unruly customers. They also knew he had a small sword for would-be robbers.

Actually, drunkards were not usually a problem at The Tabard. The Tabard typically lent itself to a more genteel kind of clientele. Most customers used the road in Southwark to travel to Canterbury and other places like Dover, to the east of London. Harry Bailly had set a standard at his hostelry that prided itself on cleanliness and service. With his commitment came a steeper price to pay if a pilgrim to Canterbury wanted his services. Harry kept his prices a little higher for room and board. The prices usually kept out the lowlifes around Southwark. If they did happen to enter The Tabard, Perkins was uncommonly good at expelling them.

Yet, there was trouble from time to time. Southwark itself had a bit of a reputation as a wild "entertainment" district. Outside the jurisdiction of London, Southwark allowed the theater and all the influences it brought, animal baiting, dog fights, and prostitution. For Harry Bailly's end, it was almost impossible to keep out all the drunks and prostitutes. His reputation and Perkins's attention to such riffraff helped Harry to run a respectable business. But every once in a while, there was a mishap.

Harry had a reputation of running an honest hostelry. He was a striking man, handsome in every way. He was taller than the average man and was known for his rather large hands. His blue eyes seemed to always be bright. In his thirties, his once-compact and strong body had gotten a little larger, mostly around the waste. Harry had a reputation as a man of action, but only as a last resort. He had opinions and was not afraid to say them. The Tabard was his domain, and he made sure his clients knew it.

What set Harry apart from other innkeepers was his ability to deal with customers and townspeople. Harry was a merry-hearted man, quick with a laugh. He was an "easy" audience, never too busy to hear a story and had a contagious laugh if someone told a joke. In addition, Harry was known for his wisdom and tact in dealing with his clients. If there were a problem, Harry always seemed to have a solution. And usually, his solution pleased his customers.

"Perkins," Harry said, pointing to some customers at one of the benches, "pilgrims?"

"Aye, Harry. Just come in."

"Have they asked for rooms?"

"Not yet, Harry. Intend to ask them soon."

"Very well, Perkins. Should have a full house by nightfall," Harry answered.

Harry walked across the tavern to where four figures were seated at one of the benches. He approached with a genuine smile.

"Good days, sirs. Welcome to The Tabard."

There were four men sitting at the bench. One man stood as Harry addressed the table. He appeared to be a Moor, for his skin was dark. The man stood but said nothing.

It was the youngest of the group that returned Harry's welcome. "Good day to you, sir. Might you be the innkeeper?" the young man asked with confidence.

"I am, young sire. I am Harry Bailly."

"Master Bailly, may I introduce my father, Sir Robert of Ganse?"

"An honor, Sir Robert." Harry bowed, showing the proper respect to a knight.

"With us is Father Leo Colman, a village priest from the Winchester parish," the young squire continued. "Standing is my father's yeoman, Hugh, and I am Thomas, squire to my father."

"A pleasure, sirs," Harry said and added, "on your way to Canterbury?"

"Indeed, Master Bailly," Sir Robert answered, still seated with Father Coleman. "We are in need of rooms for tonight, as well as care for our horses."

"By all means, gentlemen. For you and your son, Sir Robert, we have rooms especially tailored to suit your needs. For you, Father, we have rooms for clergy. And for your servant, Sir Robert, we have set aside some berths in the upper level of the barn," Harry assured them.

Thomas looked at his father, who nodded. "You will let us know the cost, Master Bailly. We shall also require dinner tonight and breakfast in the morning," Thomas said. "There will not be a problem housing Hugh, will there?"

"Why do you ask?" Harry asked.

"Some inns do not house men of his color or those who look like Moors," Thomas said as a matter of fact.

"No need to worry, Master Thomas. Your servant will be treated as any other servant," Harry answered. "I expect a crowded inn tonight, gentlemen, but please be assured, you will be taken care of. Now if you excuse me, I have chores to attend. I will send one of my servants to escort you to your rooms when you are ready. Feel free to take your horses to our stable and have them rested for your journey tomorrow."

Thomas was quick to answer, "By all means, Master Bailly. We all know The Tabard has a solid reputation as an inn of quality."

Harry smiled, bowed to Sir Robert, and left the room.

As Harry Bailly left the back of the bar to check in the kitchen, the front door of the tavern opened, and five men walked into the tavern together.

Sir Robert took notice of them at once. Hugh had gone to care for the horses. Father Colman had his back to the front door and did not see them come in. Thomas had excused himself from the table and had gone to relieve himself. Others in the tavern were busy with drinking and conversation. No one but Sir Robert noticed the men enter.

Sir Robert did not stare, nor did he pretend to witness their entrance. But he did look, and he did notice the men. They were wearing new clothes, and they seemed to have badges attached to the fronts of their shirts, indicating a sign of the newly formed guilds. There was something about the men that seemed odd. Sir Robert could not put his finger on what seemed out of place. Was it his imagination, or did they seem bigger and thicker than the average man? Was it his imagination, or did they come through the front door in such a way that no one seemed to notice that five men had just entered the tavern, surveyed the entire room, and sat themselves at a bench near the far wall? They seemed to move in unison as one. And that was what bothered Sir Robert the most.

The hair on the back of Sir Robert's neck was standing. He did not know why, but he respected the feeling. He had not lived through fifteen major battles without recognizing dangerous men. And now they were seated behind him. Nonchalantly, he stood, moved around the table, and took Thomas's empty seat. Now he could see the men gathered around one of the tables. They were in his view. Sir Robert was cautious not to stare at the men. But from time to time, he studied them.

"Mind if I join you, gentlemen?" a stranger asked Sir Robert, breaking him from his thoughts of the five men in the corner.

Sir Robert looked up before he answered. The stranger was young with curly brown hair and a beard. And he was obviously drunk. As he awaited Sir Robert's answer, the man slowly swayed as if he were going to topple at any second. The mug of ale he had was tilting with him and was spilling small amounts of its contents onto the table in which Sir Robert and Father Colman sat.

"How about I help you, sir?" Thomas said with a friendly but firm voice. He had just returned from the privy.

The young man with the curly brown hair and beard did not seem to understand that Thomas was addressing him.

Instead, the young man said to Sir Robert, "Are you going to Canterbury, sirs?" Without waiting a reply, he continued, "I am Albert, a cook by trade." He tried to bow to the table but stumbled, spilling a good portion of his ale at Sir Robert's feet.

Thomas was quick to act and pushed the man away from the table. Grabbing the man by his shirt and his belt, Thomas quickly rushed the man to an empty bench. He sat him down and gave him a friendly warning, "Friend, we will be happy to meet you when you sober up. But do not approach my father in your condition again. Do you understand?"

Albert looked up at Thomas, nodded, and put his head on the table, using his arms as a pillow. He did not move.

Some of the patrons at the bar observed the incident, but no one interjected or said a word. Sir Robert was quick to note that the five men seated in the corner had witnessed the entire event. They watched but did nothing to interfere.

Thomas came over to his father's table and sat down. He did not question his father's changing seats. Sir Robert nodded an appreciation of his son's help, and they continued to sip their ale and watch as others began to arrive at The Tabard.

CHAPTER 15

MEETING THE MILLER

Since leaving the Langley Inn, Merek was pleased with the group's progress toward Southwark and The Tabard. Father Smithton led the group the entire way. He kept a steady pace, and the group found itself on the outskirts of Southwark ahead of schedule. Fortunately, the road was open, and there were no treacherous woods to venture through. It was a calm and peaceful trip.

It was also a trip of lively conversation. The prioress seemed to think it was her duty to ask questions of everyone in the party, give opinions when she felt they were needed, and mix in a story or two of her own. After Merek's confrontation with the friar at the Langley Inn, he felt the trip with the two added priests would be loathsome. But Merek was wrong. Thanks to the prioress, the time flew by.

There was an order in which they rode. Father Smithton led the group out in front by himself. Behind him, the monk and the friar rode together. The prioress and Sister Anne were next in line, but after a few miles, the prioress asked Merek to ride with her and Sister Anne. The road was wide enough for three horses to ride side by side. Father Gilbert Towns carried up the rear. He seemed content to be in the back, said nothing, and kept a vigilant eye.

"And in the end, the young maiden took the knight to be her betrothed. So, you see, gentlemen, that a woman's intuition is not to be taken lightly," the prioress said with a smile as she finished a story she had shared with the group. "Do you see?"

Father Quinn turned in his saddle and smiled. "Of course, Madam Prioress. Makes perfect sense to me."

"So it does, Father Quinn?" the prioress answered in feigned shock. "I would not expect a monk to understand or have the where-withal to understand the ways of a woman. It is my understanding you monks see so very little of them."

The monk was immediately embarrassed. "It is what I am told," the monk answered sheepishly.

The prioress laughed loudly. "By St. Loy, Father Quinn, do not be embarrassed. I am merely jesting with you." She laughed again, a laugh that was not a teasing laugh, but one meant to lighten the group.

The monk turned in his saddle and nodded to her.

"What did you think of the story, Father Merek?" she countered, directing her attention to the man riding beside her.

"Madam Prioress," Merek answered, looking into the beautifully glass-grey eyes of the prioress, "it has been a standing rule of mine not to comment on topics in which I have no experience."

"Come now, Father Merek. You are a village priest. Surely you have seen young parishioners who have fallen in love?" the prioress said with a genuine smile.

"I have, Madam Prioress," Merek answered, hoping the question of women, love, and intuition would pass. He was concerned that his all-too-real feelings for Thea might come to the surface with the prioress's questions.

"So tell the group, Father Merek, your opinion of the story I told."

"I enjoyed it, Madam Prioress, as did we all," Merek answered, knowing his answer would not pass the test.

"St. Loy, Father Merek, you seem to be at a loss of words," the prioress said loudly. "Are you shy when it comes to women, love, and marriage?" She smiled at her own cleverness.

The others in the group began to laugh at the conversation.

Merek did not like the way the conversation was going, so he took the offensive with a bluff. "Understand, Madam Prioress, that I got the calling to be a priest late in my youth. I did not begin my studies until I was in my early twenties. I must confess that in my youth I did experience love. In fact, I was to be married at one time," Merek lied.

"Oh, my, Father Merek. Please tell us more," the prioress pleaded, genuinely interested.

"I beg you, Madam. Please do not make me tell my tale. It is a sad tale, one that truly breaks my heart."

"Oh, Father Merek, I am so sorry," the prioress said with genuine sadness. "How careless of me to resurrect such sorrowful feelings! How did your lady love die?"

Now it was Merek's turn. "Die? Madam Prioress, who talks of death? The young lady in which I was betrothed ran off with a cobbler!" There was a silent pause in the group. "The sadness, Madam Prioress, is that the cobbler took my finest pair of boots too!"

The group laughed loudly, as did the prioress, who laughed the loudest for having the joke played on her. "Father Merek, touché." The prioress laughed.

And the group moved on. A few miles from Southwark, the group heard the strange sound of a single bagpipe being played eerily on the road ahead. At first, the group could not see the stranger playing the instrument. After a relaxing journey, the sound brought a little tension to the group. Father Smithton slowed the group down. The group tightened its ranks as the men drew their weapons.

The eerie sound continued as the group came to a hilly bend in the road. Father Smithton urged the group on but with great caution. As they turned the bend, they saw the cause of the sound. At first, the group saw his horse. And then they saw him.

The man was sitting against a tree, playing the bagpipes. Since the man was seated, the group could not tell too much about the stranger. Merek, like Smithton and Towns, was looking around to see if his playing were a trap for robbers or highwaymen.

As the group grew closer, the man stood, still playing the bagpipes. Merek did not know the tune he was playing, but the man's play indicated he had little proficiency with the instrument. As they approached, he put the bagpipes aside. "What in Christ's name do we have here?" he said, slurring his words.

"May we pass?" Father Smithton asked, wanting no trouble.

The stranger looked around. "What, you think this land belongs to me?" He began to laugh at his own comment.

Merek observed that the man was big, almost sixteen stone. He was broad and stout with short shoulders and had red hair and a red beard. Merek observed that the man looked strong, like one who could out wrestle a villager in a contest, where the winner would be awarded a pig or calf. Merek also observed that the man was drunk.

Father Smithton was put at ease when he saw the man was obviously drunk. "We heard your pipes, sir. We were not sure of your intentions."

"Jesus Christ, man, can't a man play his pipes when he wants?" the drunk man answered. He looked around the group. He stared at the friar, Father Hubert. "Do I know you?" he asked the friar.

Father Hubert shook his head.

The stranger looked hard at the friar. Suddenly his eyes grew large. "Christ's bones! I do know you!" the stranger screamed. Suddenly, he threw his bagpipes to the ground and rushed to the friar's horse. In a second, he yanked the friar off the horse and threw him to the ground. He sat atop the helpless priest. "Goddam you, I do know you! Last summer, you wed one of your 'girls' to my cousin's son. They were both fourteen. The girl was pregnant thanks to your stiff prick. You pawned her off to my cousin's son. Yes, I know you!" He tried to punch the friar in the face, but his drunkenness caused him to miss. The punch just glazed the priest's jaw.

Before the stranger could attempt another blow to the friar, Fathers Smithton and Quinn pulled the red-headed stranger off the friar. For his part, Merek watched with amusement, for he knew friars like Hubert and what they were capable of doing. Secretly, he was pulling for the red-headed stranger.

The stranger was momentarily moved by Father Smithton and Father Quinn but easily shook the two priests from their grasps. He pushed Father Smithton down easily and grabbed Father Quinn by the arm, swinging him off balance. Father Quinn tumbled into the road. Next, the stranger took Father Hubert by his robe, pulled him to his feet, and punched him squarely in the stomach. The friar went down fast and stayed on the ground.

"Enough!" the prioress screamed. She looked to Merek and Father Towns and commanded, "Help them!"

Towns charged the stranger who had just punched the friar. Towns tackled the stranger, and the two began to roll around in the weeds by the side of the road. Merek, for his part, took his time getting to the fray watching the two men roll around. Smithton had pulled himself to his feet, and was going to help Towns with the stranger. Merek held him back.

"Let them roll," he said calmly. "They are not hurting each other. The stranger is drunk and will soon need rest."

Quinn tried to help Father Hubert to his feet, but the friar was not ready to stand. The blow to his midsection had not only hurt but had caused a sickening feeling in his stomach. As he sat on the ground regaining his wind, the contents of his stomach came up suddenly, and he vomited on the ground beside him.

True to Merek's prediction, Towns and the stranger grew tired. They stopped wrestling, both winded, sweaty and gasping for air. As Smithton helped Towns to his feet, Merek stood over the stranger.

"Are you finished?" he said quietly to the stranger.

The man looked up at Merek and said nothing. He was still trying to catch his breath.

Merek looked back at the prioress, who was concerned about the friar's health. As Merek looked back, his eyes met Sister Anne's eyes. They had a look of satisfaction, knowing the kind of man Father Hubert was and how the stranger had inflicted injury upon him. Of course, Sister Anne would never admit this feeling that Merek had seen in her eyes. He knew the look. He felt the same way.

"Christ's bones," the stranger said, finally catching his breath and looking at Merek, "when did they begin makin' bloody priests as big as you?"

Merek smiled. "Are you done slugging the friar?"

From the ground, the stranger growled, "No promises, dammit."

Merek put out his hand to help the stranger to his feet. The stranger accepted, and Merek pulled him up.

"You are a brute, sir," the prioress scolded. "How dare you strike a man of the cloth?"

"With all due respect, your highness," the stranger said, "he had it comin'."

"Good sir, Christ teaches us to love our fellow man, not attack him," the prioress retorted, clearly out of sorts.

"Your holiness, does Christ teach men of the cloth to stick their pricks into young girls? Is that part of God's word?" the stranger came back.

The prioress was speechless. Sister Anne tried to comfort her. Father Towns was gathering himself, while Father Quinn was helping the friar to his feet. Merek instinctively knew he had to pull the stranger away from attacking Father Hubert again. Merek had a feeling the man was not finished with the corrupt friar.

"Will you walk with me, sir? Over to your horse?" Merek asked with a smile on his face.

"And if I don't?" the stranger answered in a surly way.

"You and I will have an unreasonable quarrel on the other side of these bushes, out of sight of the ladies."

The stranger eyed Merek up and down. Even though the stranger was stout, thick, and strong, he was still a head shorter than Merek.

"God's arms, I am not afraid of you, priest," the stranger said.

"I do not fight fair," Merek answered with a sly smile on his face.

The stranger became quiet and looked Merek over. Both men stood toe-to-toe. Suddenly, the stranger let out a big smile. "Saint's bones! What kind of priest even fights, let alone in an unfair way?" The stranger laughed.

Merek laughed also, and the men shook arms. "I am Robin Miller," the stranger said. "On my way to Canterbury."

"Father Merek Willson. We are all going to Canterbury. Will you ride with us?"

Robin Miller pointed to the friar. "With that turd of a man? Besides, I might not be invited," Miller said, looking at the prioress.

Merek turned to the others. Father Quinn was helping the friar on his horse. Fathers Smithton and Towns were seated on their horses. The prioress seemed to have regained her composure.

"Madam Prioress, this man's name is Robin Miller. Like us, he is going to Canterbury," Merek said.

"He shan't go with us, Father Merek," the prioress answered. "What is to stop him from assailing poor Father Hubert again?"

Robin Miller was about to speak, but Merek put his hand up. "It seems, Madam Prioress," Merek said, "that Robin Miller is going to Canterbury as an act of penance. In the confessional, his penance was to go to Canterbury and pray at St. Thomas's shrine."

The prioress looked at Father Smithton. Smithton just shrugged his shoulders.

"If this man travels with us, Father Merek, you will be responsible for his actions. I do not want any more attacks." The prioress consented.

"Indeed, Madam Prioress," Merek agreed. To Robin Miller, "Come, let us get you on your horse."

Without another word, Father Smithton led the group back on the road to Southwark. They did not wait for Merek and Robin Miller. The others were out of earshot when Merek and Robin Miller got underway.

"So tell me, Father, what was all that shit about confession, penance, and St. Thomas?" Robin Miller asked.

"Did you want to join us or not?" Merek answered.

"The road to Canterbury has a number of taverns I want to visit. That's why I go."

"So be it." Merek smiled.

Merek helped Miller gather his things and mount his horse. Merek took an instant liking to the troublesome man. There was something about him. Miller was feisty, drunk, smelled to high heaven, and was not good with the bagpipes. Yet, Merek liked his spirit, and the fact he shared the same regard for friars made Merek like him even more. In a short while, they caught up with the others.

CHAPTER 16

CHAUCER AT THE TABARD

Geoffrey Chaucer entered The Tabard in the midafternoon. He walked in with two men. All three stood in the entrance and let their eyes adjust to the dim candlelight inside the tavern. The room was not full but was busy. Although some of the many benches were full of customers, there were other tables open. Chaucer guessed the great tavern room was half full.

Chaucer's trip to Southwark was less than two hours from Sir John of Gaunt's palace. Chaucer had lots to think about. Marriage was not to be taken lightly. Nor was the idea of disappointing a man like Sir John of Gaunt. Chaucer determined that disappointing Sir John was scarier than a marriage to a woman he did not know. So before he left the palace that morning, Chaucer knew that he would go through with the marriage. It might not be the "right" thing, but it was the "smart" thing.

As Chaucer readied his horse for the ride to Southwark that morning, a house servant approached and indicated that he would have company on his way to Canterbury. Since company would be welcomed on any trip on horseback, Chaucer was delighted to accept. In addition to "safety in numbers," the conversation would make the trip appear to be shorter.

Chaucer met his travelling companions at the palace entrance. Each of the two men were friends of Sir John of Gaunt and had already met and had breakfast with him that morning. Both men were known around London. Chaucer certainly knew about each man, but he had never met them personally. Until that morning.

Josef Gates was a serjeant-at-the law, a legal servant of King Edward. Since there were only twenty such men in 1366, each served as a judge, not just in London, but in the traveling courts. Gates had a reputation as a strict and tough judge who knew the letter of the law inside and out. He had been a lawyer for over sixteen years before the king appointed him in an official royal capacity.

Chaucer knew of Gates's reputation. Wise, discreet, and very learned, Gates knew the law better than anyone in London. Because of Chaucer's many contacts in and around London, he knew that Gates was becoming quite a landowner, using the law to obtain large quantities of land. Of course, the land Gates obtained this way was very legal and done in an appropriate way. Yet, Gates had a tendency to keep the purchases to himself. He was not one to bring attention to himself.

Chaucer's other companion was a wealthy landowner, a franklin, named Charles Coleson. An older gentleman with a snow-white beard, Coleson was a genuinely happy man who happened to have a permanently red-colored face. Some had said the red face was due to his benign disposition, while others said it was from his voracious intake of wine and ale. It was said that Charles Coleson began each morning with a small piece of pastry dipped in wine.

Coleson was also a justice of the peace and served his county well in that regard. He also represented his county in Parliament and was known for the dinners he gave at his estate. His dinners were famous throughout Parliament and London for their fine food and wine. No one in London had a better collection of imported wine than Sheriff Coleson. His house was never short of homemade bread and baked-meat pies. Guests to Sheriff Coleson's house were privileged to taste his succulent partridges, bream, and pike. The special sauces his cooks produced were known throughout London. It was said that Sheriff Coleson, despite all the ways he served his king, would prefer to simply have dinner guests over to his house and enjoy the pleasures of life more than anything.

The trip to Southwark was an easy trip that morning. Both men were easy conversationalists. Chaucer, holding a high regard for both men, said little unless he was asked. Both men had concerns about certain aspects of the government but were smart enough to keep any true opinions to themselves. Both men were aware that Chaucer, although a commoner, had the ears of one of the most powerful men in England, Sir John of Gaunt.

Chaucer was amused at the way each man dressed, although he certainly kept his amusements to himself. Josef Gates, one of only twenty serjeants-at-the law, was dressed in a homely double-colored coat. The coat had a silken belt that had a pin stripe or bars pattern. It clashed to the local style. Chaucer was surprised and amused by Gates's lack of concern about fashion. In addition, Gates wore a thick beard that was unkept. Chaucer smiled to himself when he looked at the deep black beard and wondered if a bird could actually nest in it. Gates wore a common hat that covered his balding head. He was a small man, thin and older by the day's standards. Chaucer guessed him to be in his midforties.

Coleson, on the other hand, was dressed moderately, showing some knowledge of the local style. Coleson kept a small purse made of an unusually white silk that hung at his belt. In addition, he kept a small dagger at his disposal, which also brought a certain amusement to Chaucer. Chaucer wondered what a small dagger could do without the protection of a larger blade.

For his part, Chaucer had brought a sword and a dagger on the trip. Even though he was a messenger for the king, he had at one time been a soldier. Trained in the art of swordplay, Chaucer had gone to France for the king, serving in his son Lionel's army. Adept with the sword in close combat, Chaucer trained with Sir Lionel's knights and had become quite skillful with the sword. Unfortunately, he did not see much action in France. In fact, while on a foraging expedition for food for a hungry English army, Chaucer's company was surprised by a French force and was captured.

Months later, Chaucer was released from a French prison because his ransom was paid. He was later to learn that King Edward III had indeed paid a large portion of Chaucer's ransom. After he was released, Chaucer began to serve the king in a more diplomatic way, thus keeping Chaucer from the horrors of war.

Chaucer asked the men if they wished to step up to the long wooden bar, find a bench, or inquire about the rooms. Sheriff Coleson did not answer but walked right to the wooden bar. Chaucer and Gates did not hesitate and joined him. As they stood waiting for the barkeep, a young man with a brown beard and curly hair, seemingly drunk, bumped into Sheriff Coleson, nearly spilling his ale on him.

"Beg pardon, sir," the young man said.

Chaucer was quick to help, grabbing the young man's unsteady hand and guiding him away from the sheriff.

"Steady there, young man," Chaucer said, smiling. "Let me help you to a bench."

Grabbing the young man's arm, Chaucer helped the stumbling drunk to the nearest empty bench.

"Thank you, sir," the young man slurred. As he sat, he put his head on the table and appeared to fall asleep.

As Chaucer rejoined his travelling companions at the bar, he could not shake an odd feeling about the young man with the beard and curly hair. There was something about him. Yet, Chaucer could not put his finger on the odd feeling he received from helping the young man. As one who prided himself on observing the small details of people that he encountered daily, Chaucer knew there was an oddity about the drunken man. It would come to him.

But there was more to do. Since Chaucer was the "commoner" travelling with the two officials of the government, he felt it was his duty to see they were taken care of.

"While you gentlemen enjoy your ale, I shall make accommodations for you with the innkeeper," Chaucer said to the judge and the franklin.

Chaucer left the men at the bar and proceeded to another part of The Tabard. At the base of the inn was a small room with a long plank supported by two barrels. On the plank was a crude register for guests. And behind the long plank was the innkeeper, Harry Bailly. Harry had a parchment to register the guests. Two quills and a container for ink were at his ready. He also had a mug of ale beside him at the temporary bench.

Luckily, there was no one in line to register at the present. Apparently, it was somewhat early, and the travelers had spotted the great tavern room of The Tabard first.

"Yes, sir. May I help you?" Harry Bailly said with a smile. Bailly was quite astute in judging his customers by the way they dressed. He could tell Chaucer was not a lord, for he did not wear the style nor the badge of one of England's houses of nobility. But he also knew Chaucer was not a peasant, for his clothes indicated otherwise. They were somewhat new and well-made. Bailly figured him to be a merchant, a man from the newly formed "middle class" of English society.

"I travel with a judge and a franklin from London, sir. All of us are going to Canterbury in the morning and will need a room for the night," Chaucer said.

"Indeed, sir. I have a room that sleeps ten, reserved for nobles and those of similar standing to the men who travel with you. I have three openings in that room. Would you care to join them?"

"If it is possible, sir. I must confess I am not a lord, nor am I a king's official."

"Not to worry, sir. I think you'll fit in just fine," Bailly said with a smile.

Chaucer registered the names with Bailly and set the standard price. Bailly also gave information and prices for the care and feeding of the horses in the large Tabard barn. The directions were quick and efficient.

Chaucer went back into the bar to give the news to the judge and franklin. He also wanted to take care of all the horses before it became overly crowded. Chaucer returned to the great tavern room to ask Judge Gates and Franklin Coleson what they wanted from the saddle bags on the horses before he had them stabled for the night.

At first, Chaucer did not see the men, for they were not at the spot in which he left them. He looked around, noticing that the drunken young man was also not in the spot he left him. Finally, Chaucer saw the judge and the franklin seated at a bench with three men he did not know. He approached. "Good day, sirs," Chaucer addressed the group.

"Sir Robert, this is Geoffrey Chaucer, the king's special diplomat, servant to Sir John of Gaunt, and our escort to Canterbury," Judge Gates said.

Sir Robert did not get up, for lords did not need to show the courtesy. But he did hold out his arm, and Chaucer shook it. It impressed Chaucer, for a lord did not have to do that either.

"An honor, my lord." Chaucer bowed as he shook Sir Robert of Ganse's arm.

"This is his son, Thomas. Thomas is soon to be a knight," Judge Gates said.

Thomas stood and moved from the bench to shake Chaucer's arm.

"A knight? Splendid, young man! Congratulations," Chaucer said genuinely.

"Indeed, sir," Thomas said.

"And this is Father Leo Colman," Judge Gates said, ending the introductions. "He travels with Sir Robert and Thomas."

"A pleasure, Father Colman," Chaucer said.

"Come join us, Geoffrey." Sheriff Coleson smiled.

"Thank you, sir. I would, but I thought I should attend your horses," Chaucer said.

"Nonsense," Sheriff Coleson disagreed. "Come, sit. Have some ale and enjoy Sir Robert's company. The horses will wait."

Chaucer hesitated. Judge Gates nodded, as did Sir Robert, and so he sat with the men. In no time, there was an ale in front of him, and he enjoyed the company.

Chaucer was seated in between Sir Robert and Thomas. As they drank and talked, Chaucer observed and listened. He seemed to have a fairly good hold on the kind of men the judge and the franklin were. Both were competent in what they did, but they were very different men.

Sheriff Coleson was genuinely a nice, pleasant franklin. Chaucer observed that he was not particularly an intelligent man, for he seemed to left out of the majority of discussions concerning the war with France, the economy, and the king's policies. But his eyes would light up if one talked of food, game, fish, or wine. Although he seemed a good administrator, his love was of a festive nature.

By contrast, Judge Gates was stern, had no sense of humor, and was all business. Chaucer had heard rumors that Judge Gates was formidable in the courtroom and, after travelling with him, tended to believe the rumors. As it turned out, Judge Gates had helped Sir Robert in matters of the law a few years ago, and that was how they knew each other.

Chaucer was entirely impressed with Sir Robert. A knight who had fought for the king all around the Mediterranean Sea, Sir Robert was humble but had a quiet pride. Sir Robert was gracious, showed great courtesy to all around him, and never spoke of himself. Chaucer observed that Sir Robert had a scar just below his neck behind his right ear. Chaucer also noted that Sir Robert had large hands, the kind of hands that handled a battle sword.

In the time at the bench sharing ale, Chaucer noted that Sir Robert would quietly turn his head and look at a table against the wall. The table had five men seated, seemingly drinking and enjoying a meal. Sir Robert did not stare at them, but he did look at them from time to time. To Chaucer's surprise, the young drunken man with the beard and the curly hair had made his way over to the table with the five men and seemed to be in conversation with them. The young man seemed to have become quite sober again.

And then it dawned on Chaucer. What was strange about the man with the beard and the curly hair was that he appeared to be dead drunk but did not smell the part. Usually, a person inebriated to the point of passing out on one of the benches would have spilled ale on himself at one time or another. But this man did not have a hint of ale on his person. And then it dawned on Chaucer. The man was not drunken at all. It was a ruse. In a moment, Chaucer realized the man must be a thief. Chaucer checked for his own bag of coins. It was there.

"Excuse me, Judge Gates and Sheriff Coleson. Please check your money. Sheriff Coleson, do you still have your silken purse?" Chaucer blurted out.

The conversation ceased. Both men checked their belts. The franklin's eyes grew large. His money purse was not there. "No," he said with his eyes wide.

"I believe I know where it is, sir," Chaucer said, getting up from the table.

Chaucer rushed across the tavern to the young man with the beard and the curly hair.

The young man did not see him coming, but some of the men at the table saw Chaucer. Chaucer grabbed the man by the shoulder and spun him around.

"Where is it?" Chaucer demanded.

"Where is what?" the young man replied. And then, with a drunken, slur, "No idea what you mean?"

"I want the purse you stole," Chaucer demanded. Normally, Chaucer was not a physical man, but he was angry at the thief's audacity. To steal from an honest man was bad, but to stick around in the same vicinity was a way of mocking the victim.

The young man acted even tipsier. He put his hands up, indicating he had no idea what Chaucer was talking about.

"You are not drunk, sir. So stop the act. You have a white silken purse on you. It belongs to Sheriff Coleson, and I want it back."

"Believe you have the wrong person, sir," the young man still slurred, pretending to be drunk.

The altercation had caused a stillness in the room. Perkins, club in hand, stood beside the bar, waiting for something to get out of hand. Chaucer for his part was angry, knew the young man had stolen the purse when they first entered the bar, but did not know how to prove it.

Suddenly, a figure flew past Chaucer, grabbed the young man in question and pinned him to the table in which the five men sat. It was Thomas, and Sir Robert was right with him. Thomas had a short dagger at the heart of the man he had pinned on the table.

The five men at the table stood and cleared themselves of the altercation. Sir Robert and Thomas had the man on the table; Chaucer was standing behind them. Chaucer, for his part, was done with the examination. He looked around. Judge Gates and Sheriff Coleson stood beside him. Now even Harry Bailly was present.

"The purse, you cad," Thomas grunted.

The young man was suddenly sober. "Please, sir, I found it on the floor by the bar. I did not know its owner," he confessed, almost crying. Apparently, Thomas had put some pressure on the tip of the dagger at the man's chest.

"I am a lowly cook, sir, not a thief. I swear by Christ's bones, I did not steal the purse," the young man said.

"Where is it?" Sir Robert demanded.

"I will get it," the young man said, trying to reach under his shirt.

"None of that!" Thomas interjected. He took the cook's arm and twisted it in an awkward way. The cook yelled.

Thomas reached under the cook's shirt and brought out a dagger. Thomas held it up for all to see. Then Thomas reached back in and pulled out the franklin's purse. He held that up also, and the crowd cheered.

Now Harry Bailly made his move. He cleared a path to Thomas and Sir Robert. "My lord, if you please, the thief is mine!" Bailly declared.

Sir Robert touched his son on the shoulder. Thomas nodded and pulled the cook to his feet. Harry Bailly punched the cook squarely in the jaw, knocking him back onto the heavy table. The cook slid to the floor.

"Thievery will not be tolerated in The Tabard!" he bellowed.

Perkins was by Bailly's side, and they got the cook to his feet. The thief was bleeding from the mouth. As they made their way through the crowd, Perkins took his club and hit the cook squarely in the ribs. The thief went down again. He yelped in pain on the floor.

Perkins announced loudly, "Like Harry, says, 'No thievin' in The Tabard.'"

Harry and Perkins took the thief to the front door of The Tabard and threw him out onto the street. Harry gave a coin to two men and told them to drag the cook to the constable. The man would be in stocks by the morning.

Back in The Tabard, all went about their business. As Harry and Perkins dragged the cook away, Sir Robert had a closer look at the men he was studying. Satisfied in what he saw, he returned to his table.

Sheriff Coleson was most grateful to Chaucer and his recovery of his purse and money. The Sheriff assured Chaucer that he would be well-rewarded for his bravery. The others applauded and continued in fellowship.

Judge Gates, having had a little too much ale, began to tell of a court case that had absolutely nothing worth noting. Those close to him listened out of respect. Sir Robert and Chaucer, now seated opposite each other and at the other end of the bench, spoke. "How did you know he had it?" Sir Robert asked.

"He was 'drunk', but did not seem drunk," Chaucer answered. "When I saw him talking to those men at the far table, he seemed quite sober. And I remember him bumping into the franklin."

"Those men he was conversing with"—Sir Robert nodded at the table of five men dressed in new clothes—"I think they are confederates with the cook."

CHAPTER 17

THE PRIORESS ARRIVES AT THE TABARD

The prioress and her party arrived at The Tabard well before dark. After the incident with Robin Miller, the rest of the trip was uneventful. Merek had ridden alongside Robin Miller for the journey and was careful not to let the man get too close to the friar, Father Hubert. In fact, Merek and Robin Miller rode behind the others, including Father Townes, who did not seem to object to having riders following behind him.

Father Smithton was quick to aid the prioress and Sister Anne from their horses outside the great tavern room. Father Townes took care of the horses, while the monk and the friar simply tethered their horses at the rail outside the tavern. Robin Miller and Merek did the same with their horses.

For his part, Merek did not mind the company of the foul-mouthed Miller. In a way, Miller was "refreshing," not caring what he said and to whom he said it. Merek kept Robin Miller close to the travelling group, but not close enough for the group to hear what he was saying. It was a good thing for the friar that Merek kept Miller from him, for Miller truly wanted to do the friar bodily harm for the woman he impregnated and pawned off on a poor village boy.

"It wasn't the first time the bastard pulled a stunt like that," Miller growled. "Takes advantage of them village girls who don't know no better. Bastard."

Merek also knew the type, but did not agree. He did not want to fan the fire of Miller's anger. Merek diverted Miller's anger by having him talk more about himself. As it turned out, Robin Miller had been a foot soldier in the king's army. He had seen action in France, had spilled blood, and had been wounded. Merek invited Miller to tell him more about the army and his experience. Miller, sobering just a little, seemed content to tell Merek about his military experience.

"Ya, see, Father, when it comes to a battle, they put us rabble up front," Miller grumbled on the road to The Tabard. "We didn't get much trainin', ya see. But to tell ya the truth, Father, we didn't need much trainin' to beat the French. Seems they set their rabble out first too."

Merek did not say a word. He did not want Robin Miller to know that he had seen battles firsthand and knew, for the most part, Miller was correct.

"The French rabble, saints' arms, Father. They did not have a chance, 'specially if we threw the archers at them first." Miller smiled. "The French had crossbowman, but not the archers we had. Crossbowman up close can be deadly, but he has to get close to ya', Father. But the English archer, now there's a weapon we was all grateful for."

Once again, Merek just listened. To keep Robin Miller occupied during the remaining trip to Southwark, Merek was willing to listen to Miller go on about his fighting in France. In truth, it was tough for Merek. He had been there. He had seen the carnage. He had killed. He had seen friends killed. And when Miller spoke on the matter, Merek could tell the man had been there. Robin Miller had seen many of the same things Merek had seen, probably more. As an archer, Merek did not often get to the hand-to-hand annihilation that Robin Miller had seen. A foot soldier's life in a battle was on far more treacherous ground than that of an archer. As Miller talked on their journey, Merek believed the man about his survival in France. And he held a respect for Robin Miller.

"Seems you were there, Father," Miller said quietly, a big grin on his face.

"What do you mean?" Merek asked.

"I see your bow." He quietly pointed to Merek's bow unstrung on the back of his horse. "I might be a wee bit drunk, but I know a guardian angel when I see one. You was in France. You was an archer."

Merek did not say a word but nodded.

"I knew I liked you, Father. Who knows, maybe we fought in France together?"

"Fighting for me is over, Robin," Merek said quietly. "I have committed myself to God."

"Aye, Father, but you still don't fight fair."

Both men laughed at that. Not another word was said as they made their way to The Tabard. Robin Miller took hold of his bagpipes and played the rest of the way.

Tethering their horses outside, Merek told Miller he would meet him inside. Merek wanted to make sure the prioress and Sister Anne were taken care of. Fathers Smithton and Towns had seemed to have been one step ahead of Merek, for accommodations were made. There was nothing more to do than join the others in the tavern.

As Merek walked from the barn where the horses were kept next to the tavern, he saw a couple near the barn kissing passionately. He did not want to interrupt the couple, but they were in his path to get to the great tavern room. He looked for other ways to avoid the couple, but he could not. His only hope was to just skirt by them quickly. Unfortunately, as Merek tried to breeze by the couple, they moved, and Merek bumped right into them, causing them to stop.

"Beg pardon," Merek apologized.

"Father Merek?" the young man answered.

"Thomas!" Merek replied.

The men shook arms.

"Wonderful to see you, Thomas," Merek said quickly, a little embarrassed by his intrusion.

"My father is inside. So is Father Colman. Father Colman's brother is there also, just recently joining us," Thomas said, excited to see Merek.

The girl was speechless, not understanding the stoppage of their desires. She was one of Harry Bailly's barmaids and had taken a fancy to the extremely good-looking Thomas, son and squire of Sir Robert of Ganse.

For his part, Thomas did not introduce nor did he feel the need to introduce Father Merek to the girl. Nor was Thomas intimidated by a priest's presence at the time of his merrymaking with the tavern girl. As the son of a nobleman, Thomas knew there were actions he would not have to explain to any man other than his father and perhaps his king.

"I shall look for your father, Thomas. It is so good to see you," Merek said.

"Meet you inside, Father Merek," Thomas said and waited for Merek to go past them to the door before he turned his attention to the girl. "Now, where were we?" he asked as they began to kiss passionately again.

Merek finally entered the tavern. It was crowded. He looked around, first for the prioress and her entourage. He saw them all. Seated near the front, Merek saw the prioress, Sister Anne, and Father Smithton at a bench. Although it was near the front of the tavern, it was off to the side. Also near the front, in the middle of tavern, Merek spotted Sir Robert of Ganse, Father Colman, and some men Merek did not know.

Merek continued to look around. He did not see Hugh Bowman, the yeoman with Sir Robert. Merek's guess was that the man was finding a corner of the barn to bed down for the night. Merek also looked for Robin Miller. Merek observed Robin drinking a large vessel of ale.

Merek checked in with the prioress first.

"Father Merek, we have a seat for you, but please keep that Miller away from us," the prioress ordered.

"Aye, Madam Prioress," Merek answered, noting that Fathers Quinn and Hubert had already joined the prioress's bench. It disheartened Merek to think he would have to sit with the two of them for a time, let alone dinner and ale. His only consolation was that he would be at the table, so Father Hubert would not have a chance to try some licentious action on the poor young nun. "I will join you shortly, Madam," Merek assured the nun. Then he walked toward the table in which Sir Robert was sitting.

Sir Robert saw him coming and stood. A nobleman did not usually stand for a poor village priest, but Sir Robert and Merek had encountered danger, fought and spilled blood on the road to Southwark. And even though Sir Robert knew Merek was a village priest, he also knew Merek was a former king's archer who could still wield a powerful bow and arrow.

"Father Merek Willson." Sir Robert stood, smiled, and shook arms with the village priest.

For his part, Merek played his part, bowed, and said, "Sir Robert, an honor to see you again."

"I am glad you made it to Southwark, Father Merek. I am hoping we can travel on to Canterbury together," Sir Robert said.

"I am with a group that leaves tomorrow, Sir Robert."

"As are we, Father Merek. As are we. Please, let me introduce you to the men at my table. Men, this is Father Merek Willson, formerly of the king's army who has given his life to the Church and Christ's teachings. This is Judge Josef Gates, and seated to his right is Sheriff Charles Coleson," Sir Robert said.

Merek nodded, knowing that formality would not include any kind of arm shaking or bowing.

"And this is Geoffrey Chaucer, diplomatic servant to the king and personal friend to Sir John of Gaunt."

Chaucer stood and shook Merek's arm. "A pleasure, Father," Chaucer said. And added, "So glad it is a pleasure to meet a priest as large as you are. Imagine if it were not a pleasure?" Chaucer smiled. To the men at the table, he added, "I try not to anger God or my local priest. Can you imagine enraging this priest, as big as he is?" Chaucer saw that Merek took the comment in good jest and patted him on the side of the shoulder. "Good for you," Chaucer exclaimed. "A priest with a good sense of humor."

"Afraid a good sense of humor will keep me from being a bishop," Merek joked to Chaucer.

"In my observation, Father Merek, a good sense of humor will keep you alive. Being a bishop is a whole new factor to consider." Chaucer smiled.

"To be honest, Master Chaucer, I am quite happy to serve the small village in which I was assigned. I have no desires to rise above my station."

"Well said, Father Merek. A humble village priest," Chaucer commented, smiling. "So glad you will be with us on our journey to Canterbury."

"As will I. Now to be frank, Master Chaucer, I must join the party in which I travel and the Madam Prioress at her table. Please excuse me."

"By all means, Father Merek" was all Chaucer said.

Merek made his way to the table and benches in which the lady prioress sat. Suddenly, he heard his name called. Looking around, he saw Father Leo Colman seated at a table nearby. Chaucer smiled and made his way to Father Colman's table.

"Greetings, Father Colman." Merek smiled, shaking arms with the priest.

"Thank God you have arrived, Father Merek. I was, indeed, worried when you left our group. I was afraid another batch of high-waymen would find you," Father Colman said.

"'The Lord is my protector,' isn't he, Father?" Merek smiled.

"I wish for you to meet my brother, Anthony."

Anthony stood from the crowded table and shook arms with Merek. Merek immediately noticed the size of Anthony Colman's hands. They were enormous. The hands coupled with the weathered look of a man who is constantly working in the sun, Anthony Colman looked like the common village plowman that Merek saw every day back in Harper's Turn.

The men stood and made small talk, for the table was crowded with would-be pilgrims to Canterbury. Merek noticed at one end of the table a young man sat reading a book. He did not seem to be with anyone, nor did he seem to want to engage anyone in conversation. His clothes were worn, the overcoat in which he wore was almost worn through with a number of small holes on the sleeves.

By contrast, two men sat directly opposite from Father Colman and his brother. The two men were drunk and were singing in a most awful way. In fact, the men had to end their small talk because the two raucous men were singing so loudly. All three men simply stopped talking and stared at the men who were oblivious to those around them.

One of the singers was a smaller man with yellowish hair that hung down like rattails on his head. He wore no cap but had clothes that were well-made. The man had bulging eyes and a goat-like voice as he sung. His chin was spotted with a chin hair here or there, but it was evident that the man did not have to shave.

The other singer had a fire-red face with an unusually hideous blemish that marked his face and neck. The man had narrow eyes with thick black scabby eyebrows. Merek did not notice it at first, but the longer he stood near the singers, he began to notice a distinct odor emanating from the two men. Merek determined the odor was coming from the man with the countless scabs on his face and neck. The odor was a combination of ale, body odor, and garlic. It was a strong odor, and as the men continued to sing, Merek excused himself from the Colman brothers, promising to meet them later and finish their conversation.

As Merek left the Colman brothers, the singers suddenly stopped singing. Merek turned around to see Robin Miller talking with the two men. Merek did not know what Miller was saying, but both men had a somewhat scared look on their faces. Miller walked away, and the men stopped singing. Some of the customers who were near the singers applauded and thanked Miller for his interference in the spontaneous entertainment.

Merek had to smile as he went to his seat with the prioress and her company.

CHAPTER 18
OSWALD MEETS HIS CONFEDERATES

Oswald traveled to Southwark in the company of three men and a woman. It was an uneventful ride, and for the most part, Oswald was left alone. In fact, the men were somewhat quiet, for they had to be. A woman dominated the entire conversation.

In the course of their travel, the traveling woman turned the conversation toward a woman's role in a marriage. Apparently, she was an expert in the dealings of a husband and wife, having been at "the church door" five times. Oswald could not have cared less about her views on marriage, for he was a bachelor and would remain a bachelor his entire life. However, the men in the company seemed to take an interest in what she had to say. One of the men was a merchant. Another was a doctor and the third was a manciple. Each man took an interest in the lady's views. It seemed that the greater the men showed an interest in her views, the more she seemed to flirt with them.

Oswald learned the woman was from Bath. She was a cloth maker. If she had not told the men that making cloth was her profession, they would have probably guessed. She was covered from head to toe with fine scarves and veils. She wore an extremely wide hat that was also decorated with the fine cloths she wove. The woman's name was Allison, and Oswald guessed her age to be in her early forties. Not so long ago, she had buried her fifth husband and said she was making a pilgrimage to Canterbury for guidance in making the next step in her life.

Oswald was not fooled by the "mission" of her pilgrimage. It was clear to him that the lady from Bath was on the trip looking for husband number six. She had charm, a pretty face, and owned land and money accrued from being married five times. And the way her traveling companions were listening with keen interest to her every word, she was well on her way to completing her mission. Allison was adamant about marriage. Even though the teachings of the Holy Catholic Church discouraged marriage, Allison disagreed fully with the Church. She wanted definitive proof that the Bible discouraged marriage.

What really interested her listeners was her explanation as to how she controlled her marriages with her womanly ways. Each husband eventually gave her the control of the marriage because she used her guile and sex to persuade each husband to allow her to be in control. Friendly and personable, Allison drew each of her listeners into her conversation, making each man an eager listener to her personal experiences. Oswald was not taken in by her subtle flirtations with the men in the group. Perhaps he would have been at another time, but this trip was all business, and he focused on the plan at hand.

It seemed as though her company of listeners were successful in their various occupations. The merchant, whose last name was Neville, wore an expensive fur hat to go along with new, well-made clothes. The doctor, a man named Richard Howard, rode a beautiful destrier, a horse usually seen at jousting tournaments. The horse bespoke of money, for the horse would cost a small fortune to have by a commoner, like a doctor. The manciple, a man who catered to guilds and groups of lawyers, was named Simon. Oswald did not hear his last name but was impressed by the comments Simon made in the course of the trip.

Simon was a commoner who had developed a trade whereby he would produce drink and meals for various guild gatherings. He would also accommodate lawyers whenever they met as a group. Simon's business was to cater to their needs and serve the groups in the fashion in which they paid Simon. Apparently, he did quite well for himself. It made Oswald smile to himself when he heard Simon admit that he always charged way too much to his clients, who never questioned his prices and paid his exorbitant fees. A commoner out-foxing a group of "learned" men was interesting to Oswald.

The group arrived in Southwark in the late afternoon and found The Tabard with ease. The three men did not stop at The Tabard's great tavern room but took their horses immediately to the barn used to house the animals ridden on the journey. Oswald and Allison tethered their horses and walked into The Tabard's tavern room.

Oswald allowed Allison to enter the tavern first. She thanked him for accompanying her on the journey and made her way inside. Once inside, the two made separate ways. For her part, Allison looked for a table with an empty seat, preferably populated with males. For his part, Oswald looked for Thaddeus and his men. In addition, Oswald looked for Albert, the cook, and Anglicus, the shipman, who was hired to hurt the priest.

It did not take long for Oswald to spot the five mercenaries. It took a few minutes, but Oswald found the eyes of Thaddeus, the leader of the mercenaries hired to kidnap the prioress. Thaddeus's eyes widened as he saw Oswald, and with a slight motion of his head, Thaddeus hinted that he needed to speak with Oswald.

For his part, Oswald nodded and made his way out of the tavern. He crossed the courtyard outside of the tavern and waited for Thaddeus. It was only a minute when Thaddeus exited the tavern. Looking around, it did not take him long to see Oswald. He crossed the courtyard and followed Oswald farther back into an alley for their secretive conversation.

"Your men are here and intact?" Oswald started.

"All here. We are registered and will join the others tomorrow for the trip to Canterbury," Thaddeus answered.

"Very well," Oswald said.

"But there is a problem," Thaddeus stated soberly. "Your man, Albert, the cook, was arrested this afternoon for lifting the purse of an official."

Oswald did not answer right away. But there was an obvious look of disgust on his face.

"There is a chance he has compromised our mission," Thaddeus warned.

"In what way?" Oswald asked.

"When he was questioned and arrested, Albert was at our table asking of your whereabouts," Thaddeus answered. "We were seen in discussion with him."

"Goddam him," Oswald cursed. "That stupid fool."

"I am concerned about the mission," Thaddeus stated. "If the cook is associated with my men, we will be under suspicion during the entire trip to Canterbury. It will ruin our element of surprise."

"Where is Albert now?" Oswald asked.

"They escorted him from The Tabard. We learned later that the local constable in Southwark took him prisoner as a thief. Who knows, he may be in the stocks by now. Oswald, I have to ask you, will this 'cook' jeopardize our mission?"

"I will see that he does not, I assure you," Oswald answered. "We will continue as planned. Go back inside. Tell your men the plan is still on."

"As you say, Oswald. As you say. We will do our part as instructed. But I have to tell you that I think this man has jeopardized our plan. If my men and I feel others suspect us in anyway, we will remove ourselves from the trip. We will not go to jail or the gallows, nor will we engage in a plan that will fail."

"I will take care of this loose end, Thaddeus. I assure you. Go back inside now. Have dinner. Be ready to go to Canterbury and fulfill your duty."

Thaddeus nodded, left Oswald in the alley, and returned to The Tabard. Oswald waited a few minutes, made sure there were no witnesses to his conversation, and reentered The Tabard. Glancing around, Oswald saw that Thaddeus had joined his men. He also noted that the men in which he traveled had found a table and were making conversation with the others at the table.

Oswald looked around the tavern for Anglicus, not seeing the man at first. However, near the front of the tavern, sitting at the corner of the bar, Anglicus sat nursing an ale. He had been watching Oswald for a time and, at the signal from both men, agreed to meet outside the tavern.

"I see you made it safely, Anglicus," Oswald said quietly outside The Tabard.

"Arrived this afternoon," Anglicus answered.

"You do not look well," Oswald observed.

"A bit sick, you see," Anglicus answered. "Not used to riding a horse so long. Much different than being at sea. Some of you might get 'seasick' when riding in my ship, but I get 'sick' riding on a horse. Imagine?"

"Quite funny if one thinks about it. But you will notice that I am not laughing," Oswald answered.

"Enlighten me," Anglicus said.

"Albert, our cook, was arrested today for stealing. He puts our mission in jeopardy," Oswald said.

"By 'your mission,' do you mean my mission?" Anglicus answered.

"Have you spotted your man?"

"Oh, yes. I think so. His size sets him apart from all others. I observed him sitting at a table with the clergy and a woman I take is the prioress," Anglicus said.

"Do you think you can handle him?" Oswald asked.

"A priest?" Anglicus chuckled. "Yes, I think he will be hurt, as you instructed. Maybe even mortally."

"I might have another job for you," Oswald said soberly. "Seems to me the cook has suddenly become a liability."

"I am listening."

"If they put him in the stocks, he may talk. Give our plans away."

"I am listening."

"It will not be unusual to put him in stocks overnight to loosen his tongue. If they do, I will need to be assured that he will not talk," Oswald said, looking intently at Anglicus, the shipman.

"If they put him into the stocks tonight, the cook will not talk," Anglicus said.

"I will guarantee your pay will be doubled for your trouble," Oswald countered.

"Done," Anglicus said, touching the rusted blade that swung from his neck.

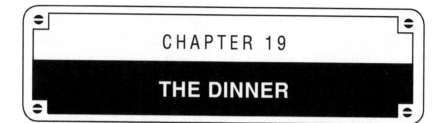

CHAPTER 19

THE DINNER

The sun was setting, and an April moon was rising in a clear sky that overlooked Southwark. As the sun was about to set, Southwark seemed to come alive. Theaters, not allowed in the city limits of London, found a home in Southwark. To take advantage of the light, performances were held in the afternoon. Patrons to the theater found their way to various taverns after the performances for food and drink. The streets became crowded in the late afternoon and into the evening. Singers and musicians, hoping for handouts from the swarming crowds, played on street corners. Certain taverns promoted gambling with dice and cards. Prostitutes plied their trade from taverns or brothels, not ashamed of their role in society. It was commonly said by Londoners that if one were to travel to Southwark, "one could make a full day of it"!

Not to be outdone, The Tabard was also a busy hostelry. For the most part, a different crowd visited Harry Bailly's establishment. Nevertheless, Harry Bailly's establishment catered to the crowd in the house that night. The great tavern room served ale and wine to its customers. The maids who took care of the sleeping quarters prepared the rooms and had to use their wits to house the overflow crowd that was in The Tabard on this night. The livery was busy with the stabling of horses and the bedding of some customers who were unable to pay for one of the rooms or whose social status demanded they sleep in the barn.

The kitchen was preparing the evening meal, and Harry Bailly was on top of the cooks, making sure tonight's fare was worthy of the tavern's reputation. His plan was to serve a healthy portion of bread and cheese to begin the meal and follow it up with venison, pork, rabbit, and mutton. The Tabard served its dinners with great reputation. The food was delicious and plentiful. It used wooden platters placed in the middle of the table. Customers would choose their food directly from the middle of the table, using the knives provided by the tavern to choose the food from the platters.

Certain sauces were used to add flavor and spice to the meat, and these sauces were also placed at the center of the table beside the large platters of meat. Customers would sometimes use their knives to dip meat into the sauces, but most customers just used their fingers. Fingers were much more precise and quick when one was famished and wished to indulge in the special sauces that would give the meat a uniquely delicious flavor.

Wine and ale were also served with dinner. Most taverns did not have enough cups to serve individual customers, so cups were usually shared by those at the same table or bench. However, The Tabard was unique in that it was able to ensure each customer would have a cup of his own. It was a point of pride in Harry Bailly that he would be able to give each customer his own cup. Of course, he also hired a man at the door to make sure the cup was left behind when the customer left The Tabard.

At the end of the meal, there was usually a hot or cold custard used as a dessert for Harry Bailly's customers. He also had live music played by local musicians who played various songs using flutes, pipes, and tabors, or the hurdy-gurdy. Once in a while, he would also bring in singers or balladeers.

On this particular night, Harry Bailly was excited about the crowd that was sitting at The Tabard for dinner. There was something unusual about the customers as a group that truly pleased Harry. By his count, there were close to fifty customers in the tavern room that night, thirty of whom were making the pilgrimage to Canterbury in the morrow. The "pilgrims" were the ones who fascinated Harry this night. He had seen many groups gather and leave for Canterbury before, but every once in a while, he ran into a group that piqued his interest. Tonight was one of those groups.

The group ate well. They were lively in spirit and seemed to have an unquenchable appetite to eat, drink, and make talk. They did not seem to be aware of the musicians playing, for they did not acknowledge the ending of one song or the beginning of the next. After an hour, when the meal was almost concluded, Harry dismissed the musicians for the evening.

In fact, Harry joined the pilgrims as they ate, sitting at a table with four men and a woman. Being a widower, Harry was interested in the heavily veiled woman from Bath. She had a handsome face, made unusual conversation, and knew the ways of "the dance"—a subject every man was interested in. It was a subject not spoken in polite society, but it was understood by all. It was about the private dealings of men and women. And this woman seemed an expert. And Harry was interested.

After the custard was served to all the tables, and the ale and wine were refilled for every customer, Harry stood and asked for silence in the hall. He wished to speak. The customers, knowing Harry's reputation as a fine host of a hostelry, were glad to give him their attention. "Truly, gentlemen, I cannot think, when upon my word, I have seen a gathering here at The Tabard that looked so full of life and energy. I tell you no lie. No, not his year! There have been groups of pilgrims who have met and began their journey to Canterbury, but none like yours." He smiled.

The customers in the tavern laughed and applauded the innkeeper.

"It just occurred to me," he continued, "to think you up some fun as you travelled to Canterbury. A thought has just occurred to me, and it will cost you nothing, on my word. You're off to Canterbury. Well, God speed! May the blessed Saint Thomas answer to all your needs! But if I have my way, before the journey is done, you will have an opportunity to while away the time in tales and fun."

Harry was interrupted for the moment by the two men sitting with Father Colman and his brother. Both men stood and began to sing in a most obnoxious way, causing those around them to physically push them to their seats and quiet them. The one man with the horrible scabs on his face was undaunted, stood again, and began to sing.

Robin Miller, sitting nearby, stood and punched the singer squarely in the jaw, sending the man to the floor of the tavern. The singer did not rise, and the crowd in the tavern cheered.

"Thank you, sir, for your utmost respect for quality singing." Harry smiled, and the customers in the tavern joined in the jest, laughing with him. "But hear me, good pilgrims to Canterbury," Harry said to the crowd. "Let me propose, for your enjoyment, a contest. If you agree to this contest, and you promise to adhere to it, playing the parts exactly as I say, tomorrow as you ride along the way, then by my father's soul, and he is dead, if you do not like it, you can have my head."

The entire tavern exploded with applause and laughter. "Go on, Harry! Tell us more!" many in the crowd yelled.

"My lords, if you please," he continued. "Now listen for your own good. This is the point, and I will make it plain. I propose that each of you tell a story, or two, on the trip to Canterbury, and one or two on the way back to Southwark. The man or woman who tells the best story, that is the story that gives the best morality and general pleasure, will be given a supper, free, at my expense, when we return to The Tabard.

Once again, there was applause and general mirth by Harry's guests.

"I am going with you to act as judge and guide," Harry said. "Is there an objection?" he asked with a smile on his face.

The crowd was warmed by his proposal and cheered him once again.

"So it shall be," Harry said. "We leave tomorrow for Canterbury. We shall have a contest of storytelling, and the winner will have a free dinner, at my expense, here at The Tabard. Godspeed all! Now, let us make merry tonight and make our way to Canterbury tomorrow."

A general applause went up from the tavern.

"My lords." Harry smiled. "Just remember, we leave early in the morning!"

Everyone laughed and continued their enjoying the evening.

"A wonderful suggestion," the woman from Bath beamed as Harry sat down.

"Thank you, my lady." Harry smiled, attracted by this older woman with a genuine smile that showed a gap in her two front teeth. "I look forward to hearing your tales."

"Oh, I hope my tales will be worth listening to," she replied.

"Indeed." Harry smiled; his attraction for this widow mounting as the night went on. He was glad to be going on the trip. He meant to find true love with this woman from Bath who called herself Allison.

It was dark when the meal, the dessert, and Harry's speech ended. Many of the pilgrims began to depart the tavern and make their way to the sleeping quarters that awaited their reservations and expense. It would be an early start, and the customers were ready to get a good night's sleep and an early beginning tomorrow.

Merek, for his part, bade the prioress good night and, along with Fathers Smithton and Towns, went to the spacious room that housed the clergy. To his dismay, Fathers Quinn and Hubert were assigned the same room, but there was enough space in the room for the men to keep their distance. Both brothers Colman also stayed with the clergy. No one minded that Anthony, a poor plowman, stayed in the room meant for the clergy.

As the men in the clergy room were getting settled, the door suddenly burst open, and the two men who were drunken and singing loudly throughout the meal appeared. The smaller man with the blond hair that hung like rattails from his hat was holding the drunken man with the horrible complexion on his face from falling.

"This for clergy?" the smaller man asked with a drunken lisp.

"It is," Father Quinn answered.

"Excellent," the smaller man answered and began to drag his companion to an open palate.

He dropped the unconscious man with the hideous scabs all about his face onto the empty palate and made his way to another near his comrade.

"Good night, gentleman," he exclaimed and suddenly passed out on the palate at his feet. He began snoring immediately.

"He's a pardoner," Father Leo exclaimed to the other priests, pointing to the smaller man with the blond hair that looked like rat tails coming out from under his cap. "His name is Gilbert. The other one is a summoner. The one with the carbuncles on his face. His name is Walter. They sat at my table tonight. Men, God forgive me, for I am not one to speak badly of others, especially fellow priests. But may I tell you, after spending a meal with these two fellows, I have a better understanding of what purgatory is."

The other priests smiled at Father Colman's remarks.

CHAPTER 20

AN OMINOUS START TO THE TRIP

Father Colman held Mass at matins, sunrise, in the closed tavern room. Word had spread the evening before that he would say Mass before the journey to Canterbury. The tavern room was a perfect spot for it was enclosed and was able to hold a substantial amount of people. Of course, Father Colman had consulted Harry Bailly, who was more than enthused about the service. Harry promised to have breakfast ready after the service was completed.

The benches in the tavern could not be easily moved, so the participants in the Mass knelt beside the tables and easily spread out throughout the tavern. Father Colman used a small table beside the bar to serve as an altar.

Anthony Colman helped his brother as a server and was instrumental in helping to carry out the minute parts of the service. Most of the men who had slept in the room assigned to the clergy were present at the Mass, including Merek, Fathers Quinn and Hubert, and Fathers Smithton and Towns. The summoner and the pardoner were not present for the Mass.

Merek was not surprised they were absent. Both had been unusually drunk the night before. Merek doubted they would even make the trip. Perhaps they would begin their journey with the next group of pilgrims to Canterbury. Merek was hoping they would. He held both of them in low regard, given their professed jobs for the Church and the way they presented themselves.

Walter, the summoner, whose scabulous appearance made him a frightful-looking character, was loathsome in Merek's eyes.

Summoners were messengers of the Church whose job it was to "summon" offenders of the Church's laws to its courts. If a priest or bishop felt a commoner or lord were in opposition to the Church's laws or teachings, it was up to the summoner to bring them the document that would tell them the time and date the accused offender was to appear in court. Merek knew the hypocrisy that went along with the summoner's job. If one did not want to appear in the court of the Church, it was known that one could bribe the casual summoner. Give the summoner a fee, and he might report back to the Church's court that he was unable to find the accused. Merek knew it was a common practice.

As for pardoners, Merek knew the practice was even more corrupt. By law, licensed pardoners could sell "pardons," whereby a sinner of the Church could purchase a lesser penance to a sin he had committed. If a man stole from his neighbor and wished to repent to a priest in the confessional, he would purchase a "pardon" from a church official like Gilbert, the pardoner on the trip, and use the pardon in the course of the confessional. If the original penance for stealing was two days in the stocks run by the Church, a "pardon" could reduce the penance to a series of prayers using the rosary, a set of beads that directed its user in a series of prayers. It would save the confessor from a stressful day or two in the stocks.

Merek knew that rich lords could commit heinous crimes against sworn enemies, purchase pardons, and be forgiven for their sins with small tokens of penance. The more money the lord was able to give, the smaller the penance. And absolution was given each time. It was a wicked practice of the Church, and Merek knew it. He was sure to forbid pardoners, summoners, and friars from entering Harper's Turn while he was the village priest. They would not infect his villagers with their hypocrisy.

Madam Eglantyne, the prioress, and Sister Anne were present for the Mass, arriving just before Father Colman began the service. To his surprise, Merek saw Sir Robert of Ganse, with his yeoman, Hugh, kneeling, waiting the start of the service. Merek was not surprised that Thomas, Sir Robert's squire, was not there. Merek imagined the squire had been up very late, keeping company with the young barmaid. Merek did not think less of Thomas, the squire, for he knew a young man's desires. What Merek did feel was a bit of guilt, for thoughts of Thomas with the young barmaid made him think of Thea and how he missed her.

As the Mass began, Merek tried to concentrate on the hymns and prayers said by Father Colman. It seemed as though Merek could not keep his mind off Thea. The more he tried to focus on the Mass, the more he thought of her beautiful hazel eyes and long flowing auburn hair. He felt ashamed that he could not shake the memory of her as the Mass was underway. He longed for Thea but had kept his feelings at bay up to this moment in his assignment to accompany the prioress to Canterbury.

As the Mass ended, Harry Bailly and his servants were ready to begin serving breakfast. Served in the tavern as well, breakfast was a positive beginning for the journey to Canterbury. After the Mass ended and breakfast began, the other pilgrims began to appear. By seven, almost all scheduled to go to Canterbury were breakfasted and were beginning to prepare their horses for the trip.

The pilgrims gathered in the courtyard of The Tabard. Horses were carefully loaded, and all eagerly awaited for Harry Bailly to give them the sign to start. Many of the travelers sat atop their horses, while others stood beside their mounts, holding the reins. Those who did not attend Mass seemed to come from all directions to prepare for the journey. Surprisingly, it did not take long to assemble the thirty odd travelers to Canterbury.

Two horses approached the pilgrims from outside the court-yard. The local magistrate and his deputy entered the courtyard with grave faces. They approached Harry Bailly as he was getting ready to mount his horse for the trip. They spoke in hushed tones. Harry listened intently to their words. He nodded and pointed to his tavern.

Then Harry Bailly addressed the crowd of pilgrims to Canterbury. "Gentlemen and ladies. Before we begin on our trip to Canterbury, there has been an incident that has occurred in Southwark. It is an incident that has affected one of the customers to The Tabard. I am afraid our departure for Canterbury will be delayed, so that we can sort out the details with our local officials.

The officials wish to question certain members of our party. I count on your patience and understanding," Harry said. "Please, join us in the great tavern room."

There was talk amongst the pilgrims, many questioning what event in Southwark could have anything to do with them. Harry tethered his horse and walked around quietly, urging the pilgrims to join him in the tavern.

"Good people," Judge Gates said, trying to help Harry with the investigation, "the sooner we meet with the local official and answer his questions, the sooner we will be able to get under way. Please, join us," he said calmly, pointing to the tavern entrance.

With the help of Harry Bailly's workers, the horses were gathered and tethered, making the assembly of pilgrims quicker. Each entered the hall and sat at one of the tables. The local official and his deputy stood at the bar and waited for the pilgrims to get settled.

Chaucer entered with Sheriff Coleson and sat at the same table he ate the night before. As Chaucer looked around, he noticed that for the most part, the pilgrims sat at the same table and with the same company they sat at the night before. The only exception was the table where the pardoner and the summoner sat. No one sat with them. The Colman brothers sat elsewhere.

Despite the circumstances, Chaucer had to smile. "Creatures of habit," he thought, thinking of how the pilgrims sat at the same table. And he smiled even more, looking at the pardoner and the summoner. The pardoner's bulging eyes were bloodshot, and his sober face indicated a night of too much ale. The summoner, on the other hand, was in pain. He kept feeling his jaw where Miller had punched him. Last night, with so much ale in him, he did not really feel the pain, but this morning was different. The pain was back.

Chaucer just shook his head at the odd pair. He smiled again, thinking the two will not be singing this morning. And he was grateful for that.

"Ladies and gentlemen," the magistrate began to the pilgrims sitting in Harry Bailly's tavern, "I must ask your forgiveness for delaying your departure. There has been a murder."

The pilgrims immediately began to talk among themselves, naturally curious about the crime and why they were involved.

"Last night," the magistrate continued, "I was summoned to Harry's tavern, for a thief had been caught in your midst. Men from The Tabard brought the thief to our jail where we questioned him. To our dismay, he would not give us much information. He did tell us his name was Albert, and he worked as a cook in a tavern on the north side of London. Other than that, he would not give us any information.

"My deputy and I, as is the custom, decided to put him in the stocks last night. We have found that being in the stocks overnight not only sobers our drunken criminals but also loosens their tongues. And we did just that. The cook was securely placed in the stocks outside our jail last night. When we left him, he was angry but very much alive. And in our rounds throughout Southwark, we did check on him twice before our duties ended.

"Lo and behold, ladies and gentlemen, when we checked on our thief this morning, he was dead. His throat had been cut in a most horrific way."

Now the pilgrims spoke loudly and began to ask the magistrate questions. Harry stepped forward to quiet the crowd, but there was no need. The magistrate had a commanding voice.

"Just a few questions, ladies and sirs, and you will be on your way," he assured them.

Sir Robert of Ganse was not protesting. He was watching the five men at the table in which they sat the previous evening. He had no proof, but he knew the men were allied with the dead cook. It was an inner feeling, a feeling he would not ignore. Without staring, he watched the five men as the questioning began.

Merek, for his part, kept his eye on a man standing at the bar. Last night, Merek noticed the man occasionally looking at him like he was studying Merek. Although their eyes never met, Merek knew the man had glanced at him more than usual. The man had a deep tan, not like one that a farmer would earn working in the hot sun. No, this man was not a farmer. He did not "look" the part.

Merek did not make it obvious that he was studying the man, who the night before seemed to be studying him. Last night, Merek had noticed the large dagger that hung on a lanyard around the man's neck. Perhaps it was the darkness in the tavern the night before, but the dagger seemed to be shining this morning, like it had been cleaned! Merek was sure it was his imagination and sat in silence and watched.

Oswald stood in the back of the tavern. He positioned himself in such a way that he could see everyone in the room. He said nothing and studied as many of the pilgrims as he could. Oswald was interested in the lord knight and his son, the squire. Oswald wanted to determine if they would be a hindrance to the plan on the trip. And, of course, he spotted the large priest who travelled with the prioress. Oswald had confidence in the ability of Anglicus to take care of the priest when the time was right, but he wondered if Anglicus underestimated the priest. By the looks of the priest, he seemed to have broad shoulders and a thick chest. The priest's hands were large and looked like they had been used in his lifetime for hard work. No, this was not an average reverend who doled out wafers on Sunday at Mass and gave blessings in the confines of a safe church.

Oswald had a strong intuition about people, and his strong inner feelings had helped him to be successful in the many duties he performed. Thaddeus and his men trusted Oswald and honored his instincts and suggestions. Anglicus was a man who really did not know Oswald, as this was his first time he had worked with Oswald. For his part, Oswald was impressed by the side job he gave Anglicus. The cook's throat was mortally cut without noise or witnesses in the dead of the night. Anglicus had performed the task as a true professional assassin.

"You, sir," the magistrate said, looking directly at Chaucer. "You accused the man of stealing. Your name, sir."

Chaucer stood. "I am Geoffrey Chaucer, foreign diplomat to King Edward III and personal servant to Sir John of Gaunt. I did accuse the man, sir, and I had good reason."

"Go on, sir." The magistrate nodded.

"The man appeared to be drunk when he approached our persons. He bumped into Sheriff Coleson," Chaucer said to the sanguine sheriff seated beside him. "Later, Sheriff Coleson discovered his imported silk purse was missing. For my part, sir, I thought the thief was pretending to be drunk as a ruse to pickpocket the sheriff."

"And so, you confronted him?" the magistrate questioned.

"Yes, sir. At first, the thief began to act as if he were drunk. He would not admit his theft," Chaucer stated.

"Begging your pardon, sir," Thomas interrupted. "My father and I came to Master Chaucer's aid, and upon further questioning of the thief found the stolen silk purse. I am Thomas, squire to the lord knight, my father, Sir Robert of Ganse."

"And where did this questioning and discovery take place?" the magistrate asked.

Sir Robert wanted to stand and point to the five questionable men at the table where the cook had stood, but he was too slow, for one of the men at the table stood and faced the magistrate.

"Sir, the thief was at our table," Thaddeus said, standing for all to see. "I am Thaddeus, a haberdasher from East London. We are guildsmen traveling to Canterbury to give thanks to God for the profits of our professions. I tell you honestly that the man was at our table when he was questioned by Mr. Chaucer."

"And why was he at your table?" the magistrate asked.

"Very simple, sir. He was asking us to buy him a pint of ale. When Master Chaucer approached our table, the thief was telling us the woes of his life. We did not know the man, sir."

"Thank you," the magistrate said, seemingly convinced that each was telling the truth. "Ladies and gentlemen, understand my dilemma. We have thirty witnesses to a thief's crime. We have a number of witnesses who saw the man being led away by Harry Bailly's men in front of the tavern. And yet, a few hours later, the thief is dead. For his murder, there are no witnesses. It is my belief that his murderer is in this room."

The crowd once again began murmuring and looking all around.

Judge Gates stood and looked at the magistrate. "Your honor, I am Judge Josef Gates. I am one of the king's serjeants-at-the law. Although I have empathy for your position, sir, I also know the law. You offer no proof that a person in this room is the murderer. And even though I am a great champion for justice, I must inform you that you have no right to hold anyone in this group from his appointed journey. Without proof, you must allow us to proceed. I say this with all due respect to your difficult position, sir."

Judge Gates had clout. And Gates knew the law better than most. His knowledge, his confidence, and his stance put the magistrate in a winless situation. The magistrate had no option. He would have to allow the trip to begin without an arrest.

However, Judge Gates offered an olive branch to the magistrate. "Sir, our group travels to Canterbury, but we shall be back within a week. Perhaps by then, you will find proof as to the perpetrator of this crime. We will be back."

"Very well, Judge," he answered. "And I may surmise if one of you does not return to Southwark with the group, it shall put suspicion on you. And so I would like each of you to give your name to my deputy. He is fully capable of writing and will gladly record your names for my records. Judge, may I do that?"

"Indeed, sir. You may."

"Well, then, step up all and give your name to my deputy. God speed to you as you visit the tomb of the holy blissful martyr, St. Thomas."

"Come on, then," Harry urged, and the pilgrims complied to the magistrate's wishes, lining up to give the deputy their names.

It was almost half past seven in the morning by the time the group was finally ready to begin the trip. Harry Bailly, seeing the group of pilgrims mounted and ready, signaled for the group to proceed.

And so the journey began.

CHAPTER 21

ST. THOMAS-A-WATERING

Robin Miller led the pilgrims from The Tabard. Wearing his white coat with a blue hood, Robin played his bagpipes as best he could. He was still drunk from the night before. He had not slept the night before but had stayed up all night drinking with a few of the locals in The Tabard and one of the pilgrims was the dark-skinned shipman who had a dark black beard and kept his dagger on a lanyard around his neck.

As Miller and the shipman drank the night away, they seemed to find a common ground in the way they went about their businesses. Robin learned the shipman's name was Anglicus, and he was the pilot to a ship called the *Maudelayne*. Anglicus had sailed to many ports and had a steady stream of customers who wanted him to either import or export goods for their businesses. Anglicus bragged to Robin that he made a handsome living in the import/export business and would often steal from his customers. He was proficient in stealing from traders, for he knew how to adjust the shipping numbers to hide the products he stole. In addition, Anglicus was an expert in being able to hide his ship when being chased. He knew inlets, creeks, and rivers that had the proper depths for him to sail when being pursued.

Robin Miller laughed heartily as Anglicus told Miller how he conducted business. Robin confessed that he also took advantage of the customers who brought their crops to his mill. Since a miller was paid by the weight of the crops he milled, Robin Miller confessed to Anglicus that he had a "thumb of gold." When the grain was being weighed, Robin would subtly press his thumb on the scale indicating there was more grain on the scale than there actually was. Customers had to pay more for his services than they really had to. It was a game to Miller, one he enjoyed playing.

Anglicus laughed heartily when Miller confessed his thievery and slapped the strong man on the back, pouring more ale in his cup. Robin Miller enjoyed his new friend's company. But as the ale continued to flow between the two men, Robin Miller began to hold Anglicus in a different regard. Even though Robin was becoming drunk, he could tell the shipman was not just telling tales or bragging. Robin knew the man meant business. He could tell Anglicus would have no problem in stealing from customers. And Robin knew the man was ruthless. He could see it in the shipman's eyes. Robin gazed at the dagger hanging around his neck and saw that it was rusted. But he had no doubt that the dagger had been used.

The men drank through the night. Even the locals who were drinking with the men gave up, left, or passed out. Robin and Anglicus stayed together telling stories, jokes and talking about women. Around three bells, Anglicus excused himself to visit the privy and was gone for what seemed to be a long time. Miller was about to leave the great tavern room and look for the reveler, when Anglicus returned. When Robin questioned him, the shipman admitted he had passed out in the privy. Both men laughed at the notion and kept drinking. Even though Miller was inebriated at the time, he did notice the dagger around the neck of the shipman looked different. The dagger seemed to have a little shine to it, like it had just been cleaned.

Behind Miller heading out of Southwark, Harry Bailly rode alongside the woman from Bath. Harry seemed to be captivated by the widow and paid attention to every word she said. For her part, Allison enjoyed the attention of the host but occasionally looked around to some of the younger men in the group, particularly Thomas, the squire.

The group travelled on Kent Road, one of the oldest roads in England. Part of an ancient Celtic path, the Romans had constructed the road almost nine hundred years ago. It linked London to Canterbury. Some called it the "Pilgrim's Way," but there was another route more to the south from Winchester to Canterbury that was also called the Pilgrim's Way. The route was thickly forested for the most part, so it bode well for pilgrims to Canterbury to travel in large groups, for the forest hid many robbers and highwaymen.

The prioress and her entourage rode behind the host. Father Smithton continued to ride in front of Madam Eglantyne, while Sister Anne rode alongside her. Father Towns continued his due diligence by riding behind the prioress. The monk and the friar rode behind the prioress's entourage.

The five men who represented the guilds rode behind the monk and the friar. The others traveled in groups of two or three spread behind the five guildsmen. The summoner and the pardoner rode together for the moment unusually quiet. Although they were both hungover from the night before, the summoner rode with a laurel of leaves around his head, held a cake as a shield, and used a broomstick as a lance as they travelled.

Oswald, the reeve, rode last, keeping all the others in his view. He rode alone the way he wanted.

Merek, for his part, rode with Sir Robert, Thomas, Hugh Bowman, and Chaucer. By his duties, Merek was to stay with the prioress but had been engaged in conversation with the group in which he now rode. He enjoyed their company and decided the prioress was in good company. It was a long trip, and he would perform his duty in due time.

"I am told, Father Willson, that you are adept with the longbow," Chaucer said as they reached the outskirts of Southwark.

"Somewhat," Merek hesitantly answered, not wanting to reveal his past.

"Come now, Father. Do not be modest. Young Thomas tells me you were an archer for the king, and that you served in France," Chaucer said in a friendly way.

"Master Chaucer, I have fought for the king. I have killed, and I have repented. My life before priesthood was wayward. And if you would be so kind, please do not ask me to relive it or give you any indication that I am proud of it," Merek said quietly.

Chaucer saw in an instant that he had broached a subject with Merek that was unapproachable. "Of course, Father. Many pardons," he answered. "However, may I tell the group of my reckless courage and bravery in France serving our good King Edward?"

"Please do," Thomas urged, knowing Chaucer was going to momentarily entertain them.

"Very well, sirs." Chaucer smiled. "At the time of my training in the arts of war, I was serving Sir Lionel, second son of our glorious king. May I tell you I was trained in the use of the sword and was quite adept at its use? Men say my stroke was swift and accurate and could cut a barbarous incision in any vine or plant." The men laughed at Chaucer's joke. "At the time," he continued, "Sir Lionel was ordered to serve his older brother, the Black Prince, in France. The Black Prince had a force of one hundred thousand that sailed across the channel to France. By accounts, sirs, only five thousand were considered combatants. The rest were servants, whores, builders, and retainers. May I say to you that I was not considered a combatant and have often wondered in which group I was assigned?"

The men laughed again at his self-deprecating humor.

"Yet, sirs, I had a vest and a light helmet of iron. I had a sword and was willing to cut a path of French with my skilled swordsmanship." Chaucer flailed his arms as if he had a sword. The listeners laughed, causing some of the other pilgrims to suddenly turn and look at the group.

"I was given a task by Sir Lionel early in our mission in France. I was a party to a foraging mission looking for cattle and other domestic animals or food, when our party was surprised by a French unit and were taken prisoner. As you can surmise, my masterful swordplay did not save me from being a prisoner of the French. As a matter of fact, my sword never left its scabbard, gentlemen. I tell you no lie." Chaucer smiled.

Once again, the men smiled, including Merek, who understood that Chaucer was diverting the attention away from a topic Merek did not want to speak of.

"And how long were you with the French, Master Chaucer?" Thomas asked.

"Months, Thomas. Months. Seemed like years. But in the end, a ransom was paid for some prisoners in which I was fortunate to be included. Good King Edward assisted in the ransom."

"Impressive, sir," Thomas said. "To have the king of England aid in your ransom is quite impressive."

"I am sure the king liked the way I served his son," Chaucer answered, smiling.

The group led by the drunken Miller came to the first stop on the journey to Canterbury. It was a traditional resting spot called St. Thomas-a-Watering. It was a crossing point across the Neckinger River. The crossing point was actually a small brook that was an offshoot of the river itself. The pilgrims stopped and rested for a short while, giving their horses a simple drink from the river.

As the group gathered and dismounted, each rider led his horse to the edge of the brook. The spirit of the group seemed high despite the delayed departure. Father Smithton led the prioress's horse to water, and Merek was quick to help Sister Anne with her horse. Harry Bailly saw to the Woman of Bath's horse.

Robin Miller had stopped playing his bagpipes a little after the group had left Southwark. Still drunk, he almost fell off his horse at the first rest stop. Likewise, the summoner and pardoner were slow to dismount, still feeling the effects of the drinking the night before.

Harry Bailly gathered the pilgrims after a few minutes, holding up a fist full of straws. "Come, gather all. It is time to begin our contest, if you please. Please draw a straw. Whoever draws the shortest cut will be the first to tell his tale. Come, come, do not be shy," he said, walking up to each pilgrim and allowing each to pick a straw. There was hesitation at first, but one by one, each chose a straw.

"Ah, I see, ladies and gentlemen. The shortest straw has been drawn by Sir Robert of Ganse, our noble knight!" Harry spoke with enthusiasm.

The pilgrims cheered, and Sir Robert began to smile.

"Are you prepared, Sir Robert?" Harry asked.

"I think I have a tale that will please the group," Sir Robert said. "I shall begin when we get on our way. By your leave, Harry."

"Of course, Sir Robert. I would say in a few minutes we will be ready to continue. Once on our way, we will be eager to hear your tale," Harry said.

The animals were watered, and each pilgrim mounted his horse. For the most part, it was a happy group, fresh in the journey. As they began again, Harry took the lead alongside Allison, the woman of Bath. Miller stayed behind and seemed hesitant to mount his horse. Merek noticed and stayed behind a bit to make sure Miller was all right. Merek saw Miller stumble to the weeds beside the brook and vomit. He must have vomited a few minutes as Merek waited at a short distance.

Soon, Miller walked to his horse, pulled the reins, and began on the trail. He saw Merek waiting for him.

"What's the matter, Father?" Robin Miller asked as his horse trotted past to catch up to the group.

"We priests have to watch the entire flock, Robin." Merek smiled.

Robin Miller forced a smile and kept riding, as did Merek. Soon they caught up to the group that was listening to Sir Robert's tale. To hear the tale, the group moved in close to the knight. Sir Robert had a fine voice, and all were able to listen.

Merek noticed that Oswald, the reeve, also seemed to be waiting for Miller to pass. Oswald dragged behind the group also. It was only after Merek and Robin Miller passed him did Oswald join the group. Merek found it odd that Oswald had to be last, as if he had to keep watch over everyone. Robin Miller slowed down when he approached the reeve. He said something to the reeve, who sneered at him, and allowed Miller to get ahead of him. Merek did not know what Miller said, but when he passed the waiting reeve, he could tell the reeve was not happy.

And the journey continued.

CHAPTER 22

A DAY'S TRAVEL

Sir Robert's story was a good one. With his fine voice and choice words, the pilgrims were entertained about his story concerning knights and their quest for fame and love. Sir Robert had broken his story into five parts, and after each part, he would pause and let the details of his story sink in to his listeners. He also allowed time for questions, but there were none. Each member of the traveling party would not think of asking a lord, a knight no less, in a trivial question about a story being told.

While Sir Robert's story was being told, the group passed the small town of Deptford, home of St. Nicholas Church. The path the pilgrims travelled was so close to the town that the large church was easy to see. Normally, certain groups of pilgrims would stop at each church along the way and give proper thanks for the safety of their journey. But Harry's group was too enthralled with the good knight's story to interrupt him. Even the clergy were quite entertained by the knight's story.

There were a few stragglers who were not entertained by the knight's story. Oswald, of course, staying behind the procession, did not seem interested in the story. The guildsmen rode close to Sir Robert, but they did not seem interested either. As the crowd laughed or were in awe of a certain point to Sir Robert's story, it was easy to see by the lack of reaction from the guildsmen that they were not listening.

For his part, Merek had missed the beginning of the tale and was somewhat lost with the names of the characters and the plot of the story. He rode along anyway, observing the company and enjoying the beautiful day. Robin Miller had not only caught up to the group but had made his way to the front, well within hearing distance of the knight's tale.

Hugh Bowman, pulled himself from the group and made his way back, trying to do so without notice. Riding close to Merek, he nodded and indicated he needed a word with Merek. Merek pulled his horse from the group. The road in which the group rode was wide, and so with little effort, Hugh and Merek were able to ride with the group but at the same time divorce themselves from the group.

"Hugh, how are you fairing?" Merek asked.

"Well, Father Merek. Well." Hugh smiled, keeping his eyes on the reeve behind them.

"Sir Robert is quite entertaining." Merek smiled.

"Aye, Lord Robert can fetch a tale when the time is right," Hugh agreed.

"Something troubling you, my friend?" Merek asked quietly, making sure he could not be heard, especially by the reeve.

"Might be nothing, Father. Want to ask you something as a soldier, not a priest," Hugh said.

"Go on," Merek said, looking straight ahead.

"Sir Robert had some concerns about the five men travelling together. The guildsmen. He asked that I keep an eye on them. He says there is something about them that does not meet the eye."

"You must have seen something," Merek said.

"Two things, Father Merek. When you get a chance, take a look at the men's boots," Hugh said.

"Let me guess. They are all the same?" Merek asked.

"They are the same. Not because the men bought them from the same cobbler but because they were issued by the army," Hugh exclaimed.

Merek looked at Hugh with surprise and did not say a word, trying to hide as much of their conversation as he could.

"That is why I need you to think as a soldier," Hugh said. "Take a close look when you get a chance. I think they are soldiers or former soldiers."

"You have a second point," Merek asked.

"Each of the five has a dagger hidden in one of his boots," Hugh said quietly.

"Probably a lot of daggers hidden on this trip by a number of the pilgrims," Merek answered.

"Aye, but these daggers are also army issued. See for yourself, Father Merek. You were a soldier. You would know."

"I will when it presents itself," Merek answered. "But the questions is why are they in disguise?'"

"I have no idea, Father, but it is my sworn duty to protect Sir Robert and his son. Therefore, I must anticipate that the men are on the trip to assassinate or kidnap the men that I protect," Hugh spoke with certainty and resolve.

Merek smiled and laughed as if Hugh had something funny just to keep the observant Oswald from surmising the topic in which they spoke. For a moment, Merek was amused that he wanted to make sure Oswald did not hear their conversation. Yet, Merek had no inclination or proof that information like this should be kept from a man like the reeve, who held high consideration in a lord's estate. Yet, Merek felt a caution about the man, a caution Merek could not shake.

"Be assured, Hugh, I will keep an eye on our 'soldiers'." Merek smiled.

Hugh nodded and rejoined the group, sidling up a little closer to Sir Robert and Thomas.

The group was well passed Greenwich when Sir Robert finished his story. All applauded the noble lord, for he set a high standard for the group's storytelling. Conversation ensued as to who would tell the next tale.

Harry Bailly stepped in and congratulated Sir Robert on his choice of stories. "Quite noble, my lord. A very fitting tale. I am afraid your tale will be a hard one to follow."

Harry looked around at the group. "Now, let's see whose turn will go next. The contest is off to a fine start. Sir Monk," Harry said, pointing at Father Quinn. "Let us hear you tell a tale as equally good as Sir Robert's."

"For Chrissake," Robin Miller interrupted, "I am next."

"Robin, dear brother," Harry said, "you are drunk on ale. Let a sober man tell his tale before you indulge in your story."

"By the arms and blood and bones of Christ, I know a noble story that will match the noble story that Sir Robert has told," Robin Miller slurred, still feeling his night of drunkenness.

"But I must insist on the man I choose." Harry tried to reason. "It is my contest."

"To hell with your contest," Robin belched. "By God's soul, I will speak or go my own way."

Harry looked to the others for some help. Father Quinn was very sensible and nodded to Harry, indicating it would be all right for Miller to tell his tale before he did. Harry also looked to Allison, the woman of Bath, for he was desperately trying to impress her. Allison also nodded, and Harry gave in.

"Tell your story, you drunken fool," Harry said. "Even though drink has gotten the better part of you, I shall allow you to tell your story."

"Now listen, one and all," Miller said. "First, I am drunk. I blame it on the ale served by our host, Harry Bailly. It was his ale at The Tabard that has sent me adrift. So, if I speak improperly, blame it on Harry, for his ale has loosened my tongue. I beg you."

The pilgrims surrounding Miller gave way and let him begin his tale. Slowly, they began on the road again as Miller began his tale.

"I shall tell the legend of a reeve who happened to also be a carpenter, and how a student made a fool of the reeve," Robin Miller began.

Suddenly, Oswald, the reeve, raced his horse to the front of the group. "Stop this nonsense at once, you fool," he said to Robin Miller. "Your drunkenness is no excuse for your ignorant, drunken vulgarity." To Harry Bailly, he requested, "Please, sir, do not allow this Miller to tell his tale. I assure you it will be rank and vulgar."

"A tale is a tale," Harry answered. "We have made no rules or conditions for the subject or material for each person's tale."

"I am sure his tale will embarrass us. Sir, may I remind you there are clergy here? There is a madam prioress with us," Oswald said to Harry.

"Take your swollen prick to the back of the procession," Robin Miller told the reeve. "It is my turn to tell the story. You'll get your turn."

The reeve was not happy but could do nothing about the drunken storyteller. He turned his horse and began to move toward the back of the group hoping not to hear Miller's tale. As he went back, he could hear Miller beginning his tale.

"And so, my lords and ladies, allow me to tell you of the older reeve who had a young wife and how she turned him into a cuckold because of a young student who boarded at their house."

"Damn you!" the reeve shouted as he made his way to the back of the group.

It did not deter the drunken Miller, for he carried on with his boisterous tale. Perhaps it was the strong drink or Miller's flippant attitude about the pilgrims and the contest, but he did not censor his tale. He said things in his tale that were considered immoral. He mentioned body parts, lust, and sex. Yet, the more he spoke, the more the guests were enthralled with his story.

Merek, along with the other clergy, listened intently. He had to admit the story was a good one. It had coarse humor, action, and the topic of intercourse. Of course, Robin Miller did not use the term *intercourse* in his story. He used a more profane synonym for the intimate act. The crowd all listened intently, even the five men who travelled together as guildsman. Yes, for the most part, the company was most interested in where Miller was taking the main characters of his tale.

Hugh Bowman was not interested in the story. He kept a watchful eye out, for the road to Canterbury, although paved by the Romans so long ago, was through some thickly forested areas. It would have been easy for highwaymen to attack a group of pilgrims on their way to Canterbury. Fortunately, with a group of thirty, predominantly with men, the odds of such an attack would be low. Yet, Hugh kept a watchful eye, always taking mental notes of the five soldiers disguised as guildsmen.

Miller's tale was not long, but it had the travelers laughing. When he finished, they applauded, asking questions and giving their opinions. Some of the clergy pretended to object to the coarseness of the tale and the talk of the intimate language of sex, but secretly, they enjoyed hearing the story.

From the back of the procession, Oswald made his feelings known. "So help me, by Christ's bones, I could very well pay back this disgusting tale with one of my own! My tale is one of a proud miller who is tricked by some fellows with whom Miller cheated. It will certainly level the score!"

"Well, tell your tale, Oswald," Harry said. "We have passed Deptford and Greenwich. We are almost halfway to Dartford, our stop for the night. You want to tell a tale about a miller, so be it! I grant you, tell your tale!"

"I will sir," Oswald grumbled. "I will make a fool of this Miller, for he has made a mockery of reeves and carpenters. By your leave ladies and gentlemen, I ask for your forgiveness, for I will use the same coarse language Miller has used. I will use his vulgar terms and hope to repay him well."

Robin Miller laughed at Oswald. "Do your best, damn you."

"I hope to God you break your neck on this journey, Robin Miller, for you are nothing but a quarrelsome drunk," the reeve spouted.

And with that, the reeve trotted his horse to the front of the group and began to tell his story. For his part, Miller rode close to the reeve. Robin did not want to miss a word, for he knew the reeve was going to repay him in full. And Robin Miller wanted to be close enough to the reeve to physically hurt him when the time was right. The procession of pilgrims continued.

"In the town of Trumpington, near Cambridge, there runs a stream with a small bridge over it. Next to the bridge is a mill, run by a miller who was both proud and crooked . . ." the reeve began.

And he continued his tale. Oswald told his tale in full, seeming to relish the thought that the tale would embarrass Robin Miller. The group listened intently, laughed sporadically, and seemed to enjoy the vulgar series of comic mishaps in the story. Like Miller's tale, it made sport of a foolish man of the trades. However, there was a big difference in the tales. Whereas Robin Miller's tale was told as a farce with the intention of getting a good laugh, Oswald's tale had more of a sardonic humor that had biting satire in it. Both stories could have been funny in their own way. Yet, Oswald's way of telling his tale had an underlying bitterness to it.

Merek enjoyed the story. It had humor, a vulgar bedroom scene, and a "moral" to it. But to Merek, it brought Oswald into a different light in his mind. Merek smiled, thinking how Harry's contest was indeed clever, for the tales told by the various pilgrims would unwittingly say something about the character of the pilgrim. Sir Robert's story of noble knights undergoing tests of courage seemed to define Sir Robert's character. And Robin Miller's drunken tale seemed to define Miller's life, attitude, and sense of humor. If the stories revealed insight into the teller's character, Oswald was giving a glimpse into the kind of man he was.

At the end of his tale, Oswald said, "See what happens to a miller who is a cheat! Therefore, the proverb is true that says: 'He who commits evil must not expect goodness.' The cheat himself was outwitted. Now I have repaid Robin Miller with my tale."

There was some polite applause from the group, but not the same kind of cheering and laughing as that of the Robin Miller's tale. It seemed the group understood the difference in the way the tales were told. Too polite to say anything, they applauded and waited for Harry to announce the next speaker.

For his part, Robin Miller only laughed at Oswald. "Saint's bones, man, is that the best you can do?"

"Just so everyone knows, my tale is true, for it has been my experience that millers, as a whole, are a crooked lot and will cheat you at the first turn," Oswald said to Robin Miller.

"Come, Oswald, goddam you. Let's you and I make a detour through these trees, so I can show you just how crooked I can be." Robin Miller challenged.

Geoffrey Chaucer stepped in before Harry Bailly could say anything. Chaucer spoke to the entire group, but his message was meant for the two men who were about to fight. "Gentlemen, may I say that it is has been my privilege to work for two of King Edward's sons. And in the time that I have served both wonderful men, I have met a number of reeves and millers. May I say to everyone here that in my experience, I have most positive experiences in working with both millers and reeves? I have seen millers of the finest integrity working with equally fine reeves in the care of his majesty's sons' estates."

The pilgrims were glad of Chaucer's interruption for it stopped an impending fight. They gave Chaucer a polite applause. Oswald, not happy, rode to the back of the group and set himself in his usual position in the back of the procession. Robin Miller began to urge his horse to follow Oswald to the back of the group but was restrained by Merek, who had cleverly taken a hold of Robin Miller's horse's reigns.

"Jesus, Father," Robin Miller said to Merek, "let me go back and blacken one of his eyes. Won't take me long."

"Stay with me, Robin." Merek smiled.

"Christ, what luck?" Robin Miller sighed. "I'm stuck with the biggest goddam priest in Christendom who doesn't fight fair!"

Harry Bailly spoke, "Ladies and gentlemen, if you do not know, we are about one-half mile from the town of Dartford. Instead of beginning a tale now, I suggest we ride along in good company to Dartford. I have sent word to my good friend at The Swan that our group would need supper and accommodations for the night. Once we are settled at The Swan, we will dine together. After dinner, our stories will continue. What say you?"

Of course, the group agreed, and the procession made its way to Dartford.

CHAPTER 23

A MEETING AT THE SWAN

Ideally, Rochester would have been a more favorable stop for the pilgrims, but it would have been another thirteen miles from Dartford. Harry Bailly had experience in the trip to Canterbury and knew the stop in Dartford would be more timely than pushing on to Rochester. Had the group made the push to get to Rochester in the same day they left Southwark, they would have arrived in Rochester tired, miserable, and too late for the dinner. Besides, Harry knew the innkeeper at The Swan in Dartford and had made arrangements for the group to stay there. His friend, Walter Brewse, was the innkeeper and promised Harry a little reward for bringing such a large group to The Swan. Harry did not think his arrangement was clouded by the "reward" Brewse offered him. It was just business.

It was early evening when the group arrived at The Swan, the largest inn in Dartford. The Swan boasted three buildings to house and feed customers on their way to Canterbury. The main house had a tavern not quite as big as The Tabard but big enough to accommodate the thirty pilgrims on this night. One house was used as both a barn and hostelry. The barn was the ground floor of the building. The "hostelry" was the loft of the barn, used for commoners who could stay for a minimal charge.

The third building was the actual hostelry. It was divided into rooms that could accommodate large numbers. Like The Tabard, rooms in the actual hostelry were pricier, with the highest-priced rooms for the lords and nobles. Clergy were also afforded rooms that were nicer than the barn loft, but not nearly as nice as the rooms held for noblemen. Customarily, sexes were separated in the rooms, but occasionally, married customers could stay in one of the rooms if they did not mind the company of others.

Walter Brewse welcomed the group to The Swan. Thanks to Harry Bailly's message, Brewse was waiting for the pilgrims when they arrived. A short, stocky man with long hair, Brewse had his entire lot of employees on hand to help with the horses and any traveling bags the pilgrims had.

"My lords and ladies," Brewse announced as his attendants helped the guests, "welcome to The Swan. My men will help you in any way you need them. Do not worry about your horses. We will attend them and make sure they are properly watered and fed. If you should like to have your horse rubbed down tonight, please tell the attendant who is helping you."

Harry Bailly had dismounted and was shaking Brewse's arm. Walter Brewse allowed Harry to announce. "Ladies and gentlemen, dinner will be served in one hour. Until that time, you may rest in your rooms, join some of us in the tavern, or do whatever fancies your pleasure. We will adjourn in the tavern hall at six bells," Harry announced.

Spirits were high as the pilgrims hustled about. Sore from their trip, some of the pilgrims took advantage of a chance to lie down, while others chose to get a head start of the evening festivities and step up to the bar.

"Father is tired," Thomas said to Hugh Bowman. "I will remain with him as he lies in his room."

"Very well, sir," Hugh answered. "I will see to the horses."

Chaucer had ended the journey with Sheriff Coleson and Judge Gates. They also wanted to rest and made their way to the room reserved for them. Chaucer was not tired and looked for a suitable companion to begin the night's festivities with.

"Father Willson, may I buy you an ale and talk about the hideous shortcomings of our Holy Catholic Church?" Chaucer smiled.

Merek smiled, getting to know Chaucer's keen sense of humor. "I am afraid you will have to buy me more than one ale to list the corrupt practices of our faith, Master Chaucer."

"Fine, Father Willson. I have enough coin for a keg tonight," Chaucer laughed as the two men went inside.

Madam Prioress and her attendants walked into the tavern also. The prioress wanted to choose a table that would allow her to have the best seat for the afterdinner activities. Once she spotted a table, she asked Father Towns to sit at it and save it for her. She thanked him, excused herself, and went with Sister Anne to a room to rest.

The five guildsmen did not allow any of Walter Brewse's servants attend their horses. They insisted on caring for their own, and each walked his horse to the barn. When they arrived at the barn, Oswald was waiting for them. With a nod, Thaddeus left the men and walked with Oswald. The two men walked past the barn to a small alleyway, just out of sight of The Swan.

"First, the damn cook stole a purse and brought it to our table. He was supposed to be our invisible eyes and ears on the trip. What good was he? And you, you have compromised your position on the trip," Thaddeus said.

"That goddam Miller," Oswald returned. "I have half a mind to kill him as he sleeps."

"Have never seen you like this," Thaddeus said. "We have worked together before, and I had never seen you lose your composure."

"I make no excuses. I might be compromised, but you have not been. As long as we are not seen together, I believe our plan is safe to continue."

"I am not sure, Oswald," Thaddeus answered. "I have noticed men staring at us."

"Who?"

"The brown-skinned yeoman, for one. He is constantly studying us. I can feel it."

"He is a bodyguard for the knight. He stares at everyone."

"I even feel the eyes of the knight upon me and my men," Thaddeus said.

"Let him look," Oswald replied.

"And the priest. The big one. He studies us too."

Oswald grinned. "Do not worry about the large priest. He is one you do not have to worry about."

"Because he is a priest?" Thaddeus asked.

"No, because he is a part of the plan," Oswald answered.

"He is with us?"

"No, I mean he is a part of the plan. Once we kidnap the prioress, the large priest will meet his end."

"Oh?" Thaddeus answered. "Are we to take care of him too?"

"No, of course not. I have a special man on the trip who has been assigned the large priest. Once your part of the plan is underway, my man will take care of the large priest. It is a separate contract. So do not worry about the large priest."

"Let me get this straight, Oswald. You have one man assigned to the large priest?"

"Aye."

"And this man is going to dispose of the priest as we kidnap the prioress?"

"Aye."

"And kill the priest?"

"Maybe. Harm him badly, aye."

Thaddeus thought for a little, looking around to see if the two men were being spied upon. "Have you ever known me to give you advice?" Thaddeus asked Oswald.

"No, not really," Oswald answered.

"This advice is free. One man is not enough for that priest."

"I do not understand," Oswald said.

"I study people too, Oswald. Have you really observed this priest, this large priest?"

"I have seen him," Oswald answered.

"Seen him, aye. Have you observed him?"

Oswald did not know what to say.

"Observe him closely, Oswald," Thaddeus said seriously. "He is a large priest. Have you observed that his cassock seems truly small in his chest and shoulders? Have you observed that he carries an untethered longbow in his saddle? Have you seen his professional arrows he keeps hidden under his saddle bag?"

Oswald listened.

Thaddeus continued, "Did you see the way he subtly handled the drunken Miller's horse's reins? Did you see how the bold Miller backed down from attacking you because the priest whispered something to him? Oswald, the priest was a soldier. It is my guess that he was an archer in the king's army."

"What is your point? The man is merely a priest now," Oswald answered, getting angry at the harsh tone in Thaddeus's voice.

"One man will not be enough to subdue the priest," Thaddeus said.

"And that is your advice?"

"It is."

Now it was Oswald who said nothing. He was thinking. It had nothing to do with the priest. He had complete faith in Anglicus, the shipman, to do his appointed duty on the priest. What Oswald was thinking was whether or not the element of surprise in kidnapping the prioress was lost. If it were lost, the kidnapping would be more difficult. Blood would be shed. The element of surprise was their biggest ally. Was Thaddeus correct? Were the five guildsmen compromised? Did the yeoman and the knight suspect them?

Normally, Oswald might have called off the kidnapping. He had done it before. When a plan was set in place, it had to be followed step-by-step. His plans had gone correctly in each enterprise he undertook. And when parts of the plan did not come through, Oswald would always cancel before any damage was done or crime committed. But the kidnapping of the prioress involved a steep pay of money, more than he had ever made.

"You are thinking?" Thaddeus interjected.

"Aye. Thinking that if we lose our element of surprise, we lose the mission," Oswald said.

"And?"

"I am afraid we cannot wait. To travel to Canterbury, visit the shrine, and return might be three to four days away."

"And?"

"If you and your men are being scrutinized now, imagine how it will be in four days? No, our chance is now. Now, before we completely lose our element of surprise."

196

"Are you saying tonight?"

"Tonight. By leaving from Dartford, our travel west will not be as far. If we wait until tomorrow night, our meeting point will be farther. And if we wait until the return trip, our element of surprise will most likely be compromised."

Thaddeus was surprised by Oswald's decision. Yet, he kept his composure, thinking rapidly how his men could pull off the kidnapping cleanly and without hurting anyone.

"Can you and your men accomplish the task tonight?"

Thaddeus did not answer right away. He was thinking. Oswald did not press for an answer. He liked the fact that Thaddeus was thinking. This was a man of careful deliberation. Oswald waited patiently.

"We can," Thaddeus said with confidence.

"Very well," Oswald said. "We will stick to the original plan. Bring the prioress to the first meeting sight. I will be awaiting there for you at dawn. Then we will travel together to the lodge and await the ransom."

"We will make our move in the deadest part of the night," Thaddeus said. "I must go back, inform my men, and then we must make the layout of The Swan known to us."

"But you must be at dinner," Oswald urged. "Keep the element of surprise."

"Done," Thaddeus said.

"At dinner, I will give you the final word," Oswald warned.

"Will it be a sign?"

"Aye," Oswald grinned. "I will simply nod my head to you."

"Easy enough," Thaddeus said. "See you at the meeting point."

Oswald nodded. And said nothing, thinking to himself. It was a risky venture, but the reward was great. As Oswald returned to The Swan, he had to find Anglicus. Another plan had to be put into effect, and quickly.

CHAPTER 24

THE WOMAN OF BATH

Chaucer bought Merek an ale, but they decided to sit at a nearby table instead of standing at the bar. It was Chaucer's idea. He did not want to put Father Merek in an awkward position. A priest standing at a bar drinking ale was not the picture the holy church would have approved. The table had an open bench, and the two men sat with their cups of ale.

"Many thanks, Geoffrey," Merek said, taking a large gulp. "It tastes fine after being on the road all day."

"Aye, Father," Chaucer agreed, clanging his ale cup to Merek's.

Fathers Quinn and Hubert entered the tavern but upon seeing Merek moved to the other side of the room where they sat together at a table. Merek nodded to Father Towns, who was sitting alone at a table. Father Towns had nothing in front of him. Merek excused himself from Chaucer and bought an ale for Father Towns. Chaucer took it to his table and placed it in front of the solemn priest. Father Towns was caught by surprise at the offering and nodded a thanks to Merek. Merek returned the nod and made his way back to Chaucer.

Father Leo Colman and his brother Anthony entered, asking to sit with Fathers Quinn and Hubert. Merek saw them enter and hoped they would join Chaucer and him. But they did not. Deep down, Merek felt unworthy of Father Colman's company. Leo Colman was a humble, God-fearing priest who served his villagers as if he were a shepherd. Merek felt he served the villagers at Harper's Turn well but, after that, could not compare himself to the humble village parson.

"May I join you, gentlemen?" a somber-looking man asked Chaucer and Merek. Both men had seen the man riding with them during the day, but neither had had a chance to meet him.

"Please sir, join us." Chaucer smiled, standing.

The man placed his cup of ale on the table and sat next to Chaucer. "I am Richard Howard from Weyridge." He smiled.

Both men introduced themselves to Richard Howard, who told Merek and Chaucer that he was a doctor. Without prodding, Howard told the men he was capable of prescribing medicine and performing surgery. Dressed in blood-red garments with stripes of bluish-grey, the doctor was wearing taffeta. Chaucer, who had done some travelling and had witnessed many styles of clothing, had never seen a man wearing the fine fabric. Usually reserved for woman for its soft silken nature, Howard was wearing a colorful shirt made of imported taffeta.

Richard Howard was a talker, and at once, Merek and Chaucer were unhappy the man sat with them. Howard told them all about his profession, which was interesting at first, but when the doctor began inserting names like Aesculapius, Dioscorides, Galen, Rhazes, Hali, Avicenna, Constantine, John of Gaddesdon, and Gilbertine, the discussion turned into an egotistical lecture.

Neither Chaucer nor Willson could get a word in when another figure approached the table. It was the bearded man who had been tanned brown by the many days in the sun. He was the one who wore a lanyard about his neck. Unlike the doctor, he was not well-dressed, for the bearded man wore a simple woolen gown. "Please it you, sirs. May I join you?" Anglicus asked.

"Please do," Merek said swiftly.

As Anglicus sat down, Chaucer was quick with a question, for the new man had interrupted the doctor's droning about the four elements that made up the human body.

"I am Chaucer, this is Father Merek Willson, and our friend the doctor is Richard Howard," Chaucer said with enthusiasm, thankful that someone had rescued them from the boring physician.

"I am Anglicus, a shipman, from Dartmouth. I am in port and wished to make a pilgrimage to Canterbury to thank God for my safe arrival in England," he said, sitting next to Merek.

"Well-said." Chaucer laughed. "Especially in the presence of a priest."

The table laughed. Even the doctor smiled, although he was secretly irritated that he had lost his audience.

"A shipman, Father Willson." Chaucer smiled. To Anglicus, "I'll bet you have seen the world."

Anglicus feigned modesty. "I must admit I have been all around the Mediterranean. However, most of my trade is with France, so I have limited stories and sights to pass on to you, gentlemen."

"I detect modesty, Father Merek." Chaucer smiled. "Come, sir, tell us of your travels. Tell us of the sights you have seen," Chaucer urged.

More and more of the pilgrims were entering the tavern, for it was time for dinner. The tables began to fill. As Anglicus was entertaining the table with his stories of an incident in Carthage, Gilbert, the pardoner, and Walter, the summoner, approached the table. "May it please you, sirs? Are these seats taken?" Gilbert asked.

Anglicus did not miss a beat. He turned to the two intruders, "Sorry, gents, but these seats are promised. You'll have to go elsewhere, I am afraid."

Gilbert looked at Walter and blinked. Both nodded, and they moved on, seeking a table elsewhere.

Anglicus looked at Merek. "Forgive me, Father. I just lied to those men. I must confess I saw their act last night and would not enjoy my dinner and your company if they sat at our table."

Merek smiled. "Not only are you forgiven, Anglicus, but I will say an extra prayer for you tonight for keeping me from sinning. For surely, if those two had sat with us and began their atrocious singing, I would have sinned."

The table laughed, even the doctor, who had witnessed the glaring voices the night before. Soon, two men did approach the table, and Chaucer accepted them as old friends. One was the cleric, who had his cherished books under his arms. The other was the quiet merchant, whose forking beard hung halfway down his chest. Although all introduced themselves to the two newcomers, Merek could not remember their names.

Dinner was served. Walter Brewse, with the advanced warning from his friend, Harry Bailly, served up his finest victuals. The hungry pilgrims ate from large platters set on the tables. The platters boasted large swans, geese, and capons that satisfied the hungry pilgrims. Hot pastries of venison were also served with the customary breads and cheeses. The ale and the wine flowed throughout the supper, and all were satisfied by the food, drink, and merriment. Brewse had served an excellent feast, and the pilgrims did not seem to mind the steep price they paid for the meal.

No one seemed happier with the meal and the glow of the evening than Harry Bailly. Seated with Allison, the woman from Bath, he glowed with satisfaction and newfound love. He could not keep his eyes from the cloth maker from Bath. She seemed smitten also, for her desire on the trip was to meet husband number six. In Harry Bailly, she found all the characteristics she needed. Harry was a little younger than she, had money and a profitable inn, and was handsome. Secretly, her only reservation was whether he would agree with her philosophy of marriage. She would not broach the subject with Harry until he pressed her for marriage.

The meal ended, and more wine and ale were sent around to the tables. Harry Bailly stood, and the crowd grew quiet. "Ladies and gentlemen, if you please," Harry announced and waited for the crowd to be still. It did not take long, for the pilgrims were ready for the contest to continue. "Thank you. Before we continue the contest, ladies and gentlemen, how about a hand to our host, Walter Brewse, for the immaculate feast he served?"

The crowd cheered in unison. As they cheered, Anglicus slipped a potion into Merek's wine. It was a subtle move, one he had done many times before to other victims.

"May I tell you, ladies and gentlemen," Harry continued, "that the contest will continue with the next storyteller." Here, he stopped, purposely teasing his audience. Harry looked all around the room until his eyes came upon his newfound love. "Our next storyteller will be Allison, our cloth maker from Bath!"

The entire room came alive with applause as the woman from Bath stood and faced the room. She had a lovely smile, not afraid to show the wide gap between her two front teeth. She waited for the applause to end and started. "Ladies and gentlemen," she began. "Since I was but twelve years old, I have had five husbands at the Church's door. All were fine men, called to God before their time, I assure you. But having been married five times, I believe I have the experience and the authority to speak of the troubles in marriage." Allison spoke in a sweet way, and even if one did not agree with her words, her sweet smile and good sense of humor drew her audience to her subject.

The room became very quiet for it was understood that Allison, the woman from Bath, was going to touch on subjects not spoken of in mixed company. It was plain to see that she had indulged in some wine, but so had most of her audience. The audience was primed for a good story and only hoped Allison could deliver.

Allison knew the rules of the Church. The Church did not discourage marriage outwardly, but in subtle sermons mentioned that the path to heaven was better paved with those who focused more of the sacred part of life rather than being bogged down with marriage. It was a hypocrisy the Church preached, for many of its own sacred clergy indulged in sex and unholy unions. But having been married and widowed five times, Allison felt it was her time to tell the clergy in the audience that marriage was not against God or the Bible.

Allison challenged the clergy in her audience, "Show me a text where God forbade marriage. Show it to me. Let me see it! Thank God, I married five. Welcome the sixth whenever he comes. When a husband of mine has gone from this world, some other Christian man will take me on. So says the apostle, I am free to wed in God's name whoever I please. He says it's not a sin to marry."

Suddenly, the pardoner stood up and said, "Madam, by God and by St. John, that is noble talk. No one could surpass such preaching. I was about to take a wife recently. Alas! But why would I enter into a union that would punish my flesh? I have decided there would be no marriage for me this year."

The crowd laughed at the pardoner's comments mostly because the pardoner was drunk, and the crowd highly doubted the man had a female interested in marrying the likes of him.

"You wait, sir," Allison went on. "My story has not yet begun. You will taste another brew before my tale is done. In that time, you will hear of all the tribulations man and wife can have. I believe I am an expert, and after you hear my tale, you can decide if you want to drink from this barrel called 'marriage'."

The pardoner said, "Madam, I put it to you as a request. Please continue your story. Instruct us younger men in your technique."

The last comment brought more laughter, especially when the pardoner addressed himself as a "younger" man. He was probably the same age as Allison.

"Gladly, "Allison replied. "I will go on, since it pleases you. But I must say to the company, I beg you not to be vexed by my opinions. Please do not be offended by my views. I offer them only to amuse the company."

She stopped, and the crowd applauded. Allison smiled at Harry Bailly, who encouraged her to continue.

"Now, gentlemen, I will tell my tale. And as I hope to drink fine wine, I'll tell the truth. Of the husbands I married, three were good and two were bad. The three good ones were rich and old. They could hardly keep up with me. I held them in the palm of my hand. Listen, I will tell you how I held them in my hand. You knowing women can understand what I say. To hold a husband in the palm of your hand, you must first put him in the wrong and out of hand. No one, no man that I know of, can be as bold as a woman can at telling lies and swearing as a woman can. A knowing wife, if she is worth anything, can always prove her husband is at fault."

The crowd laughed again. Allison was in her element speaking to a crowd of eager listeners who were very interested in her topic, the relationship between a man and a woman. Although she claimed to be an expert, Allison surprised some of the audience by revealing how she used sex to control her husbands, a subject not spoken aloud in mixed company. And even though the subject was forbidden, it was also the most interesting. And so she continued, all eyes and ears upon her, as more wine and ale were served.

Finally, after telling of her experience in marriage, she finally began her tale about a knight who must search for the answer to the question: What do women most desire?

In the end, her tale was well-received. The crowd inside The Swan applauded loudly for the entertaining hour the woman from Bath had entertained them. There was great clamor and discussion when Allison was finished. Each table seemed to have several opinions about her torrid topic.

Harry arose to make an announcement before the discussions ran too deeply. "Ladies and gentlemen. A hand for our dear lady of Bath. If the men in the audience paid strict attention, they may have learned something!"

The crowd, having drunk a sufficient amount of wine and ale, laughed and applauded.

Harry added, "We leave at dawn in the morrow, good pilgrims. We have a long day. Be aware of the time, and I will see you in the morrow."

He and Allison left the tavern, arm in arm.

Others began to leave. The five guildsmen left as a group, nonchalantly walking out together. As they left, Sir Robert nodded to Thomas, who walked over to the table where the guildsmen had been sitting. Thomas studied the table and returned to his father.

"Their ale cups are still full," Thomas said. His father nodded and watched the door in which the men left.

"Father," Anglicus said, seemingly drunk. "Will you hear my confession?"

Merek was not feeling well. His head hurt, and he was suddenly tired and achy. He must have drunk more ale than he had thought. "Perhaps, tomorrow, Anglicus, when our heads are clearer," Merek said painfully.

"Please, Father Merek. It will not take long. There is something I want to get off my chest. I will sleep better tonight. Please, Father."

"Very well. Come, let's find a quiet spot." Merek had a hard time focusing. He was sleepy, and his mind was swirling. With great effort, he addressed Chaucer and the doctor, "Good night, gentlemen. See you in the morrow."

Merek did not hear the men's responses for it was awkward for him to get up from the table. Anglicus helped Merek and guided him out a side door of the tavern. Merek felt himself stumbling as Anglicus kept talking quietly about confessing his sins and how it would help his soul. Before Merek knew what was happening, the two men had left the grounds of The Swan and were walking on a desolate alley away from The Swan.

They came to a run-down barn where Anglicus guided Merek in through the back door. Merek was completely out of sorts when they entered the barn. His head was swimming, and he only wanted to sleep. How much ale did he drink?

"This will do, Father Merek," Anglicus said. He got down on his knees and said quietly, "Bless me father for I have sinned."

At that moment, Merek was struck in the back by a wooden board. He fell immediately, unconscious and thankful for the much-awaited sleep.

CHAPTER 25

THE KIDNAPPING

When Father Colman awoke, it was still dark, especially in the room he shared with his brother and the other clergy. Father Colman needed to use the privy and was worried that if used the pot in the room, he would awaken the others. So he took it upon himself to make his way to the privy located outside the tavern.

Father Colman exited the room and instantly felt the chill of the cold spring morning. He wondered what time it was and guessed it must be close to the time of matins, prayers said at sunrise. He was surprised by how dark it was in the hallway leading from the clergy room to the outside. He used his outstretched arms as a guide as he slowly made his way down the hallway. As Father Colman passed the room that housed the female clergy, he noticed there was a body lying on the floor.

Not thinking too much of the still body, he stepped over it, his foot splattering a liquid around the body. *Oh my God,* he thought. *The poor drunk has wet himself. What a mess.* Without another thought, the parson kept going and made his way out the door and past the courtyard to the back of the tavern and the privy. Fortunately, the privy to the hostelry had a customary candle lit that would help the customers for such an occasion. As he relieved himself in the privy, he thought it quite strange there was no other movement in the hostelry. Perhaps it was earlier in the night than he thought.

As Father Colman finished his business, he buttoned his cassock. His eyes fell to his boots, still wet from the puddle around the man lying on the floor in the darkened hallway. Father Colman looked a little closer to his boots. Taking the candle from its holder, he used the light to check on the wetness of his boots. As he bent over with the candle, he did a double take. A red liquid had stained his boots. And then it dawned on him—blood! He had stepped in a puddle of blood!

Father Colman did not put the candle back in its holder. Carefully guarding the flame, he hurried from the back of the tavern, crossed the courtyard and into the hallway leading to the guest bedrooms. Just outside the lady clergy's room, he knelt down with the candle and examined the man lying in a puddle of blood. With a gasp, Father Colman saw the dead man was Father Towns. His throat had been cut so deeply that his head was barely attached to his body. Upon seeing the gruesome cut, Father Colman gasped and vomited to the side of the body.

"Help," he pleaded, but his voice came as a whisper. "Help," he tried again. Still a dull whisper. He blessed himself then blessed the corpse. "Help," he said a little louder. And then, "Help" in his normal voice.

The hallway was still dark and quiet. No one stirred.

"Help!" he suddenly shouted. "Dear God, someone help me!"

Finally, there was movement. His brother heard him and made his way down the darkened hallway as quickly as he could.

"Leo, what is it?" Anthony asked. "What do we have here?"

"Evidence of the devil's evil, brother," was all Leo Colman said. He gave the candle to his brother to look upon the dead body.

Other feet were heard.

"What goes on, I say?" Harry Bailly arrived, buttoning his trousers. He looked down and saw what Anthony Colman was looking at. "Dear God, what has happened? Brewse! Brewse!"

There were more feet converging on the noise. Other pilgrims were awakening and making their way to the hallway. Soon, Walter Brewse arrived.

"Get the constable, Walter," Harry said. "There is murder here."

"Dear God," Walter Brewse said, blessing himself and running down the hallway. As he exited the building, he could be heard shouting to his attendants to get the local lawman.

"Father Towns, poor bloody man," Harry said. "What the hell happened do you suppose?"

No one said a word.

"Is it odd that he should lie dead in front of the room for the lady clergy?" Judge Gates asked, standing in the crowded hallway.

"Father Towns posted himself outside the prioress's sleeping quarters last night. He felt it was his duty to protect the lady prioress from all danger," Father Smithton said, kneeling down beside the body and blessing himself.

"Maybe that is why he is dead," Judge Gates said.

The men suddenly looked at the door that led into the room for the lady clergy.

Harry took the lead and knocked gently. He knocked again. No answer. "Who roomed with the lady prioress last night?" Judge Gates asked in front of the many bystanders. By now, the majority of the pilgrims had made their way to the hallway next to the lady clergy's room.

Father Smithton answered, "Along with Lady Prioress, there was Sister Anne. And I assume that, since Allison, the woman of Bath, was the only other lady on our trip, she would be in the room too."

Harry quickly said, "The woman of Bath had other arrangements tonight. She was not in the room." Harry immediately felt embarrassment for his admission to where she truly stayed, but no one commented or actually thought anything of his comment. They were too horrified by the scene in front of them.

Harry took the candle from Father Colman and opened the door to the room where the lady clergy slept. He walked in and was followed by Father Smithton. Judge Gates entered also but told the others to stay out. He had a voice that convinced the others to listen.

Sunrise had begun, and a faint light was beginning to show in the sky. The coolness of the morning had not left yet, but no one in the hallway or in the room that housed the lady clergy seemed to notice. All were too horrified by the sight of a dead priest to think about the coldness of the morning.

Inside the room, Harry looked at the bed in which the lady prioress slept. It was empty. There was no sign of her. It was as if she had never slept there. None of her belongings were seen. If she had nightclothes, they were not found. Even though the room could have housed up to eight women, there had only been the prioress and Sister Anne. Sister Anne was there.

Sister Anne was tied at the ankles and wrists. She had a gag in her mouth, and when Harry approached her, she screamed through her gag. Even when she saw it was Harry Bailly, her hysterics did not end. She cried and screamed as Father Smithton and Harry untied her.

Before Father Smithton tried to calm Sister Anne, he noticed she had a blackened eye and a swollen cheek on the side of her scarred face. Evidently, her attackers had knocked her unconscious before they tied her up. Father Smithton tried to calm her and had to resort to holding her close to get her to calm down.

"They took her!" Sister Anne screamed. "They took her!"

"Who, Sister Anne, who?" Harry asked.

Sister Anne only whimpered as Father Smithton tried to comfort her. Sister Anne cried into Father Smithton's arms, scared, hurt and feeling as though she had not done her duty in protecting the prioress.

Finally, she calmed herself to say, "I cannot say who, but there were a few men in this room. It was dark. They barged in the room before we knew what happened. They took the lady prioress before I could help her," she cried. "I did not do my duty, Father," she cried to Father Smithton.

"Oh, Sister Anne, it was not your fault," Father Smithton said, trying to console her.

"Sister Anne, you can help us," Judge Gates interjected, "by telling us more. Think. Tell us what you saw or heard."

Sister Anne cried some more but tried to regain her composure.

"The men came in and gagged the lady prioress and myself. I heard the one man say to the prioress, 'Come quietly, and we will not hurt the nun. One loud word from you and my man will slit her throat. Do you understand?' Apparently, the lady prioress agreed, for they did not cut my throat. The men made her dress, gathered up all her belongings, and left with her. Before they left, one of the men took me aside and punched me, knocking me out so they could get away cleanly. That is all I remember, sir," Sister Anne said, beginning to cry again.

"What do you think, Judge?" Harry asked Judge Gates.

"I think we need to assemble in the tavern," the judge said.

"Let me in!" Sir Robert shouted outside the room. A path was cleared, and he entered the room. "Harry, what goes on here?"

"I am afraid it is bad news, Sir Robert. Madam Prioress seems to have been abducted. The crime is compounded by the murder of good Father Towns and the assault on Sister Anne," Harry answered.

Sir Robert said nothing, but his mind was churning.

"I agree with Judge Gates. We should assemble the group in the tavern. Has the local constable been summoned?" Sir Robert asked.

"Aye, Sir Robert," Harry answered.

"See to that woman, Father," Sir Robert said of Sister Anne. "You men, get a litter, and get the body out of the hallway. Take him to the courtyard for the constable to inspect."

There was a scuffle of footsteps as the men complied with Sir Robert's orders.

***

Earlier in the middle of the night, Thaddeus and his men had made their move. Thaddeus had paid Walter Brewse for a private room where the five guildsmen were to sleep. The room was perfect for the plan. Thaddeus and his men were isolated from the rest of the pilgrims. They were able to put their plan in action without worrying about sneaking out of a crowded room of sleeping pilgrims.

At four o'clock, there was a stillness in the air. It was cold and dark. Not a sound was heard. And the five guildsmen were on the move. The youngest, Jack, was assigned to gather the horses. His job was to ready them for the quick departure. Once the prioress was kidnapped, the men would need a swift getaway. Thaddeus had chosen Jack, not because he was the youngest, but he was the best man to handle the horses. It would be important that the gathering of the horses would not cause a stir. Jack had a talent of calming animals, particularly horses.

The private room in which the guildsmen stayed was in a separate building from where the other pilgrims slept. The private building was opposite the tavern. Thaddeus and his men quietly exited their room, went down the narrow stairway that led to the courtyard by the tavern. It was here that Thaddeus posted his second man, David, with a longbow. David's assignment was twofold. One was to be a lookout for the group. The second was to cover the group's exit once they had the prioress. David had been an archer in the king's army and was proficient with the longbow.

Thaddeus and his two companions entered the building that was housing the majority of the pilgrims. Thaddeus knew, in a general way, where the prioress was sleeping. He had asked the innkeeper which room he could have for his guildsmen in the building where the majority of the pilgrims were to be housed. Without knowing, Walter Brewse had given Thaddeus the information he wanted.

"So you want to room just for your men?" Walter asked Thaddeus, who had requested a private room in the building where the pilgrims were to sleep.

"Yes, Master Brewse. Do you have such a room?" Thaddeus asked.

"Let me see," Walter Brewse answered, thinking aloud. "The lady clergy have the first room. The male clergy will have the second room. I will house the nobles in the third room, and some of the commoners will be put in the fourth room. The others will sleep in the loft of the barn. Come to think of it, sir, I do not have such a room in that building. But I do have a room elsewhere on my property."

With the knowledge that the prioress was in the first room, Thaddeus and his two companions crept toward the first room. Stopping outside the door, Thaddeus paused. He had heard a noise. His companions did the same. Backing against the wall, the kidnappers stood like statues. They waited. The noise had ceased.

Thaddeus took a breath and moved toward the door of the room in which the prioress slept. Just as he stepped forward, a figure appeared. The hallway was dark, so the figure did not see the men approaching the door. The figure inadvertently bumped into Thaddeus, just as Thaddeus was about to open the door. The figure was a man, a big man.

The figure did not say a word but merely grunted. Thaddeus, taken by surprise by the sudden encounter, froze. The man pushed Thaddeus against the wall, his strong hands grasping for the neck of Thaddeus. Thaddeus, known by his men as a man with strength, could feel the strength of the hands around his neck. For his part, Thaddeus did not panic. Thaddeus was sure it was one of the priests who travelled with the prioress. It was the short, thick priest who hung behind the prioress in the pilgrim's procession to Canterbury. He was not concerned about his physical well-being. His real concern was creating a clamor that would awaken all the other pilgrims.

The priest finally had a firm grasp of Thaddeus's neck and was beginning to squeeze it. Suddenly, there was a spray of blood in Thaddeus's face. At the same time of the sudden warm spray of blood, the taunt grip of the priest lessened. And then it let go. The priest fell to the floor without a noise, for the other two kidnappers had grabbed his sagging body and eased its fall. Benjamin, one of Thaddeus's men, dagger in hand, dripping with blood, helped his comrade lower the dead priest to the ground. He had used the knife to slice the priest's neck wide open. The attack on Thaddeus was unexpected, and in the darkness of the hallway, Benjamin had cut into the priest's neck too deeply, almost slicing the man's head off.

The intruders stood silently next to the fallen body. They waited in silence, listening to any movement that would endanger their mission. Satisfied that their mission was not compromised, Thaddeus opened the door to the room where the prioress slept. He entered, and his two companions followed, shutting the heavy door behind them without a noise.

The room had no light and was even darker than the hallway in which they had just left. Thaddeus knew they had to find the prioress, gag her and spirit her away now. Someone would encounter the body of the dead priest in the hallway at any time. The kidnappers stood statue still, trying to hear the breathing of the sleeping occupants. Thaddeus could only hear the quiet but gentle breathing of one of the occupants in the room. He knew there were at least two or three. Why could he only hear one?

"Someone is awake," he whispered to his men.

There was a sudden shriek and movement in one of the corners of the room. Benjamin was the closest to the sound and grabbed the woman who was desperately trying to get up from her pallet. He grabbed the lady and pinned her to the palate with his body, his hand covering her mouth. She tried to scream and break his hold, but he was too strong.

"I have a knife and will use it if any noise comes from your mouth," he whispered. "Do you understand? Nod your head."

Sister Anne was terrified. She had been awakened by the strange noises in the hallway. When the men entered the room, she had pretended to be asleep. Panic set in, and she made a rush for the door. And now one of the intruders was lying on top of her, threatening to kill her if she made a noise.

"Do you understand?" he whispered again.

She nodded. Although he could not see her very well, he could feel her head nod.

Thaddeus had found the bed in which the prioress slept. Kneeling down, he covered the mouth of the prioress. She opened her eyes, still heavy with sleep. Suddenly, her eyes darted open, wide awake at the man beside her with his hand over her mouth. She attempted to scream, but the kidnapper's hand muffled the volume of her shriek.

"Do as I say, Sister, and you will not be harmed," Thaddeus said quietly. By now, he knew there were no others in the room.

The prioress tried to scream again, but Thaddeus increased the pressure on his hand over the woman's mouth, muffling it. His hand continued to press harder on her mouth. Using his other hand, he dug his finger against her throat, instantly causing pain to the woman.

The prioress felt the pain and tried to cry out, but the man was now almost on top of her muffling the noise.

"Listen to me. Listen," he said quietly as she struggled to get his hand away from her face. "My man will kill your companion if you make another sound. Do you hear me?"

The prioress said nothing but continued to struggle.

"Bring her here," Thaddeus ordered.

Benjamin grabbed Sister Anne and pulled her to her feet. With force, he shoved her toward the bed where Thaddeus had the prioress. She fell beside the bed. Sister Anne was so frightened she could not speak or cry out. In an instant, Benjamin lifted her to her knees and put his knife to her throat.

"You see, Sister? Look closely," Thaddeus asked. "Make a sound, and she dies."

Even though it was dark in the room, the prioress could see the figure of Sister Anne beside her. She could not really see Sister Anne's face, but if she had, she would have seen a terrified face.

The prioress stopped struggling and lay in silence.

"I am going to take my hand away," Thaddeus said. "If you cry out, she dies. And maybe you too. Do you understand?"

The prioress nodded. Thaddeus slowly took his hand away, yet kept it close in case she did try to cry out.

"What do you want?" the prioress asked.

"You," Thaddeus answered. "You are coming with us. If you cooperate, no harm will come to her."

"And what is to become of me?" the prioress asked.

"We are taking you with us. That is all you need to know. No harm will come to you either if you do not fight us."

"How do I know that? How do I know that you intend to harm or kill me?" she asked.

"Sister, if I wanted to kill you, you would already be dead," Thaddeus said, getting up from the bed. "Tie her up," he said to Benjamin, meaning Sister Anne. To the prioress, "Put on your habit, Sister, you are going for a ride."

"But my thing," she protested.

Thaddeus did not answer her but guided her to the door as she struggled to get the long habit on. Benjamin had finished tying and gagging Sister Anne. He laid her on the bed gently. He lifted her head gently then quickly punched her below the eye, knocking her out. "Sorry, Sister," he said quietly.

The third kidnapper opened the door and made sure the hallway was clear.

"Clear," he said, turning his head toward his comrades.

Thaddeus pulled the prioress close.

"Remember, one word, one sound, one noise from you, and the young nun will die. And so will you. Understand?"

The prioress nodded.

Thaddeus took her by the arm and led her out into the hallway. Led by the lookout, Thaddeus followed with the prioress. Benjamin brought up the rear. After carefully stepping over the dead Father Towns, they made their way down the corridor and outside. They crossed the courtyard and made their way to the stables, where Jack had the horses ready. Jack knew which horse the prioress had ridden on the trip, and that horse was waiting too.

David, bow in hand, joined as the men mounted the horses.

"Sister, if you cooperate, you can ride sitting up," Thaddeus said quickly. "Or I can tie you up and lay you across the saddle. Which will it be?"

The prioress hesitated, then put her hand out. Thaddeus took it and helped her mount her horse.

Without another word, the men left with the prioress. At first, they walked the horses away from the inn. Once they had gone a little way, they quickened their pace and made their way out of town.

CHAPTER 26

TORTURE IN THE BARN

Oswald had passed Thaddeus's advice on to Anglicus concerning the size of Merek Willson. Anglicus assured Oswald that he could handle the large priest himself and that the deed would be fulfilled. But after having observed the large priest for a day, Anglicus had decided he might need some help.

In Dartford, Anglicus searched for a place to hurt the priest. It had to be close to The Swan and private, yet far enough away that screams could not be heard. The pain he was going to inflict on the priest was going to be the cause of intense screaming, even if the victim was going to be gagged. It did not take Anglicus long to find an old barn two blocks from The Swan that would suit his needs.

As a bonus, the owner of the barn had a brother. Anglicus hired the owner of the barn and his brother to help with the priest. Anglicus would drug the priest and bring him to the barn. There, the hired brothers would knock the priest out, help Anglicus tie him up to a central beam in the barn and then make themselves scarce. When Anglicus inflicted his pain on the priest, he did not want an audience.

Merek was in a deep sleep. He was dreaming of Thea. In his dream, the couple stood in a grassy field outside the village. They were face-to-face so close he could feel her breath. Merek kept staring into Thea's beautiful eyes, wanting to kiss and to hold her. She smiled at him, moving closer so their lips could touch. As they held each other and kissed, Merek could smell wild lilacs that surrounded the couple in the open field. Merek felt an overwhelming happiness as they kissed. There were no worries about God, the priesthood, and his holy orders. It was only Merek and Thea.

In the dream, it began to rain. Merek and Thea were embracing for another kiss when a flood of water separated the two lovers. At first, Merek did not realize the cause of the sudden flood of water. It was not rain. And then he slowly awoke. Someone had taken a bucket of water and drenched him with it. Merek spit and coughed, for some of the water had gone up his nose and into his throat.

He tried to open his eyes, but it was hard. His coughing and gagging from the water quickened his awakening, and he opened his eyes, not knowing where he was. He tried to use his hands to rid the water from his eyes and face, but they were bound behind him to the beam in which he was tied. Merek tried to move his legs but discovered they were bound too.

"Did you have a nice sleep, Father?" Anglicus asked. The dagger that hung around his neck was now in his hand.

Merek did not answer, his mind still foggy from the drug slipped into his ale. He blinked his eyes, trying to get them to focus on his surroundings. He saw two lights, two candles burning at either end of the barn in which he was tied. Merek could smell the old hay thinly scattered on the barn floor all around him. There were no animals in the stalls of the barn, and by the looks of it, there had not been animals in the barn for a long time. The candle at the other end of the barn was lit and attached to a thick oaken beam. Merek was tied to another oaken beam at the other end of the barn. He saw a lit candle on a post at one of the stalls. The barn had a low ceiling; the place was in need of a general demolishing.

Merek's wit was coming back now. He was in a barn, tied to a beam. And then it all came back to him. Anglicus needed a confession. The men leaving The Swan. After that, he could not remember how he got to this barn and how he was tied to a beam. Why was he tied to a beam?

"You did not like the penance I gave you?" Merek said, coming out of his drugged state. "You tied me up, for the penance was too harsh?"

Anglicus gave a genuine laugh. "No, Father, there never was a confession, so to speak."

"Then what is the meaning of this?" Merek answered, understanding that he was in danger. His adrenalin was beginning to fire his body and enable him to become sober much faster. "Have I wronged you, sir?"

"Me? No, not in the least, Father," Anglicus replied. "Actually, I enjoy your company, Merek."

"Then why I am bound to a beam?"

"Pain, Father. I am about to inflict pain on you," Anglicus replied, punching Merek squarely in the ribs on his left side.

Merek tried to double over from the blow to the ribs, but the bindings did not let him. He gave a grunt of pain and felt the heat of anger rising in him. Before he knew it, Anglicus hit him again in the same area, this time using the butt end of his dagger. Merek grunted again, his head flooded with pain.

"Aye, it hurts, Father?" Anglicus smiled. "We are only getting started, I assure you. When I am finished with you, you will beg me to kill you."

"Why?" Merek asked, trying to catch his breath. As he spoke, he tried to work the bindings of his hands. If he could just get them to loosen, he might be able to set himself free. They were tight. Whoever tied him to the beam knew how to tie a knot. It dawned on Merek that a sailor could tie such a knot.

Anglicus came close to Merek and began to unbutton his robe.

"Let's see what pain we can conjure from inside your cassock, Father," Anglicus said.

"Why do you do this?" Merek asked. He looked at Anglicus, who seemed to be enjoying the moment.

With Merek's chest exposed, Anglicus took his dagger and drew a thin line across Merek's chest. Blood began to trickle where the fine cut was made. Merek winced in pain, fully sober now, all his faculties working. He tugged at his bindings, but could not free himself. His anger was causing his adrenalin to surge through his body.

"I say again. Why? Why me?" Merek spit out quietly with anger, feeling his blood trickle from the eight-inch cut on his chest. The cut was not deep, but drew blood and caused pain to Merek.

Anglicus smiled and drew close to Merek. "A Father Gilbert Berners wanted me to say hello for him."

"Berners? You know Berners?"

"Never met the man, I assure you," Anglicus said suddenly, punching Merek squarely in the stomach.

Merek grunted with pain but could not double up because of the bindings. When he looked up, Anglicus punched him on the side of the face.

"No, I never met this Father Berners. But he must hate you for some reason, Father. He hired me to hurt you, and hurt you badly. In fact, he gave me permission to kill you, if I choose," Anglicus said, looking at his dagger and then at Merek.

Blood was rushing from Merek's mouth. He spit at Anglicus, hitting him in the chest.

"Get on with it then, you murderer!" Merek yelled, his words slurring due to the blood.

"It puzzles me, Father. I must admit. You Christians speak about love for your neighbor, yet I am hired by a priest to hurt, maim, and possibly kill another priest. Does that make sense? Is this world mad?"

"Get on with it!" Merek yelled, trying to move toward the assassin. Because of his size, strength, and anger, the beam moved slightly with his effort. Merek immediately pushed back against the beam, causing it to rock slightly. It was a movement only Merek could feel.

Anglicus held his dagger for Merek to see.

"Yes, we shall get on with it, as you shall see," Anglicus said. "There is a custom amongst men of my trade to take a trinket, a small item to remember a special occasion. Since this is a special occasion, I hope you will understand."

Without warning, Anglicus put his left hand to Merek's face and turned it away. Swiftly, he took his dagger and cut off Merek's left ear. Anglicus's dagger was not sharp, so the cutting of the ear was not only painful, but did not take the entire ear. Merek let out a loud scream. Anglicus let go of Merek's face and stepped back, showing Merek the souvenir he took from Merek.

"Now, we can begin to get to work, Father." Anglicus smiled. "But if you are going to scream and shout, I shall have to remedy that."

Anglicus pulled out a rag. He approached Merek and roughly used the rag to gag the bleeding priest. Anglicus went around to the back of the beam to tie the gag to Merek. As he stepped behind Merek to tie the gag, Merek pushed back with all his might, trying to cause the ancient beam to fall. The beam creaked for a moment and then suddenly gave way. Anglicus felt the beam giving way and stepped back as the beam fell toward him, Merek still attached. As the beam went down, part of the small roof of the barn came with it.

Anglicus had stepped away from the falling beam, but he could not escape the part of the roof that fell. Although it was mostly a thatched roof, it was interspersed with boards. The combination of boards and thatch fell on Anglicus, knocking him to the ground.

Lying on the ground with the beam to his back, Merek was able to free his legs from the broken support. Kicking fiercely, the bindings on his legs came free. As Anglicus struggled to get himself free of the fallen roof, Merek began to shinny himself toward the broken end of the beam. With his legs free, Merek could use his leverage to work himself to the broken end of the oaken support.

Anglicus freed himself from the fallen roof as Merek was freeing his hands from the bindings that loosened as he made his way to the end of the beam. Merek was bleeding from his chest, mouth, and ear. His body ached from the vicious punches he took, and his ear would not stop bleeding, but his anger and adrenalin were hiding his aches and pains. He did not care about the blood.

Merek cleared the rest of the bindings as Anglicus approached him with his dagger in his hand. They went to the center of the barn where there was minimal damage from the fallen beam. As Anglicus approached, Merek looked for protection.

"Seems I will have to kill you now," Anglicus said. He and Merek began a slow circle of defense.

"You can also leave," Merek said.

"Afraid I cannot. I have made a deal. I must finish the contract."

Wiping blood from his mouth, Merek felt the wound to his ear. "Was hoping you would stay." As he circled, Merek spotted a fallen plank and picked it up. He spat more blood from his mouth. "Want to warn you. I do not fight fair."

Anglicus moved in with his drawn dagger. He feigned a wide sweep and brought the dagger in for an upper stab meant for Merek's abdomen. Merek moved the plank toward the wide sweep but was quick enough to ward off the sudden upper sweep. The board checked the dagger's thrust. Anglicus backed away, seeking another way to attack the wounded priest.

Merek decided to go on the offensive. Plank in hand, he moved quickly toward Anglicus. Concentrating on the dagger, Merek used the plank as a shield. Anglicus, surprised by the sudden counterattack, panicked and made a wild thrust with the dagger. Merek saw it coming and hammered down on the wrist of Anglicus. The dagger flew to the near wall of the barn.

Merek heard footsteps. It was the owner of the barn and his brother.

"Help me, and I will pay you handsomely," Anglicus told the men.

Both men looked at each other and nodded. They began to spread out, taking daggers from their belts. Anglicus was still holding his wrist from the plank impacting on it. He stood directly in front of Merek. The two other men walked to either side of Anglicus.

"I fear you have broken my wrist, Father," Anglicus said. "But now, with my two new friends, I believe I will be able to accomplish my task."

"No need for you to get hurt," Merek said to the two men as blood continued to escape from his mouth and ear. His ribs hurt from the blows, and his chest ached from the cut inflicted by Anglicus, but he was still furious about the threat on his life. And to think Berners had ordered it!

"Quite correct, sirs," another voice spoke behind the attackers. "Leave now, and there will be no retribution." The attackers turned and saw that Geoffrey Chaucer had entered the barn. His sword was drawn, and he was slowly moving toward the attackers.

"Master Chaucer! So glad you could join us," Merek said, feeling instant relief.

Chaucer approached the man on his left, who turned and faced Chaucer. The other two men directed their attack on Merek.

"Here is the thing, my good man," Chaucer said to his opponent. "You have a dagger. I have a sword. Unless you are adept in throwing the dagger, I suggest you run from this place."

The attacker looked at Chaucer, then at his brother and Anglicus. Chaucer continued to slowly walk toward his opponent, forcing the issue. Taking the dagger, he threw it wildly at Chaucer. Chaucer ducked but did not have to, for it was a wild throw and did not come close to his person. And now the attacker was trapped, for Chaucer stood between the man, and the only way out of the collapsed barn.

"Down!" Chaucer yelled. "Lie flat on your face, you cur! Or I shall make swift work of you!"

The man obeyed and fell to his knees. Chaucer used the tip of his sword to urge the man to lie on his stomach.

The other attacker and Anglicus went after Merek. The man who owned the barn attacked first. Using the board, Merek swung freely, catching the attacker on the side of the arm in which he held the dagger. Upon hitting the attacker, Merek quickly used the plank to ward off a swing by Anglicus, catching him in the chest and knocking him to the ground. Merek swiftly went to the owner of the barn and used the plank to ward off his thrusting dagger.

Taking the plank from its end, he shoved it into the belly of the attacker. As the man doubled over, he took the plank and smacked him soundly on the head, sending him to the floor in a heap. Merek immediately went after Anglicus, who had gotten to his feet. At that moment, Anglicus wished to escape and run for his life, but Chaucer, sword in hand and standing over his prisoner, blocked his escape.

Anglicus backed up to the nearest wall. Merek approached him, plank still in hand.

"Who was your agent?" Merek asked.

"Agent?" Anglicus answered.

"You said you never met Berners. Yet, you were hired to hurt or kill me. Who was your contact?"

"I am not at liberty to say, Father," Anglicus answered, still holding his broken wrist.

"You will tell me what I want to know," Merek said.

"And if I do not?" Anglicus said confidently, knowing that a priest would not truly hurt him.

"Do you understand I was not always a priest?" Merek said quietly but with force. He was beginning to feel wary from the pain and the blood loss. There would be time to question Anglicus. The adrenalin was beginning to wear off.

"Master Chaucer," Merek said, directing his attention to Chaucer. "How did you find me?"

Chaucer continued to hold his sword over his prisoner lying on the floor.

"Luck, I suppose. I have been searching for you for hours. I must say the barn roof collapsing helped immensely," Chaucer said.

"But how did you know to look?" Merek asked.

"Believe it or not, it was our dinner companion, Richard Howard, the physician. After you left with Anglicus, he told me that he had sold a sedative to Anglicus, who had told the doctor that he was having trouble sleeping. At the end of the night, Father Merek, you seemed to have had too much to drink, yet I did not see you drink that much ale. Anglicus asking for a confession late in the evening seemed strange. It was Howard who suggested to me that you were drugged.

"I began to follow you from the tavern but was accosted by the drunken summoner and pardoner. I could not escape them. The summoner kept blabbering in Latin, *questio vid juris, questio vid juris*. By the time I escaped their company, I lost you into the darkness of the night."

"I thank God you arrived when you did, Geoffrey. I will be forever in your debt," Merek said, still close to Anglicus, who was trapped against the wall. Now he turned to Anglicus, feeling a small burst of energy. "You have injured me and have threatened my life. I want to know your contact."

"This is not a confessional. I will not tell." Anglicus managed with a smile.

Merek threw the plank aside and charged Anglicus. He grabbed the shipman by the throat and lifted him from the ground. His ribs, chest, and stomach ached from the wounds inflicted earlier, but he was angry and wanted answers.

"You think I am a priest and will turn the other cheek?" Merek said, not caring that his spittle, filled with blood was splashing the face of his enemy. He punched Anglicus in the stomach, then stood him up, and punched him again in the face.

Anglicus fell to the floor with a thud.

"I need to know who ordered my torture and death, Master Chaucer," Merek said, trying to explain his plight to Chaucer.

"By all means, Father Merek. Do what you must," Chaucer replied, still standing over his prisoner.

Merek picked Anglicus to his feet and pressed him to the wall.

"Give me the name of your contact, and I will show you mercy," Merek said slowly face-to-face with his enemy.

"I will not. I know you cannot hurt me. You are a priest," Anglicus said.

"Enlighten me," Merek said, holding Anglicus tightly and pressing the pressure points in his neck. "Tell me how a man like you knows so much about the priesthood."

Anglicus grunted with the pain. He could not understand the strength in the priest's hands. The grip was unlike anything he had ever encountered. As Merek slowly tightened his grip, Anglicus could feel his breath beginning to become more and more shallow. Merek was going to choke him to death.

"I need a name," Merek whispered, slowly using his large hands to choke Anglicus to death.

Anglicus knew fear. It was a professional hazard in stealing goods from customers who had threatened him for the misdeeds he had committed. Yet, he had never been at arm's length facing death as he did now. This large priest was going to kill him. His mind told him the priest would not kill him, but after seeing the look in the priest's eyes, he knew his mind was wrong. He was going to die.

He nodded to Merek that he would talk. Merek loosened his grip and lowered the shipman.

"Oswald, the reeve," the shipman said, gasping for breath. "He was the contact. He set the price. He made the arrangements."

Merek loosened his grip. He had his answer. Even though he wanted to hurt this assassin more, his good senses were beginning to come to grips with his torture and hurt. No, do not kill this man. Turn him over to the authorities. Let them deal with him.

He removed his hand from the assassin. Anglicus felt immediate relief as he fell to the floor below Merek.

Suddenly, Merek grabbed him again, pulled him to his feet, and thrust him back against the wall. He drew the shipman close, so close the blood from Merek's face smeared on Anglicus.

"I want it back!" he said with anger. "My ear!"

Anglicus lowered his hand and pulled the piece of ear from his pocket. He held it up to the smothering priest. Merek took the ear, looked at it, and punched the shipman as hard as he could in the stomach. The shipman went down with a heavy thud, gagging over the sudden loss of air in his body.

"We will turn the three over to the local constable," he said to Chaucer. "Let them deal with the assault."

Chaucer nodded, still standing over his prisoner lying prone on the ground. He looked over at the fallen owner of the barn. That man did not move.

"You will need to see Doctor Howard when we get back to The Swan," Chaucer said to Merek.

"Aye," Merek said, still debating on what to do with the assassin. The adrenalin was wearing off, and he was beginning to feel the pain from his ribs, his chest, ear, and face. His cassock was torn, and there was blood from his wound to the chest, ear, and mouth.

"What kind of priest are you?" Anglicus muttered, finally regaining his breath. He was still holding his broken wrist. His neck was already showing the deep bruise marks from Merek's large hands.

"Not a very good one," Merek answered. "God forgive me."

Using his sword, Chaucer made his prisoner rise from the dirt floor of the barn. He directed him to the area where Anglicus sat. Then he went over the unconscious owner of the barn and turned him over. The man was still out cold.

"I am going for help, Father. Thought it best if we kept them together. I shall leave you my sword," Chaucer said. "In case they try anything."

Merek went over and pulled the unconscious man by the legs and dragged him across the barn to the other prisoners. Then he picked up the plank he had used to battle Anglicus.

"Take your sword, Geoffrey. Still dark outside. You might need it," Merek said. He pointed the plank at Anglicus. "You better hope your friends here behave. If they try something, I am breaking your legs."

Anglicus said nothing, still clutching his broken wrist. He merely looked at the other conscious prisoner.

"I shall return, Father. If I can, I will bring the physician."

Chaucer left quickly and entered the street. It was still very dark. He judged the time to be around four bells. There was no one on the streets. He did not know where to find a constable, so he headed toward The Swan. The innkeeper would know what to do.

As Chaucer approached The Swan, he heard a group of horses walking away from the hostelry. He could not get a close look, for as soon as they were a short distance away, they picked up their pace and were gone. Although he did not get a close look, he counted six riders.

Someone was getting an early start.

CHAPTER 27

ORGANIZING A RESCUE

As the riders left the vicinity of The Swan, Chaucer made his way to the courtyard of the inn. He had no idea where Walter Brewse had his quarters. There was no movement in the hostelry, for it was just after half past four bells. Chaucer's mind raced as he tried to remember where the innkeeper would be staying. He knew it would be foolhardy to try to find the local constable at this early hour. He had never been to Dartford and would have gotten lost easily once out of sight of The Swan.

As Chaucer stood in the courtyard trying to decide what to do, a lonely figure approached him. Chaucer said nothing, letting the figure get closer. He had his sword and did not feel threatened in the courtyard of The Swan, but one never knew. The figure came closer.

It was Thomas, Sir Robert's son. He was making his way to the building where his father's room was located. He saw Chaucer but was not sure who it was. He slowed his pace and approached cautiously.

"Thomas?" Chaucer was first to call out. "Is that you?"

"Aye. Master Chaucer. You are up early," Thomas said politely, coming close to where Chaucer stood.

"Afraid I have not turned in yet, Thomas," Chaucer said grimly.

Thomas missed the tone of Chaucer's answer. "Nor have I," Thomas said with a smile Chaucer could not see in the dark. "I met a maiden tonight and kept her company. Felt it was my duty to keep her warm on this cool spring night."

227

"I have not been so lucky, Thomas. I need your help," Chaucer said.

Thomas recognized there was trouble in the air.

"What is it?" Thomas asked. "I am at your service, Geoffrey."

"Father Merek was attacked tonight by an assassin—" Chaucer started.

"Merek? Attacked? Is he—"

"Let me finish, lad. He is hurt. We were able to subdue his attackers. He guards them in a barn down the road. I told him I would try to get a constable, but at this hour, I know not where to look."

"Take me to this barn. I will help Father Merek until the light shall direct us to the authorities."

"Have you a weapon?"

Thomas had a dagger and showed Chaucer. Even though it was still dark, the blade scraped his belt as Thomas brought it out.

"Come then. There were three attackers. With you, we will have an equal number. I think we will escort the prisoners to The Swan."

They began to run quickly from the courtyard onto the street. Chaucer gave Thomas more of the details of the drugging, the long search, the roof collapsing, and the fight in the barn. By the time Chaucer finished with the details, they entered the barn.

Both men had their weapons drawn as they entered the barn. Chaucer hoped that Merek had not passed out, or the three men had not overpowered the priest. When he left, he felt the situation was under control, and the prisoners were injured sufficiently to make a counterattack an impossibility. He breathed a sigh of relief as he saw Merek still had the men under control.

And it dawned on him that he had not brought the physician.

"Father Merek!" Thomas said. "You are hurt and need attention." Thomas swiftly went to Anglicus who was sitting against the wall with his two confederates. Thomas kicked Anglicus in the ribs, doubling the assassin over. "I knew there was something evil about this tanned bastard." Thomas took his dagger and put it up to Anglicus's neck. "Give me a good reason not to end your worthless life right now!"

Merek could not stop the young nobleman. He was hurt, aching, and tired. His swollen cheek made it difficult for Merek to speak. He looked to Chaucer.

"We must bring him to justice, Thomas," Chaucer said, trying to calm the angered young squire. "I suggest we bind these men and march them to The Swan. At first light, we shall seek the local officials. Justice will be served, young sire."

Thomas hesitated. Having travelled with his father around the Mediterranean, he had witnessed shipmen like Anglicus before. Pirates. Brigands. Heartless bastards who stole and found safe havens at sea, in rivers and creeks. Many had no allegiance to any country. Their only loyalty was to their kind, and that was fostered with robbing and pillaging.

"We need to get Father Merek to The Swan. He needs the attention of Doctor Howard," Chaucer said, relieved that Thomas had unhanded Anglicus, pushing him back against the wall. Thomas stepped back and looked at Merek.

"Father, can you walk?" Thomas asked.

Merek nodded.

"I say we tie the two scoundrels together and leave them here. We will walk the pirate back to The Swan," Chaucer said. "The two are local. Even if they escape our bindings, they have nowhere to go. What say you, Thomas?"

"It shall be done," Thomas said, looking for something to tie the men.

The brothers were tied and bound and left in the barn. They did not bind the shipman. His one arm was useless and hung, causing him to wince in pain. He had trouble holding his head straight, injured from Merek's strong grasp. Thomas had broken the shipman's rib with his angry kick. The shipman was in pain and not going anywhere.

For his part, Merek's wounds began to heighten as his adrenalin began to subside. He had to be helped to his feet. His bruised ribs ached everytime he breathed, the cut on his chest needed cleaning, and one side of his face was swollen. His torn ear still bled. The parade to The Swan began just as the dawn was beginning.

The walk was slow. Chaucer, sword out, kept the shipman in front of him and led the men. Thomas walked with Merek and helped him whenever he felt faint from his wounds. None of the men had slept, and the walk back to The Swan reminded each man in his own way that he was tired. As dawn was beginning, there was unusual movement on the street. Men seemed to be running to and from The Swan. The flurry of men was a strange change from the solitude of the streets earlier.

The first thing Chaucer noticed as he entered the courtyard of The Swan was the noise and clamoring from within. The shouting, arguing, and loud voices were coming from inside the tavern. Chaucer guided his prisoner and the rest of the parade into the tavern. It was his hope that the innkeeper and Doctor Howard were in the tavern. He would need both.

Inside the tavern, the men crowded around the tables nearest the bar. They were shouting and arguing about the newly discovered kidnapping and murder. Each was trying to understand the crime and who was involved. Harry Bailly was attempting to keep order but found it difficult with so many opinions and guesses as to who the culprits were.

The door of the tavern opened, and Anglicus was seen. The hall became silent at the sight of the wounded man. Chaucer entered, sword drawn, followed by Father Merek and Thomas. The men in the room did not know what to say. They saw the shipman "under guard," yet physically beaten, and they saw Father Merek, face swollen, the bloodied torn ear, and his torn cassock.

"See to the priest!" Sir Robert yelled.

The men did not hesitate. They hurried to Merek, helped him to a table where he lay down on top of it. Richard Howard was there and began to attend the injured priest.

"Master Chaucer," Sir Robert said. "What has happened to our dear friend, Father Merek?"

Sword still pointed at the shipman, Chaucer told the others of Merek's torture at the hands of Anglicus. When he finished, the men stared at the shipman, who showed no emotion.

"Walter has already been sent for the town's officials," Harry said, confusing Chaucer and Thomas.

"You sent for them already?" Chaucer asked. "We just arrived."

"I am afraid there is more bad news," Harry said. "There has been a murder, a kidnapping, and a beating this early morning. We have sent for the constable."

"Judge Gates," Sir Robert addressed the eminent judge, "are you able to preside over this shipman in a quick and speedy trial?"

"Out of my jurisdiction, I am afraid, Sir Robert," the judge answered. "Have no fear, sir. I know the judge in Rochester. This is his territory." Judge Gates pointed at the shipman. "He will be hanged at the judge's earliest convenience."

Chaucer was confused. "A murder? A kidnapping? A beating?"

Harry was quick to give Chaucer and Thomas with the latest news. He told of Father Towns's murder, the kidnapping of the prioress, and the beating of Sister Anne. The men had gathered to decide a course of action.

The physician continued to work on Merek with the help of some of Walter Brewse's workers. Howard spent most of his efforts in cleaning the wounded ear. Merek tried to listen to the update on the goings on at The Swan. It upset him that members of the clergy had been attacked. It angered him that they were members of his party, people he was supposed to protect. He felt a personal responsibility for the crimes against the prioress and Sister Anne.

"Seems too much of a coincidence, gentlemen, if I may?" Chaucer said aloud after being briefed on the crimes at the inn.

"Coincidence?" Harry asked.

"The crimes here in The Swan and the attack on Father Merek. It is too much of a coincidence, I think. Perhaps our captured assassin can shed some light on the subject?" Chaucer asked.

The men's eyes went to the shipman, who was allowed to sit at a bench, guarded now by Hugh Bowman and Robin Miller.

"And why would I want to help the likes of you?" Anglicus said sarcastically. "I am doomed to the gallows."

Without a word, Robin Miller took the shipman by the back of the neck and slammed his forehead on the table. Anglicus screamed in pain. Robin Miller picked the shipman's head up for all to see. The pirate's nose was bleeding all over his face as he cried in pain.

"Ask him again," Robin Miller said.

"Anglicus?" Chaucer asked.

The shipman was holding his nose, trying to stop his nose from bleeding. He was in pain but clearly did not want his head slammed again. He put his good hand up as if to say he would help.

"I do not know about the kidnapping and murder," he sputtered through the blood running down his face. "I was hired to hurt the priest. And I was told when to hurt the priest just last night."

"Who gave the orders?" Harry asked.

There was a small pause.

"Oswald, the reeve," the shipman said.

"Goddam him!" Robin Miller shouted, once again slamming the shipman's face into the table. "That bastard!"

Anglicus fell to the floor writhing in pain. No one in the room attended to him. They left him there as they tried to sort of the rest of the crimes.

"So who took the prioress and killed Father Towns?" Sheriff Coleson asked. He, like Judge Gates, had no jurisdiction in this part of England.

"I can tell you the five guildsmen were in on it," Sir Robert said. "Anyone with eyes could see they were mercenaries."

"But mercenaries are hired. They follow orders," Judge Gates surmised.

"Led by Oswald," Chaucer finished.

"But why the prioress?" Harry asked. "And why did they kill Father Towns?"

"A ransom, no doubt," Chaucer said. "They want to hold the prioress for ransom."

"How do you know that?" Harry asked.

"If they had been hired to hurt or kill her, they would have done it already."

"What? Are they going to demand a ransom from the Church?" Harry asked.

"My guess is that the prioress has family. A well-to-do family. Someone is holding her ransom against her family," Sir Robert said.

"So the mercenaries are hired by someone who wants to get back at the family of the prioress," Chaucer said.

"A reeve?" Thomas asked.

"Too ambitious for a reeve, Thomas," his father said.

"But why murder Father Towns?" Father Smithton asked.

"In his zest to protect the prioress, poor Father Towns got in the way," Chaucer simply said.

William Horn, the local constable, arrived with his two deputies. He was apprised of the crimes and of the actions of the assassin. He ordered his men to take the bleeding Anglicus to the brig and chain him to the wall in the brig. Then he ordered the deputies to return to The Swan. Horn, an older man, was competent, but not very ambitious. When asked if he was going to lead in the search for the kidnapped prioress, he told the group that since the kidnappers had escaped Dartford's town limits, he could not follow.

Judge Gates scolded him for his ignorance of the law. "Sir, they may have left your jurisdiction, but they committed the crime here in Dartford. By English law, you can follow them to Hades if you choose!"

Horn did not know Judge Gates, nor was he intimidated by him. "Do not interpret the law for me, sir. I have been at this job for twenty years! I know what I can and cannot do!"

"So what becomes of the kidnapped woman?" Sir Robert asked.

"I will send my deputies," Horn said. "Once they secure the shipman in our brig, they will be back. I will send them after the kidnapped woman."

"Do they have experience in apprehending criminals?" Harry asked.

Horn did not answer right away. Inwardly, he smiled. "They can do their duty. The Pierce brothers are very able, I assure you. They will be like hounds after a fox." Horn said. To Walter Brewse, "May I see you in the kitchen?"

Walter nodded, and the two men left the room.

"Two deputies? That will not do," Harry said to the others in the room. "I am the host. I am the leader. I cannot go back to The Tabard with the knowledge that a pilgrim under my escort was lost to kidnappers. I am going with these deputies. I must bring that dear lady back."

"I shall go with you," Sir Robert said. "And I will pledge my yeoman. He is an excellent man in the ways of the forest. He will track these mercenaries."

"I will be included," Thomas said. "I go where my father goes."

"I pledge my sword to the mission," Chaucer added. "Count me in."

"By the bones of all the saints, I will go. Promise me that I can get my goddam hands on that bloody reeve," Robin Miller said.

"You will not leave without me," Merek said, sitting up on the table as Doctor Howard was wrapping a bandage around his head, covering the lost ear. "You will need my bow."

Chaucer wanted to talk Merek out of going with them. So did Sir Robert and Thomas. But when they saw the look and determination on Merek's face, they did not say a word.

CHAPTER 28

THE KIDNAPPERS TURN SOUTH

Once the kidnappers were away from The Swan, they set their pace a little faster. They hurried their horses on the cobblestones of Dartford. Because it was not quite dawn, they had to be careful with their horses. As the kidnappers left the town of Dartford, they veered from the main road and made their way through the dark forest. Entering the forest, the fleeing party slowed to a walk and formed a single line. The kidnappers had trouble seeing the path off the main road. The footing of the ground for the horses also forced the group to slow. A lame horse could jeopardize the entire plan.

Mason was the name of the fifth guildsmen. It was he who would lead the kidnapping party to the designated lodge where the prioress would be held for ransom. Mason had been a proper forester before serving in the king's army. He had an uncanny of way of finding his way from forests to towns. He also had a knack for finding freshwater when needed and could navigate through forests at night. Thaddeus did not understand Mason's ability to guide, but he depended on him and trusted in him. Both men had served together in France.

The lodge in which they were to deliver the prioress was east of Winchester. The mercenaries did not know the exact location of the lodge, but were assured that Oswald knew, and that he would get them there. From Dartford, Oswald had estimated the trip to the lodge was almost ninety miles. The men planned to make the five-day trip in four days.

As Mason led the way through the forest, he was followed by young Jack. Jack was the newest member of the group. He had not served in France with the other kidnappers, but his brother Rodney had. Rodney did not return to England with the others, the victim of a French crossbow. But while in France, he had pleaded with Thaddeus to seek out his younger brother if Rodney did not return. True to his word, Thaddeus found the small village and the tiny cottage where Rodney grew up. Thaddeus met young Jack and offered him a place in the group. Jack agreed and followed. Thaddeus knew the young man lacked fighting skills the others had, but took him in and trained him personally. Thaddeus found Jack to be an able student, strong and eager to please. For two years, he travelled with the group. They trusted him and were impressed with Jack's ability to handle horses.

Benjamin was behind Jack in line. Benjamin was the oldest of the kidnappers. Noted for his use of the dagger, Benjamin was a fierce fighter. None of the kidnappers would dare challenge him, even Thaddeus. Benjamin had a temper and was ruthless at times. Yet, for some reason never explained, he respected Thaddeus, obeyed his directions, and followed him without question. There was a simple explanation for his loyalty, an explanation Thaddeus never knew. In France, during a pitched battle in which both ranks broke into a chaotic fight, Benjamin was overtaken by two French men-at-arms. One pinned him to the ground while the other brought a spear aimed at the English soldier's head.

Before the French warrior could stab the prone Benjamin, Thaddeus stepped in and killed the soldier with the spear and decapitated the French soldier pinning Benjamin to the ground. Thaddeus did not stop to see who he had saved but continued to fight the next opponent. He never stopped or acknowledged his deed with the fallen English soldier. Benjamin did, however. He saw his savior and would be forever indebted. Afterward, by chance, he found the resting Thaddeus under a copse of trees with his men. Benjamin introduced himself and never left Thaddeus's side from that day on.

The prioress followed Benjamin with Thaddeus very close. David followed, his bow strung and ready for anyone who followed.

Keen with the art of the bow, David was a deadly archer. Tall and thin, his small chest belied the awesome strength in his arms and hands in using the great bow. David was a quiet man with a cool demeanor. It was hard to rile him, and that was what impressed Thaddeus about his second-in-command. Davis could be a killer, but did not have to kill.

"Hold," Thaddeus ordered, and the men stopped. The prioress did not understand, but Jack grabbed the reins of her horse to bring her to a halt. "Listen," he said quietly.

The men listened for anyone behind them. Thaddeus wished to know if searchers had been sent to find the kidnapped nun. The men listened but only heard the natural sounds of the forest. The birds had awakened and were communicating to each other of the new day. Dawn was coming, and it was a little easier to see on the path Mason led the gang.

"Stay and listen," Thaddeus said to David. "Once we are on the small hill ahead, come join us."

David nodded, and Thaddeus ordered the gang to continue.

"Prithee, sir," the prioress said to Thaddeus. "I am in need of a place to make water. I am about to burst. I have been a model prisoner to this point. Please, sir."

Thaddeus thought for a moment, then nodded. As far as he knew, the group was not being followed, and they were off the main road, heading to the location arranged to meet up with Oswald.

"Make haste, Madam Prioress," Thaddeus said.

"I suppose I will have to go here in forest," she said with angry tone.

"There are plenty of trees, Sister," Thaddeus said without emotion.

The prioress waited for one of the men to help her dismount, but no one moved. With a huff, she dismounted and made for the trees.

"Go with her, Jack. In case she has an inclination to give us away with loud noises or shouting," Thaddeus said.

"If she does?" Jack asked.

"Quiet her, but try not to harm her," Thaddeus said.

"And if she should run away?" Jack asked.

"She will not get far, my friend," Thaddeus said. "She keeps her size hidden underneath her black habit."

Jack dismounted and followed the nun into the woods. He stopped when she stopped behind some trees.

"Are you spying on me, young man?" she asked.

"No, Sister. Wild animals out here. Just here to protect and be sure you make your way back to the horses," Jack answered.

"Poor excuses to spying on a lady, a nun for our Lord's sake," she said with frustration. She blessed herself and took care of her needs.

Afterward, Jack escorted the nun back to the group. Jack helped the nun mount her horse, and Mason led them over a small hill covered with thick trees. The others followed. David stayed behind, listening for a search party approaching from the rear. He heard nor saw anything. As the gang faded from the hill, he kicked his horse to catch up with the group.

Oswald and Thaddeus had chosen the escape route after considerable discussion with Mason. Oswald had wanted to stay on the main road, thinking that if they had a good head start, any posse would not be able to catch them. Oswald's idea was to retrack the route from Southwark. He maintained that by staying on the main roads, they would make better time.

Thaddeus disagreed. By staying on the main roads, they would draw attention by the many travelers they would encounter. What would people think if the saw five middle class guildsmen travelling with a nun, a prioress? Furthermore, if a search party were to pursue them, it would be easy for the search party to follow, for there would be many witnesses to answer the description of the gang with the nun in tow.

Thaddeus wanted to take the prioress off the main roads through the dense forests and stay away from the popular roads that took travelers to Canterbury, Southwark, and London itself. Mason agreed with Thaddeus and assured both men he could lead the group through the dense terrain. His only worry would be the occasional bands of rogues, bandits, and highwaymen they might encounter.

Thaddeus was willing to take his chances with robbers and brigands than with a search party that would easily find them on the main roads. Thaddeus had confidence in his men's abilities to defend themselves. Most had been in the king's army and had seen combat. All had killed men. All had seen the face of the devil. A natural leader, Thaddeus had been an officer in the king's army. As a man-at-arms, he had commanded troops in the war with France. Now he led a small group of mercenaries who had to perform a lucrative mission. If successful, Thaddeus would be able to change the lives of the woman he loved and their two children.

David was an expert with the longbow. Jack and Mason were experts with the glaive, a pole-like weapon that could stab an enemy from a safe distance. Each had his own glaive and daggers to go with it. Benjamin was an expert with a bollock, a dagger but could also handle a sword with proficiency. Thaddeus preferred a sword in fighting and was the most skilled of his men. Robbers would rue the day they attacked this group of travelers.

And so they made their way through the forest to a town called Sevenoaks. Almost ten miles from Dartford, Sevenoaks was noted for its flourishing marketplace. The small town derived its name from an Old English name for the chapel that stood near seven impressive oak trees. The chapel was called Seouenaca and was known for bringing the Christian faith to the local tribesman. Eventually, a strong marketplace formed, and a town was started.

Thaddeus and his group arrived in Sevenoaks close to eight bells. The market and the town were busy. Before they entered the town, Thaddeus had to warn the prioress about her behavior. He assured her that his men would not harm her, but if she spoke out or tried to escape, they would do her harm and possibly kill her. To make sure she understood his seriousness, he had taken the point of his dagger and had pressed it against her thigh. He was sure to draw a pin prick of blood to ensure her of his serious intentions.

The men dismounted, and Jack took care of the horses. Benjamin helped the prioress to dismount, and they made their way to a small inn for a quick breakfast of bread, cheese, and beer. Each man took his turn in the privy, and one was assigned to escort the prioress when it was her turn. Jack joined the group, and they ate quickly.

As they sat and ate, Thaddeus spotted Oswald, who was sitting in the corner of the small inn. Oswald had been waiting for them. They nodded to each other, and Oswald approached the table. He sat with the men and nodded to the prioress.

"You are with them?" the prioress asked.

"Aye, Sister," Oswald said quietly. "We are to take you to a meeting. I assure you that you will not be harmed in anyway."

"Say, you, sir! I have been rudely accosted in the middle of the night. My aide was beaten and bound before my eyes, and one of my protectors has been brutally murdered!" the prioress said loudly.

Sitting beside her, Thaddeus grabbed the nun by her elbow and squeezed it tightly. The prioress winced in pain but became quiet.

"Eat, Sister," Oswald said quietly as Thaddeus kept squeezing her arm. "Any trouble?" Oswald asked Thaddeus.

"Nothing my men and I could not handle," Thaddeus said with confidence. "When did you arrive in Sevenoaks?"

"I was here at break of day," Oswald answered. "It is a busy but a quiet town. You will have no trouble here. Were you followed?"

"We do not think so. We had a clean start and deviated from the usual roads. No trouble through the forest. Thanks to Mason, we made reasonable time."

"It will be imperative that we push on, when you and your men are ready," Oswald said.

"We will not be long," Thaddeus said, looking at the prioress. "We are not as swift as we wish to be, but I feel confident the woman will pick up her pace."

"Very well," Oswald said. "When you are ready, we will head to Edenbridge."

CHAPTER 29

THE SEARCH BEGINS

At daylight, it was drizzling. There was a breeze with the rain, and the combination of the two elements made the morning cold. The rescuers were still trying to organize themselves. Those who were a part of the rescue mission were given a hasty breakfast of bread, dried beef, and ale. Horses were gathered, and the men checked their provisions. The summoner and the pardoner entered the tavern late and were confused by the flood of movements. They had slept through the kidnapping and all the mayhem that went with it.

It was decided that Judge Gates and Sheriff Coleson would lead the remaining pilgrims to Canterbury. Some of the pilgrims were hesitant to continue the journey, but with the judge and sheriff leading, they consented to keep going. They would leave The Swan later in the morning.

Allison, the woman from Bath, did not want to continue. She wanted to accompany the rescuers, so that she could remain by Harry's side. Apparently, she was content with Harry as husband number six! Harry denied her going, promising to meet her at The Tabard when she returned from Canterbury. Allison was not happy about the decision, but had no other choice.

The two deputies from Dartford arrived. Their horses were equipped with ropes, chains, and various weapons, including a bow. The deputies were ready to pursue the criminals. One of the deputies had a halbeard, a weapon with an ax-like cutting blade and a sharp pointed spike. The other brother had a poleax, a unique weapon with a blade combining an ax, a hammer, and a spike.

It was easy to see the deputies were brothers. Both had the same red hair. One, who appeared to be older, wore a full beard. It was red like his hair. The older brother had a solemn face with a hawk-like nose. Other than the unusual amount of weapons secured to his horse, he looked like a commoner.

The younger brother had the same tone of red color in his hair as his older brother, but he wore no beard. He seemed a little smaller than his brother. He, too, had the pronounced nose and solemn face. The younger brother was missing one of his front teeth but had a wildness to his eyes that his brother lacked. They did not smile, nor did they seem friendly in anyway as they approached. They rode up to the group, not aware they had a posse.

"I am Nathan Pierce. This is my brother, Griff. Will Horn, the town constable, has assigned me and my brother to track them down and bring the kidnappers back here for trial. Was hoping to get some information of the men we are chasing," Nathan Pierce looked at he group and waited.

Griff sat next to him and said nothing.

"You and your brother. The two of you are going to bring six criminals back for trial?" Thomas asked.

Nathan stared at Thomas. "We can hold our own. We chased down criminals before. I ask again. Information?"

Chaucer spoke up, "As I ran to The Swan just before dawn, I saw the riders from a distance. They were on the main road and were heading west."

Nathan Pierce nodded, his way of saying "thank you."

Harry spoke up, "There's some of us who want to go along."

Nathan Pierce shook his head. "Too dangerous."

Sir Robert, who had fought in fifteen major battles, knew all about danger. "Young sir, let us decide what is dangerous and what is not. We want to help you apprehend these criminals and bring them to justice. Not to mention, save a dear friend of ours."

Nathan looked Sir Robert up and down. He looked to his brother. Griff did not say anything. He seemed to be studying the group.

"By Christ's bones, man, we are going," Robin Miller burst out. "Whether you like it or not."

"You have no authority," Nathan Pierce said simply. "We represent the law."

"Good sirs, let us be your helpers," Chaucer said, trying to be a peacemaker. He felt the conversation was creating a rift with the two young deputies and the men who wanted to ride along. "We will help you with your pursuit of the criminals."

Sir Robert added, nodding to Hugh Bowman, "My man is an excellent woodsman. He can track and provide for us in the forest."

Nathan Pierce looked at his brother, Griff, who said nothing. After thinking on the matter, Nathan began to nod his head.

"Could be dangerous. Me and my brother have tracked more dangerous criminals than the ones you seek. One way or the other, we bring them back. Some dead. Some alive," he said. "Just keep up and do not get in our way. Figure they have two hours head start." After nodding to his brother, they slowly left the courtyard and began walking their horses west along the main road.

The "posse" quickly mounted their horses and began to follow. Chaucer and Thomas helped Merek mount his horse.

"Father Merek, would it be wise to take on this deed?" Chaucer asked.

Merek, mounted on his horse, nodded. After quickly checking his bow and arrows, he joined in line as the parade left the courtyard of The Swan. Led by the Pierce brothers, Sir Robert and Harry rode just behind the deputies. Chaucer and Thomas rode on either side of Merek. Robin Miller brought up the rear. Hugh Bowman, for his part, rode to and fro, apparently looking for tracks of horses.

Just outside of Dartford, the Pierce brothers stopped and dismounted. They were looking at a set of tracks just off the main road. Hugh Bowman rode to them, dismounted and joined in their investigation. The rest of the posse stayed mounted. The Pierce brothers and Hugh engaged in conversation that none of the other men could hear. Chaucer noticed the men seemed to be listening to Hugh when he spoke. Even the silent Griff was in on the conversation.

Finally, they stood up and began to mount their horses. Hugh went straight to Sir Robert.

"The tracks indicate that the men left the main road here and travelled south, Sir Robert," Hugh said loud enough for all the men to hear. "They seem to have a distinctive trail. One of their horses has a shoe that is loose." Hugh did not offer how a loose shoe looked in the dirt compared to a regular shoe.

Sir Robert nodded and began to follow the brothers, who had not waited for the group, but had already turned their horses south off the main road. They entered the thick forest. The rain had stopped, but the wind continued to blow, making the morning cold with air that seemed to make its way to the bones.

Because they were on a narrow path, they had to travel in a single line. Griff Pierce led the group, apparently the better tracker of the two brothers. Sir Robert held his place in line and nodded for Hugh Bowman to be up in front with the brothers. Sir Robert then followed. Next came Harry Bailly, Chaucer, Merek, and Thomas. Robin Miller still brought up the rear.

A few miles into the forest, Griff stopped the parade and dismounted. Hugh joined him. Nathan stayed mounted on his horse. Griff and Hugh conferred and began to walk off the path to a group of trees. No one else in the posse followed, but waited. After a few minutes, both men returned to their horses.

Hugh walked up to Sir Robert's horse holding a set of rosary beads. The rosary beads were made of coral and had large green beads for the *Pater nosters*. Attached to the rosary beads was a brightly shining golden brooch with a Latin phrase etched in its surface. "They stopped here, Sir Robert. These are the prioress's beads."

"Very well," Sir Robert said. Back at The Tabard, he remembered seeing the rosary beads attached to the habit of the prioress.

Once Griff mounted, they began again.

Merek was suffering, but said nothing. His ribs pounded each time the horse had to make a sudden move because of the uneven trail. His chest was still numb from the special salve in which Howard had dressed his wound. His face was still swollen, and once in a while, he spat blood. The tear where the ear had been ripped was aching also, but the bandage with the special salve dulled the pain. At first, he drank water, but Robin Miller shared a flask of wine with him. In small amounts, the wine numbed his pain.

It was just after eleven when the posse entered Sevenoaks. As they rode through the busy marketplace, there were stares and guarded remarks at the strange group of riders. It was a true spectacle for the simple citizens of the small village. The parade provided a wide array of riders, from the heavily armed brothers leading the group to the large gruesome man in the back of the procession. In between, if one looked closely, one would have seen noblemen and a priest. It was an uncommon group for the small village of Sevenoaks.

Nathan Pierce informed Sir Robert that he and Griff were going to seek a local official, and that the group should have respite in the small inn. Sir Robert nodded and informed the others. They drew up to the inn, dismounted and tethered their horses. They entered the inn. As his custom, Hugh stayed outside and looked out for the horses. He saw they received some water and some oats to eat.

The inn was small, but was not very crowded, and the group was able to find a bench together on one side of the room. Harry took the lead, and with the help of Chaucer, went to the bar to order ale and food for lunch. The others rested, used the privy and drank the unusually good-tasting ale. Some of the group had not slept the night before, and the ale reminded them that they were tired.

Soon, Nathan Pierce entered the inn and sat with the group. He announced that the kidnappers they were following had been through Sevenoaks. The constable had plainly seen them but had not known they were wanted for kidnapping or murder. The constable said the group did not make a disturbance, paid their bill for breakfast, and moved on without any trouble.

The problem was that the constable had not noticed in which way they left Sevenoaks. Did they go west to Oxted, or did they go south toward Edenbridge? Or did they go in a direction completely contrary to that of common thought?

Once Nathan gave the group the news, there was immediate discussion about the next move. To find the actual tracks in a busy marketplace at midday with constant traffic would be impossible to find. Would they split their group and pursue two trails, or perhaps divide into three groups and send a group back north?

Thomas sat and listened to his father, Harry Bailly, and Chaucer give opinions about the next move. As he listened, Thomas observed a young barmaid. She was a little younger than he but was definitely a young woman. She made eyes with him and smiled. He smiled back. Thomas excused himself from the table for the use of the privy. As he began to exit, he nodded to the barmaid to meet him outside. She did.

Thomas took her hand and went to the back of the inn where there was very little traffic. From there, they hurried to a small walkway between two buildings. No one was around.

"What is your name, my sweet?" he asked, holding her hands.

"Rose," she said shyly.

"I am Thomas, my lady, and may I say you are quite a flower to see on such a day."

She smiled and continued to hold his hands.

"Does your father own the inn, Rose?"

"No, it is my uncle," she answered, smiling with all of Thomas's attention. "My father is passed."

"Sorry to hear," Thomas said. "Tell me, my sweet. Were you working this morning?"

She nodded yes, and Thomas gave her a small kiss on the lips. She kissed him back.

"Did you happen to serve a group of men, say five or six, travelling with a woman?"

Rose did not hesitate. "Aye, I remember them well. The lady seemed to be a nun, but I could not understand why she would be travelling with so many men."

Thomas kissed her again, letting his lips stay a little longer on hers. She did not pull back. "By chance, were you privy to any of their conversation?" Thomas asked.

"Like what?" Rose asked, putting her arms around Thomas's neck. This time she kissed him, opening her mouth and using her tongue to explore his mouth. It was a long, wet kiss.

Thomas tried to compose himself after the kiss. He was searching for an answer, and at this rate, it would take longer for him to get the answer. And if Rose continued to kiss him like she was, he would have to take longer than he wanted to extract the information he needed.

"Rose," he said a little out of breath, "did the group mention where they might be going when they left your inn?"

"They might have," she teased.

Thomas took the challenge and held her in his arms. They kissed for a long time, no care in the world as to witnesses or interlopers. Finally, Thomas stopped, pulling himself away from Rose. "My sweet, please tell me. Did they say where they were going?" he asked.

"Funny, the group always became quiet when I served them. Like they was keepin' a secret from me. Yet, at the very end of their breakfast, as they was getting' up to leave, I heard one of them say Edenbridge."

"Oh, you are the best, sweet Rose!" Thomas said with enthusiasm. He gave her a quick peck on the cheek and sprinted back to the inn. Thomas entered a side door and took his place at the table. His father seemed to be the only one who noticed how long he was away. Sir Robert gave Thomas a disapproving eye. Thomas, for his part, simply nodded. The men were still discussing the whereabouts of the kidnappers and which way they were going in search of them.

There was a moment of silence, and Thomas said aloud, "Edenbridge. They went to Edenbridge."

"Edenbridge? Are you sure?" Harry Bailly asked.

At that moment, Rose entered the tavern and walked behind the bar. She gave Thomas a deep smile, a smile Sir Robert saw and had witnessed before.

"He's sure," Sir Robert said. To Nathan Pierce, "I suggest we travel to Edenbridge."

Nathan nodded and got up. The others followed. Merek was slow to get up, but the rest, the food and ale had helped his miseries. Sir Robert went to pay the bill as the men began to drift outside. Thomas waited till the men had left the table. He pretended to be adjusting his belt, but was waiting for Rose to come and clean the table. When Rose approached the table, Thomas got up slowly, went behind her, and whispered something in her ear. She smiled and looked at him with doe eyes.

A set of hands grabbed Thomas and pulled him toward the door. It was his father. "Come, lad," he said. "She gave us what we wanted."

Thomas waved weakly to her as he and his father exited the tavern. She smiled and mouthed the words "come back."

Outside, there appeared to be trouble. A dozen soldiers were gathered around the posse's horses. Their leader, a large man with big shoulders and a black beard, was having words with Griff. Two of the soldiers had Hugh by the arms, as if he were arrested. It seemed they had plans to take Hugh away.

Sir Robert and Thomas were last to leave the inn, so they entered the scene late. They could hear the members of the posse protesting to the soldiers.

"There must be a misunderstanding," Harry told the soldiers.

"No call for this, men," Chaucer tried to reason.

Nathan Pierce took charge, gently moving his brother aside and standing up to the soldier in charge. The soldier was tall, for Pierce had to look up to him.

"Say again why you are taking this man," Nathan said, nodding to the men who held Hugh Bowman captive.

"As I said to this chap," the lead soldier said, looking at Griff, "I am under orders to arrest all Moors and bring them to the garrison in Oxted."

"You'll not take this man," Nathan Pierce said. "I am a deputy constable, duly assigned by Will Horn, chief constable of Dartford, in pursuit of criminals, and this man is a part of my posse."

"Well, your posse will be short one man," the head soldier said, smiling. "I have my orders."

"I assure you, captain, this man is not a Moor," Sir Thomas butted in. "He is my yeoman, an English citizen just as you and I."

"Just who are you?" the captain asked in a cocky way.

"I am Sir Robert of Ganse, a lord noble of King Edward. I am also a part of Nathan Pierce's posse."

"I do not know you, sir. For all I know, you could be a pie maker from London." The captain's men laughed at the comment.

Sir Robert could feel the anger rising in him. "Listen to me, Captain. I have fought for the king. I have been all over the Mediterranean for England. How dare you question me, a lord of our good King Edward?"

The captain was not intimidated. "Look, I have my orders. I don't care who you are," he said to Sir Robert. "And I don't give a fig about this deputy constable either. The Moor's coming with us."

Nathan Pierce had had enough. With his index and middle finger, he suddenly struck the captain squarely in the Adam's apple. The captain fell immediately grabbing his throat and choking. As if on cue, Griff jumped into three of the soldiers standing behind the captain, knocking them all to the ground. Jumping to his feet, Griff kicked one man in the ribs, punched another who had risen from the ground, and kicked the third in the groin.

Hugh took the cue from the Pierce brothers. He quickly stepped back and pulled his two guards together. They banged heads and fell to the ground. Dazed, the two men tried to rise. Merek grabbed one, and despite the pain in his ribs and chest, pinned the man against the wall. The soldier, seeing Merek's size, put his hands up in surrender. Hugh took his soldier and threw him in the dust. He followed the man who took a wild swing at Hugh. Hugh blocked the punch and hit the man squarely in the jaw, knocking him to the ground. The man did not move.

For his part, Robin Miller welcomed the fight. He had circled around the crowd as the arguments were brewing. When the Pierce brothers began the fight, Robin Miller began in the back of the crowd of soldiers. One by one, he approached the soldiers from the back, spun each victim around and punched him squarely in the face. He knocked three soldiers out in that fashion.

Sir Robert and Chaucer had swords drawn and were herding the fallen soldiers against the wall of the inn while the fighting continued. Fortunately, the beaten soldiers had no fight left in them and did not challenge the swords of either man.

A soldier approached Harry Bailly, but the large tavern keeper was up to the task. He dodged the soldier's first volley of fists, blocking each, then sent the man to the ground with a solid uppercut. Thomas got in on the action, diving onto a pair of soldiers who were closing in on Griff Pierce. The soldiers got to their feet but were no match for Thomas's quickness and combat training. He kicked one, blocked the punch of the other, and countered with yet another kick. As the first man got to his feet, Thomas punched him, spun him around, and pushed him to where his father was standing. The soldier lay in the dust when he felt the tip of Sir Robert's sword inviting him to join the other soldiers against the wall. In a few seconds, Thomas brought the other soldier, bleeding from the nose, to his father, who put him with the others.

When the dust settled, some of the soldiers were left on the ground with an assortment of bruises and injuries. The others were lined against the wall facing the swords of Sir Robert and Chaucer. A small crowd gathered as the posse mounted their horses. Before they left, Nathan Pierce went up and kicked the choking captain.

"You would do well in the future to take heed of the local law enforcement deputies," he said to the ailing captain. "And know when a lord of the realm is speaking to you, you should honor his word."

And the posse left Sevenoaks. Edenbridge was eight miles away.

CHAPTER 30

EDENBRIDGE AND BEYOND

Edenbridge was known for its ironworks, so Thaddeus and his group could smell the fires and the smelting of the iron from outside the town limits. The town had grown along a section of an otherwise-unused Roman road that used to cross the River Eden and went straight to London. In 1366, it was known for its ironworks and the mills that ran along the river.

The trip from Sevenoaks had been considerably slower than Thaddeus would have liked. The prioress was holding them back. She did not keep pace, had to stop to relieve herself, and began to talk and ask questions. Finally, Thaddeus threatened to tie her up and lay her across the saddle if she continued to hold the group back. She did not believe him at first, but when he began to pull some small ropes from his saddlebag, she got the point.

As they entered Edenbridge, it was almost noon. Thaddeus told David to stay back along the trail in which they travelled and to listen for anyone following them. David found a spot in the woods where he could observe the road. He waited one half hour. Satisfied they were not being followed, he joined the group as they entered Edenbridge.

"We will only stop for the horses and to allow the nun to use the privy," Thaddeus said.

"Saints be praised," the prioress said. "Am I permitted to speak now, sir?" she asked with sarcasm.

"Mind you, Sister, that if we catch you speaking to a commoner, or anyone else for that matter, we will have to kill the person in which you speak. Are you clear about that?" Thaddeus said with a calm voice.

"Will you allow me a visit to the chapel over there? I missed my morning prayers," she asked.

"Pray as you ride, Sister. God hears all prayers. He does not care if prayers are spoken in a church or in the forest, does He? Is that not what you preach?" Thaddeus smiled. "Benjamin, escort the lady to the tavern where she might find a privy."

"Come along then, Sister," Benjamin said with a tired kind of patience. He had his large dagger with him, not to mention a smaller one he had tucked in his boot. He did not like the part of the job where he had to watch over the victim. It was slow and tedious work. His preference would have been to be a highwayman, where the action would be instantly rewarded with stolen goods or money. Yet, he knew he would be handsomely paid for his job. He trusted Thaddeus. And so he escorted the lady prioress to the privy.

While Jack attended to the horses, Oswald conferred with Thaddeus.

"We have slowed considerably," Thaddeus warned.

"Has your man detected someone coming after us?" Oswald asked.

Thaddeus looked at David, who shook his head. "No, not yet," Thaddeus said. "But it is only a matter of time."

"Think about it," Oswald said with thoughtful confidence. "Do you really think someone will come after her? Who? Certainly not the local authorities. They have no jurisdiction where we are going."

"Have you thought about the group in which we travelled? What about the knight? And his son? They travel with a forester. We studied him. That man could track us," Thaddeus said as a matter of fact.

"You worry too much," Oswald said. "That is my job."

"And that priest. The big one. The archer. He could be formidable," Thaddeus said.

"I truly do not think you will have to worry about him," Oswald said with confidence. "He has been taken care of."

"What do you mean?" Thaddeus asked.

"Trust me. If there is a group following us, the priest will not be among them. I assure you."

Benjamin returned with the prioress, and the horses were assembled.

"Is there no respite?" the prioress asked, looking at Oswald.

"Not yet, madam Prioress," Oswald said, mounting his horse.

Benjamin helped the woman mount her horse. Thaddeus gave the word, and Mason led them out of Edenbridge. On the edge of the village, they passed the Haxted Mill. The miller, an older man with grey whiskers and a bald head, stopped his work to study the group as they left. When they passed, his eyes met the eyes of the prioress. She gave him a slight nod, and he blessed himself.

From Edenbridge, the group followed the road west. Lingfield was about five miles from Edenbridge, and despite being tired from the events of the day, the group kept going. The prioress, still understanding that she was going to travel with them either on or across the saddle, cooperated, mostly in fear.

In Lingfield, they passed the Church of Saints Peter and Paul, a beautifully built church near the center of the town. They did not stop in Lingfield. As they passed the town's center and the magnificent church, they saw a "punishment cage." A body was in the cage but was clearly dead. The inhabitant had been a local criminal who was locked in the cage, which was hung high above the ground for all to see. The man was left to a slow death, probably succumbing to the lack of food and water. He must have died recently, for the birds were still feasting around his face.

Not one man in the group thought twice about the dead criminal in the cage. Yet, each man knew he could end up in such a cage if he were caught for the kidnapping. Each man believed he would not get caught. Each man only wished for the rich reward he would get for the mission accomplished.

The prioress saw the executed criminal and blessed herself. For her part, she should have been frightened by the rude awakening in the middle of the night, the flight from Dartford and the discomfort of men pushing her along a trail she was unfamiliar. Yet, as she traveled with these men, she was not truly afraid of them. They were not desperados. They were not mad, angry, and bloodthirsty. They were mercenaries doing a job in which they would be paid.

Yet, the prioress was not naïve. She knew these men could kill if they had to. Thaddeus had assured her that no harm would come to her if she cooperated. He had kept his word. But she knew deep down that if he did say he was going to tie her up and throw her across the saddle, he would do it. Thaddeus, trying to calm her fears, had given her the basic plan. The men were stealing her and using her as a pawn in the negotiations of two nobles, one being her father.

Once passed Lingfield, the group continued west heading toward another small town called Copthorne. It was important to get past Copthorne before dark, for the town housed an uncommon amount of smugglers from the south coast who would store their stolen goods in the woods around the village. Copthorne was almost six miles from Lingfield, so the group arrived well before dark.

Mason knew about the smugglers and the hidden caches of goods surrounding the town and had warned Thaddeus of the need to be cautious in and around Copthorne. In addition to the den of smugglers, the town was known for its making of charcoal, where the workers would strip to their waste while they worked. After working with the development of charcoal for a time, the workers' bellies would turn yellow from the smoke. Hence, people who lived in Copthorne were known as Yellowbellies.

By design, the group gathered as they rode slowly through the town. Mason still led but was followed by the prioress, who had Thaddeus on one side and Benjamin on the other. Jack and Oswald rode directly behind the prioress, and David brought up the rear. It was a tight formation, and they would maintain it through the town. There had been discussion about avoiding the town altogether, but Mason felt it was more dangerous on the outskirts of town than going straight through.

At the edge of town, they were approached by a priest. The priest was middle-aged. His scraggy beard was peppered with gray. His cassock was brown and dirty with numerous holes around the shoulders. His sandals were also old, held together with old strips of cloth. He walked with a limp and hailed the tight formation to stop. He approached with a broad smile.

"God bless you, sirs," he said, smiling and making the sign of the cross. And seeing the prioress. "And to you, Sister. May God bless all of you on this fine day."

Thaddeus tossed him a coin, thinking him a friar, a begging priest.

"Thank you, sir," the priest said, fetching the coin from the dirt. "Many thanks to you, kind sir. And blessings upon you." He put the coin in a small bag tied to his waist that also served as a belt of sorts. "However, I do not stop your party to beg but to offer advice."

"Advice?" Oswald asked.

"I am warning all travelers this day that the bridge that crosses the Alben Creek is out. Washed away by a sudden flood just a month ago. It is just a mile ahead. If you continue, you will see that it is impossible to cross, and you will have to return here to Copthorne."

No one said a word.

"Just trying to save you time, sirs, that is all," the priest said.

"Is there another way?" Oswald asked.

"Aye. Actually, there are two ways, sirs. One is to take the path south of town through the forest. It is a bit longer but will get you back to the main road in due time."

"In due time?" Thaddeus asked.

"I am afraid it is a few miles out of the way," the priest said.

"You mentioned a second way?" Oswald asked.

"There is a path north of town that will allow you to cross the creek and get back to the main road in a shorter time. But . . ." the priest said.

"But?" Oswald asked.

"You will have to cross the bridge next to the Martell Mill. Gregory Martell owns the mill and has rights to the bridge. There is a hefty toll, especially since the bridge has been out."

Mason spoke up, "I say we ride the main road. I have not heard of a washed-out bridge."

"I will be here when you get back," the priest said simply, looking hard at Mason but smiling.

Oswald looked at Thaddeus. "The south path would put us too far behind schedule. To go forward would be futile. Seems we pay the toll and use the bridge. What say you?"

Thaddeus looked at Mason. Although he trusted Mason, he could not make a mistake involving time. They had to keep on schedule just in case they were being followed. Thaddeus nodded to Oswald.

"Where is this north path and the bridge?" Oswald asked the priest.

The priest gave the simple directions, gave them a blessing, and watched as the group turned their horses and followed the north path out of town. They stayed in a tight formation as they recrossed their path through the town. In the middle of the town, they turned north and followed the path as directed. About one-half mile out of town, they saw the mill and the bridge beside it. The mill was running, but the party did not see anyone to attend the bridge.

A man appeared from the mill and walked up the small hill from the mill to greet the strangers. He was a small man but had thick shoulders and a long black beard. He wore a patch over one of his eyes and carried a large stick. It was for defense. "Good day," he said in a friendly way. "If you wish to cross the bridge, there is a toll."

Mason stopped the group just short of the bridge.

"How much?" Oswald asked.

"A shilling each, sirs," the miller said politely. "The lady travels across free." He smiled.

"A shilling? That is robbery, sir," Oswald said.

Mason turned on his horse and looked at Thaddeus. Thaddeus knew the look. Thaddeus shook his head. The miller never knew how close he came to dying that day. Mason was ready to kill him.

"We will give you five pennies each." Oswald bargained.

"Ten, sirs," the miller countered.

"Eight," Oswald said.

The miller looked at the men in the group and the nun. He had run the toll for years and knew when to negotiate and when not to push against the "wrong" customers. One look at the group knew they were formidable men, so he would take their price.

"Eight it is," he said, and Oswald paid him.

The group passed over the bridge to the other side. Mason led them. Once passed the bridge, the path diverted sharply to the left and went deeply into the woods. It was after five in the afternoon when they entered the thick woods. It was Oswald's hope that the group would get through the thick forest before nightfall. The group was barely a mile into the forest when they heard a voice. "If you will, sirs, be kind enough to stop," the voice said.

The group stopped, setting their formation close to the prioress. They drew their weapons. An arrow thumped into a tree next to Thaddeus.

"We will be collecting a toll, sirs," the voice said. The man could not be seen.

"Just paid a toll," Thaddeus said. He and his men, including the prioress dismounted. At least they could use their horses for coverage for an enemy they could not see.

"For the bridge, yes," the voice said. "But now you travel through our forest. We will charge you a toll."

"We were not told of a toll, sir," Oswald said.

Thaddeus added. "Show yourself so that we can see who owns such a beautiful forest."

The men in Thaddeus's group had their weapons drawn and were peering throughout the trees, trying to get a glimpse of how many bandits were hiding from them. There was a sharp whistle, and the group emerged. Since the trees in the forest grew so closely together, the robbers emerged from all sides of the intended victims, some as close as ten feet from the horses. Thaddeus made a quick count of the highwaymen, totaling sixteen men. The men had a variety of weapons. Only a couple had swords, while he could see daggers in the hands of others. Oddly, only one man had a bow, and it was a regular bow, not like David's longbow.

"We do not want trouble, sirs," the leader exclaimed. He stood with two others on a grassy mound flanked by large oak trees. He was a tall, thin man with a balding head. He was clean-shaven and had a large bulbous nose.

"Trouble?" Oswald questioned. "Sir, take a good look at the men with whom I travel."

Thaddeus looked around, studying the highwaymen. His companions did the same. What they saw was a ragtag band of robbers. Their clothes were rags, their weapons old and rusty. Some carried wooden staves as weapons, and even they were crooked. They had a wide variety of ages amongst them. At least two of the men were old, well into their forties.

Thaddeus looked at David, who still had an arrow ready for combat. The other men with Thaddeus were ready also. The prioress stood amongst them, scared, and trying not to cry aloud. Oswald made sure he stood next to her. He had a dagger in hand.

"Madam, we don't wish to scare you." The leader smiled. "No harm will come to you if your men pay the toll." To Thaddeus, "Funny, when we first spotted you entering our forest, I took you to be merchants! But I see by the weapons you carry that you are not the easy prey I thought you would be."

"Your observation is keen, sir. You would be wise to be wary of us," Thaddeus said directly.

"Since it is your forest, sir, you can also give us a free toll. That way, no one gets hurt," Oswald said, his sword still in hand, looking at the three robbers standing just ten feet away.

"That will not do, sir," the leader said. "I am afraid the toll must be paid."

"What is the charge?" Thaddeus asked.

"Ten shillings each," the leader announced, and his men laughed at the outrageous price. "We have families to feed tonight."

Oswald, like the others, kept his weapon poised to strike. "I warn you, sir, these men are not to be trifled with."

The leader smiled. "I thank you for your warning, sir. But as you can see, we outnumber you."

"Tell me something," Thaddeus said. "The priest in the village. Is he with you?"

"Priest?" the leader asked. And then he laughed, as did the rest of his robbing crew. "You mean Archie? My cousin, you see. Born actor, you know. Hope he didn't hear your confessions or give you communion!" The men roared with laughter at that.

While they laughed at the joke, Thaddeus turned and gave David quiet instructions. The leader saw Thaddeus turned and motioned to his man with the bow. The bowman stood on an old stump and cocked his bow at the group, specifically the prioress.

"Any trouble, sirs," the leader said, "and my bowman will shoot the lady. Nothing personal, my dear," he said to the prioress. "We must take precautions. Now, gentlemen, what will it be?"

Thaddeus looked at the leader. "Do you trust your bowman?"

"He is a fine shot," the leader said with confidence.

"I trust mine too," Thaddeus said. And with that, David took his huge bow and pointed it at the leader. "That, sir, is a longbow, and from this distance, my man will not only hit you, but his arrow will go right through you."

"You jest with the lady's life?" the leader said hesitantly.

"I do not jest, sir," Thaddeus said. "Now!"

David loosed the arrow. It hit the leader squarely in the chest, knocking him off his feet and off the mound. As Thaddeus gave the signal, Oswald pushed the prioress forcefully from where she stood. The push knocked her to the ground, allowing her to escape the robber's futile arrow aimed at her. The arrow buried itself in a small tree.

Mason thrust his sword at the man nearest to him, catching the man in the upper thigh. Pulling it back, he whirled the weapon at a highwaymen attacking with the stave. Dodging the stave, his sword found the man's open stomach and killed him instantly.

Benjamin took the nearest robber to him by the cloth and punched him squarely in the face then used the stunned man as a shield when another robber approached with a dagger. The robber inadvertently stuck the dagger into his fellow robber. Benjamin dropped the stricken robber and made a clean swipe of the throat of the second man, spilling blood everywhere.

Jack put his sword to use, skillfully holding off three bandits wielding old daggers. Jack dodged the first man's thrust, took his sword to the second man, almost cutting the man's wrist from his body. The third man moved in to stab Jack from the back, but

David's arrow caught the man in his side, piercing all the way to his heart. He dropped immediately.

Thaddeus killed two men who had tried to make their way to the fallen prioress. Thaddeus caught the first one in his upper torso with his sword and then was able to pull it cleanly in time to chop down onto the second robber as he tried to attack the prioress.

The fight had not lasted more than two minutes, but there were nine bodies lying all about the forest floor. The others had fled, most of them carrying some type of wound with them. During the fight, the prioress had stayed on the ground, hurt and terrified of the fighting going on all around her.

When the forest grew quiet again, Jack and Mason went around inspecting the bodies. David kept a vigilant eye out for a counterattack, bow and arrow always ready. Thaddeus helped the prioress to her feet, giving her some ale they had brought along for the journey. She was weak with fright and seemed to need Thaddeus to lean on.

When the men were certain there was no more danger, they mounted their horses. Jack and Benjamin helped the lady prioress on her horse. The men had inspected the bodies of the dead, hoping to find a weapon or a coin of value from the robbers. They found nothing worth taking, not even the men's weapons.

Mason was ready to leave. "Which way, Thaddeus? You want to go back into town? It would be my guess that the bridge we're supposed to take is as good as the day it was built."

"No doubt, the 'priest' lied. But if we go back, we backtrack. Too risky. Can you get us through this forest back to the main road?" Thaddeus asked.

Mason thought a moment. "Aye, a bit out of our way. But it will work."

David was still angry. "Send me back, Thaddeus. From a distance, I will be sure 'Priest Archie' will not send any more travelers to this neck of the woods."

"Tempting, David. Tempting," Thaddeus said. "But we have to stay on schedule."

The men and the prioress were mounted, ready to proceed, except for Benjamin. He had disappeared over the mound in which the leader had stood and was shot with David's arrow. He appeared momentarily with something in his left hand. He held it up. It was the leader's head. He put it on a stump for all to see.

"See if they come after us now," he said to the group.

The prioress saw the decapitated head and was about to faint. Jack steadied her and handed her some ale.

"Mason. Lead the way," Thaddeus said.

Mason took the lead and led the group on the narrow path that led them through the thick forest. They kept careful watch as they went, knowing the dead men back on the trail had family and friends that might want vengeance. But no one came after them, and they proceeded safely through the forest. They had lost time, but Thaddeus felt fortunate to have escaped the highwaymen with no injuries, particularly the prioress. She was shaken from the experience but physically unharmed.

CHAPTER 31

NEWS FROM THE KING

Father Berners sat on the edge of his bed, wiping the beads of sweat from his face. He turned his head to the naked girl who was tied to the four corner posts of the bed. She was whimpering, trying to catch her breath, knowing that if she cried out or were too loud, the priest would hurt her more. Berners said nothing to the girl but got up from the bed and began to dress.

There was a soft knock on the door.

"Speak," Berners said with quiet authority.

"Prior, one of our young priests has just delivered a message," Father Richard said on the other side of the door.

"Come in," Berners ordered.

Father Richard walked in with the parchment that held the message. He looked at the girl and then to Father Berners. Father Richard gave Berners the parchment. It had the Bishop of Winchester's seal.

"See to the girl. Get her out of here. Use the back door," Berners said, opening the message. He read it silently.

Father Richard walked over to the bed and threw the girl's woolen kirtle on top of her to cover her naked body. Then he began to untie the binds around her hands and feet.

"Seems the bishop has had a message from the king himself," Berners said aloud. "Wants me to his office at my earliest convenience."

Father Richard had the girl to her feet and was helping her dress. She was trying not to cry, but tears were streaming from her eyes. She shook and had trouble standing. Father Richard propped her up and gave her a small glass of wine. He put it to her lips and made her drink it.

"Get her out of here," Berners ordered, suddenly angry at her presence. "You will not say a word to anyone, will you, my child?"

The young girl did not know what to say. She had been asked earlier in the day to deliver kindling for a fireplace to a small house on the southern edge of Winchester. It was a small cottage in a quiet end of Winchester, where there was little peasant traffic. She had knocked on the door and to her surprise was greeted by a priest. She brought the kindling in, placed it by the fireplace, and was paid for her trouble.

What happened after that was a blur to her. Now she was being escorted from the small cottage by another priest who warned her not to say a word to anyone about the encounter. He even gave her another coin as she left through the back door. She was only twelve.

Father Richard returned to the bedroom where Berners was dressed in his cassock and putting on his boots.

"We will make our way to the bishop's, Father Richard. You shall accompany me."

"As you wish, Father Berners."

And they left the cottage. From the many bribes and favors Berners had accumulated over time, he was able to purchase the small cottage for his personal use. He enjoyed its solitude, its way of giving him a break from the day-to-day duties of the priory. It was also useful for his strong proclivities. It was a haven only he and Father Richard knew about.

The priests made their way to the cathedral and the office of Bishop William Edington. The office was in the cathedral. Berners and Richard were unable to enter the spacious nave of the cathedral from the front, for Bishop Edington had made arrangements for repairs and remodeling of the nave. The cathedral in Winchester, whose groundbreaking began in 1079, was one of the largest cathedrals in Europe. Its nave, the main body of the church, was the largest Gothic nave in all of Europe. Bishop Edington wanted to make it the grandest nave in Europe also.

Father Berners announced his presence to one of the bishop's secretaries and waited outside Edington's office. Berners did not usually like to wait on people, but for Bishop Edington, he would make an exception. Bishop Edington was not only his boss, so to speak, but also a famous man in all of England for his service to the king and the Holy Mother Church. And Berners knew the bishop was not a man to trifle with. Berners would wait and would gladly answer to the great bishop's needs.

Finally, the door opened, and Berners was ushered in. Father Richard knew his place and waited outside the office. As Berners entered the office, William Edington was seated at his desk, signing a parchment.

"Your Excellency," Berners greeted the bishop, walking toward the massive desk. The bishop held out his hand, and Berners gently took the hand and kissed the ring that stood for the bishop's rank in the Church.

"Father Berners, good of you to come. Please, sit down," the bishop said.

"Bishop Edington, I received your message, and I am here. How can I be of service?"

The bishop put down the quill in which he was using, took the parchment, and set it aside. He folded his hands and let them rest on the desk.

"Our good King Edward has called on me."

"Again, the king calls on you, your excellency?" Berners asked. "Have you not gone above and beyond in the service to our king?"

"It is not a service, so to speak, Father Berners. It is more of an appointment."

"Appointment?"

"Appears King Edward wants me to be the new Archbishop of Canterbury," William Edington stated, looking closely at Father Berners.

Father Berners was no fool. He knew the bishop was telling him the news personally for a reason. Was the bishop looking to see his reaction? Would Berners go along with the bishop to Canterbury?

Would Berners become the new bishop of Winchester? Was Berners going to receive a promotion?

Berners blessed himself. "It is a great honor that the king has chosen you for the coveted title, Bishop Edington. Congratulations," Berners said with an even voice. He smiled also, trying not to over-play his joy at such news.

To be the Archbishop of Canterbury was to be the most pow-erful churchman in all of England. By church law, the only man the Archbishop of Canterbury had to answer to was the pope in Rome. The only question in Berners's mind was "What do I get out of this?"

"Thank you, Father Berners. I am humbled by the appoint-ment. My reason for sending for you is that I wanted to tell you personally. I have also called Fathers Johnson and Whitehead to tell them the news."

Father Johnson was the priest who ran the day-to-day goings-on in the cathedral, and Father Whitehead was in charge of the town itself. With Father Berners, the three were invaluable to Bishop Edington in the running of the cathedral in Winchester. It was no coincidence that all three priests lived well and benefitted from each other. For instance, it was Father Whitehead who had helped Father Berners get his small cottage on the southern end of town.

"May I ask a question, Bishop Edington?" Berners asked.

The bishop nodded.

"With your leaving for Canterbury, will there be changes here?" Berners asked boldly, hoping to hear of a promotion.

"Oh, yes, Father Berners. There will be changes." The bishop smiled. "There will be a new bishop appointed to my post." Bishop Edington paused for a moment. "But I do not think the changes will affect you," he said simply. "I will recommend that you continue your work as the prior of the monastery."

Berners held back his emotions. "Do not let him see your disap-pointment," he said to himself.

"Is something wrong?" Edington asked.

"No, excellency. No," Berners said with great discipline.

The bishop smiled. "Father Berners, you seem to thrive in matters dealing with the running of a monastery. I would not think of taking you from that position."

"Is there another way in which I can serve you in your new position?' Berners asked.

"I think not, Gilbert. It might be better if we distance ourselves anyway."

"Oh?"

"I hear rumors, Gilbert. I hear rumors of habits, expenses, and secular wealth. I do not know if any of these rumors are true. I have no proof. You serve me and monastery in a most able way, and we will leave it at that. But there is no way would I recommend you to be raised to a higher position, nor would I take you with me. I only hope the new bishop will not take the rumors for truth and usher an investigation."

Father Berners sat quietly, staring at William Edington. Berners did not know what to say. He felt that any words coming from his mouth would make matters worse. In his mind, he felt rage and embarrassment. He could feel his face redden. His nose seemed to drip more, and he absently took a kerchief to it.

"I think we understand each other, Father Berners. If there is nothing else, you are dismissed."

Berners sat for a second and thought of a response. He had none. He stood, took the hand of Bishop Edington, kissed his ring, and left the door. The heavy oaken door closed loudly behind him.

CHAPTER 32

THE POSSE GAINS GROUND

After the skirmish in Sevenoaks, the posse rode hard for a few miles in case the members of the small militia decided to give chase. Nathan had ordered Griff to ride behind the group as a lookout for any pursuing militia. Griff did what he was told and let the group ride ahead. He waited for the group to disappear on the trail and then rode a little ways back to Sevenoaks to spy on any would-be followers.

During the fight, Merek had felt surprisingly good. His ribs and jaw had stopped their aching as the fight occurred. They did not ache on the sudden rush from the town. But now with the adrenalin wearing off, the pain returned. Although he did not say a word, Merek's wounds were unbearable. The cut on his chest was bleeding. Blood was spottting on the bandage on his head. The skirmish had opened the wound at his missing ear. His face was swollen and had begun to turn black and blue. Fortunately for Merek, Nathan had ordered the group to stop to give the horses a short rest. Merek needed the respite. They were a few miles from Edenbridge.

Hugh Bowman noticed Merek inspecting the wound on his chest. Helping Merek off his horse, Hugh sat Merek down at the base of a large oak tree. Hugh bent down and slowly took the bloodied dressing off Merek's chest. Then he unwound the bandage on Merek's head and let it bleed a little. Hugh dabbed the dressing on the wounds and told Merek to hold the old dressing on the wound at the ear. Promising to return, Hugh went into the forest.

"Father Merek," Chaucer said, "how can I be of service?"

Merek simply nodded as a thank you and kept the dressing close to the wound. The soreness was coming back in larger volumes of pain. The area of the ear was especially aching.

"Have a swig, Father," Robin Miller said, offering his jug of wine.

Merek nodded and took a long pull of the wine. It felt good as it went down. He took a second pull, longer than the first.

"Aye, Father," Robin Miller smiled. "That will cure the evils haunting you."

Hugh Bowman returned with some plants and roots. He took the dressing from Merek and began to rub the wet roots over the bleeding wounds. Merek had no idea what the roots were, nor did he care. He felt instant relief from Hugh's application. Merek was sure the wine helped too. He felt a little better.

Hugh Bowman dressed the wounds, and soon, Merek was fit to ride again. After the short rest, the men mounted and were about to begin when they heard the sounds of a horse riding to them. Several of the men drew their weapons but put them away when they saw it was Griff. Griff did not say a word to the group. He only looked at his brother and shook his head.

"Seems the militia is not interested in pursuing the yeoman," Nathan Pierce announced. "They are not following."

"And I thank you, gentlemen. Each of you. For your assistance," Hugh said solemnly. "I shall be in your debt. All of you."

"Family and friends owe no debt, Hugh Bowman," Thomas announced.

"I second that," Sir Robert said. "You owe us nothing."

Hugh only smiled. And the posse continued in its pursuit.

In the middle of the afternoon, the posse entered Edenbridge. The small town was unusually quiet in the middle of the afternoon. Nathan halted the procession to water the horses, buy some supplies, and take a short break.

Merek needed the break. Although Hugh's dressing had helped his pain with cut in the chest and ear areas, his ribs and swollen jaw were aching. Thomas and Chaucer were quick to help him from his horse. Merek spotted an old tree stump outside a small tavern and quickly sat down on it. Noticing the ground near the stump was full of grass, Merek lay down. With his back on the ground, he used the precious moments to allow his body to rest.

Thomas put a coin in Robin Miller's hand and whispered something to him. Robin Miller nodded, smiled broadly, and walked into the tavern. Chaucer followed Robin into the small tavern, while Thomas stayed with the ailing Merek.

Griff Pierce approached Thomas and nodded toward Merek.

"Just a quick rest, Griff," Thomas answered, still baffled that Griff would not utter a word to the men. "He will be ready when Nathan gives the word." Thomas assured the silent deputy.

Griff nodded and walked away.

Harry and Nathan purchased some need supplies from a merchant. Sir Robert had given them some money for the expenses. Hugh Bowman saw to the horses, finding a stable and buying the grain and use of the water trough from the livery master.

Nathan Pierce gathered the group, and they were ready to leave Edenbridge within an hour in which they stopped. The rest, along with Hugh's natural dressing, did wonders for Merek. As they mounted their horses, Robin Miller, with a fresh flask of wine from the small tavern, offered Merek a pull. Merek accepted the offer, took a long swig, and thanked Miller. Taking the flask from Merek, Robin Miller winked at Thomas, whose coin purchased the flask for "medicinal" purposes.

Nathan led the group, and they trotted their horses out of the town. At the edge of town, the posse passed Haxted Mill. The old miller was standing next to the road, as if he were waiting for the posse. "A good days, sirs." He nodded as they passed.

"Have you seen riders today?" Nathan asked, halting the parade.

"Aye, sir, a few," the miller said humbly.

"Seen a group of riders with a solitary woman?" Harry Bailly asked.

"Aye," the miller added simply.

"How long ago?" Nathan asked.

"Few hours," the miller said, looking at the sky for the positioning of the sun. "Aye, a few hours, I'd say."

"Thank you, sir," Harry Bailly said.

"She is in trouble, sirs," the old miller said. "She looked at me."

"I do not follow," Harry Bailly said.

"As they passed, the lady did not say a word with her mouth," the miller explained. "But her eyes were frightened. They spoke to me. I ask your forgiveness for not helping her. May God forgive me?"

"You need not be forgiven," Merek intervened. "You did nothing wrong. On the contrary, you have helped us. You have indicated we are on the right trail. God will bless you for your aid, my brother." Merek made the sign of the cross.

The old miller made the sign of the cross, bowing his head in deep humility. His head was bowed as the posse continued by him. No one looked back as they left. For his part, the old miller watched the posse until they were out of sight. Satisfied they were gone, he walked slowly back to he mill.

Outside of Edenbridge, Nathan decide to quicken the pace. The posse seemed up to the task and kept up. It was Nathan's goal to ride into Lingfield before dark. He knew the kidnappers would have to stop somewhere before nightfall, and both the kidnapping and the rescuing would have to take a rest for the night. Nathan felt that if they were able to enter Lingfield early in the evening, they could get to rest earlier and arise early to begin the search again. He truly hoped the prioress was slowing the kidnappers.

The sun was beginning to set as they entered Lingfield. A small town, it had no accommodations for the travelers. Nathan Pierce gathered the posse to organize the setting up of a camp. With no accommodations, it was the only choice. Merek interrupted with an idea. Since the posse was duly appointed and a part of the law, they could seek shelter in any village cottage they chose. But Merek proposed a simpler solution. Why not ask the priest in charge of Saints Peter and Paul's Church if they could make their accommodations inside the church? Nathan had no answer, so he agreed to let Merek intercede to the local pastor to let the men sleep inside the holy church.

As they rode their horses to the church, they passed by the punishment cage and the remains of the criminal who had died most recently. There were no birds feasting on the corpse at this hour, but the stench of the decaying body was overwhelming.

Merek met with the priest of Saints Peter and Paul and was given consent to allow the men to sleep under the cover of the roof of the church. They tethered their horses outside the church and made their beds inside. There were few pews in the church itself, for pews were expensive. Sir Robert and Merek were given pews, as the others were glad to rest their heads under the cover of a roof.

Hugh Bowman slept outside near the horses. Merek assured Hugh that he was most welcome inside the church with the others, but Hugh politely refused. Merek noticed that Griff Pierce was also setting up his makeshift bed to sleep outside also.

"Do not worry, Father Merek," Sir Robert said as they entered the church. "Hugh has slept outside more than he has slept with a roof over his head. He is more at home outside than inside. He will be fine."

Merek, for his part, was too tired to argue. He began to arrange his things on the pew to make it somewhat comfortable. His body ached, yet the fatigue was far stronger and seemed to pull him down to the pew without fully making it comfortable. As he lay down, he could hear Harry talking to no one in particular that he was in love. And that when this was all over, he was going to make Allison, the woman from Bath, his wife.

It made Merek think of Thea. As he closed his eyes to sleep, he saw her eyes. They were staring into his. They had that look. The look he tried to avoid as a priest, but the look he wanted as a man. Now in the comfort of his fatigue, he did not fight his priestly vows. He let the memory of her look linger. He let the memory of her look make him feel that he wanted to take her in his arms and kiss her. And as he drifted off to sleep, he was indeed holding Thea in his arms.

Thomas was asleep before he lay on the floor. He had not slept in twenty-four hours, and the excitement of the day had kept his adrenalin moving. But now, with the day ending and the quietness of the church, fatigue was closing in.

Chaucer, for his part, was also exhausted. Like Thomas, he had not slept in twenty-four hours. Yet, his training as a servant had taught him to ignore his own fatigue and continue with a job at hand. So as the others began to settle down, Chaucer went around to each man to make sure he was settled.

"Sir Robert, is there anything you need?" Chaucer asked the nobleman.

"Thank you, Geoffrey, but I am fine," Sir Robert answered.

"Sleep well, sir," Chaucer said quietly as he moved about the room.

Robin Miller was on the floor of the church propped up against one of the large beams holding up the roof of the church. His flask of wine was beside him, and he was unusually quiet. Near him, on the floor, Harry was stretched out with his eyes closed.

"Good night, Robin," Chaucer said quietly.

"And you, Master Chaucer," Miller replied. "Just remember, when we catch them bastards, I get the reeve."

"You get the reeve, Robin Miller. You get the reeve." Chaucer smiled.

"And I get to go home to Allison," Harry Bailly said, not turning from his side.

It made Chaucer smile. So that is the sound of love? It made him think of his own situation. If he were to marry Philippa, would he feel this love? He had already made up his mind to marry the maid in waiting. The marriage would help his standing with John of Gaunt and ensure a pension for his future. It was his hope that he and Philippa would someone learn to love each other. He envied Harry Bailly. He envied anyone who could feel the emotions of love. He knew of Philippa but did not know her. And to think of a marriage to a woman he did not know worried him. And those were the thoughts Geoffrey Chaucer took to his makeshift bed. He fell asleep immediately.

It had been a long day.

CHAPTER 33

CONTINUING THE PURSUIT

As tired as Merek was, he did not sleep well. When he finally lay down on the pew to sleep, he had thought of dear Thea and the loving look she would give him when they were together. Most times, Merek would try to avoid her eyes when she peered at him, but as he fell asleep, he pretended to look back at her with the same look. He wanted her to see he was in love with her too.

Yet, it did not last long. As he drifted off to sleep, the look of Thea morphed into the bearded face of Gilbert Berners. Merek was caught in a nightmare. Merek found himself tied to a beam in a small room, and Berners was standing as close to Merek as he could without actually touching him. Berners had a knife in his hand and was laughing, drawing the knife across Merek's chest and smiling as the small stream of blood emerged from the cut.

Merek tried to scream but could not. The dream prohibited it. The dream would not allow him to cry out in pain. He could only watch as the knife sliced his skin. And then he saw the young girl. She was tied to the four corners of the bed. She was naked, scared, and crying. Berners momentarily put the knife down and moved over to the girl. He laughed as he looked back at Merek, a laugh that said Merek could not stop him, could not help the innocent young girl.

That was the worst part of the dream. In the dream, he did not feel the knife make the incision on his chest. He did not feel the bindings that held him to the beam. But he could feel the anger for Berners as the priest smiled while cutting Merek. As Berners moved to the bed, Merek could feel the anger and hate rising in him for the monster who pretended to be a priest. Merek pulled and pulled at the bindings holding him back. It seemed the harder he tried to set himself free, the tighter the bindings became. The harder he tried to free himself, the louder Berners laughed.

And Merek awoke in a sweat. Fortunately, he did not awaken the others. He took a few deep breaths to try and calm himself. The room was dark. He did not know the time of the early morning. Slowly, he lay down and tried to close his eyes. It was just a dream, but it had stirred his hatred and desire to seek out Berners.

After his escape from Anglicus in the barn, Merek had not thought too much of the man who had commissioned Anglicus to harm him. Merek was grateful to be alive and feeling the pain of the wounds inflicted by the hired assailant. But as the day progressed, and they pursued the kidnappers, Merek had had time to think about Berners. Merek tried not to think too deeply about the evil man. He tried to use other means not to dwell on what he wanted to do to Berners. But he did want to hurt the evil priest.

These thoughts would haunt Merek as he travelled with the group. Occasionally, he would engage in conversation with the other pursuers, or his aching wounds would beg his attention. But in the back of his mind was the thought of how he would repay the man. At first, his priestly vocation would settle his mind and tell him that God, in all His judgment, would deliver Berners to the fires of hell. But as the day progressed and the aches continued, Merek began to think that it was he who should deliver Berners to hell in a most personal way. It was not a priestly way to think, but Merek found that his hatred for Berners helped ease the pain of his wounds. God help him.

It was not yet daylight as Merek lay quietly on the pew thinking of Berners. Despite feeling tired, Merek knew he would not be able to return to sleep. And so he prayed the rosary, trying to focus on the love of God and the death of Christ. If Jesus could forgive his executioners, could Merek do the same? It was a question Merek could not answer, and so he prayed harder.

Just before daybreak, Hugh Bowman and Griff entered the church and awakened Nathan Pierce. Nathan was quick to rise and began to move about. The stirrings caused Chaucer to awaken quickly. In his years of being a servant, he had been accustomed to awakening quickly and getting right to his duties. As Chaucer began to gather his things, he tried to awaken Robin Miller, who was sleeping soundly near him. It was of no use, for Miller was deep in sleep.

Chaucer, for his part, gathered his things and gently nudged the sleeping Miller with his boot. It took a couple of nudges, but Miller awoke with the usual gruff profanity.

"Jesus, is it goddam morning already?" he grumbled, looking up at Chaucer.

Chaucer nodded, gathered his things, and walked to the door of the church. He was joined by Sir Robert, who had awakened his son. Thomas was slow to rise and was just stirring when Chaucer and Sir Robert left the church.

Outside, Hugh Bowman and Griff Pierce had the horses tethered and ready to go. Off to the side of the church, Hugh had a small fire going with an open pot atop the fire. He had made a broth of local herbs and was heating it for the men to drink. As the men exited the church, Hugh had bread and cheese for them and the hot broth to drink. Sir Robert had given Hugh a few coins to secure the morning meal. It would be a long day, and Sir Robert felt it wise to make sure the men had a strong breakfast.

"What is it?" Harry Bailly asked as Hugh Bowman gave him a ladle full of the hot broth.

"Something to warm your belly and help digest the bread and cheese, sir," Hugh said quietly.

Harry Bailly took a sip of the broth, swirled it in his mouth, and swallowed. He smiled. "It is good, Hugh," he said. "Might need the recipe when I get back to Southwark. Could be a staple of The Tabard's early breakfast drinks."

Hugh bowed to Harry as the other men stepped up for their portion of the meal and broth. Robin Miller was last to exit the church and join the others. All stood around the fire, enjoying its warmth and taking in their breakfast. For the most part, they ate quietly, even Robin Miller.

"What is the plan, Nathan?" Sir Robert asked.

Nathan took a sip of the herbal broth. He looked at the men before he spoke.

"'Bout six miles to Copthorne. Tough town, Copthorne. Smugglers about. They might think we are after their loot and give us trouble. Got to be careful."

"Do you think we have gained ground on the kidnappers?" Sir Thomas asked.

"Aye. They had to stop and sleep too. By the way, the old miller talked back there in Edenbridge, I'd say we gained a couple of hours on them."

"Think we can catch them today?" Harry Bailly asked. "We ride hard and the prioress slows them down?"

"Lucky, maybe. First, we do not know exactly which route they will take. Depends on the tracks. Second, Copthorne. Got to be careful. Ride in slow. Ride out fast. Lots of trouble around there." Nathan Pierce warned.

"Why not ride around Copthorne?" Harry Bailly asked.

Griff shook his head but said nothing.

"Ride around Copthorne, you are asking for more trouble. Smugglers hide their goods all around the town. Ride around the town, you will encounter the smugglers. No. We ride through it and hope no one asks questions."

No one said anything. Each finished his breakfast. They doused the fire, mounted their horses, and left Lingfield. The Pierce brothers and Hugh led the posse. Robin Miller and Merek rode as the rear guard and the group left at a brisk pace. It was their hope to enter Copthorne by eight in the morning.

About a mile out of Copthorne, the group began to be aware of the peculiar smell that was associated with the town. It was the unique smell of the burning of wood to create charcoal. The Pierce brothers slowed the posse as they neared the town. It was their goal to traverse the center of town and continue on to the town of Crawley, seven miles away.

The posse had made good time and entered the town before eight. There was a hustle and bustle about the town, but the group was able to continue through without incident. At the very edge of town, a beggar of a priest approached the Pierce brothers, who were leading the posse. It was "Father Archie."

"Father Archie" was aware of the last group he had directed into the ambush awaited by their leader, Amos Remstead. Archie knew Remstead and others had been killed when the ambush went awry. Nevertheless, the surviving members of the foresters had reformed, appointed a new leader, and had directed "Father Archie" to detour travelers to the site of the ambush. The foresters were confident that they had encountered an unusual group of travelers, and that the odds of entertaining another group of skilled warriors was too great to pass up. So they had quickly reorganized and sent "Father Archie" to set the trap.

"Brothers! Brothers!" he shouted, looking at the Pierce brothers and the group they led. "Father Archie" walked directly in front of the Pierce brothers' horses, holding a cross and begging them to stop.

The Pierce brothers stopped, as did the rest of the group.

"Brothers, before you leave the town of Copthorne, I have some bad news for you. No less than two miles up the road, the bridge leading to Crawley has been damaged so severely that it is impossible to cross," Archie said with all the humility he could muster.

"Why do you tell us?" Nathan Pierce asked. "How do you know we travel to Crawley?"

"Sir," Archie said. "I only guess, as the road in which you are to venture on heads right to Crawley."

"And your purpose, Father?" Thomas spoke, bringing his horse to the front of the group.

"Well, as a servant of the Lord, I feel it is my duty to help my fellow man, young sire," Archie said, trying to convince the group of his sincerity.

Thomas looked the man up and down. The man wore a threadbare cassock, had rosary beads that served as a belt, and wore a cross hung around his neck. Furthermore, his hair shorn very short, giving more evidence that he was a monk.

"And you say the bridge is out farther up the road?" Thomas asked.

"Aye, sire. I feel it is my duty to report the catastrophe to your group and any group that travels the road of the bridge washing away in a storm a few weeks back," Archie countered.

"And what are you proposing to the travelers you warn?" Thomas asked, not believing the man.

"There is a detour in which I would gladly show your group, sire." Archie smiled in his most humble way.

Thomas looked at Nathan Pierce. Then he looked at Griff.

"Nathan, you and Griff know this area better than we. What do you think? Have you heard of any detours or bridges out?" Thomas asked.

Nathan did not answer right away. He looked at Thomas then to "Father Archie." Finally, he looked at his brother. Griff shook his head.

"Tell me, brother," Merek said, bringing his horse to the front of the group and stopping just in front of Archie. "Where did you study the word of our Lord?"

"Father Archie" saw the cassock and knew Merek to be a priest.

"Studied here and there, Brother," Archie said, not convincingly. "I am only a humble servant of the Lord, like you, Father."

"Will you pray the Lord's Prayer in Latin with me, Father?" Merek asked.

Archie was beginning to panic. In the past, travelers did not question the bridge being out. Nor did they question his "priesthood."

"Father?" Merek asked. "Will you lead us in prayer?"

Archie began, "Our Father . . ."

"No, Father, please in Latin," Merek asked. "Let us use the language of the Holy Catholic Church."

Archie stopped and looked at Merek, who was smiling.

"Please, save us time and tell us the truth." Merek smiled. "Is the bridge destroyed?"

"Yes, of course, it is! Do you think I would lie? I am a friar, a priest, a holy servant of the Lord," Archie said, backing away from the group. He was panicked and knew the group had discovered his lie.

Griff acted suddenly and drove his horse directly at the retreating "priest." The horse knocked Archie to the ground. Before Archie could gather himself, Griff was off his horse, pulled Archie to his feet, and punched him squarely in the mouth. Before Archie fell, Griff pulled the man forward, put him on his shoulder, and laid him across the saddle of his horse. Griff mounted the horse, Archie lying in front of him.

"Let us go see if the bridge is out," Nathan announced. The group followed, leaving Copthorne, with Archie draped over Griff's saddle.

None of the men protested Griff's sudden action. Each knew the "priest" was lying, particularly when Merek had called him on the Lord's Prayer. It was ironic that Archie was asked to lead the men in reciting the Lord's Prayer in Latin. Except for the Pierce brothers, each man could have said the Lord's Prayer in Latin, even Robin Miller. Yet, the counterfeit priest could not even fake the prayer to keep his secret.

It was not quite two miles out of town when the group came to the "destroyed" bridge. Although it was old and used, it was not destroyed and could be crossed without a problem. By now, Archie had regained consciousness but was not allowed a more comfortable riding assignment by Griff. Archie was too smart to protest, too scared to yell. He was at the mercy of the group.

As the group was about to cross the bridge, two men appeared and stopped them. Both men had yellow bellies. They were shirtless, and the yellow across their abdomen seemed like a type of soot from making charcoal. Both men had swords and stood on the bridge.

"Morning, gents," the older man said, hoisting his word over his shoulder. "Must say, we have had little travelers venture this way lately."

"State your business," Nathan Pierce asked, not looking for small talk.

The older man with the sword and the yellow belly looked at his partner.

"Appears our visitors are not want for small talk," the older man said. He seemed to be a learned man, a man who would keep his wits about him. "Well, sirs, to cross the fine bridge will cost a toll."

"What's the price?" Nathan Pierce asked.

"A pound each," the man with the yellow belly and sword said.

"Too much," Nathan Pierce remarked, moving his horse across the bridge toward the two toll collectors.

Suddenly, the older man put his fingers to his lips and whistled. In an instant, the woods surrounding the bridge became alive. Now, instead of looking at two men, there seemed to be twenty men with an assortment of weapons surrounding the posse. Swords, daggers, bows, and other weapons threatened to attack the posse.

Chaucer was quick to react. He moved his horse to the front near the Pierce brothers. He addressed the leader on the bridge.

"Sir, if I might," Chaucer asked. "Would you consider a deal?"

"A deal?" the leader asked.

"It is only a guess, sir. But I guess the traffic through this part of the woods from Copthorne has been minimal lately."

"Meaning?" the leader asked.

"The thoroughfare of business across this bridge has been scant lately," Chaucer said.

"And how do you know?" the leader asked.

Chaucer nodded to Griff who pushed "Father Archie" from his horse. "Father Archie" fell to the ground in a thud and stayed there.

The leader looked at the fallen man and said nothing. He looked back to Chaucer.

"The population does not use this bridge anymore. This man," Chaucer said, pointing to Archie on the ground, "lures travelers like us away from this bridge and detours them elsewhere. There, his confederates rob and pillage them. If your women and children are starving, his group has taken your tolls away with his lies and deceptions. He and his group are the cause of your woes."

The leader of the group looked at Chaucer and then at the "priest" lying on the ground. He did not say a word. He was thinking. Chaucer saw this and was relieved. A "thinking bandit" was one that would negotiate.

"We must exact a toll," the leader said.

"Let us cross the bridge, and you can have him," Chaucer said, pointing to Archie lying on the ground. "It is my guess that he will explain how his group works, what tolls they collect, and how his work in Copthorne diverts travelers from the bridge you clearly own. He will be yours to do with what you want."

Archie heard the bargaining and began to cry.

"Please, sirs, I am only doing what I have been instructed to do. I have no ill feelings toward any of you."

The leader standing on the bridge nodded to one of his archers who loosed an arrow toward Archie. It hit Archie in the thigh. He fell at once and began to scream.

"You may pass, sirs," the leader spoke above the wailing of the wounded Archie. "We agree to terms. Your passage for this sham of a priest."

Nathan Pierce led the way, and the group proceeded across the bridge. As Merek passed the fallen Archie, he made the sign of the cross.

The leader of the group saw Merek's sign of the cross.

"God bless you, Father. This man," he said, pointing to Archie, "will discover the pains of purgatory and the fires of hell tonight. And then God will take his soul."

Merek nodded and followed the rest of the posse across the bridge. No one looked back.

CHAPTER 34
THADDEUS MAKES A HARD DECISION

The skirmish in the forest was quick and deadly. The highwaymen were no match for Thaddeus and his men. Trained soldiers, they knew how to engage and attack an enemy. And they knew how to kill. As a sign, they left the head of the leader of the robbers on a broken stump to warn others not to seek vengeance. It was a gruesome reminder of the art of killing.

In the skirmish, Thaddeus had pushed the prioress to the ground to prevent the robber's arrow from hitting her. During the fight, the prioress stayed on the ground and covered her head with her arms and curled in a ball so that no horses would step on her in the excitement of the battle. Luckily, none did. She tried not to cry out or make a sound as she heard the fighting continue all around her. And then, suddenly, it grew quiet. She felt an arm tug at her. The prioress slowly looked up and saw that it was Thaddeus. He was not smiling but had his hand out to help her to her feet.

One of the others helped the prioress mount her horse. Although the prioress was not hurt physically, she was shaken by the experience. Up to this point in her life, Eglantyne had led a very simple life away from the poor, the crowds, and the life of violence. And despite the times, she had been sheltered from the day-to-day tragedies that befell the common people around her. Inside Norwood, she had led a protective and secure life without the day-to-day dangers others experienced.

As she sat on her horse waiting for the men to lead her deeper into this strange forest, her emotions began to unravel. In less than a day, her whole world had crumbled. Kidnapped in the middle of the night, she saw her servant beaten and a priest murdered. She had been forced to ride against her will at a pace she had never ridden, gone without food for most of the day, and was treated roughly like a common prisoner by men who were no more than pagans. And now, she was witness to a bloody confrontation where men were savagely beaten and killed in her presence. Seeing the decapitated head on the stump completed her emotional breakdown.

The prioress leaned from her horse and vomited upon seeing the head on the stump. The men did not think anything of her expulsion and continued to lead her horse deep in the forest. She wiped her mouth with a cloth and began to cry. She tried to hold it back but could not. Thaddeus had the reins of her horse and was in front of her. He heard her begin to cry and turned to look at her. The prioress did not look up but cried into the cloth she held to her mouth. Thaddeus looked at Oswald and shrugged his shoulders. He did not know what to do. He turned on his horse and looked toward Mason, who was leading the group down a grassy path in the forest.

As she tried to hold her crying back, it only worsened. The floodgates of her emotions opened, and she began to sob. Now Thaddeus turned on his horse again and tried to say something, but his quiet voice could not be heard over the sobbing Eglantyne. She was having a tough time staying on her horse, as the men were moving through the unchartered forest as swiftly as they could. A few times, Thaddeus had to stop in fear she would fall from her horse. The noise of her crying and the unsteadiness of her riding made the kidnappers come to a halt.

"We cannot go on like this, Thaddeus," Mason said. "There might be other highwaymen around, and this women only announces our arrival."

"Aye," Thaddeus answered. He pulled his horse to the side of the prioress, who was leaning forward with her head against the neck of the horse. She was now crying hysterically.

"Madam, you must stop," Thaddeus pleaded. "There are others around this forest who would find us and attack. We must move quietly."

The prioress did not look up. She only cried further. The build-up had been too great. She had tried for the better part of the day to keep her emotions in check. She was tired, hungry, and scared. Her emotions were out of control. And so she cried loudly.

"Do something!" Oswald demanded.

From his horse beside the prioress, Thaddeus quickly grabbed the prioress and shook her. He said nothing but shook her. Then he slapped her hard across the face. "Enough!" he said with a quiet rage. Had it been a man, he would have knocked him out.

The prioress momentarily stopped crying, shocked at the assault. She had never been struck before.

"We are in peril in this forest. Men will search for us for what we have done back there. Your emotional outburst gives our presence away. One more word, one more sound from you, and I will tie you up and throw you over the horse. Do you understand?" he said in earnest.

The look he gave her was frightening. Before an hour ago, the prioress had a vague idea of why she needed to be frightened of these men. They had kidnapped her. She had seen what they had done to Sister Anne and Father Towns, but she did not think they would harm her. And then she had witnessed the short battle in the forest. These men were brutal, capable of killing without a thought. And afterward, they showed no remorse, no sorrow for the killings. And now she was struck by the leader!

The prioress looked at Thaddeus a moment, still feeling the pain of her cheek where she was struck. She narrowed her eyes, took a deep breath, and screamed at the top of her lungs. It was not a long scream, for Thaddeus used the back of his hand to knock her from her horse. She fell with a thud and did not move.

"You killed her!" Oswald shouted, jumping from his horse.

Thaddeus joined him as the others kept a sharp eye out for visitors. Thaddeus checked her breathing as Oswald, kneeling, lifted her upper torso into her arms. Fortunately, the ground on which she landed was grassy and soft from the recent rain.

"She breathes," Thaddeus said quietly.

"Thank God," Oswald remarked, looking at the swollen cheek where she had been struck.

"Give her time. She will come to," Thaddeus said quietly. He stood and went to his horse for ropes.

"What are you going to do?" Oswald asked, still cradling the woman in his arms.

"Whatever it is, Thaddeus, make it fast," David said. "Her cry must have been heard."

"Come, help me." Thaddeus ordered.

Jack was first off his horse. He took the legs of the prioress, and Thaddeus took the upper torso from the lap of Oswald. Together, they lifted the unconscious lady and lay her across the saddle, face down.

"Tie her ankles together. I will get her hands. Oswald, find a soft cloth for her mouth."

As the men tied the ankles and the hands of the woman, Oswald found a small cloth from the saddle on the horse of the prioress and gave it to Thaddeus. Thaddeus immediately tied it around the woman's neck and stretched it so that it created a gag. Thaddeus made sure the gag did not hinder her nose from breathing. When she was ready, Thaddeus, Jack, and Oswald returned to their horses. A nod from Thaddeus, and Mason led the way through the forest.

From a distance, the kidnappers heard men approaching. They were not sure if the men were from the family of robbers who had attacked them earlier, or they were men investigating a woman's scream. Nevertheless, Thaddeus and his men made sure to go in the opposite direction of the men's voices. And with the prioress subdued, the band of kidnappers were able to make their way through the forest with great haste and without incident.

It was not long before the prioress awoke. At first, she was confused by her inability to move her arms, her legs, and her awkward position on the horse. Upon awakening, she felt the movement of the horse and the ground in which her eyes could see. It was uncomfortable and hurt her stomach and ribs. When she tried to release herself from the movements of the horse, she found that her feet and hands were tethered. She tried to cry out, but the gag was tightly wound. She made noise, but no one seemed to hear her. Finally, she realized she was tied over top the saddle.

The men did hear her, but the sounds she made were muffled by the gag. For his part, Thaddeus rode aside her horse and made sure she stayed across the saddle. He did not want her to fall again.

Mason led the men outside the forest, and the procession climbed a hill barren of trees or foliage. The land had been tilled recently, but they saw no evidence of the farmers who worked the land. By now, it was dark, and they moved as swiftly and as safely as possible.

"Down there," Mason said quietly to the group. "That is Crawley."

In the distance, the kidnappers could see a few fires and what looked like a small town. It was about a mile from the hill in which they travelled.

"What do you want to do?" Mason asked Thaddeus.

Oswald wanted to go to Crawley, find some hostelry, and get some sleep. He was exhausted.

"Is that where the main road is?" Thaddeus asked.

"Aye," Mason answered. "Once we get on the main road, we will make much better time."

"What is after Crawley?" Thaddeus asked.

"Horsham is about another eight miles," Mason said.

"Come, Thaddeus. Let's stay in Crawley for the night. The horses are tired. I am tired. This poor woman must be exhausted." Oswald whined.

The prioress made some noises but was ignored.

"We lost too much time with that damn detour. No, I say we move on. Keep going," Thaddeus said.

"Lost time?" Oswald questioned. "May I remind you that we are ahead of schedule?"

Thaddeus looked at Oswald in the growing darkness. "I am thinking that if we are being pursued, they would have gained ground on us with this skirmish and detour through the forest."

"But we do not even know if someone is following us. You yourself sent David back to make sure we were not being followed." Oswald pleaded. "No one is coming."

"Nevertheless, we keep moving," Thaddeus said, not to Oswald, but to his men. "We will go through Crawley, find the main road, and make our way to Horsham. Just outside of Horsham, we will get off the main road and grab some sleep. Any questions?"

"We are with you," Thaddeus's men all seemed to say.

"Well, I disagree." Oswald complained.

"Listen," Thaddeus said, "you want to sleep in Crawley tonight. Go ahead. No one is stopping you. But we will move on. We will meet you in Petersfield tomorrow night."

The procession moved on without another word. Mason led them down the hill toward the town of Crawley. For his part, Oswald said nothing. He was too tired to argue. The prioress was motionless, either asleep or unconscious. The hill was steep, but Mason found an easier slope for the party to find the path leading to the town.

There was no movement in the town as they entered. A few of the cottages had a trace of light from a solitary candle, but most of the buildings were dark. A tavern on the eastern part of town seemed to have life. Men were singing, and a woman was laughing as the men passed the tavern. Suddenly, Oswald veered his horse from the group toward the tavern.

"See you tomorrow night in Petersfield," he said in a quiet voice. "There is a tavern in Petersfield called The Thistle. That is where we will meet."

"The Thistle it is," Thaddeus echoed, and his men continued on with the stolen prioress.

Oswald dismounted his horse and watched the men leave through the growing darkness. Satisfied they were through the town, he entered the tavern.

The tavern was small with a low ceiling. It had no windows. Oswald did notice there was a door opposite the entrance and made note of it. The tables and benches were scattered throughout the room. All looked worn and ramshackled. Oswald saw the tavern keeper in the left corner serving customers from a long board supported by two large kegs. Oswald counted five customers surrounding the serving board. They were all sharing the same cup, singing an old English drinking song, and standing very close to a woman who seemed drunk and friendly.

"Welcome sir," the tavern keeper announced. "Please join us."

Oswald nodded to the tavern keeper and walked close to the board with the barrels.

"Thirsty, sir?" the tavern keeper asked.

Oswald nodded and threw a coin on the wooden board supported by the two old kegs. The tavern keeper took the coin and gave Oswald a cup full of ale. Oswald took the cup and hoisted it in a mock salute to the company of strangers. The strangers laughed and hoisted the cup they shared, taking turns sipping from it. They began to sing again.

The lady had seen the coin Oswald gave to the tavern keeper and made her way to the end of the board where Oswald stood. "Always good to be in the company of a gentleman," she said with a provocative smile. "Want some company, sir?"

The other men at the bar laughed at her remark. They made some rude comments about the lady, and each laughed at the comment each made. It seemed that the ruder the comment, the more the men laughed.

The woman was not dismayed by the comments of the men. She edged closer to Oswald, smiling at him and placing her hand on the cup from which he drank. "Will you share, sir?" she asked with a smile.

Oswald took another gulp of the drink and handed her the cup. She took the cup, looked at the men who were mocking her, and drank from Oswald's cup. The men cheered.

"Another," Oswald demanded, throwing another coin at the tavern keeper. The owner refilled Oswald's cup. Oswald drank plentifully. The ale went down smoothly. The day had been eventful and exhausting, but the ale made it all seem worthwhile. He took another long drink from the cup.

"Easy, sir." The lady smiled. "The night is young," she said, moving closer to Oswald and letting her breast brush up against his arm resting on the board supported by the two barrels.

"Do you have a room?" Oswald asked the tavern keeper.

"For one or two?" the tavern keeper asked, all the men laughing at the joke.

Oswald stepped free of the woman clinging to his arm. He pushed the cup with ale in it toward her, nodded and stepped to the side.

"I need lodging tonight," he said, beginning to feel the exhaustion of the day setting in.

"All I got is the loft above the bar," the tavern keeper said. He pointed to a ladder that led to a loft that overlooked the bar.

"How much for a spot?" Oswald asked.

"A shilling, sir," the tavern keeper answered, trying to keep a straight face.

"I have five pennies. Will that do?" Oswald asked, knowing the loft was up for negotiation.

"Five will do." The tavern keeper smiled. He took a candle from the bar, lit it from another candle, and gave it to Oswald. "Gets dark up there, sir. This will guide you."

"Thank you," Oswald said, accepting the lit candle.

"Mind you, sir, be sure to extinguish it properly. Wouldn't want a fire in this tinderbox," the innkeeper warned.

Oswald nodded. "Good night, all," he said to the group.

The group wished him a good night and forgot about him. The men at the bar began singing again as Oswald approached the ladder. Oswald climbed the ladder and inspected the loft. It was not very big but could accommodate four grown men if needed. The floor was lined with straw. With the candle, Oswald made a thorough investigation of the room. Finding a spot that suited him, he took his personal pack, lay it out on the straw. Oswald took off his boots and lay down. He fell asleep instantly and slept soundly.

An hour later, he was unaware that someone had joined him.

CHAPTER 35

A DISCOVERY IN CRAWLEY

Oswald slept in the loft of the small tavern longer than he had planned. It was his intention to awaken and be on the road at first light. His exhaustion from the hectic day before plus the welcomed ale at night made his sleep welcome, and he gave into it. He slept peacefully and was only awakened by the noise of busy market town.

Crawley was a small town. In Roman times it had been an important iron-working village used by the Romans to fortify its armory in helping to settle the land. Recently, Crawley's location made it a popular market town. Fields of various crops surrounded the town, while a little distance south, fishermen were able to sell their wares without travelling too far for their goods to spoil. Farmers, fishermen, merchants, and buyers all came to Crawley to do business and make money.

Oswald heard the early-morning buzz of the merchants, fishermen, and farmers setting up their booths to sell goods, but he did not awaken to the noise. Instead, he slept. As he slept, he found comfort in a body sleeping next to him. He was not consciously aware of the body, but as he slept soundly, he could feel its presence. It actually comforted him. The comfort of the body and the way it seemed to snuggle next to him encouraged him to sleep longer.

Suddenly, he awoke. It was daylight! For a moment, he felt an urge to panic, knowing he was almost two hours late in keeping with his schedule. He looked around the loft. It was empty except for the body that lay beside him. The body was hidden under the blanket

Oswald kept rolled up on his saddle. He quickly pulled the blanket down to discover a woman sleeping beside him.

He jumped to his feet, startled at her presence. With Oswald's sudden movement, she too awoke. She rolled over on her back and looked through bloodshot eyes at the man she found comfort in. It was the woman who was entertaining the men at the bar the night before.

"Good mornin' love," she said without a smile. "Mind if I use the blanket? Not quite ready to greet the mornin'."

"How dare you lie beside me?" Oswald sputtered. He tried to keep his voice low, but his anger at her intrusion into his privacy angered him.

"Oh, my sweet. You didn't seem to mind my company last night. It got chilly up here, and you did not mind when I snuggled close."

"I was sleeping!" Oswald began. "I never agreed to lay with you."

"Lay with me?" she laughed. "You did not 'lay' me, or the charge would be higher."

"Charge?" Oswald asked, trying to battle her nonsensical words and his urge to run. It was daylight. Someone might see him!

"Come on, sugar," she said, sitting up. "You can afford my price. I saw the coins you showed the barkeep last night. I only want one."

"You want me to pay you for lying beside me last night?" Oswald asked in disbelief.

"Just one coin, sir, or there will be a commotion," she said with a smile. "I can raise my voice if I have to. I can be quite loud and proclaim to all the merchants below that you took advantage of me. You would not want that kind of trouble. Would you?"

Oswald's mind was racing. This woman was blackmailing him for money. He was late to leave the town. Many people would see him. Even though he did not believe they were being followed, somewhere deep in his mind, Thaddeus had convinced him that they were indeed being followed. What he did not need was for this woman to be screaming and calling attention to him.

He took a coin from his small leather purse and tossed it to her. She caught it and examined it immediately.

"Come to think of it," she said coyly, "maybe one coin will not do."

Now the panic left Oswald. Her comment angered him. It suddenly made him think clearly. "Another coin?" he asked, pretending to show a little fear at her threat.

"Maybe three more will do." She smiled, feeling the man was at her mercy.

Oswald reached back in his coat and pulled out the purse. He feigned a smile. "For more coins, should I not get more comfort from you?"

The lady smiled at the notion. "Why yes, we can work something out," she said, standing. She wore a large but loosely linen shift that left her legs exposed.

Oswald moved closer to the woman. "Can we start with a kiss?"

"The comfort I provide will cost you five coins, plus the three coins for the warmth I gave you last night," she said, still a few feet away from Oswald.

Oswald pretended to think for a moment. He looked at her, then at his swollen purse. "Very well," Oswald said, still holding his purse in hand.

"Payment first, if you please, sir," the woman said, holding out her arm.

Oswald counted the coins from his purse and put them in the woman's hand. She took them, counted them, and smiled. She advanced closer to Oswald, who took her in his arms. She was ready to kiss him when he suddenly pushed her back and punched her squarely in the left temple. She fell to the straw-covered floor. She did not move.

Oswald acted quickly. He grabbed the coins that had fallen to the floor and quickly put them in his purse. Then he made for the blanket he had shared with the woman the night before. She had fallen on the blanket after the assault. He merely rolled her body over and pulled the blanket free. He rolled it up and made for the ladder to descend to the main floor. He did not bother to see if the woman were alive or not.

At the bottom of the ladder, Oswald was greeted by the barkeep. "How was yer rest, sir?" he asked with a toothy grin.

"It was fine," Oswald said quickly, walking toward the entrance of the bar.

"Did the lady give comfort?" the barkeep asked.

Not wanting to cause any more commotion, Oswald stopped, took a coin from his purse, and flipped it to the barkeep. The barkeep caught it in the air and nodded in thanks. "Is the lady resting presently?" the barkeep asked.

"Indeed," Oswald said as he left the bar. The barkeep said something and began to cross the room toward the ladder as Oswald left. He did not hear what the barkeep said, but he knew he had better leave quickly.

The street beside the tavern was bustling with business. Merchants were announcing their wares amongst the noise of patrons haggling over prices. Farmers held vegetables in their hands, selling to a throng of villagers. Fishermen's stalls were busy with their owners trying to sell freshly caught bream or pike. Livestock seemed to be everywhere, complete with sounds and smells. It was the beginning of a beautiful spring day, and the small town was alive with commerce.

Fortunately, Oswald found his horse where he had left it. He mounted the horse and, for a moment, forgot his bearings. Which way was the correct way out of town? It took him a moment to gather his thoughts.

And then there was a commotion. Among all the noise of the merchants and busy customers, someone was shouting. At first, Oswald was not aware of the strong voice shouting. He began to notice some people of the dusty village street looking at him. Then Oswald heard the loud voice. It was the barkeep! And he was shouting at Oswald.

"Stop that man! I say, stop him!" The barkeep shouted, pointing at the mounted Oswald. "He has assaulted my wife! I say, someone stop him!"

Oswald looked around, saw the crowd beginning to point at him, and spurred his horse. The animal sensed the urgency of the situation and raced in the direction Oswald wanted. He left before anyone could question or capture him. His accuser began to run after him but never got close. The barkeep watched as the stranger left the village on the galloping horse.

The market town went back to its usual business. People went back to examining the goods on display, as merchants boasted of their products. Children chased loose livestock and laughed at the entertainment. The barkeep looked around. None of them seemed to care that his wife had been assaulted, knocked cold by the fist of a stranger. He shook his head. It was if the stranger had never been there.

He walked back to the tavern to see to his wife. He hoped she was not injured badly. It would be bad for his business. Her "comfort" was a profitable side business to running the tavern. He closed the door behind him and locked the door. He would not open for business until later in the morning. Perhaps his wife would be feeling better by then. He needed her and the "comfort" she provided to his customers.

The barkeep had hoped someone would have stopped the man who had assaulted his dear wife. He had hoped his shouting would spur the local citizens in helping him to catch the stranger and bring him to the sheriff's office. He wanted justice for his wife's assault. More importantly, he wanted the coins inside the stranger's purse. The coins would have soothed the swollen face of his poor wife. But alas, no one came to his aid. It was the barkeep's opinion that no one in the village had even given the stranger a strong look. No one.

But the barkeep was wrong. Someone had seen the stranger. Someone took notice of him. Someone even knew the man. Hugh Bowman had just entered the edge of the village when the shouting began. As the shouting man pointed, Hugh fixed his eyes on a man mounted on a horse across the street from the tavern. It was Oswald!

Sent ahead of the others, Hugh was to look for signs of the kidnapping party and a place for the others to eat and replenish supplies. After Copthorne, the trackers had lost the trail. Ned, Griff, and Hugh went in separate directions to try and find the trail, agreeing to meet again at noon at a designated point along the road travelled by the others in the posse.

Hugh saw Oswald and froze. He could not believe his eyes. His immediate reaction was to approach him, capture him, and bring him back to the others. But Hugh was a hunter, and instinct told him to hold back. It was important not to make a sudden move, blend in with the busy crowd. Observe. Where were the others? Hugh was tempted to stand in the stir ups of his saddle and look for the prioress. The shouting continued. As Hugh slowly made his way toward the kidnapper, Oswald fled on his horse. A man from the tavern ran after him but stopped in a short distance.

Recognizing that Oswald was alone, Hugh quickened the pace and brought his horse to the tavern where the shouting had begun. Hugh looked down the road and could see the fleeing Oswald. Now it was up to the yeoman to make a decision. Go after the kidnapper, capture him, and bring him to the others, or mark his path, trail him for a time, and report back to the others. Without deciding which was more prudent, he began to follow the road on which the kidnapper fled.

As he rode, his decisions had drawbacks. Hunt the man down by himself, and he might run into the whole kidnapping party. If that occurred, he might be captured without the posse ever knowing what became of him or the kidnappers. The other choice was to let him go, mark his trail, and report back to the Pierce brothers. The negative to that notion was that the trail might grow cold, or for some reason, Oswald would simply disappear. These thoughts raced through Hugh's mind as he quickened the pace.

The road turned a half mile out of town, and when Hugh could no longer see Oswald, he slowed his horse and became more cautious. He did not want to be seen. His element of surprise was his biggest ally. As he slowed, Hugh realized he did not have to make a definitive choice at the moment. Follow the kidnapper for a bit. Try to get a sense of the direction in which he was going. Hugh knew the road Oswald exited the town was the main road heading west. If he continued for another two or three miles, Hugh felt it was safe to assume the kidnapper would stay on the same path. So that was the plan: follow for at least two miles in a cautious and invisible way and see if the man stayed the course.

Hugh calculated he was a mile out of town. In the distance, the road had become straight, dissecting wide-open farm fields. Most of the fields were cleared, for it was spring, and the planting had recently been finished. The openness of the fields caused Hugh to slow down considerably. With his fine eyesight, he could still see Oswald up ahead, still riding hard. Hugh paced his horse, allowing the animal to open its gait, but not come to a gallop. By contrast, Oswald's horse was at a full gallop. It had not slowed since it had left town. Hugh Bowman made a decision. Capture the reeve.

Hugh smiled as he thought of a plan. It was simple and would work. There was one drawback, and Hugh was willing to gamble. He drew his horse off the main road and veered about fifty yards into the open field to the left. In this way, he could still see the fleeing kidnapper, stay parallel to the main road, and stay out of sight if Oswald happened to look back. A man fleeing on his horse was apt to glance at the road behind him to see if he was being followed. If Oswald would look back, the road would be clear.

And so he continued to follow, picking up his pace a little. Before they had gone another mile, Hugh could see that the kidnapper's horse had slowed considerably. Now was Hugh's chance. He was far enough away to quicken the horse's pace, yet far enough for Oswald not to hear him. Still in the fields beside the road, Hugh drew nearer to the kidnapper.

Oswald suddenly stopped his horse and began to dismount. As Oswald's feet hit the ground, Hugh went to a full gallop. By now it was clear that the other kidnappers were not around, so with that in mind, Hugh drove his horse hard toward the dismounted reeve. At the same time, he guided his horse closer to the main road, where the path would be faster.

Only a few seconds on the ground, Oswald knew something was amiss. He was not sure, but his instincts knew. A horse! He heard it before he saw it. And then he saw it! Coming from the fields, it was making its way to the main road and toward him. The rider was wearing green. It was not until he saw the brown face that panic set in. It was the yeoman who travelled with the knight and squire! Thaddeus had been right all along. They had come for the prioress!

Oswald was on his horse quickly, kicking the horse in the ribs to spur it ahead. The horse whinnied, kicked its two legs high and raced west. Oswald looked back. The forester was at a distance but coming hard. Oswald yelled and kicked his horse again, urging him to gallop faster. For a quarter of a mile, Oswald's horse did just that. But the horse was spent after the earlier getaway from the town. With almost no rest, the horse was losing its energy fast. Oswald could hear its heavy panting as it began to slow considerably. He kicked harder and yelled at the horse to continue, but it did not help.

Hugh Bowman was close and bearing down. Normally, Oswald would have ridden his horse into the woods and tried to hide, but out here there were no woods, only fields. His horse was walking now, panting and snorting for oxygen. He turned and saw the yeoman gaining. Oswald was trying to think fast. He had no weapons other than a dagger. He should not have needed one. He was travelling with mercenaries! Besides, weapons on pilgrimages brought looks of doubt and suspicion.

The forester was two hundred yards away and coming fast. Oswald decided to dismount and use the horse as a shield. Perhaps he could negotiate with the yeoman. Talk to him, get him close where he might get a chance to use his dagger. After all, the forester seemed to be alone. Take care of the man in green and continue on his journey to the designated meeting place.

At one hundred yards, Hugh Bowman saw the reeve dismount and place his worn horse between Hugh and himself. Hugh immediately slowed his horse down and approached the reeve cautiously, allowing his horse to walk the rest of the way. Twenty paces from the reeve, Hugh stopped and took out his bow. He strung it calmly and readied an arrow.

"Why are you chasing me?" Oswald asked. "Your sudden appearance has spooked my horse and given me a scare. Are you chasing me because I chose not to finish the pilgrimage? Is there a law against not finishing a pilgrimage?"

The yeoman did not say a word.

"Is that not why you are here? I left the procession of the pilgrimage to Canterbury because I did not like the company. I am on my way back to my lord's estate," he said, still hiding behind his horse.

Hugh nudged his horse with his knees, and the animal moved closer to the reeve.

"You cannot shoot me for leaving the procession," the reeve reasoned, trying to see if the yeoman knew of the kidnapping.

Hugh kept the arrow ready in the bow, but did not pull back on the cord.

"Do you speak the king's language? Do you speak at all?" Oswald said, frustrated by the forester's silence.

"You will come back with me," Hugh said quietly.

"For the pilgrimage?" Oswald asked, still hoping the forester knew nothing of the kidnapping.

Hugh did not smile. He merely shook his head. "There are some men who have some questions for you."

"About what?" Oswald asked, continuing to move the horse between himself and the forester.

"I think you know, sir. It is my duty to return you to the authorities," Hugh answered, swiftly gliding from his horse. Bow in hand, he also had a dagger and small sword at his waist.

"Before I relent, I must know what I am being hunted for," Oswald said with force, trying to bully the forester. "I will not go with the likes of you."

"You are going with me, sir. There is no doubt about that. You can either sit on top on the saddle or be draped over it. But you are coming with me."

"And if I refuse?" Oswald demanded, keeping the horse between him and the yeoman.

"I will subdue you and hurt you. I will break one or both of your arms or legs. Or I will just shoot you with the bow."

"Why do you follow me?" Oswald asked one last time.

"The prioress has been kidnapped. You are to blame."

"Me? Why, I never . . ."

Hugh shook his head and waited for the reeve to become quiet.

"Anglicus told us everything. We know you are the ring leader."

Oswald did not say a word. He pulled the horse away from the forester. There was nothing between the two men now. Oswald held his hands out as a sign of submission.

Hugh took the bow and stretched the cord. The arrow was poised to strike the reeve.

"Toss your dagger and any other weapons you have in the dirt, over there. One wrong move, and my arrow will strike you."

Oswald took his dagger and threw it in the dirt. He turned slowly so that Hugh could see he had no other weapons. Hugh relaxed the cord on the bow.

"I will bind your hands and place you on the horse. We will ride back to where the others await. I must warn you that if you try to escape, I will hurt you. Do you understand?"

Oswald nodded. Hugh put the bow and arrow down momentarily. Keeping an eye on his prisoner, he went to his horse and pulled out a small rope. With the rope, he approached the reeve, who held out his hands as if to comply. As Hugh began to bind his hands, Oswald made a sudden move, pulling his hands back so that Hugh became unbalanced and drifted toward the reeve.

Oswald pulled the forester close to him and tried to knee him in the groin. Although he was off balance, Hugh was able to avoid the knee to the groin. It glanced off his thigh. Grabbing the reeve by one arm, the falling forester was able to pull the reeve over his shoulder to the ground. They wrestled in the road, the reeve trying to punch the yeoman, who took the blows as he entangled the reeve with his strong legs. The forester was able to work himself on top of the reeve, who was trying desperately to grab the dagger in Hugh's belt.

Hugh, sitting astride the reeve's waste, where his legs could do no damage, pinned one of the reeve's arms with his left leg. He punched Oswald squarely in the face, the blood of his broken nose splattering everywhere, dotting the forester's green cloak with dabs of red. Not finished, the forester struck again, further pushing the Oswald's nose farther from its original position.

Oswald screamed, the fight taken out of him and lay without a struggle. Hugh Bowman was not done. "Did I not say that if you resisted, there would be pain?" he said with anger, almost spitting in the bloodied face of the reeve.

Still astride the fallen reeve, Hugh took out his dagger. He placed it under the left ear of the reeve. With a quick swipe of the blade, he cut off the reeve's ear. Oswald screamed in pain. Hugh Bowman rose and looked at the reeve writhing in pain on the ground.

"That is for my friend, Merek," he said quietly. "Give me more trouble, and I will cut off the other ear."

Cutting a strip of Oswald's tunic, Hugh made a bandage for the bloody side of the reeve's head. He let the nose bleed freely as he bound the man's hands and helped him mount his horse. Once on his horse, Oswald groaned, cried in pain and almost lay on his horse as Hugh led them back toward the town.

Hugh made sure to avoid Crawley as he returned to the posse. He did not want to lose his prisoner at any cost. There were too many dangers in going through the town. Perhaps the tavern owner had a real charge against the reeve. He would be taken by the authorities. On the other hand, Hugh knew the land and its people. Seeing a man with brown skin leading a white man as a prisoner would draw suspicion. He wanted to hurry back to the posse with his prize possession but knew he had to be cautious in his travels. And so he was.

CHAPTER 36
THE POSSE GAINS A BARGAINING CHIP

The night before Hugh Bowman discovered Oswald in Crawley, Nathan Pierce made a decision to branch out the posse's search for the kidnappers. Knowing the kidnappers had been tricked into taking another trail by Archie and his bandits, Nathan was not sure in which direction the kidnappers headed from the deceiving detour in town.

Nathan sent Hugh Bowman on the main road from Copthorne to Crawley. Hugh's task was to see if the kidnappers had found the main road from the detour they had been deceived in taking in the nearby forest. Hugh was up early and on the road before dawn, estimating that if the kidnappers had returned to the main road, it would have been a mile or two from Copthorne. By the time he was at his estimated spot, there was enough daylight to keep an eye on the trail for the kidnappers.

Hugh made it all the way to Crawley without a visible sign. As he entered the busy market town, he had the good fortune to hear the tavern keeper screaming for help with his wife's attacker. Hugh had then seen Oswald and went after him.

Nathan sent Griff and Chaucer back along the trail the kidnappers had taken. Just outside of town, they came to the mill with the toll bridge. The man who collected the tolls came out and demanded some coins to cross the bridge. Griff ignored the man and simply rode slowly across the bridge. He waited for Chaucer on the other side.

"We ride for the Constable Horn out of Dartford," Chaucer said.

"What's that to me?" the man said. "Cross the bridge, pay the toll."

Chaucer reached into his tunic as if searching for coins.

"By chance, do you remember a group of men and a single woman crossing this bridge yesterday?"

"Maybe I do, maybe I don't," the man said coyly.

"Sir, the woman has been kidnapped. We pursue those who took her in hopes to free her. Any information will be helpful."

The man smiled, thinking he would be clever with Chaucer. "Why would I want to help some rich noblewoman who does not give a tinker's dam about the likes of me?"

"So she did cross here with the men?" Chaucer stopped and repeated to the man they were on official business for the court of justice. The man became angry and began to argue with Chaucer.

But Griff kept going. Once on the other side, it did not take him long to come across the bodies of the outlaws who had attacked the kidnappers. Griff dismounted and took a closer look at the bodies. He shook his head, knowing the bandits were just poor thieves trying to make a living. He shooed the birds from the head sitting atop the stump and looked at the somber visage of the lifeless face. He kicked the head back into the bushes, mounted his horse, and continued into the forest. He had found the trail and did not want to stop.

Chaucer, having negotiated the toll for the bridge crossing, caught up to Griff. "If we pursue the trail into this side of the forest, we will surely meet the friends of these outlaws," Chaucer cautioned Griff who seemed to focus solely on finding a trail.

At first, Griff did not seem to hear Chaucer, studying the path that led to the ambush.

Chaucer saw the dead bodies that lay on the path. "The kidnappers came this way and were met with opposition," Chaucer said to Griff. "By the looks of it, the kidnappers have mettle. They not only escaped the ambush, they decimated their foe and continued on," Chaucer observed. "We have competent foes, Griff."

Griff continued to study the trail. He turned and looked at Chaucer.

"We need to find them," Griff said quietly. It was the first time Chaucer had heard the deputy speak. "The trail is right in front of us."

"Yes, and so is the threat of the bandits. If we follow the trail, we will encounter more bandits. They will be upset about their lost comrades, and there are only two of us. I suggest we backtrack to Copthorne and meet up with Nathan and the others. We will be able to figure out the route the kidnappers took," Chaucer said quietly, trying to reason with the quiet Griff.

Griff thought a moment then nodded. They would return through Copthorne and join Nathan and the others. They had found the trail and were confident they could figure out the detour the kidnappers had taken. So the two men reversed their path and made their way back to town. It was a fortunate decision they made. Two hundred yards down the road, another batch of bandits awaited their next victims.

Once Nathan had sent Hugh Bowman, Griff, and Chaucer on their way, he and the others stayed near the bridge they had traded Archie for a toll to cross. Nathan made small talk with some of the forester bandits and asked about the detour the kidnappers had taken. One of the men drew a crude map in the dirt, showing how the detour could have pushed the kidnappers northwest to Guildford. He also was quick to point out that the trail through the forest could also branch west and come in the back way to Crawley.

As the men talked and drew in the dirt, trying to help Nathan's cause, the others took a long rope and flung one end of it over a thick branch of a tree. Other men guided the weeping Archie, hands bound to the tree in which the rope hung. They tied the rope around Archie's neck, said some remarks, and gave Archie a chance to speak. He was whimpering by then. Without another word, four men pulled on the loose end of the rope, lifting the suffocating bandit whose legs kicked freely as he slowly strangled.

Merek looked on without emotion. As a priest, he did not try to talk the men from the hanging. Nor did he ask Archie if he wanted to make a confession. He simply let the act begin and end. He did not even go over to the swinging body and make the sign of the cross as it swung lifelessly in front of the foresters. Merek felt nothing. It was as if he were back in France fighting the French, where blood and death were common, and the only way one survived the horrors was to turn off his emotions and let it go. It had been a long time since he felt the indifference to the horrors of death. But it was all catching up to him. The kidnapping, the killing, the torture by a man hired by a clergyman, the hypocrisy of the Church all made him question his vocation and priestly vows.

Sir Thomas and Robert did not try to help or interfere with the hanging. They too knew the ways of the real world. Archie had, in essence, taken food from the families who had control of the bridge and the toll road. They both understood the need to hang the man. It was not vengeance as much as it was a warning.

Harry, too, knew not to interfere with the execution. He stood near Merek and watched the man dangle from the rope. As the man died, Harry tapped Merek on the shoulder and nodded toward the flask of wine. Merek handed it to him without a word. Harry Bailly took a long pull and gave it back to Merek, who also drank deeply.

Robin Miller was one of the four men who pulled the loose end of the rope to raise the criminal from the ground. The men of the forest had asked his help, and he gladly joined in. Once the criminal was hoisted, one of the men secured the rope so that the others could let go of the loose end. Robin Miller stood with his hands on his hips as Archie dangled. He did not smile yet held a look of satisfaction.

Nathan was satisfied with his conversation with the foresters. He mounted his horse, as did his posse. They nodded to the men near the bridge and continued down the road. None of the posse spoke. They rode in silence. Even Robin Miller did not even have the desire to play his bagpipes.

In less than an hour, the posse was at the designated meeting point made earlier by the men. It was not an exact point along the main road but was an estimated halfway point between the main road the detoured route the kidnappers must have taken earlier. Nathan's idea was to send Hugh Bowman quickly down the main road in hopes of spotting any sign of the kidnappers. Hugh was to ride to Crawley, investigate, and circle back. Griff and Chaucer, on the other hand, were to take the bogus trail, pick up the trail of the kidnappers, and try to get a reading on the direction they were heading.

Nathan guessed the kidnappers were fleeing west, but he had to make sure they were not going back north. Hence, Griff was sent to make sure the trail he found did indeed go west. Hugh was sent ahead to quicken the search if there was any sign the kidnappers had entered Crawley.

Harry was confused by Nathan's plan but said nothing. In fact, he had no idea where they were. The group was not on the main road anymore but had entered the forest and was proceeding down a small path that led to a thick copse of trees by a small stream. Surprisingly, there was an ancient mound of stones by the stream. To Harry, the mounds of stones were arranged in such a way as to seem like an altar of worship. It was a strange sight in the dense woods.

"This is where we wait for Hugh, Griff, and Chaucer," Nathan said, dismounting. "The stream is clean and fresh. Use the water to fill your daily flasks."

"You know this place?" Thomas asked, dismounting, like the others.

"Heard of it," Nathan said. He pointed to the mound of stones. "Supposed to be an ancient Christian altar that was here before Hastings. I dunno, really. That is what they say."

"What's is called, Nathan?" Sir Robert asked, walking toward the altar. He kneeled in front of the altar and blessed himself.

"St. Anselm's Corner is what is called. It is an easy landmark to find. We wait here for Hugh, Griff, and Chaucer."

With hesitation, Merek walked to the ancient altar. He stood behind the praying knight for a moment. He quietly knelt despite the pain and lowered his head in prayer. He wanted to listen for God's voice. He wanted direction; he wanted to feel God's presence. Quietly, he prayed to God to send his Holy Spirit and rekindle Merek's waning faith. He continued to kneel for some time, listening, hoping for an answer. All he felt was the pain in various areas of his body and the beating of his heart.

And then he heard the horses. The others did too, and so the men quickly took weapons in hand. Merek went to his horse and readied his bow. Thomas and Harry hid behind trees. Nathan, Sir Robert, and Robin Miller stood near the horse to greet the intruders. The horses moved slowly, and as they came into view, one horse was leading the other.

It was Hugh Bowman!

At first, the men could not tell who was on the second horse. The rider was lying on the horse with his face away from the posse. Hugh nodded to the men and gave the reins of the second horse to Nathan Pierce.

"Found him in Crawley," Hugh said.

Robin Miller knew who it was. He ran to the second horse and yanked the rider off the saddle. The reeve fell heavily to the ground and groaned in pain.

Robin Miller kicked the reeve squarely in the ribs. Then he lifted Oswald to his feet and brought him up close.

"You bastard! Thanks be to Christ in high heaven that you have been delivered to my arms," Miller smiled, smacking the reeve sharply across the face. "What happened to your ear, mate?" He smiled.

The men looked at Hugh Bowman, who simply said, "For you, Father Merek. Not quite an eye for an eye."

Robin Miller took out his dagger. "Seems to me he still has one ear too many. I can remedy that."

"No," Nathan Pierce interrupted. "This man has valuable information. We need him awake and in control of his senses." He walked over and took the reeve from Miller's grasp.

Robin Miller put his dagger down. He smiled at the wounded reeve. "There will be time for you, you goddam weasel." He spat on the ground.

The men gathered around the fallen man. The reeve said nothing. He was in pain but fought to show it. He did not show fear but on the contrary looked contemptuously at his captors. He was confident they would not kill him. He had too much information. Information the posse needed.

Horses were heard. It was Griff and Chaucer making their way to the meeting point. They rode up to the group with their weapons drawn, for they could not see the man in the middle. Once they got close enough to see, they sheathed their weapons.

"Oswald," Chaucer said in amazement. "How the devil—?"

"Our friend, Hugh, ran across his path," Harry interrupted. "We were just about to get some information from the turd."

"A stroke of luck, no doubt," Sir Thomas said. "With Oswald here, we also have a bargaining chip with the kidnappers."

"And if I do not want to cooperate?" Oswald said from the ground.

"Come, sir, you are smarter than that," Sir Robert said. "Look at these men. Do you think they will not let you cooperate? No, I think you will give us the information we need. No need for more bloodshed."

"Your bloodshed," young Thomas was quick to remind.

"I will die first before I give up my men," the reeve said with resolve. He was still confident the men would not kill him. After all, there was a nobleman and a priest in the group. They might rough him up, but they would not seriously harm him. As for the yeoman who took his ear, he promised himself he would repay the brown faced man.

Nathan Pierce interrupted his thoughts by suddenly placing a knee on the reeve's chest. He had a dagger in his hand and held it close to the Oswald's nose. He put the blade just inside the reeve's left nostril.

"We will not let you die, Reeve," Nathan said, "before you tell us what we want to know. Death is a gift right now. Death is your only way out. How soon you die will depend on the answers you give."

The reeve saw the look in the deputy's eyes and was suddenly desperate. "You heard Sir Robert. Am I not a bargaining chip?"

"Not to me," Nathan said, using his wrist to flick the point of the dagger to slice the nostril of the reeve, who screamed in pain. Nathan got up, Oswald's blood on his tunic.

None of the men said a word but let the reeve wallow on the ground, his hands covering his bloody nose.

"Bleed, ya' ruddy bastard," Robin Miller said as the men walked over to the altar of St. Anselm's to confer. Robin Miller volunteered to watch the bleeding Oswald.

CHAPTER 37

ON TO PETERSFIELD

Thaddeus and his group had left Oswald on the outskirts of Crawley. Even though it was dark, they continued west on the main road. Tired, hungry, and thirsty, they ventured on, relying on the discipline they had earned from serving in the king's army. It was well into the night when Thaddeus decided it was time to stop and rest. They had travelled through Horsham and were just outside of Billingshurst when he guided them from the main road.

The group settled in a solitary copse of trees. They did not make a fire but settled their packs near the ground and readied themselves for an abbreviated sleep. No man complained. Each was used to a soldier's life. Two of the men helped the prioress off her horse. She was in bad shape. From riding draped over the saddle for hours, she was cramping in her legs and arms. Her cheek was swollen from the blow she received. In all, she was somewhat in mild shock when the men released her bindings and helped her to a spot on the ground where she was to sleep.

The men shared hard biscuits and warm ale, making sure the prioress was given a portion. At first, she declined, too tired and sore. Thaddeus helped her, making sure she took in what he thought would be a sufficient amount of ale. The prioress nibbled on a biscuit but put it down in favor of some much-needed sleep.

David took the first watch. Arming himself with a bow, he disappeared from the group among the trees. In two hours, Mason would relieve him. Thaddeus and Benjamin slept near the prioress, one on either side. It was Thaddeus's idea to keep the bindings off her at night. He felt confident that if the two men slept on either side of her at a small distance, she would not try to wander off. Jack slept near the tethered horses. He made sure they were watered and fed. As tired as Jack was, he would awaken in an instant if one the horses would move or nay suddenly.

The group was up at dawn with no incident to report. As they packed, they ate more biscuit and prepared for the next part of the journey.

Thaddeus nudged the prioress with his foot to awaken her. "Sister, time to go," he said quietly. She did not stir, and for a brief moment, Thaddeus was worried that she was dead. He knelt beside her and turned her on her back. He gently shook her.

Her eyes slowly opened. "You are a beast," she said quietly. "May God send your soul to hell."

"Not today, Madam Prioress. Not today. Come. Time to go."

"I cannot ride. I am hurt. I need a physician."

"You will ride, Sister. I give you the choice on the method in which you ride," Thaddeus said grimly. "We can bind you and drape you over the saddle again, or you can ride upright. Which will it be?"

The prioress knew she had no choice. She tried to close her eyes and say a short prayer, but Thaddeus interrupted her.

"Which will it be?" he asked.

"By St. Loy," she said, shaking her head, "Help me to my feet."

In an hour, the group had passed through Billingshurst. Once through Billingshurst, the main road went through an unusually thick forest. Thaddeus, as a precaution, assembled his team in a tight formation as they traversed the dense forest. It slowed the travel time, but they passed without a hint of highwaymen or thieves. By late morning, they entered Petworth.

Petworth was a small town with a small population. Thaddeus ordered the group to stop for a respite. No one in the town seemed to notice the armed group of men with a solitary woman in their midst. If someone did notice, he was smart enough not to make an inquiry. Petworth was so small village, there was no local constable to guard and protect.

After the stop in Petworth, the kidnappers continued on the main road west to Petersfield. For her part, the prioress kept up with the pace. She had to keep up, as the men took turns riding in front and beside her. The man in front kept hold of her horse's reins, and the man beside her made sure to keep her upright.

Just outside of Petersfield, the main road ran through the ancient burial grounds, rumored to be thousands of years old. Some had said the burial grounds were from the most ancient people of England. In 1366, they appeared as rolling mounds on both sides of the road. Thaddeus was glad the group was passing during the daylight hours. He had heard that the area was dangerous to cross during the dark, not because of the bandits and highwaymen, but because of the evil spirits that haunted the mounds.

In the late afternoon, the group entered Petersfield. Petersfield was a town of prosperity. It was another market town known for its local cottage industries. Leather, wool, and other commodities were sold by the locals from their homes. It was also an unusual town in that the local taxes were kept at a minimum, thus promoting more trade and industry.

"Stallage," a tax on erecting a stall to sell goods, was exempt in Petersfield. Outside merchants were encouraged to sell their goods in Petersfield without the usually heavy tax on erecting a stall. Also, "murage" and "pontage" were not charged in Petersfield. Unlike other towns, merchants were at the mercy of town councils on various "local" taxes. Murage was a tax to merchants to help the town repair a wall or fortification. Pontage was a tax to help the town fix a bridge. Each tax was a way for local town councils to add to their slim treasuries to help in maintaining needed repairs. But Petersfield held none. And it was prosperous. Merchants came from miles to sell their wares.

The agreement was to meet Oswald at The Thistle. Thaddeus led the group through the busy town, a bit surprised by the amount of people on the street. Merchants' stalls lined one portion of the street, while other merchants opened their "cottages" to would-be buyers. Thaddeus felt unusually secure in the crowd knowing that his group of men and one woman would not be noticed among the crowd of merchants and buyers.

The Thistle was in the middle of Petersfield. It was an unusually large building, much like The Swan in Dartford. As the group rode up to the main entrance, they saw the tavern on the left. The main entrance had an opening for horses to enter. A barn stood in the back of the main entrance to The Swan. Thaddeus figured the building to his right was where the inn was located.

As they tethered their horses, Thaddeus had orders. He gathered his men. "This is where we meet Oswald. The lodge where the ransom will be exchanged is not far from here. We are very close, men. A small fortune awaits each of us. But we wait here for Oswald at this tavern. Jack, you will take care of the horses. Stay with them. Mason, you and David will walk about the town. Get a feel for it. Look for someone following us. Once you are sure we have not been followed, join me in the tavern. I will go inside and arrange a room for the prioress to rest. Benjamin, you will get her to her room and secure her. We will wait for Oswald. I pray to God the bastard gets here tonight."

"And if he does not show?" Davis asked.

"I have a map where the lodge is located," Thaddeus said. "Precautionary step. Just to be sure. Any more questions?"

The men had none and dispersed. It was not yet four o'clock.

***

The bleeding reeve was tied to a tree near St. Anselm's altar. The blood from the slice on his nose had coagulated, but none of the men had wiped the old blood from Oswald's face. Combined with the dried blood from his missing ear, the reeve's face was a gruesome sight. Gagged, he did not fight the bindings that held him to the tree. He knew his only hope in living was the honor of Sir Robert and the mercy of the priest, Merek.

Sir Robert and Thomas approached Oswald and removed the gag.

"Come sir," Sir Robert began. "There is some information you can give us without giving away your men."

"Bloody hell," Oswald managed to say.

"I, for one, am interested in who paid you to orchestrate the kidnapping," Sir Robert said calmly.

The reeve just shook his head. He paused and shook his head again.

"Our guess is that a nobleman, just like myself. Am I right? Come, sir. I am not asking for a name. Am I right?" Sir Robert said.

The reeve thought a moment. He blinked his eyes and nodded.

"Very good." Sir Robert smiled. "You see, that was not bad. Thomas, give the man some wine."

Thomas took a flask of wine and put it up to the reeve's lips. Oswald drank deeply. The wine seemed to soothe his wounds immediately.

The other men of the posse stayed back and watched. It was determined that Sir Robert and Thomas would try to gain information from Oswald with reasoning and wine before Nathan Pierce began his forceful methods of interpretation. Robin Miller disliked the plan but deferred to the group's decision. Secretly, he hoped Sir Robert was unsuccessful. He wanted to see the reeve suffer.

Thomas took the wine away from the lips of the reeve.

"I am curious, Oswald," Sir Robert continued. "The prioress. Obviously, she was your target. What I want to know is were you told *why* you were to kidnap her? Before you answer, please think about it. It is a very important question."

Oswald did not answer. He, too, knew it was a critical question.

Before he could answer, Thomas interrupted. "Come, Father, we waste our time. Why would a nobleman trust a lowly reeve with important information? I ask you."

Thomas tried to hit a nerve with the reeve. After all, he had spent time observing Oswald and the others on the trip from Southwark. He had heard the reeve's tale about a crooked miller. He knew the reeve had an uncommon air about himself. Thomas knew Oswald to be arrogant and proud. He hoped his comment stirred the reeve's pride.

Oswald looked at Thomas and glared through the crusty blood that caked his face. Thomas knew in an instant he had made a dent.

"You see, Father, he is just a lowly pawn to some powerful noblemen. I venture to say he was hired to kidnap the prioress and merely bring her to designated spot. He would collect his pay and go on his merry way. The noblemen would not trust detailed information with the likes of a man like Oswald," Thomas said in the most sarcastic way he could summon.

Sir Robert listened intently, and he, too, noticed the marked reaction in Oswald's face. Sir Robert played along.

"Yes, what was I thinking, Thomas? I am certain the nobleman would not disclose his plan to a man like this. We waste our time." He and Thomas began to walk away.

"Lord Berkley trusted me with the entire plan, you fools! Just like other nobles who have hired me before!" Oswald suddenly cried out.

Sir Robert and Thomas turned and looked at the angry reeve. They smiled at him. "He is all yours, Nathan," Sir Robert said, looking at the deputy constable.

Oswald's eyes widened. He knew in that instance he had been tricked. As he inwardly cursed himself, Oswald knew his immediate future was in jeopardy. "I wish to make a deal," he said quickly. "I have information."

"The deal has already presented itself." Nathan approached, his large dagger drawn and ready for use. "Give us the information, and we will make quick work of you."

Oswald suddenly realized he was going to die this day. For a man like he was, who was so organized, calculating and proficient in what he did, it was a realization he could not handle.

"Father Merek, can you help me? For God's sake?" the reeve pleaded, trying to keep his composure.

Merek stepped forward. "Am I to understand that you also hired Anglicus to torture me?"

"It was nothing personal, Father. It was a contract. At the time, I did not know you. I had no idea what it all entailed," Oswald said still tied to the tree.

"I will hear your confession, and I will bless your body when we are through," he said without emotion. "May God have mercy on your soul, Oswald?"

"What about Christ's promise of forgiveness?" Oswald pleaded.

"You can ask Him yourself," Merek said and turned away.

In the end, Oswald told all. He told what he knew of the Berkley-Appleton land dispute, the meeting of the kidnappers in Petersfield, and the hidden lodge where the prioress was to be brought. Nathan Pierce did very little to persuade the reeve to talk. Oswald knew his end was near, and despite his pride and intellect, his grasp of the reality that Nathan Pierce was going to inflict more torture was too much for him to bear.

Satisfied that the reeve had told everything, Nathan Pierce turned to Miller and handed him the dagger. Robin Miller took the dagger and without a moment of hesitation stuck the knife in the abdomen of the reeve. With a firm grasp, he pulled the hilt of the dagger and thrust it upward to the reeve's sternum. As the entrails of the reeve poured out to the ground, he died, as promised, quickly.

CHAPTER 38

ENCOUNTERS IN THE THISTLE

As the sun went down, Thaddeus became concerned about the whereabouts of Oswald. Seated at The Thistle with David and Mason, he kept his eye on the door of the tavern. David was seated in a way that looked toward the rear of the tavern, while Mason kept watch of the stairs that led to some of the rooms where weary travelers could spend the night. All three men had cups of ale in front of them. Each nursed his drink waiting for the reeve to meet them.

Earlier, Thaddeus had secured a solitary room for the prioress. It was indeed costly, for most inns hosted rooms where a number of travelers could share. To get a single room was expensive, and Thaddeus had made a deal with the tavern keeper. He would pay half the cost in advance and the rest in the morning when the group left. It was Thaddeus's intention to leave The Thistle as soon as Oswald arrived, so the price did not concern him. If the plan went as scheduled, he would only have to pay a portion of the cost.

Benjamin was assigned the prioress, and so he sat outside her room. At first, he was content to sit on the floor of the hallway. But as the hours progressed, he began pacing the hallway. When Mason was sent to check on him, Benjamin requested a chair from the tavern. Mason obliged and brought him one. While he waited in the chair outside the door, Benjamin whittled with his large dagger. He was proud of his skill with a knife and prided himself on the sharpness of the blade. Like Thaddeus, he wondered what had happened to Oswald.

By six, The Thistle had a small crowd of men standing at the bar or seated at the benches openly enjoying the house ale. The Thistle had a fine bar made of a lighter pine. Over the years, spilled ale had turned the pine a darker color in some of the areas of heavy use. If one were to look at the bar from the stairs leading to the upper level of the tavern, the bar would look spotted. It was a noisy crowd as some of the men at different benches were competing with an assortment of tavern songs. All seemed to be in a cheery mood, drinking and singing in the early evening.

As men entered the tavern, Thaddeus and his men watched with great attention. Each time the door opened, it was in anticipation that the next man to enter would be Oswald. Each time a different man arrived, there was a certain disappointment registered with each of the kidnappers. The kidnappers were disappointed when two men with red hair entered The Thistle at half past six. They strode in like regular customers and approached the bar. Thaddeus and his men watched, but did not think anything of the men. It was clear to Thaddeus that the two men were brothers. After watching them a few moments, he turned his attention elsewhere.

Nathan and Griff stood at the bar and began to sip their ale. They were the only members of the posse Thaddeus and his men would not know. Once Oswald had told them of the meeting place, it was decided the Pierce brothers would enter The Thistle and get a glimpse of the layout. Hopefully, the brothers would be able to spot the kidnappers and, if lucky, would see the prioress with them. The posse calculated that the prioress would not be in The Thistle with her kidnappers, at least seated in the tavern with them. It would be unusual for a lady to be in the company of a group of men, particularly as the sun went down. Ladies were not seen in taverns after dark unless it was a part of their profession. The posse figured the prioress would be held captive elsewhere.

After Oswald had given the information about the plan, who was involved and how it was to proceed, the posse decided to split as they entered Petersfield. The ride to Petersfield had been a long and strenuous ride, for they had many miles to cross in order to get to The Thistle. Along the way, a plan was formulated. As the men rode, they bounced ideas back and forth as to the best way to proceed. Nathan Pierce wanted to descend on The Thistle as a group and attack the kidnappers. Chaucer suggested a subterfuge to trick the kidnappers, hoping to avoid bloodshed. Sir Robert suggested a more complex plan, one that would not only rescue the prioress and arrest the kidnappers but trap the nobleman who had begun the whole affair with the plan to kidnap Madame Eglantyne. Sir Robert's plan was met with enthusiasm by the entire group, even the Pierce brothers. Once in Petersfield, the group separated to set the plan in motion.

Sir Robert and Thomas were sent ahead in one direction, while Harry Bailly and Chaucer went another. Each set of men had a designated goal they hoped to achieve before midmorning. Each would have to continue riding hard into the night to accomplish each goal.

The Pierce brothers were to enter The Thistle and try to spot the kidnappers. Hugh Bowman, Robin Miller, and Father Merek Willson stayed outside the tavern and give support to the Pierce brothers when needed. The element of surprise was crucial to rescuing the prioress unharmed. As they reached the outskirts of town, Merek, Hugh Bowman, and Robin Miller split up, keeping to the back streets and alleys. The brothers continued into town together, not worrying about who saw them. Merek looked for the highest point in the town of Petersfield. Spotting the local church tower, he made his way to it.

Hugh Bowman and Robin Miller made their way into town separately. Hugh was to find a spot outside the tavern itself and keep himself hidden. Robin was to make his way to the barn and put on an act as if he were drunk and needed a place to lie down for a while. Nathan had figured that at least one of the kidnappers would be stationed in the barn to keep the horses ready for Oswald's arrival. Robin Miller rode slowly into the barn, nodding to the barn keeper. He struggled getting off his mount. He did not have to act as if he were drunk. He had been sipping on a flask of wine the entire way.

When Robin Miller entered the barn, he kept his hood tightly over his head, just in case one of the kidnappers was in the barn. The man in charge of the barn approached Miller and asked for coins for the keep of the horse. Robin Miller grunted and seemed reluctant to pay the man but did so. As he paid the fee, he nonchalantly looked around and saw the kidnapper guarding the horses. Jack was looking right at Miller. Robin Miller was quick to turn his horse, so the kidnapper could not see his face.

Although Robin Miller had been drinking, his wits were about him. He knew there was a kidnapper staring at him. Robin recognized the young man from the trip to Canterbury. He only hoped the young man did not take notice of him. Trying to diffuse the young man's scrutiny, Robin Miller suddenly fell beside his horse, landing in the hay of a stall. As he lay in the straw, he began to snore heavily, hoping the young man would feel at ease as a drunk man was in his presence.

Jack thought he recognized the man who entered the barn. Even though the man's hood was up, there was something about him that put Jack on alert. When the man in the stall began to snore, Jack's attention went from the rider to the horse. And then he saw them—bagpipes! It was Miller from the trip! What was he doing here? Was it a coincidence? Was he really following the kidnappers?

Jack needed to inform Thaddeus that a member of the procession to Canterbury was here in Petersfield. It could not be a coincidence that Miller had made his way to this barn in this town so soon after the kidnapping. No, he had to tell Thaddeus, but he could not let Miller out of his sight. Even though the man seemed inebriated and unconscious in the straw beside his horse, the soldier in him knew not to take a chance. He would bind the sleeping Miller and then seek Thaddeus in the bar.

Jack approached the sleeping man with care. He had grabbed some rope from the stall in which he kept the horses of the kidnappers. The snoring Miller made Jack comfortable to move quickly toward the man without fear of too much noise. Standing over the snoring Miller, Jack nudged the sleeping man's leg. He did not budge. Jack bent to Miller's waist with the rope, intending to tie his hands first.

As he slowly grabbed one of Miller's hands, Robin Miller's other hand shot up in an instant and grabbed Jack by the throat. Instantly, Jack let the hand of Miller go and was quick to attack the hand around his throat. As strong as Robin Miller was, the angle in which his body lay could not support the strangling grip of his hand. Jack pulled away and tumbled in the straw. He was on his feet facing Miller ready for attack.

Robin, too, was on his feet. Both men faced each other, no weapons in hand. Jack had let the rope drop when he was surprised by Robin Miller's hold. They moved about the stall slowly, looking for an angle in which they would attack. Robin's horse had moved to the side of the stall and limited the direction in which the men moved.

"Where is she, lad?" Robin Miller asked, no evidence that he was drunk.

"How did you find us?" Jack asked, moving slowly about the stall.

"By Christ's bones, I will break every bone in your body, boy." Robin Miller promised.

Jack pulled a knife from behind his waste. He waved it in front of Robin Miller.

"I am going to take that knife and stick it up your arse," Miller said, moving closer to Jack.

Jack waved the knife and suddenly thrust it at Miller. The thrust was not close, and Robin Miller did not back down.

"You gonna wave that thing or use it, lad?" Miller said, smiling.

Jack waved the knife and thrust again, this time nicking Miller in the fabric near his elbow. The nick drew blood. The sight of blood encouraged Jack, and he went on the offensive, moving closer to Miller, who gave way and began to move backward.

When Jack saw Miller moving backward, his confidence grew, and he became more aggressive. He came at Miller waving and thrusting the knife more rapidly. Each rapid stroke became longer, and it was the long motion that Miller looked for. As Jack thrust at Miller with a long stroke and missed, Miller attacked. He ran right into the chest of the kidnapper and bear-hugged him. Lifting the kidnapper from his feet, Robin Miller squeezed with all his might.

Jack was surprised by the large man's quickness. He was also not ready for the man's strength. The Miller's bear-hug was a force in which Jack had never experienced. As Jack was lifted off his feet, he could feel his ribs ready to burst. Taking his knife, he stabbed Miller in the side in the only motion his arms were allowed to move. His motion was short, but he kept jabbing the knife into Miller's side.

As Jack thrust the knife into Miller's side, the pressure from the bear-hug increased. He pulled the knife and thrust again. Miller did not relent but kept on squeezing. Jack thrust again but could feel himself losing his breath. Jack's thrusts became weaker as he tried to cling to his breath. He could feel Miller's breath on his face and Miller's whiskers against his cheeks. The man would not let go. Jack could not thrust the dagger anymore. He was losing oxygen. He lost control of his hand and let the knife go. It remained in Miller's side. Miller continued to squeeze, breathing heavily, trying to hold on longer than the young soldier could breathe.

Jack went limp in his arms, but Miller continued to squeeze, feeling the broken ribs on the young soldier. Suddenly, Robin Miller let the lifeless body of Jack fall into the straw. The body fell with a thud and remained motionless. Miller bent over, trying to catch his breath. He knelt, hoping he would remain conscious. He took his hand and with a sudden pull took the knife from his side. He was bleeding. Using the knife, he cut a strip from the tunic of the dead man and used it to plug the hole in his side.

"Goddam you, you bloody bastard," he cursed at the dead soldier. Robin took the knife and wiped it on the dead man's tunic. Then he staggered over to his horse and reached for the flask of wine. Finding it, he took a long drink, fell to his knees and lay in the straw. He needed to lie down. He felt weak from the fight and the blood loss. Just a short rest, he thought, and he would be ready for the rest of the bastards.

***

Merek felt he could help the group by finding the highest point in the town and use his longbow from a distance. When he got to the church and its high tower, he knew instantly it would not work. The church was not too far from The Thistle, but there was a small building standing between The Thistle and the church. Merek decided to forego the high ground and find a vantage point outside the large tavern.

He tethered his horse near the church, took his bow and his sheath of arrows and walked back toward The Thistle. The street was not busy. It seemed the only traffic was going in and coming from The Thistle. Merek's new plan was to hide in such a way that if the kidnappers exited the tavern through the front door, he would have the perfect angle for a shot.

Merek had just settled himself between two buildings near The Thistle when he felt a slight touch on his shoulder. He turned in an instant to see the smiling face of Hugh Bowman.

"The church tower was no good?" Hugh asked.

Merek shook his head. "Was not as good as I wanted. Figured this was a spot that would cover the front door."

"Aye. A good spot," Hugh agreed. "I will make my way around the building and look for another possible exit."

Merek nodded. The men shook arms. Hugh left in an instant, making his way to the other side of the building.

Inside The Thistle, Nathan and Griff were ready to make their move. Having studied the crowd along the bar and at the various benches, Nathan was sure of the kidnappers. There were three. They were only sipping their drinks and kept a watchful eye on the front door. Each time it opened, they studied the new entrant.

Nathan nodded to Griff, and they took their large pints toward the table of the kidnappers.

"Mind if we use the other end of your bench?" Nathan asked, setting his drink loudly on the table. Griff set his mug down and immediately sat.

The kidnappers nodded and moved their drinks closer to their end of the table. Thaddeus, trying not to draw attention to themselves, nodded for the men to join them. He did not like the intrusion but felt his group had to keep a low profile. No need to cause a stir because the two red-headed men wanted to join them.

Nathan and Griff sat at the other end of the table and observed the rest of the bar. They did not look at or try to make conversation with the three men. They sat and drank in silence. Each time the door opened to The Thistle, Thaddeus and his men watched intently, waiting for Oswald. Nathan and Griff could feel Thaddeus and his men watching the door, but they did not let on.

Hugh Bowman found the back entrance to the tavern. He knew it would be too risky for him to enter the tavern, so he found a spot in which to hide and wait. He settled into his spot and waited. His spot was settled, and there was not much traffic coming through. Growing impatient, Hugh decided to make his way to the barn. He knew Miller had been assigned the area to keep watch. Hugh made his way to the barn carefully staying in the shadows. He could not afford to be spotted by the kidnappers.

The barn was unusually quiet. There seemed to be no attendant. Hugh entered the barn cautiously and found the bloody stall. He saw the dead kidnapper lying motionless in the red hay. Then he saw Robin Miller lying on his side close to the edge of the stall. His side was bleeding, and he was not moving. Foregoing any worry of being spotted, Hugh ran to Miller.

Hugh knelt beside Robin Miller and tried to awaken him. At the same time, he tried to get to the wound in Miller's side that was still bleeding. Miller was unresponsive to Hugh's attempts to awaken him. Holding his head in his lap, Hugh gently tried to slap Miller to get him to open his eyes. It was futile. Hugh leaned in closer to listen for Miller's breath. There was none. Robin Miller was dead.

Back in the tavern, Nathan slammed his mug on the table. "What are you talkin' about?" he said loudly to his brother. "I saw it first!"

Griff immediately stood and shouted back at Nathan. The tavern suddenly grew quiet as the brothers drew closer to each other.

"I say, I am right, and there will be no argument." Nathan shouted.

And Griff pulled the knife.

"And what are you goin' to do with that?" Nathan said loudly. "Stab me?"

Griff took the knife and suddenly thrust it downward. With an unusual precision, he stuck the knife into the hand of David, the kidnapper nearest to him. The knife pinned David's hand to the table, and he let out of with a painful cry.

Nathan and Griff attacked the other two kidnappers. Nathan jumped across the table and flew into the surprised Thaddeus. Griff went after Mason and tackled him to the floor. The tavern watched in awe, thinking it was merely another brawl instigated by too much ale. The customers were accustomed to tavern brawls and stood back and watched. Each knew to interfere was a way to invite unwarranted injury or even death.

Outside, Merek could hear the sudden outburst of clatter and mayhem. He did not hesitate. Bow and arrow in the ready position, he moved toward the front entrance of the tavern. He guessed the element of surprise had been compromised and decided to enter in the hopes of helping the Pierce brothers. Entering the tavern, he saw the commotion. The two brothers were on the floor wrestling with the kidnappers. Merek saw one of the kidnappers trying to pull a knife from his hand stuck to the tavern table. Merek was too far away to prevent the kidnapper from freeing his hand. As David freed his bleeding hand from the knife and table, he began to move toward the end of the table to help his comrades. Merek's arrow pierced David's neck just below the ear and made its way through to the other side of his head. David was dead before he hit the ground.

Mason was no match for Griff, who landed blow upon blow to the man. Mason tried to protect himself from the wild attacker, but he had been taken by surprise and could not find a way to fend off the numerous blows that Griff inflicted. Sitting atop the fallen kidnapper, Griff repeatedly struck the man about the face, blood pouring from the broken nose and open mouth that Mason could not defend.

Nathan had a more difficult time with Thaddeus. At the first instant, Thaddeus had been fooled by the brothers' ruse as an argument. When Nathan attacked Thaddeus, the surprise was momentary, but Thaddues was quick to recover. As Nathan leapt to the offensive, Thaddeus had instinctively repelled the attack by rolling backward and letting the atttackers' momentum carry him past the kidnapper.

Quick to his feet, Thaddeus pulled his knife and readied himself for Nathan. The two men sized each other up as Griff and Mason wrestled on the floor.

"Where is she?" Nathan asked, steadying a knife at his opponent.

"Dead because of you," Thaddeus answered, wielding his own knife. "My man will have killed her by now because of your senseless attack."

"Then there's no use in keeping you alive," Nathan said.

The arrow hit Thaddeus on the side of the chest under his right armpit. He fell immediately. Merek had hit his mark. Nathan jumped on the fallen man and held his knife to Thaddeus's throat.

"Where is she?" Nathan asked.

"Go to hell," Thaddeus said. "Kill me and seal the woman's fate."

"As he wishes," Hugh spoke loudly from the balcony of the tavern. He was standing next to the prioress!

After finding Robin Miller dead, Hugh made his way back to the tavern and the inn. Finding a stairway to the inn of The Thistle, he made his way to the unusually large second floor. Quietly, he walked the floors, hoping he would stumble across the kidnapper who guarded the prioress. He felt doubt in his notion, thinking the kidnappers would keep the victim elsewhere. Hugh hoped the kidnappers were under the delusion that no one would be pursuing them. He wanted to be sure the prioress was not at The Thistle.

As cautious as he was, Hugh encountered Benjamin, who was sitting in a chair outside the room housing the prioress. Both men were surprised by their encounter. Hugh tried to act nonchalantly as he walked by the guard, but it did not work. Benjamin was alert and swift to ready his knife at his opponent. The encounter was too close for the use of a bow and arrow, so Hugh discarded them in an instant. Each man drew his knife. Benjamin was an expert with the knife, and Hugh could tell from the onset that he was a perilous opponent.

"I only want the woman," Hugh said as the two men faced each other. "Let me have her. You walk away."

"Will not do, you brown-faced bastard. I have my orders."

"Do you have orders to die?" Hugh asked.

"If that's what it takes," Benjamin said grimly.

The hallway was too narrow for the men to move anywhere but forward or backward. Benjamin waved his knife, displaying his dexterity and skill. For his part, Hugh remained steady, staring at his opponent's face. Hugh took a pouch from his side and held it in his left hand. With a twirling motion, he let the pouch wrap around his hand. He would use it to help block Benjamin's attack.

Benjamin swiped quickly at Hugh, who tried to avoid the blow. Hugh was not quick enough, and the knife nicked his forearm drawing blood. Benjamin came back quickly with another thrust, but Hugh used the pouch to fend off the blow. Benjamin thrust a third time, faking a sideways cut and bringing the dagger upward, trying to catch the yeoman in the stomach. Hugh was fooled by the feint, but was able to step back from the fatal thrust. Still, the dagger caught him in the area of the stomach. Fortunately, his clothing took the brunt of the knife, and no blood was drawn.

Hugh decided he could not stay on the defensive. His opponent was quicker and more adept with the knife. His forearm was bleeding, but not badly. Benjamin was being more aggressive now, feeling his opponent could not match him in skill. With a quick step toward Hugh, Benjamin thrust his knife directly toward Hugh's side. This time, Hugh saw it coming. As Benjamin's knife drew close to the yeoman, Hugh made his move. With his hand protected by the pouch, Hugh simply grabbed hold of the blade of Benjamin's knife. Hugh squeezed the blade and twisted. Even with the pouch protecting his hand, he could feel the knife piercing his skin.

Benjamin looked in surprise by the move and fought Hugh's twisting motion to grab the knife from him. But when Hugh fell to his knees and let Benjamin's knife free, it threw the kidnapper off balance for a moment. That was all Hugh needed. In that instant from his knees, Hugh struck his knife into the belly of his opponent. It was a deep strike, and Benjamin gave out a scream. Hugh stood and drove the knife higher into the kidnapper's chest. Benjamin could only lean on the yeoman as he died. Hugh let him fall.

Hand and forearm bleeding, Hugh made a quick bandage for his arm, made sure the kidnapper was dead, and slowly opened the door to the room of the prioress. It was dark, but there was a small candle lit in the small room.

"Madam," Hugh said softly. "We are here to take you home."

The prioress did not understand at first. She did not recognize the yeoman, for it was dark where he stood. But then, she saw the body of her kidnapper outside in the hall, lying motionless.

"Father Merek is with me," Hugh said softly. "Come, madam, we must get out of here."

At the sound of Merek's name, she came to her senses and recognized the good yeoman who travelled with Sir Robert of Ganse. She gladly went with the yeoman.

CHAPTER 39

THE PLAN IS SET IN MOTION

Merek smiled when he saw the prioress with Hugh Bowman. She was dirty, shaken, and seemed exhausted and was clearly puzzled and out of sorts. Merek was confident the Pierce brothers were in control of the two wounded kidnappers on the floor. He made his way to the creaky stairs that led to the balcony where Hugh stood with the prioress. As he came close, she drew herself to him and threw her arms around him. She cried in his arms, and he let her.

While he let her cry in his arms, Merek looked at Hugh and saw the wounds on the yeoman. Hugh shook his head, indicating to Merek that he would be fine. Merek put out his arm, and the men shook arms.

"Have you seen Robin?" Merek asked as the prioress continued to cry in his arms.

"He is in the barn with one of the kidnappers," Hugh said quietly. "Neither man is alive."

Despite the woman hugging him, Merek instinctively made the sign of the cross. He closed his eyes for a brief moment. Another worthless death.

Down on the floor of the tavern, Nathan had taken charge, announcing to the crowd that he and his brother were deputy constables, and the two men on the floor were kidnappers under their custody. After the fight, no one in the crowd was going to argue and make a fuss. Nathan did ask the tavern keeper to send for the town official, and so the town marshal was summoned.

It did not take long to put the full story together. With the town marshal in complete understanding of the situation, matters for exiting the town were quickened. The dead men, including Robin Miller, were to taken care of. Whereas the kidnappers' bodies were to be hung just outside of town, Robin would be given a proper burial in the local churchyard.

Mason's badly beaten face and loss of blood were a gruesome sight, but he would travel back to Dartford to be hung properly. Thaddeus, on the other hand, was dying. He and Mason had been dragged to the street after the fight. Merek's arrow had pierced the lungs of Thaddeus, and he was slowly suffocating. As the story was being put together and preparations for leaving the town, Thaddeus died quietly on the street. His body would hang with the other kidnappers.

A local physician was called to tend to Hugh's wounds. At first, the physician was skeptical to help a man with brown skin, but Griff assured the doctor that he would help Hugh Bowman to the best of his ability or find himself trying to heal himself with a wound Griff would give him. Surprisingly, the physician did a wonderful job helping the yeoman.

Oswald had told the posse the entire plan, even the location of the lodge where the prioress would be taken and kept for the negotiations of a ransom. Oswald, with urging from the Pierce brothers, drew a crude map of the lodge's location two miles south of Petersfield. It was half past seven when the remaining members of the posse and the prioress were riding out of Petersfield. All matters had been cleared with the town marshal, and despite the darkness, the posse felt confident they could be at the lodge in less than an hour. Mason was tied across a horse and would travel with the group. The Pierce brothers could have opted to keep him in the Petersfield jail, but they decided to bring him along.

The trail to the lodge was not hard to follow. Fortunately, there was a new moon, and with the light from it and Hugh's guidance, they came to the dark lodge before nine o'clock. Even in the dark, it was an impressive building. Built entirely of stone, it stood in an opening surrounded by tall trees on all sides. The roof was not thatch, but actual wood, giving evidence of the lavish costs to build it.

Each side of the lodge had a glassless window boarded by planks to keep intruders out. The Pierce brothers, using their poleax and halbeard, made short work of the planks on one of the windows, and they gained entry. Inside, the men made a fire in the hearth and began to settle in for the night. The lodge was one great room with two rooms used as bedrooms and another as a kitchen, so the men designated one of the bedrooms of the lodge for the prioress to sleep.

The prioress was still shaken and needed Merek's comfort, even as they rode to the lodge. Once inside, Merek tended to her every need and assured her he would be close by if she needed him. She hugged him close and held on, not letting him go as he said good night to her. He offered to pray with her, and they quietly said their nightly devotions. The prayers seemed to calm her, and she settled into the bed Hugh had prepared for her in one of the bedrooms.

Merek kept his word and settled on a bench outside the nun's bedroom. As he lay down, he could not help remember how her arms felt around him. Although he was merely comforting the prioress, the woman's closeness was comforting to him too. It made him think of Thea and how he wished he could hold her like that.

As usual, Hugh slept outside, hidden from any unwanted intruders who would find their way to the lodge. The Pierce brothers secured Mason for the night, tying him to the main beam of the lodge. He was groaning from the pain all about his body, so after an hour of groans, cries, and gurgling breaths, Griff dragged him outside and tied him to a tree. He did not care if wild animals happened to find the wounded kidnapper tied to the tree. Griff would take what was left of him back to Dartford when the time was right.

Nathan Pierce made a special effort to tend to Hugh Bowman's wounds. Following Hugh's suggestion, Nathan used a mixture of roots and leaves to make a salve that would help the healing of Hugh's wounds. Once the ointment was applied to his wounds, Hugh made his way outside the lodge and prepared himself for sleep. Griff had done the same. The two men slept at either end of the porch.

Inside the lodge, the prioress continued to cry but soon fell to sleep. Nathan slept on the floor of the great room near the fire. He was bruised and injured with the fight with Thaddeus but did not let on. It was part of the job. Merek tried to sleep but was troubled by the death of his friend, Robin Miller. Merek tossed and turned on the bench outside the room of the prioress, trying to understand the unnecessary deaths he had witnessed recently. Eventually, Merek moved from the bench to the floor in an attempt to get some sleep. The move seemed to work, for he finally fell asleep.

***

Riders approached the lodge by noon the next day. Led by Sir Robert and Thomas, the posse felt at ease as the second part of the plan was coming together. It had been an uneventful night for the men and prioress in the lodge. In the morning, the men scrounged up a breakfast and prepared for the visitors. Mason made it through the night, though he did not get any rest from the uncomfortable way he was tied to the tree. No animals attacked him in the darkness. When Nathan cut him loose from the tree, Mason merely fell to the ground and tried to sleep.

Sir Robert and Thomas had ridden hard to Lord Appleton's estate near the Alban River. Without difficulty, they were granted an audience with the powerful nobleman. Both father and son were escorted to the great room of the manor house where Lord Appleton greeted them.

"Lord Appleton, I am Sir Robert of Ganse. May I present my son, Thomas," Sir Robert said with the confidence a nobleman has speaking to another.

"Welcome, gentlemen. Please, have a seat. What brings a nobleman and his son to my manor?"

"It is with grievous news that we come, Lord Appleton," Sir Robert began.

"Oh?" was all Lord Appleton said.

"Your daughter, Lord Appleton, the Prioress of Norwood . . ."

Lord Appleton stood immediately. His eyes seemed to pierce the two men in front of him.

"She has been kidnapped, sir," Sir Robert said in a most serious tone.

From there, Sir Robert told the rest of the story. The trip to Canterbury. The kidnapping. The pursuit. The culprits. And the plan. At first, Lord Appleton was furious and seethed with anger at his neighbor, Lord Berkley. But he came to his senses when Sir Robert told him of the second part of the plan. Lord Appleton agreed to go along with the plan and began immediately to make preparations to accompany Sir Robert and Thomas to the lodge. Sir Thomas only hoped the first part of the plan had worked, and the men had rescued the prioress.

In the clearing to the lodge, Sir Robert and Thomas rode alongside Sir Appleton. Behind them, Sir Appleton had formed his own band of men. Although Sir Appleton's two sons were fighting in France for the king, he brought two of his sons-in-law, both noblemen and warriors, with him. Each of the sons-in-law had brought a dozen knights. Combined with Lord Appleton's personal knights and foot soldiers, the parade marching to the lodge was in excess of fifty men.

Father Merek Willson stood with the Pierce brothers outside the front door of the lodge. He still wore a bandage around his head to cover his lost ear. There were bruises on his face, and one side of his face was swollen. He did not look like a priest; he looked like a survivor. Merek waved as the large party drew near. Hugh had been hiding in the woods but moved in sight when he saw the riders were friendly.

"Welcome, Lord Appleton," Merek said as the men drew close to the lodge, still mounted on their horses. As Sir Robert, Thomas, and Lord Appleton stopped, the other riders in their party fanned out and soon drew close to the lodge.

"It is good to see you, Sir Robert. Thomas," Merek said as the party moved closer toward them.

"Lord Appleton, this is Father Merek Willson. The men with him are deputy constables, Nathan and Griff Pierce. They were the men given charge to free your daughter," Thomas said, taking a cue from his father to introduce the men. He only hoped that the men indeed had the prioress. He was a little worried for he did not see her.

"Gentlemen, I am honored to meet you. By the looks of you, you have gone to a great deal of trouble to rescue my daughter. Forgive me, but is my daughter safe?" Lord Appleton asked.

Nathan stepped back and gently knocked on the door. It opened, and the prioress walked out.

"Father?" she asked, beginning to cry.

Merek immediately took hold of her, steadying her as her father dismounted and ran to her. Lord Appleton hugged her and let her cry.

"Well done, men." Sir Robert smiled. "Well done." He dismounted and came over to Merek. They shook arms. He did the same to the Pierce brothers.

Thomas was also off his horse and congratulating the rescuers. Hugh walked over and joined in the small reunion. Lord Appleton's sons-in-law dismounted and introduced themselves to the rescuers. All the while, the prioress cried in her father's arms.

Thomas looked around. "Where is Robin Miller?" he asked.

Merek looked at Thomas and shook his head.

"Gentlemen"—Lord Appleton finally smiled—"I owe you a debt of gratitude for saving my daughter. And you will see my debt of gratitude has no bound. Sir Robert, you are a man who makes me a proud knight of our king!"

Sir Robert smiled but cautioned. "We are not yet finished, Lord Appleton. We have one more step in finishing this business. Please, join us inside so that we prepare for our next group of visitors."

***

Geoffrey Chaucer and Harry Bailly were given the task to summon Lord Berkley to the lodge. With Chaucer's experience in dealing with noblemen, it was thought he would be the ideal man to deliver the news to Lord Berkley and bait the trap at the lodge. In reality, it was risky business. Lord Berkley did not know Chaucer and would cast doubt with a messenger he did not know. Nevertheless, Chaucer and Harry Bailly rode in blind faith, hoping the first part of the plan went on schedule with the rescue of the prioress.

After some hard riding, Chaucer and Bailly entered the principal estate of Lord Berkley. Chaucer was able to use his elaborate gift of speech to make his way to the manor house. Just outside, he asked for an audience with the lord of the manor. When asked about his business, Chaucer only said the word *Oswald* and was granted entrance. It was agreed beforehand that Harry Bailly would remain with the horses and let Chaucer weave his words in setting the trap.

"Greetings, Lord Berkley," Chaucer bowed as he entered the private study of the large and proud warrior. "I bring news for your ears, lord," Chaucer added, implying his staff and servants should leave the large study.

"Before I send them away, sir, I shall know your name and your purpose for a private audience with me," Sir Berkley said, sipping from a mug of wine.

"Of course, Sir Berkley. Of course. Although my name is not important, I bring news from your servant Oswald."

"Oswald?" Sir Berkley asked. He took a large sip from his wine. "How am I to know the name Oswald?"

Chaucer looked around at the men-at-arms and servants standing by. He feigned to be embarrassed by the question and stammered a bit before he answered. "Oswald, sir. Your humble servant has sent me with an urgent message, lord." Chaucer looked around, pretending to be nervous. Little did Lord Berkley know the man before him had served two of the king's sons and had many times been in the presence of the king and his high court. Chaucer, for his part, was a bit nervous about his part in the plan to set the trap but enjoyed his playacting in front of the warrior lord.

Lord Berkley smiled, took another long sip from his mug of wine, and dismissed the servants and men-at-arms. In no time, it was only Chaucer and Lord Berkley in the room.

Chaucer waited until the room was empty. He bowed again to Lord Berkley, saying, "Lord, the plan is set. Oswald sends me to tell you that his mission is accomplished."

"Mission?" Lord Berkley laughed. "My good man, I am confused. What in Saint Michael's name are you talking about?"

Chaucer straightened up and looked at Lord Berkley directly. Now that they were alone, he could act like the mercenary he was supposed to be. He made sure his voice had the confidence he needed to set the final plan in motion.

"Lord Berkley, with all due respect. You hired us to acquire a negotiating piece for you to regain a valuable piece of land from your neighbor. I am only here to inform you that the lady you requested has been obtained and will be at your lodge two days from now."

Lord Berkley let the news sink in. He did not say a word but slowly drank from his mug.

"Where is Oswald? He is the man I deal with. Just who are you?"

"My name is Chaucer, lord. I am one of the mercenaries hired to carry out the plan. Oswald felt it prudent to stay with the woman and send me and a fellow soldier to give you the news. Oswald knew you would want to be there when the party arrived at the lodge. Oswald also knew you would want to begin the negotiations as soon as possible and send messengers to the opposition to meet you at the lodge. It was Oswald who wanted to set the plan in motion by telling you first, lord."

Lord Berkley grinned at Chaucer. "I deal with Oswald. How can I trust you?"

"Lord Berkley, what cause would I ride into your beautiful manor and lie to you? How would I know of Oswald, the prioress of Norwood, and the trip to Canterbury? I tell you, sir, I am here to move the transaction forward. My men and I are anxious to get paid for the deed we have done. Oswald and my comrades will arrive at your lodge in two days. They will await you there."

"This lodge, you say. Do you know where it is?" Lord Berkley asked.

"I have not been to the lodge," Chaucer said with honesty. "But I know it is two miles south of Petersfield. I have a map. My comrade and I will join the others there after my audience with you, lord, is over."

Lord Berkley laughed. "So it is, so it is." He paused and finished the wine in his mug. "My men and I will be there in two days. The woman? Is she all right?"

"Yes, lord. We were under strict orders to care for her properly," Chaucer answered.

"Good. Very good. Do not worry, sir. When I arrive in two days, you and your man will be handsomely rewarded."

"Thank you, Lord Berkley," Chaucer answered. He bowed and turned to leave.

"Tell me something," Lord Berkley asked, causing Chaucer to stop and turn. "Was there a priest travelling with the nun?"

Chaucer did not answer right away. He thought. "Actually, Lord Berkley, there were three priests who travelled with the nun," Chaucer answered.

"By chance, was one of them a big strapping man?" Lord Berkley asked.

"Aye," Chaucer answered quickly. "I am afraid he was mysteriously attacked on the trip," Chaucer said, thinking of Merek. "Not sure if he lived, lord. Badly injured."

"Too bad," Lord Berkley answered. "Will let Father Berners know when I see him next," Lord Berkley said aloud, almost talking to himself.

Chaucer pretended not to hear the side comment.

"In two days, Lord Berkley," Chaucer said as he bowed and left.

Outside, he and Harry Bailly rode off. The last part of the plan was in motion. He had no idea if the first and second parts of the plan had come through. But his part was accomplished.

CHAPTER 40

CONFRONTATION AT THE LODGE

Lord Berkley was in a good mood. By the end of the week, he planned to regain the valuable land his great-grandfather had squandered away to the Appleton's one hundred years ago. He had confidence in his plan and was even thinking of negotiating for more than the land he had lost. Lord Berkley knew of two prosperous mills owned by the Appleton's that operated near the land in question. Perhaps he would gain the two mills. in addition to the land he wished to regain.

After Chaucer had left the manor, Lord Berkley summoned his reeve who sent messengers to Lord Berkley's local noblemen. He wished to have added insurance in his negotiations with the soon-to-be-angry Lord Appleton. He would call upon his lords to gather some knights and men-at-arms and accompany him for a few days. The word was out. They would leave in the very early morning.

Lord Berkley also sent one of his most trusted messengers to the estate of Lord Appleton. The messenger took a sealed letter sealed to Lord Appleton himself. The letter was carefully written and spelled out the need to meet at the lodge to negotiate the release of his daughter. Even though she was a nun, her blood was still royal. Lord Berkley was sure Lord Appleton would agree to the meeting. Lord Berkley instructed the nobleman to arrive in two days. It would give Lord Berkley plenty of time to make all his arrangements.

Lord Berkley also sent for Jacob Worley, a renowned serjeant-at-the law. Like Judge Josef Gates, Jacob Worley was one of only twenty judges who were considered the king's servants in upholding the law. Each oversaw the local courts in his territory, making each of the judges powerful men. Lord Berkley knew Judge Worley well. They had dined together on many occasions. Lord Berkley made sure to present the judge with small presents each time they met. He never asked the judge for favors or special rulings. Lord Berkley was too clever to ask the judge for small favors. He could ask the judges in the lower courts for help if he needed it. Judge Worley was a deal breaker. And now Lord Berkley would use their friendship for a special favor. With Judge Worley at his side during the negotiations, Lord Berkley had a powerful chess piece in his game with Lord Appleton. Judge Worley's presence would assure that all signed papers would be legal and binding in the highest court in England.

As the men gathered at Lord Berkley's estate that night, Jacob Worley was among them. He was Lord Berkley's special guest. There was a bountiful dinner for the noblemen and the judge, all gathered to ride with Lord Berkley the next morning. In all, Lord Berkley had gathered a troop of men numbering sixty. They would leave the estate at first light.

***

Lord Appleton and his men awaited Lord Berkley at the lodge. Chaucer and Bailly had found their way to the lodge the previous evening and had given the news that Lord Berkley was on his way in the morning. Chaucer and Bailly were glad to reunite with their friends. They were relieved that the rescue of the prioress was successful but were saddened by the news of Robin Miller's death.

Lord Appleton sent his best scouts to monitor the roads through Petersfield and around the lodge. With the scouts reporting directly to the lodge and Lord Appleton, the trap would be set for Lord Berkley and his men.

Riders returned to the lodge indicating that Lord Berkley and his troop of men would arrive by ten in the morning. Lord Appleton's scouts were thorough and estimated the number to be between sixty and seventy men accompanying him. Lord Appleton was satisfied with the reports and sent the men back, warning them to stay out of sight. The element of surprise was critical to outcome of the day.

It was a little after ten when the first riders from Lord Berkley's command entered the clearing leading to the lodge. It seemed deserted, save four men standing in front of the lodge by the large door. They appeared to be armed, but their swords or daggers were still sheathed. They seemed to be awaiting Lord Berkley's arrival.

Sir Robert, Thomas, Chaucer, and Harry Bailly stood in front of the lodge pretending to be the kidnappers. Nathan Pierce and Hugh Bowman were in a copse of trees just to the left of the lodge. Beyond them, twenty of Sir Appleton's knights, mounted and armed, were ready for a charge. On the other side of the clearing just inside the tree line, Merek was ready with his bow and arrows. He had placed his entire sheath of arrows at his feet, arrow points sticking in the soil, shafts ready for his rapid fire. Beyond him, men-at-arms were hidden, waiting for word to charge if needed. Griff was behind the lodge with Mason. Mason, gagged and tied, was a gruesome sight. Griff kept his dagger near the kidnapper's ribs, lest he make a sound.

Inside, Lord Appleton waited with his most trusted knights. He was teeming with anger and wanted Sir Berkley's head. Yet, he knew Lord Berkley to be a hardened warrior and would have to be careful in how he would seek justice. The prioress was not present. She had been taken to the woods and hidden by Lord Appleton's most trusted knight and two of his men-at-arms.

One of the riders stayed at the edge of the clearing to keep an eye on the men, while the other rode to Lord Berkley. He reported what he saw, and Lord Berkley advanced into the clearing with his men. He rode confidently through the clearing toward the men standing in front of the lodge. He recognized Chaucer as the man who had given him the message, but he was a little surprised he did not see Oswald. Perhaps Oswald was inside with the nun.

"Welcome, Lord Berkley," Sir Robert began dressed in clothes borrowed from one of the men-at-arms. Both he and Thomas had donned the clothes of the common foot soldier to hide their class.

Lord Berkley nodded as he brought his horse close to the men standing in front of the lodge. Judge Jacob Worley and a few of Lord Berkley's most trusted nobles pulled their mounts around Lord Berkley so that he sat in the middle of them all.

"Where is Oswald?" Lord Berkley asked. "And the nun?"

Sir Robert took a step forward. "Neither are here, lord."

Lord Berkley narrowed his eyes. "What, you scoundrels want more money? You have hidden the nun so that I will pay you more?" He could feel his anger rising.

"No, Lord Berkley. We only seek justice," Sir Robert said.

And with that, the knights inside the lodge came out. The last to come out was Lord Appleton.

Lord Berkley could not believe his eyes. He had been duped. His mind was racing as to his next move. He took a deep breath. Lord Berkley kept his composure. He was a hardened warrior, had been in battles. He had seen death and destruction. His first instinct was to attack the men and kill them all. He took another deep breath. After a moment, he began to chuckle.

"Quite a ruse." He laughed looking directly at Chaucer. He looked back at Lord Appleton. He continued to smile. "And here we are, Appleton. Ready to negotiate?"

"Negotiate, you cur? After what you had your men do to my daughter! We will negotiate, Berkley, on how I will kill you!"

Lord Appleton's men spread themselves out facing Lord Berkley's small army. One of Lord Berkley's men gave a signal, and his men fanned out around the front of the lodge.

"How about you and I settle this man-to-man? Let your men see you for the coward that you are," Lord Appleton said through clenched lips. "Get down from that horse! By Christ's bones, I will kill you!"

Lord Berkley smiled at Lord Appleton. "We can arrange for you to meet your Maker today, but not before you sign these papers. Do you know this gentleman, Lord Appleton?" Lord Berkley said calmly, pointing to Judge Worley. "He is the region's serjeant-at-the law. He has papers you need to sign to give my family its rightful land your great-grandfather stole from my family one hundred years ago."

"Come, sir, get off your horse. Grab your sword. I shall sign those papers with your blood," Lord Appleton said. His sword was ready for a fight.

"I am curious," Lord Berkley began. "What happened to Oswald and the kidnappers?"

"Oswald is no longer among the living, sir," Thomas announced proudly. "He told us everything about you and the plan to kidnap Lord Appleton's daughter."

At that moment, Griff brought the wounded Mason from behind the lodge. He presented Mason to Lord Berkley's group by throwing him on the ground in front of the visitors.

"He is what is left of the kidnappers," Thomas said.

"You, sir," Sir Robert spoke to Jacob Worley. "Do you know the name of Judge Josef Gates?"

Jacob Worley was surprised to be addressed so directly by a common foot soldier. But he was taken aback by the name of Gates. Of course, he knew Gates, the strongest and most powerful of the serjeants-at-the law. How would this commoner know Judge Gates?

"I am Sir Robert of Ganse. Forgive me for the rustic appearance, but it was necessary to help Lord Appleton's cause. Let me be direct, Judge Worley. I am indeed a personal friend of Judge Gates, and if word gets back to him that you are a part of this scheme to force Lord Appleton into the signing of a document proposed earlier, I am sure Judge Gates will take the necessary legal proceedings against Lord Berkley and you, sir!"

Judge Jacob Worley said nothing, completely baffled by this man dressed as a man-at-arms who spoke like a true nobleman.

Lord Appleton saw the look in the eyes of Judge Worley and said, "Even the judge is not with you, Berkley. Come let us fight. Your blood for the suffering you caused my daughter."

"Maybe I am ready for a fight, Appleton. Maybe I just kill you and your noblemen and take all of your land," Lord Berkley said, pulling his sword from his sheath. "I do hope you have men hidden in the woods, Appleton. Otherwise, this is going to be quick."

Lord Berkley raised his sword with his left hand. At that moment, an arrow struck one of Lord Berkley's nobles, and he fell from his horse. Another arrow thumped into the chest of a second nobleman, and the fight began.

Nathan and Hugh raced toward the enemy. As they did, the knights who were mounted raced past them and entered the battle. Hugh's hand was too injured to use a bow, but he did have a sword, joining Nathan as they battled.

Merek fired at will, using the many arrows as well-aimed missiles. Behind him, the men-at-arms rushed from the trees into the open field and joined the battle. Sir Robert and Thomas had pulled their swords and were fighting but were at a distinct disadvantage as they were not mounted fighting knights on horseback. Father and son fought together until the mounted knights from the woods joined in and came to their aid. Now, Sir Robert and Thomas fought the men-at-arms who happened forward, or they fought knights who had been thrown from their horses.

Griff was quick to jump on the back of a knight's horse and topple the rider from the saddle. Once on a mount, he rode the mount headlong into other mounts, trying to knock riders from their horses. Nathan ran at an unsuspecting knight and dove at the mounted man, knocking him from his saddle. Hugh slashed at horses' legs causing them to jump or throw their riders.

On a mount, Lord Berkley was having his way with Lord Appleton, who could only defend himself against the mounted warrior. One of Merek's arrows found its way into the neck of Lord Berkley's horse, and rider and horse went down in a heap. Lord Berkley, despite his age and large girth, was nimble and able to get to his feet before Lord Appleton could take advantage of his fall. Both men fought on their feet, each using a sword that had been in the family for ages and had been used to kill before. Lord Berkley, with the use of only one hand, was still a powerful opponent. Since his youth, Lord Berkley had been adept with either hand, and so when he lost the use of his right hand, he lost little skill in transferring his sword to his left hand.

Thomas used his quickness to kill his adversaries. The men-at-arms were no match for his swordplay. Sir Robert was tired as he fought by his son's side but used his skill and experience to bring down his opponents. Father and son fought back-to-back, protecting each other from unseen enemies.

Lord Appleton's surprise attack had left the Berkley army vulnerable, and it was paying off. The knights and the men-at-arms were gaining control of the middle ground. Berkley's men were fighting with courage, but as they fell to the attacks on their flanks, they began to surrender.

When Merek ran out of arrows, he ran to the attack. His purpose was to pull arrows from bodies or trees and use them again. Not adept at the use of a sword, he could not sit back and watch. He was pulling an arrow from a lifeless knight when one of Berkley's men-at-arms ran at him with a sword. Merek used his strength and hoisted the dead body from the ground, using it as a shield. The charging man thrust his sword into the dead body. Merek pushed the dead body forward on to the attacker. The attacker fell backward with the weight of the dead body on him. Merek jumped on top of the man and killed him with his dagger.

Appleton and Berkley swung and thrust their swords at each other with great strength and skill. But they were older now, and each man's strength and endurance began to wane. It became an effort for each man to lift his sword. But neither would give in. Lord Berkley had cut a small wound in Lord Appleton's thigh, and it bled. For his part, Lord Appleton had stuck the tip of his sword into the side of Lord Berkley. Although it was a glancing blow, it also managed to draw blood.

Griff's ramming horse was killed by a man-at-arms who had witnessed Griff's bizarre fighting style. As he used his sword to kill the horse, Griff was able to jump on the killer of his horse and do the same to the man. Unmindful of his own body, Griff unleashed himself on other riders, knocking them from their horses so that Lord Appleton's men-at-arms could battle them on equal ground.

Sir Robert and Thomas fought back-to-back as long as they could, using their superior skill in arms to outlast opponents. As Thomas thrust his sword into the belly of an opponent, he was suddenly knocked down by a running man-at-arms fleeing from a charging Griff. Thomas quickly regained his footing but lost his father, who seemed to be in the midst of small but ferocious fight. Moving toward his father, Thomas was engaged with a hard-fighting knight. Each man challenged the other, but in the end, Thomas was able to better him with a thrust through the lower abdomen. The man fell in death. Thomas looked around. He had lost sight of his father!

Judge Jacob Worley used all his skills as a horseman to ride from the lodge as fast as he could. Once the fighting began, he fled directly to Petersfield and beyond. He actually hoped no one would come out of the fight alive and tell Judge Josef Gates that he had been a party to Lord Berkley's deception.

Lord Appleton was losing to the more powerful Lord Berkley. Each blow seemed to bring Lord Appleton closer to losing his sword or his footing, each meaning he would die. Lord Appleton decided to attack the more powerful lord differently. As Lord Berkley approached with his sword held high, Appleton feigned an upward thrust then quickly used his sword to come down on Lord Berkley's left foot. The blade caught the elder lord in the middle of his foot, and the blade almost severed his foot. Lord Berkley fell to the ground screaming in pain. Taking advantage of the fallen opponent, Lord Appleton swung fiercely at Lord Berkley's other leg and cut it to the bone just above the knee. Now Lord Berkley was on his back. Lord Appleton stood on top of Lord Berkley, using his foot to hold down Lord Berkley's arm that held his sword. Taking his sword, he rammed it through Lord Berkley's throat. He was too tired to say anything. He let the sword speak for him. Lord Berkley watched a geyser of blood rush from his own throat. He looked at his killer as his eyes began to lose their focus. He was dead. Appleton thought of taking the man's head, but he was too tired. He sat beside the body and watched the carnage all around him.

More and more of Berkley's men were surrendering, and once they saw that Lord Berkley himself was dead, the battle ended quickly. The knights and men-at-arms from Lord Berkley's side were gathered in the middle of the clearing and were separated from their weapons. Lord Appleton's knights were taking charge of the surrendering warriors, taking each man's weapon and making them stand as one in the center of the clearing.

Merek helped organize the prisoners, yet at the same time, he looked for his friends. Griff was bloodied all about his person, but it was not his blood. Nathan had a wound from an errant sword, but the wound had nicked his arm. Chaucer and Bailly found Merek, and all shook arms, glad each was alive. And then they heard Thomas scream!

Rushing to the area from which the scream came, they found Thomas, holding his dying father in his arms. Sir Robert had taken a sword to the back, and the cut had been long and deep. The nobleman was bleeding to death. As they stood there in horror, Hugh Bowman ran and squatted next to the dying man and his son. Face bloodied from the battle, Hugh's tears at the sight of the fallen lord were genuine. He, with Thomas, cried as Sir Robert began to fade.

Instinctively, Merek fell to his knees and grabbed his rosary beads. Blessing the dying man, he began to give Sir Robert the sacrament of extreme unction. Merek said his prayers quickly, hoping to finish before the man perished. Sir Robert said nothing as he died, merely looking in Thomas's eyes with love and pride as his spirit left his body. Thomas cried out and threw himself on his father's chest. Hugh Bowman also wept.

CHAPTER 41

THE POSSE DISPERSES

After the battle, Lord Appleton directed his highest-ranking knights to take charge of the battlefield. The knights organized the prisoners, collected weapons and had them gather in the field in front of the lodge. Messengers were sent to Petersfield to bring any and all local physicians to help with the wounded. Many of the wounded were brought to the lodge. Some were allowed inside, while the others sat in the late afternoon sun. It was odd, but Lord Berkley's men were not mistreated in any way. They were considered loyal men to Lord Berkley and had acted in his bidding. And, after all, they were Englishmen. Had they been French prisoners, it would have been a different story.

Merek helped Thomas and Hugh Bowman with the fallen knight. It was Thomas's intention to take his father north to their own estate and bury him there. Of course, Hugh Bowman would accompany Thomas. The men were able to use a large cloak to wrap around the body, and they secured it to a horse. Thomas wanted to leave immediately, and so he did. All shook arms before the men left. The men of the posse had a bond that was strong. Each man felt a relief that the ordeal was over, but there was also a sadness at the loss of life and the departing of dear friends bound together through the heat of battle.

After Thomas and Hugh left with the body of the knight, the Pierce brothers were next. They had bound Mason by the ankles and wrists and draped him over a horse.

"Griff and me are obliged for your help," Nathan said, mounted and ready to leave the clearing of the lodge. He said nothing more.

Griff simply nodded and began to lead the horse with Mason toward the main road. Both men still had bloodstains all over their faces and clothes. With their bloody prisoner, the trio was a gruesome sight.

"God speed, Pierce brothers." Chaucer waved.

"Remind me never to break the law in Dartford, Geoffrey," Harry Bailly said out of earshot of the Pierce brothers, who were riding toward the road to Petersfield. "Would not want those two after me."

"Well said," Chaucer replied, grinning at Harry. "Father Merek, will you join us? We make our way back to Southwark and await the pilgrims from Canterbury."

"Might need your priestly vocation to perform a wedding for me and the cloth maker, Allison." Harry Bailly smiled. "Would be obliged if you did the honors, Merek."

Merek shook his head sadly. "I have business in Winchester, Harry. I am sorry."

Chaucer knew exactly what the "business" was in Winchester. When Chaucer had returned from setting the trap with Lord Berkley, he had shared Lord Berkley's comment about hurting the big priest and how Father Berners would be pleased. Anglicus had told them as much, but Chaucer's report about Lord Berkley's comment confirmed his belief.

"Merek. Father Merek. Is there a way I can talk you out of this business?" Chaucer asked.

Merek stuck out his arm, and both men shook it.

"I will not continue to look over my shoulder for the rest of my life, Geoffrey," Merek said as he shook their arms. "I need to see a priest."

"Then let us come and help you," Chaucer said.

"I assure you, it is a one-man job," Merek answered. "But I thank you."

With that, Merek checked his unstrung bow and mounted his horse. He directed his horse to the horde of prisoners gathered in the middle of the clearing. Merek approached the knights who stood guard of the prisoners. Chaucer and Harry Bailly saw him talking with the guard. Soon after, Merek dismounted and approached the prisoners.

"Now what is the good father up to?" Harry asked Chaucer.

"Let us hope he is only going to bless the poor men." Chaucer smiled, and both men turned away.

Geoffrey Chaucer and Harry Bailly watched the large priest make his way among the prisoners. Neither man said a word.

"I will always be in your debt, gentlemen," a voice said, interrupting the quietness.

Both men turned to see Lord Appleton. He was standing by his horse surrounded by his personal knights.

Both Chaucer and Harry Bailly bowed, saying the word "lord" at the same time.

"My daughter is being taken back to my estate. She will remain with me until she feels well enough to return to the convent in Norwood. She apologizes for not thanking you and your men personally. I would not let her return to the battlefield and see all this." He pointed, referring to the dead bodies being gathered.

"Lord Appleton, it was our honor to help you and your daughter," Chaucer said in a most elegant way. "Our only thanks is that she is safe and under your care."

Lord Appleton nodded to one of his knights who brought a small sack of coins from his saddle and gave it to Chaucer.

"My thanks." Lord Appleton smiled. "I only wish I could have given the others a share."

Chaucer handed the sack to Harry Bailly, who felt its weight. He dared not look inside with Lord Appleton and his knights present. "We will see that each man gets a portion of the reward in this bag, Lord Appleton," Chaucer said.

"Very well," Lord Appleton said and came close to the men. He held his arm out to shake. It was an uncommon gesture, for lords did not shake arms with the common man. The two men hesitated. "Come, shake my arm," Lord Appleton commanded. "You clearly are not common men."

He took turns shaking each man's arm.

Mounting his horse, he gave a slight bow to the men who returned the bow. Lord Appleton and his circle of knights slowly rode through the clearing to the trees that led to the main road and Petersfield.

Chaucer and Harry Bailly watched them leave just a short while since Lord Berkley and his men had entered not two hours before.

"This sack is heavy, Geoffrey." Harry Bailly smiled.

"Aye," Chaucer returned. "Guess we will have to go through Dartford now to split this with the brothers."

"It is on our way," Harry Bailly said.

Both men mounted their horses and began to lead them to the clearing, being sure not to get in the way of the knights and men-at-arms who were clearing the ground of dead bodies and helping with the wounded. Both men suddenly felt tired as their horses entered the trees that would lead to the main road. The adventure was over, and both men needed rest.

CHAPTER 42

MEREK VISITS A PRIEST

As Merek left the company of Chaucer and Harry Bailly, he saw Lord Berkley's prisoners being herded into the clearing that stood in front of the lodge. Merek was set to make his way to Winchester, but a thought suddenly occurred to him that it would be easier for him to travel in the guise of a man-at-arms instead of a priest. Therefore, he made his way to the captain of the guards.

"May I ask a favor, sirs?" Merek asked the knights guarding the prisoners.

The knight in charge of the prisoners turned and looked at the large priest on the horse. He did not answer directly until he saw the longbow on the priest's saddle. In an instant, he looked at the priest again. All of Lord Appleton's knights were aware of the archer who had aided their battle that day. There had been rumors that the archer was a priest, but there was always exaggerated talk after a battle. The knight in charge knew in an instant that the man on the horse had been a welcomed ally in the fight.

"Ask your favor, Father," the knight said.

"As you can see, my cassock is tattered and torn. Since I have a long journey ahead, I was hoping one of these men would be willing to give me his clothes as a gift to a humble village priest," Merek said.

The knight almost laughed. "Humble village priest, huh?" the man thought. "With the way you handle a bow, I'll bet your village is crimeless and sinless," he thought with a smirk.

"What say you, sir?" Merek asked again.

"By all means, Father. I am sure these men will gladly give you the smocks off their backs," the knight said.

Merek dismounted and began to walk among the prisoners.

As Merek dismounted, the knight was surprised by Merek's size. "I do hope we can find a prisoner of your size, Father," the knight remarked, walking with Merek as a bodyguard amongst the prisoners.

Merek sought the largest man of the group huddled in the middle of the clearing and stood before him.

"I will need your clothes, sir," Merek said not as a priest but in the tone of a soldier.

The soldier did not say a word. He saw the knight with a drawn sword standing beside the largest priest he had ever seen and began to undress. Merek took his clothes and changed in front of all the prisoners. He let his cassock lay on the ground as he mounted his horse and rode from the clearing. He did not look back but did check his arrows. He had recovered many. For his next job, he would only need one arrow.

Merek took the two-mile path that led to Petersfield. From there, he would find the main road and travel west to Winchester. Thoughts raced through his mind as he headed toward Petersfield. He still hurt from his wounds, was tired from the rush of events from the past few days, and felt a burning desire to seek his tormentor. He no longer felt like a priest. Merek was a soldier again. Even though he was not in France, his mind was set. He was going to vanquish an enemy.

In his travels through the woods to Petersfield, he did not let his conscience talk him out of what he needed to do. No longer would he let his conscience dictate his life. He no longer felt a debt to God for his deliverance from war in France. He no longer felt a desire to serve God as a priest. Merek wanted to live the life he wanted to live. God would have to wait. After dealing with Berners, he would return to Harper's Turn and seek out Thea.

Merek entered Petersfield and headed westward to Winchester. Once on the main road, he would be able to make better time. Winchester was fifteen miles from Petersfield, and Merek rode undeterred, entering the city at dusk. He immediately sought the cathedral, for he knew there would be a place where the homeless could shelter for the night. The cathedral was not hard to find, for the steeple could be seen from miles around.

Merek found a stable where he secured his horse for the evening and made his way to the cathedral. With his disguise as a man-at-arms, he travelled unnoticed through the city. As he walked, he purposely hunched his back a little so as not give away his size. In the back of the cathedral, he entered and found a spot amongst the other vagrants. He had one of his saddle bags with him and used it as a pillow. He found a corner of the church and settled down for the night. He drifted to sleep fast despite the many thoughts of Berners, Thea, Robin Miller, and Sir Robert. He could see their faces as he closed his eyes.

He was awakened in the morning by a small tugging near his head. He fought the tugging gently, but it became more intense. Merek awakened to find a homeless man trying to steal his saddle bag right from under him. Merek shooed the man away by raising his hand. The beggar scampered away. It was just before dawn.

Although Merek had never been to Winchester, it did not take him long in the early morning hours to find the monastery connected to the great cathedral. As the sun was rising, Merek walked the perimeter of the monastery. He wanted to find all the entrances to the building beside the great cathedral. There were a number of entrances, yet only one seemed to point to the middle of the city. Merek decided he would wait at this entrance for a glimpse of Father Berners.

From a small food stand on the square, he bought some bread and cheese and sat. He waited, watching the traffic of people coming and going from the city to the cathedral and back. He was sure to keep his untethered bow and sheathed arrows hidden beneath the cloak he had taken from the prisoner near the lodge. Merek guessed that Father Berners's habits had not changed, and that he kept his activities away from the cathedral and the adjoining monastery. It was Merek's hope that he would see Father Berners leaving the monastery and venturing into the city. Merek's plan was to follow him into the city, find Berners's dwelling, and kill him.

Merek waited all morning for signs of Berners. As he waited and watched, he could not help but think of Harper's Turn, his vocation, and Thea. Guilt tried to creep up on him and remind him of his duties to the Church. But each time it entered into his mind, he was quick to squelch it with thoughts of the corrupt officials he had encountered ever since he entered the priesthood. Thoughts of Thea ended any notions of Merek making the wrong decision. No, the man waiting for Berners to show was no longer a priest. He was an archer, a soldier for the king's army.

And then Merek saw Father Pauls! Pauls left the entrance of the monastery and began to make his way into the city. He walked briskly, as if he were in a hurry. Merek followed. It was almost noon, and the streets of the city were crowded. It was not a problem for Merek to follow Father Pauls unnoticed. Berners's chief aide seemed to be in a hurry and was intent on going through the crowded streets as quickly as possible.

The walk was long, for it crossed the main market of the city and continued to the other end of the city line. Merek kept the pace with the hurrying priest, who was walking toward a group of cottages on the edge of the city. There were a number of cottages in a row. They were small and sat in a row along a street that did not have much people traffic. Merek was quick to note that they had entered into a part of the city that was less populous, so he was more cautious in following the priest.

Merek stopped when he saw Father Pauls approach a man and a young girl. Merek saw the priest approach the couple and speak briefly to the man. The man nodded, and Father Berners handed him a small purse. With his hand, the man guided the young girl to go with the priest. Merek could see the girl resisting and trying to stay with the man. The man patted her head and pushed her toward the priest.

Finally, the girl relented and began to walk with Father Pauls toward a cottage at the end of the row. Merek kept his distance watching the priest and the man who released the girl. Once Father Pauls and the girl had gone a short distance, Merek slowly approached the man who was walking away from the row of cottages. The man did not see Merek approach, for he was counting the money in the purse. They entered one of the side streets.

"I say, sir," Merek said, walking up to the man.

The man immediately put his hands holding the coins behind him to hide them from the stranger.

"A question for you, sir," Merek said, allowing his size to threaten the man. "Was that your daughter you just turned over to the priest?"

"None of your goddam business," the man said, not sure if he should raise his voice to a man the size of Merek.

"I will take that as a yes," Merek said. He punched the man squarely in the face, breaking his nose and sending the man to the street on his back. He lay there in a torrent of blood, the coins from his hand scattered all about the street. "See a priest before the day is out. Confess your sins and be glad I did not kill you today, you wretch," Merek said. "If your daughter is harmed in any way in the next hour, I shall find you and send you to our Maker in heaven."

Merek left the man in the street and headed back toward the cottages. At the end of the row, Merek saw Father Pauls talking with the girl just outside the cottage door. The girl seemed to be crying. Father Pauls had both his hands on the girl's shoulders and was shaking her, trying to get her to stop crying. He did not raise his voice, but Merek could see the priest talking quietly but sternly to the girl.

Finally, the girl stopped crying and became quiet. Merek approached cautiously, noticing the girl's shoulders quaking as if she were trying to get her emotions under control. Father Pauls had his back to Merek and was too worried about the girl to notice he was being followed. The priest put one of his arms around the girl's shoulder and led her to the door of the cottage. The priest opened the door and guided the girl through the entrance. When the door closed, Merek ran the remaining distance to the cottage at the end of the row and stood statue still against the wall beside the door.

Merek waited. He was hesitant to break in the door in fear the men inside would panic and hurt the girl. He felt he could not attack right away, for Father Pauls would warn Berners, who might escape. Merek decided to wait a few minutes. His guess was that if the cottage were similar to the house in Witton that Berners owned, there would be another private room for the prior.

Merek decided a few minutes would be too long. His blood was up. It was time. Using his bow, he knocked on the door staying out of sight beside the door. He knocked again, a little louder this time. He could hear steps approaching and stood still against the wall. He leaned his bow against the wall and took out his dagger. Father Pauls opened the door a crack, and not seeing anyone at the entrance, opened the door a little wider. The opening was all Merek needed.

Like a cat, Merek jumped from his position and grabbed Pauls's cassock and pulled him halfway out the door. With the dagger in his other hand, he stuck the blade through Pauls's stomach, at the same time putting his large hand around the stricken priest's mouth so he could not call out. Pauls screamed at the attack, but his voice was muffled by Merek's large hand. With his hand still on the dagger stuck in the priest's stomach, Merek backed the priest into the cottage. Once inside, Merek pulled up on the knife, opening his abdomen all the way to the man's chest. Pauls was not dead as he saw his stomach and intestines fall on the cottage floor. Merek kept his body from dropping to the floor. He eased the dying man to the floor, where he bled out in seconds.

Merek wiped his bloody hands on the cassock of the dying priest and went to the partially closed front door to retrieve his bow and arrows. He quietly closed the door and made his way to the back of the cottage. From inside the back room, he could hear the girl crying. Perhaps it was her crying that kept Berners from hearing the commotion in the front room. Merek could hear Berners admonishing the girl.

Merek knocked quietly on the door. The girl continued to cry in the bedroom. He knocked again.

From the other side of the door, Merek heard Berners, "What is it? You know I do not like to be disturbed."

Merek knocked gently again. When he heard the latch for the inside lock move, Merek burst through the door. His sudden entrance caught Berners at the door and knocked him to the floor. Merek stood over the prior, whose eyes showed immediate shock and fear.

"Get out!" Merek said to the girl. "Never come back to this cottage again!"

The crying girl, who was still mostly clothed, gathered her things and ran past Merek. She ran through the front room and slipped on the blood from the dead Father Pauls. She screamed when she saw the dead priest, opened the front door, and ran out still holding some of her clothes.

Father Berners looked up at Merek. His mind was racing. How did Merek find him? Better yet, why was Merek not gravely injured? Why was he still alive?

"You will let me up!" Berners called out, summoning his most commanding voice.

Merek took the end of his bow and slammed it into the priest's stomach. Berners doubled up on the ground, his breath taken away from the blow. He coughed and gagged trying to keep his midday meal from erupting. He continued to lay on the floor at Merek's feet.

"You will not give the orders today, little man," Merek said to the gagging man. "I should think you should save your voice. You will need it later today."

Berners stopped gasping and used all his might to regain his composure. "You are turning me into the authorities?" he managed to say. "They will hear my voice. I should warn you that I am a powerful man—"

"No," Merek interrupted. "I am not turning you into the authorities."

"My voice. You said I would be heard," Berners said, not sure what Merek meant.

"Your plea will be with God today, you bastard. I will be sending you to hell shortly, so if you want to pray for your worthless soul, you should begin."

"You cannot kill me," Berners said, almost pleading. "You are a man of the cloth. A priest, for God's sake."

"A priest. Like you, eh?" Merek said with a smile. "A priest like you who rapes young girls on a regular basis? A priest like you who hires men to hurt and kill fellow priests? Yes, I am a priest, just like you, Gilbert. And, therefore, I am going to send you to a place where little girls will never fear you again."

Merek suddenly dropped his bow and reached down, grabbing Berners by his unbuttoned cassock. He pulled the prior to his feet. Merek used the back of his hand to slap the priest across the face. With his other hand, he held onto the prior, so the man would not fall. He punched the prior in the stomach, doubling him over. This time, Berners could not keep his stomach settled. He vomited on the floor as Merek pushed him toward the bed. Father Berners was still trying to catch his breath as Merek threw the man in the middle of the bed. Using the same ropes Berners used to tie girls to the four corners of the bed, Merek tied Berners's hands to the posts by the bed. Berners was too weak to put up a fight as Merek tied each of his legs to corners of the bed.

"I have gold. It is yours," Berners said, regaining his breath from the blow to his stomach. He watched as Merek took his bow and strung it.

Merek grabbed one of his arrows and placed it in the bow. He walked to the foot of the bed. Berners lay in front of him, spread eagle.

"You cannot just kill me like this. It is nothing short of murder!" Berners cried.

Merek pulled back on the string as far as his might would allow. He loosed the arrow. It struck Berners in the chest, the shaft going through his heart and sticking into the boards that made up the bed frame. Only the feathers of the arrow could be seen sticking out of the chest of the dead man.

"Aye, call it murder if you want. Take it up with God when you see him today," Merek said quietly.

CHAPTER 43

A ROYAL VISITOR

Bishop Edington was alone in the vestibule behind the great altar in Winchester Cathedral. He had just said Mass to a throng of people. The new additions to the nave were finished, and the cathedral was more magnificent than ever. As the bishop began to disrobe, he began to think that he would miss this beautiful cathedral when he took on his new role as the Archbishop of Canterbury. The appointment was a great honor, and he looked forward to the appointment when his new post would begin in the fall.

The overcast day made it unusually chilly for early May. Bishop Edington loved the month of May in Winchester. The gentleness of the month seemed to agree with the great cathedral and monastery. The sun brought out the beautiful colors of the stained-glass windows, the gardens surrounding the cathedral. The warm air seemed to make the bricks glow when the sun shone on them. Yet, today was not one of those days.

A young priest helped him with his vestments, making sure they were hung properly. The priest was one of two personal servants to the Bishop of Winchester. He would take both of them to Canterbury when his new position took effect. Both priests were skilled in writing, spoke French, Latin, and Italian and were trustworthy.

The second priest entered the vestibule.

"Gabriel, what is it?" Bishop Edington asked.

"Your Excellency, you have a visitor," the young priest said.

"You know I do not see visitors after mass. I will have my breakfast."

"Your Excellency, forgive me. Your visitor. He is the king's son," Gabriel stammered. "He wishes to see you at once."

Bishop Edington was surprised. A royal visit? An unannounced royal visit? Perhaps the king's son was just in the area and wanted to drop in to congratulate him on his new appointment? That must be why. He could not think of anything else.

"Take him to my study, Gabriel."

"Bishop, he is already there," Gabriel said as an apology. "He insisted on waiting in your study. I could not say no to him. Forgive me."

Bishop Edington smiled. "Do not worry, Gabriel. You did the right thing. When a member of the royal family visits us, we must indulge him. Come, lads, help me to get ready."

Both young priests aided the bishop as he changed from his vestments to his daily cassock and boots. When he was ready, both young priests escorted him to his study. The large oaken door was closed, so Gabriel opened it slowly. The bishop peered inside. There were two men. He did not recognize one of the men. But he did recognize Edward's son, Sir John of Gaunt.

The bishop entered the room, and Gabriel closed the door from the outside. John of Gaunt stood and greeted the bishop with a smile.

"Your Excellency," John of Gaunt said, taking the bishop's hand and kissing his ring. "Thank you for seeing us. May I introduce my personal servant, Geoffrey Chaucer?"

Chaucer took the bishop's ring, kissed it, and stepped back. Your Excellency," he said and bowed.

Bishop Edington was put to ease immediately by Sir John's easy smile and gracious air. "Please be seated, lord," he said to Sir John. With his hand, he also invited Chaucer to a seat behind Sir John.

Chaucer nodded in gratitude and took the seat.

"Bishop Edington," Sir John said with a smile, "before we begin, will you do us a favor and kindly send a blessing to Geoffrey, for he is to wed this summer."

"Of course!" The bishop smiled. He waved for Chaucer to approach. "Congratulations to you."

Chaucer went to his knees before the bishop, who made the sign of the cross and touched Chaucer's head. Chaucer stood, bowed in thanks, and took his seat behind Sir John.

"Master Chaucer is a lucky man, Bishop. He will marry one of the queen's maids-in-waiting. She is educated and a real beauty, eh, Geoffrey?"

"Aye, lord. I am indeed a lucky man." Chaucer smiled, looking from Sir John to the bishop.

"You came all this way for a simple blessing?" the bishop asked.

"No, Bishop Edington. No, we did not. But we are thankful you were gracious enough to give Master Chaucer the blessing of our Lord Jesus Christ," Sir John said. "I am here because of your new position."

"Ah." The bishop smiled, thinking they were here to congratulate him.

Sir John of Gaunt was not smiling now.

"I am not here on my father's request. In fact, good King Edward does not know about this meeting, Bishop Edington. This meeting is between the two of us."

Bishop Edington was confused and looked back at Chaucer.

"Just between you and me, Bishop. Master Chaucer has my upmost confidence. He will not utter a word about this meeting."

"I am confused," the bishop started. "Why are you here? And why the secrecy?"

"I am here for your resignation, Bishop Edington. Master Chaucer has a document that I want you to sign, resigning from the position as Archbishop of Canterbury."

Bishop Edington did not say a word. He let the words from the nobleman sink in before he answered.

"Sir John, why would I resign? I have not even begun yet?" The bishop smiled, thinking it were some kind of joke.

"Bishop, you will resign because of health reasons. In essence, you will tell my father, our king, that you are unable to hold the position of Archbishop of Canterbury because of your declining health," Sir John said, holding the document that Chaucer had unrolled from a sleeve and given him.

"My health is good, lord. Why do you do this?" the bishop asked.

"In the past, you have served country and King well, Your Excellency. You are a good man, a pious man," Sir John said sincerely. "But you do not run a clean ship."

"A clean ship?" Bishop Edington asked.

"On the outside, Winchester Cathedral is beautiful, perhaps the finest religious monument in all of England. But beneath the surface, it is rotten."

"Rotten?" the bishop asked.

"Father Johnson?" Sir John of Gaunt asked. "How do you explain his exorbitant lifestyle in the city of Winchester? How do you explain the two women he lived with?"

"I . . . I did not know until he was arrested," the bishop tried to explain.

"You must have had meetings with him every day, Bishop. How did you not know? And what of the grisly murder of Father Gilbert Berners and his assistant?" Sir John asked.

"The murders are still under investigation," the bishop said. "God bless us, but the men's deaths were gruesome."

"Bishop Edington, we heard that Father Berners was staked to a bed and an arrow was driven through his heart. His assistant, a Father Pauls, lay dead in the next room, gutted from the nave to his chest."

Chaucer was sure to keep a straight face in front of the bishop. He was sure to show no emotion or knowledge of the double murder. But he knew who committed them.

"A terrible thing. Our constables are still baffled by the murders," the bishop said.

"And yet you did not know that Father Berners purchased the cottage in which he was murdered with church funds? He used the cottage regularly to assault and rape children with the help of Father Richard Pauls. You did not know these things?" Sir John said with a raised voice.

"No, no, none of it," the bishop said, closing his eyes and pounding his desk. "I knew nothing of it, I swear to Christ himself!"

"Then I ask you, Father, why did you *not* know these things?" Sir John asked, quieting his voice.

"I . . . I . . . have no answer," the bishop said, holding his palms open in bewilderment.

"Hence, running a clean ship," Sir John said. "As the bishop of the Winchester See, you have a responsibility to maintain a spiritual order from your lowest servant to your highest-ranking priest. And yet, you let criminals operate right under your nose, Bishop Edington. I do not know how you can simply blame ignorance on your part. How would I expect you to hold the highest-ranking position in the Catholic Church in England as the Archbishop of Canterbury if you cannot control the priests right under you domain?"

Bishop Edington did not answer the question. He looked at Sir John of Gaunt, frustrated and not knowing what to say.

"You will sign the paper, and Master Chaucer and I will deliver it to my father," Sir John continued. "He will be deeply disappointed but will understand your position and keep you in high regard. Once more, you will stay in your present position and continue to do the good work of God. And no word of this will ever leak to the king, the public, and your family. Do I make myself clear, Bishop Edington? You are a good man, but you let too many rats on your ship. And that will not do if you are to be the Archbishop of Canterbury. Now sign!"

Sir John of Gaunt handed the parchment to the bishop who hesitated but signed it. Sir John stood, took the parchment, and exited. Neither man kissed the ring of the bishop, nor did they ask for his blessing. Chaucer was sure to slam the large oaken door when they left.

CHAPTER 44

RETURN TO HARPER'S TURN

Merek did not waste time leaving Winchester. He had been tempted to set fire to the cottage in which Berners plied his evil trade, but he was concerned that the fire would spread to the cottages nearby. There was no need in making others suffer for the misdeeds of the two priests. Leaving the cottage, he retraced his steps back toward the cathedral. He kept an eye out for the father of the girl he had assaulted earlier, but did not see the man.

Back near the cathedral, Merek secured his horse from the stable, paid the owner, and set off from the city. He figured it would be about fifty miles to Harper's Turn from Winchester. It was early in midafternoon when he reached the outskirts of the city. Finding the main road, he headed north and east toward Harper's Turn. He knew he would not make the entire trip by nightfall yet made up his mind to go as long as he could before it became too dark to travel.

As he travelled, he encountered others on the road. For the most part, no one bothered him. In many cases, it was if he were invisible with his disguise as a man-at-arms. Merek kept his bow untethered and his arrows in his sheath as he travelled, hoping not to have to use them. For a while, he rode with a group of merchants who were leaving Winchester and making their way home. He stayed behind the group and did not engage in the conversation. At first, the group was cautious about his presence, but after a mile or two, Merek assured them that he was simply going home too.

Merek stayed with the group for a good ten miles. As the road split and they continued north, Merek thanked them and continued on the road that pointed more to the east. It was almost dark when the group separated, so Merek kept an eye out for a place to shelter for the night. Alone, he knew it was a dangerous risk to be caught on the road alone. After travelling a mile by himself, he dismounted from his horse and entered the woods. He needed a safe place to rest for the night.

There was no moon, and it grew dark quickly. Merek was tempted to get back on the main road and take his chances, but was too tired from the day. Walking quietly with his horse, Merek stumbled on some loose rocks and almost tripped. The loose rocks were from an ancient Roman wall that stretched out in front of Merek. The wall was about three feet high and in bad repair. With his hands, Merek found a portion of the wall that was still intact and decided to spend the night with his back against the wall. And so he did.

Rising in the morning, Merek was cold and stiff from the uncomfortable way in which he had slept. He awoke thirsty and hungry but was grateful for the uneventful night. He led his horse back to the main road and began to make his way back to Harper's Turn. Along the way, he stopped at a small tavern near a crossroads connecting Weybridge and Windsor. There he had a proper meal and saw to the needs of his horse.

Before Merek returned to Harper's Turn, he had to make a stop in a small town called Tolworth. There he had to see William Kint, the man who was the local constable in charge of the territory that included Harper's Turn. He was a friend of Merek's, and Merek needed a favor.

It was the middle of the day when Merek entered the town of Tolworth. After asking one of the townsmen about Kint's whereabouts, Merek rode to the man's small house located in the middle of the village.

"Father Merek!" was Kint's response to the soft knocking on his front door. "Do come in, Father."

The men shook arms.

"William, I hope you are well," Merek started.

"I am, Father. You are back from your pilgrimage? I was in Harper's Turn two weeks ago and was told you were on a trip to Canterbury."

"Aye, Canterbury," Merek answered. "I felt a need to seek you out before I returned to Harper's Turn."

"Do sit down, Father," William Kint said, offering a chair to the priest. "Now how can I be of service?"

"I need a favor," Merek said. "It is a big favor, and if you decline my request, I will certainly understand."

"All you need is ask, Father," Kint said.

Merek looked solemnly at the constable. "I want you to report me dead to the bishop."

Kint did not say a word for a moment. He merely looked at Merek.

Merek repeated, "I am asking you to tell the bishop that Father Willson went on a pilgrimage to Canterbury and never returned."

When Kint did not say a word, Merek went on to tell the story of his trip to Canterbury, the kidnapping, and the posse's pursuit of the criminals ending in a battle outside of Petersfield. Merek told the whole story, even telling how he had been captured and tortured. He showed Kint his deformed ear and the cut across his chest. However, Merek did not tell Kint of his trip to Winchester and his visit with Berners.

But he did tell Kint of his desire to quit the priesthood yet remain in Harper's Turn as a citizen and possibly the proprietor of the popular tavern, The Harp. Kint took the story in, did not ask questions, and merely listened to the fascinating tale. He did not question the tale or its validity. He knew Merek too well. And besides, who could make up such a story?

"And you want me to tell the bishop you are dead?"

"I want you to tell him that I never returned to Harper's Turn. I want him to send a replacement for me to tend to the villagers' spiritual needs," Merek said plainly.

Kint did not say anything and seemed to be thinking.

"What say you, William?" Merek asked.

"Will you continue to teach the villagers the use of the long-bow and continue with the practice of said weapon?" William Kint smiled.

"I will, William, but not as a priest." Merek smiled.

"So be it," William Kint said, holding his arm out. The men shook.

***

It was early evening when Merek entered The Harp. He was still dressed as a soldier and came in unnoticed. He stood to the side of the room and watched. He did not see Thea. Emellye was serving a table of men a large tray of food. There were other patrons, but it was not crowded. Many benches were vacant.

Merek took a seat at one of the empty benches and waited. For the most part, he kept his head down, not wanting to be recognized. He did not wait long for Emellye made her way to his bench.

"What are you having, sir?" she asked, not recognizing him.

Merek kept his head down. "Ale," he said simply. And as she began to walk away, he added, "And I want to see the owner."

Emellye paused, but did not respond. She walked away to fill his order.

Sometime later, a mug of ale was slid in front of Merek, who continued to keep his head low.

"There's your ale, sir. You wanted to see me?" It was Thea.

Merek did not look up right away. He kept his head low. How much he had waited for this moment! He let his mind take in the experience; he wanted it to last.

"Come, sir, I have chores," Thea said impatiently. "What is your business?"

Merek kept his head down. "I understand you are looking for a partner?"

Thea looked closely at the man with his head on the table. It did not take her long to recognize Merek. As thrilled as she was, she could not help but play along. "A partner?" she said. "Aye, I need a partner. But not one who eats and drinks all the profits. Not a big man. I need a wee one. Know anyone like that, sir?" It took all she had not to acknowledge his presence and hug Merek.

"I just might," Merek said, keeping his head down.

"And I want a partner who won't go throwin' priests into deep water," she said, trying not to smile. "And I want a partner who does not go on long pilgrimages to Canterbury."

"Those are tough demands," Merek said, suddenly understanding now that she knew to whom she was speaking. "Is there anything else?"

Thea casually walked to the other side of Merek, looking at him, wanting to celebrate his homecoming. Then she saw his damaged ear, the jagged skin from where it had been cut. She paused and put her hand to her mouth. Most of his ear was missing! How she wanted to press herself to him and hold on! She gathered herself and gave one more command: "Aye, there is one more thing. My partner better have two good ears so that he can hear me when I give him orders," she said, wanting to tend to the ear and give it proper caring.

With that comment, Merek looked up and stood.

"Do you know of a man with all of those qualifications, sir?" Thea said as she approached Merek. She put her arms around Merek and held him tightly.

For his part, Merek did not say a word. With her arms around him, Merek kissed Thea with his entire being, allowing the dreams he had wanted come true. Thea, surprised by the embrace and kiss, gave back without question or remorse.

After the embrace, Thea pulled back and gave Merek a long look. She gently touched the bruises on his face. She tilted his head and inspected what was left of his ear. There were tears in her eyes.

"I did not know that going on a pilgrimage was so dangerous," she said quietly, still holding his face with her hands.

"Wrestling with Satan is never easy," Merek tried to jest. "There is evil everywhere, even on a pilgrimage."

"But you are home now," Thea said quietly. She reached up and kissed him again.

"Dear Thea," Merek said when they were finished kissing, "I have thought long and hard about your offer of partnership. Does the offer still stand?"

Thea's hazel eyes widened as the smile on her face expanded. She kissed Merek again long and with great emotion. When they finished, Thea stepped back. "Of course, there will be some more negotiations," she said. "First of all, did you bring back my horse?"

Merek smiled. "I brought back our horse." He took her in his arms and kissed her again.

Emellye would be in charge of closing The Harp that night.

EPILOGUE

Geoffrey Chaucer married Philippa Roet, a lady-in-waiting of the queen in the summer of 1366. She bore a child less than nine months later. Sir John of Gaunt, one of the richest men in England and rumored to be her lover, provided her an income for the rest of her life. He made sure Chaucer had a job, an income, and a pension for the rest of his life too.

William Edington, Bishop of Winchester, died after a brief illness in October 1366. Although King Edward had been disappointed with Edington's resignation as the Archbishop of Canterbury, he praised Edington's dedication to church and state. Reverend Simon Langham was appointed by the king as the new Archbishop of Canterbury.

Harry Bailly married Allison, who helped him run The Tabard. Unfortunately, Harry died less than five years after their marriage. Allison would find husband number seven a year after Harry's death.

Both Anglicus and Mason were hanged in Dartford at the judge's convenience.

Sir Thomas of Ganse took over his father's estate and hired Hugh Bowman to be his reeve. It was the first time on record that a man with brown skin held such a post in England.

The Pierce brothers stayed in Dartford and continued to hunt down criminals. Today, if one visits Dartford, do not commit a crime. For if one does, expect to be arrested by a formidable law enforcement official with red hair.

ABOUT THE AUTHOR

Vince Pantalone is a retired high school English teacher. He was inspired to write *Incident on the Road to Canterbury* after teaching *The Canterbury Tales* for twenty years. Coach Pantalone has also written, directed, and produced eight plays for young adults. His published play, *Wooing the Rich Widow* was cowritten, produced, starred, and directed by his son, Nick. Nick and Coach Pantalone have also published *Keep Moving Forward: A Boy's Journey Riding the Rollercoaster Called Cancer*, a journal of Nick's fight with cancer.

Presently, Coach Pantalone is the defensive coordinator for the Lebanon Valley College football team. He and his wife, Carla, have five children and five grandchildren.

CPSIA information can be obtained
at www.ICGtesting.com
Printed in the USA
BVHW03s1857270818
525748BV00001B/8/P